TRUE
TO HER
WORD

Printed in Australia

Cover and internal design by New Found Books Australia Pty Ltd
Images in this book are copyright approved for New Found Books Australia Pty Ltd
Illustrations within this book are copyright approved for New Found Books Australia Pty Ltd

First printing: SEPTEMBER 2024
New Found Books Australia Pty Ltd
www.newfoundbooks.au

Paperback ISBN 978 1 9231 7243 2
eBook ISBN 978 1 9231 7255 5
Hardback ISBN 978 1 9231 7267 8

Distributed by New Found Books Australia and Lightning Source Global

 A catalogue record for this book is available from the National Library of Australia

We acknowledge the traditional owners of the land and pay respects to the Elders, past, present and future.

LORIE BRINK

TRUE TO HER WORD

Author Bio

Lorie Brink's eclectic secretarial career has fuelled her adventurous spirit and imaginative passions, extending to culinary delights which creates characters with a delectable outlook on life. Describing herself as a prolific novelist, she has several more works demanding her attention.

Her well-fed travel bug has taken her across Australia several times and to exotic countries in both hemispheres, although her insatiable appetite for sleek aircraft and fast cars haven't played a role in these expeditions... yet!

Lorie Brink lives and works from home in Australia's tropics which she shares with two pooches, one piano and a man who enjoys her cooking.

To my very own devil's advocate, my family and my friends,
thank you for your love and ongoing support.

To my team at Shawline Publishing, job well done!
To my readers, this is the beginning of a terrific relationship.

To quote Chanakya –
"The fragrance of flowers spread only in the
direction of the wind but the
goodness of a person spreads in all directions."

CHAPTER ONE

Although the shock had long since subsided, the bitter, two-year-old feeling of indignation simmered just below the surface. Not the kind of anniversary she wanted to remember, yet it still haunted her. Sighing heavily, she remembered the awful day where instead of reading the proposed menu for their engagement party, she had read the cessation of their twenty-year de facto relationship, along with the legal financial separation contract. Again, she fought back tears of humiliation as she recalled his cruel words.

Now we each have a ticket to freedom. You're the motivational speaker, so practice what you preach. Anyway, you bore me, Darlene. Have a good life. This is goodbye.

The division of the investment domestic portfolio was without doubt the olive branch. She had retained ownership of her beloved fully restored 1990s V8 Jeep Wrangler Renegade and acquired her favoured investment property, which bordered the state-owned rainforest west of Mackay.

And that was where Darlene Adams was headed to.

She yawned, stretched out each arm individually then arched her back, craned her neck and read the odometer. Exactly five hundred kilometres and the long-range fuel tank registered half on the gauge. Winding down the window, she rested her head on the door pillar, breathed in the crisp air of the darkest hour and listened to the comforting rumble of the V8 engine. A smile softened her tight-set lips as she reminisced about her most recent work experience.

The remote dry-land agricultural and livestock property took on whoever they could, but getting past the Boss Lady was the biggest hurdle she had ever faced. The suntanned, strong-jawed, much older woman had taken one look at the thirty-nine-year-old standing in front of her at the base of the windmill and laughed herself silly. With cargo pants and chambray shirt modestly fitting her size fourteen figure and waist-length blonde hair tied back in a ponytail

1

under a broad-brimmed hat, she was as spick and span as her work-boots. Short, clean fingernails and not a splash of makeup, just healthy skin, albeit with large hazel eyes framed with naturally long lashes and arched eyebrows. Darlene was just a bit too attractive.

'We're not looking for a pleasure toy for our workers, girl,' the station owner had said without malice. 'Go back to where you came from. This is no place for you.'

With every ounce of self-assurance that she could muster from deep down within her shattered soul, she had set about convincing them. Eventually, they had negotiated a one-week trial after she'd vowed that she was definitely not of the entertaining type. Having the ability to cook and bake, drive a tractor, shoot accurately, do basic accounting and stay quiet amongst the predominantly male crew put her in good stead to remain employed. Granted, her aloofness encouraged several nicknames, yet her willingness to pitch in with the dirty work afforded her an acceptable level of respect.

It had been the most challenging time of her life. From being a motivational speaker and event coordinator wearing corporate clothing to mucking in with some hardworking, true-grit, down-to-earth country folk. The diverse experiences had forced her to learn a lot about herself and life. Fortunately, her reputation of being a champion pistol competitor gave her the opportunity to fire the tranquilliser rifle from the ringer's helicopter.

Then all the fighting started. The fighting off wandering hands, fighting the urge to retaliate against insults, fighting against the weather to reap crops, fighting the fear of being trampled to death by rogue bulls and fighting to save the lives of breached calves and their mamas. Darlene had proved herself a versatile and valuable employee and as such, the transformed semi-detached laundry became her sanctuary. Hers and hers alone. One week out of every month, she was responsible for catering for the fifteen-strong staff on the station.

Then just last month, the Boss Lady's future daughter-in-law made her presence known. Even though Darlene had always kept her nose out of everybody's business and had worked damned hard, the high-maintenance mademoiselle did not think it fitting she remain in the employ of the family-to-be.

With reluctance, the Boss Lady and the Big Boss bade her farewell with a glowing reference, way too much farm-butchered packaged beef and bacon, a $500 fuel card and two full jerry cans, plus a full tank of fuel in her Jeep.

She swiped a little tear away and swore under her breath as she nearly cleaned up a wayward kangaroo. The approaching dawn, along with little ponds of slushy ice on the highway verge, made for some very cautious driving. She had always called that time of the morning the 'tragically expensive hour'.

It was a very cold winter in Central West Queensland. Her breath was a dragon's as she topped up the fuel tank. Under the spectacular dawn sky, Mother Nature sure painted a pretty picture for Darlene. Farm fences were coated in solid ice, with the barbed wire strands wrapped in clear frozen water. Spider webs sparkled like enormous diamonds under the bright sunrise. Staring along the fence line which disappeared into the golden horizon, she eventually brought herself back to reality and secured the empty jerry cans onto the rear door with a loud sigh. The first day of the rest of her life. Well, a new chapter in it, anyway, with three goals to achieve. One: drive to Western Australia. Two: take out the national pistol championship over there. Three: swim with the dolphins. She had already swum with the platypus.

After wiping her competition off the board at the Queensland State Titles shooting competition several months earlier, she had retained the championship title in all her preferred pistol disciplines and had immediately registered to participate in the WA-based challenge. A trophy she'd had her eyes on for many years. She pushed the horrible Oliver Cady out of her head. She didn't want to think about him. Instead, she focused on her reward, which had always been a three-day spa and holistic retreat, and this year's was long overdue. Except this year, she was going to climb her tree house and do something she hadn't done since she was a kid. Stare at the clouds during the day and sleep under the stars.

Her smile broadened as she thought of Jimmy, her old hippie neighbour and property caretaker. He'd carved and hollowed out the most amazing wind chimes and played the flute beautifully. They had hit it off immediately fifteen years earlier when she stood in awe, listening to his rendition of Chopin's *Nocturne in E Flat*. Her favourite classical piece of music. Her mobile ringtone, in fact. After she'd applauded him loudly, she'd casually strolled up the meandering path, stood at the bottom of the tree house and hugged the tree, sobbing her heart out. Her dream had come true. The rolling green hills in the background gradually merging with the rainforest and her tree house. The second half to the painting her favourite niece held in her possession. A one-off. A masterpiece. A collectable.

3

Darlene wanted to surprise Jimmy, but the closer she got to the rainforest, the stronger her instinct was telling her to call him first.

'I don't know this number, so you have five seconds to tell me who you are.'

'It's me, Jimmy. How're my platypus?'

'Wow! My beautiful dreamer, Darlene Adams! It's been ages since I heard your lovely voice. Our platypus are nesting further upstream – a true sign of an early cyclone this year. But right now, talking with you, I can see the crystal-clear waters making colourful rocks shimmer when sunlight kisses the gentle ripples.'

Her tears threatened to overflow at how frail his voice had become. 'Beautiful words, so poetic. How is your book coming along?'

'It's at the publishing house as we speak, babe. My agent has been tremendous. I knew perseverance would pay off, and you know something?'

'Tell me, Jimmy.'

'You're the only one who believed in me. The cover of the book is a view from the middle step of your tree house overlooking the valley. I've included a spiral staircase around the tallest tree fern. A symbol of my eternal gratitude to you, as is my book... I've dedicated it to you.'

Wiping the tears that had trickled down her cheeks, Darlene said, 'Bless you. Oh, Jimmy, I'm flattered. Thank you, but gee, man, congratulations! So well deserved.'

'Thanks, my beautiful dreamer. But before we hang up, there's something else you need to know.'

Darlene listened with a heavy heart as Jimmy told her he was in end-of-life care losing the battle to pancreatic cancer. The shining light was his book of poetic ramblings, which would be published posthumously. He declined her offer to be his executrix for the sole reason he'd already bequeathed his meagre assets and the future proceeds of all book sales to her. But of greater concern was the state government's push to buy back all property bordering state and national parks. He'd left her correspondence at the post office, along with his certified final wishes, but she had to seriously consider removing her belongings from the tree house. He'd found termites in his cottage and writing nook, which was actually a hammock slung between two massive rain trees, and was happy to contribute his belongings to the forest.

She burst into tears. 'Oh, Jimmy, I am so sorry. Why, Jimmy, why?'

'Darlene, babe. It's me that's sorry. I should never have withheld it from you, but I couldn't wait for you to come home. It won't be long now.'

Sniffing softly, she said, 'Are you in Mackay?'

'Yes, my beautiful dreamer. Where are you?'

'On my way to see you. Please wait for me, Jimmy.'

'I'm in the departure lounge of the hospice by the foothills south of the township. Will you do me the honour of joining me for supper?'

'It would be a privilege.'

'Good, I'll wait. Speed safely now!'

The sound of his smoker's raspy chuckle stayed in her head for the next few hours. A disused rest area on the outskirts of Mackay provided her the opportunity to pull over and burst into tears. She had to cry it out without witnesses. Nobody had ever seen her cry.

Swiftly changing gears and navigating through the increasing traffic, she was remarkably composed by the time she key-locked her Jeep. Wheeling her trusty pale blue hardcover suitcase ahead of her along the winding path under the rambling rose arches, Darlene tried to steady her breathing. A matron met her at the door of the sanctuary, blessed her then led her into Jimmy's suite. She held back a loud sob. His withered, jaundiced frame broke her heart.

Squeezing his hand softly, she whispered, 'Hello, Jimmy.'

His eyes fluttered open. 'You're an angel! Wow. If I were thirty years younger and had all my strength, you would be in a lot of trouble. How can you go away and come back looking younger and prettier, I ask you?'

Blushing under his gaze, she smiled. 'You always knew how to say the best things! What did you order for dinner?'

He chuckled, coughed a little bit and chuckled again. 'Your favourite. We'll share a filet mignon, pepper sauce and loaded potato.'

Darlene climbed onto his bed, lay beside him and whispered, 'Thank you for all the wonderful lessons you taught me. For being my friend, having my back and sticking with me while I failed miserably at pottery!'

They shared a good laugh. Her pottery attempt had looked like a demented calabash. Jimmy gave her some more useful tips before nudging her solidly.

'How was the shooting comp?'

'I won! Jimmy, I wiped the floor with my opponents... um... I've always had my eyes on a trophy in the west.'

'Congratulations! There's something else you're not telling me, but that can wait. How will you get across the country?'

'I'm going to drive, with my trusty blue suitcase and two best friends right beside me.'

'Consider shipping your V8 over on a car-carrier and hiring a motorhome. Less wear and tear, and it'd be better if you're independent. But please, pay attention to your surroundings, beautiful dreamer. Watch out for spiders and snakes. Most of all, be careful... a lot of women go missing along the bottom of the country.'

Trying not to think about the negatives or his breathlessness, but liking the suggestion, she said, 'Yeah, that's a great idea. I have a little over three weeks to sort things out before I absolutely have to leave.'

'I need to look into your eyes, Darlene. There are some things you have to know, and they shouldn't wait. Please sit up.'

As she did so, a quiet knock on the door interrupted their conversation. A buxom matron with a kind face, knowledgeable eyes and a gentle smile wheeled a dinner trolley over to them. They both helped Jimmy to sit up and plumped several pillows behind his back. He clutched at the older woman's hand and brought it to his lips.

'You are an earth angel, ma'am. Bless you for your kindness.'

'Oh, Jimmy Mann, you'll leave a mark on this world that will follow you to your next life.'

Darlene observed the interaction silently. Being kind to a fellow human was the simplest of gifts anybody could give and everybody should. Jimmy picked politely at the perfectly cooked meal and imparted knowledge about the platypus, his cherished lyrebirds and cyclone preparation while she ate most of the food. Then the subject got around to the land.

'Honestly, sell it for the highest amount you can get out of the government. I know our furniture isn't of any value, and who cares if the forest reclaims her own? I believe it's a sign, for the platypus haven't returned. They're further upstream, where the water is better, the air is cleaner and the mountain blue butterflies dance across the ancient tree ferns.'

He stole the last tiny morsel of steak off her plate, winked and savoured every gram of the succulent meat but swallowed hard. Smacking his lips loudly, he coughed, chuckled then spoke in a very quiet voice while holding her hands tightly and focusing on her eyes.

'My beautiful dreamer, the tree has grown since you last accessed our tree safe. I made it easy for you. You'll know what to do.'

He took several deep, shuddering breaths and shook his head when she went to say something. 'Get to the post office. As soon as you can. Remember how we made the wind chimes? It's all... there for you. Thank you for being my friend, Darlene... I'll love you forever. I'm getting tired now. I'm not in any pain... I had to say all that, thank you for listening... keep talking to me, please... I want your sweet voice to be the last thing I hear...'

Tears trickled down his face, following the deep creases of life's experiences until they plopped onto the bed sheet. Her own eyes blurred.

Holding back a sob, she said, 'I'm going to miss you awfully. You'll know when it's time to get your wings. Next time I'm gazing into the blue sky, I'll imagine the round fluffy clouds being you and your fellow angels from a bygone era enjoying a toke on a reefer. Your wind chimes will be wherever I am... I'm right here for you, as you have been for me.'

The matron returned, tweaked something on the machine beside the bed and gently wiped Jimmy's brow. 'He's resting his eyes, but he's fading. Say what you both need to say...'

'My beautiful Darlene, my beautiful dreamer,' Jimmy murmured, 'thank you for being in my life. Stay true to yourself. You will have to find somewhere else where the platypus play, maybe somewhere far away where you and your heart can stay. Love and light, beautiful lady.'

'Oh, Jimmy.' She sniffled and held his hands firmly. 'I love you. It's not goodbye. You're transitioning and will be free of all pain. You'll be a forever-young hippy, and we'll meet again in another life...'

'Earth has no sorrow that heaven cannot heal,' the matron said gently. 'It won't be long now, dear child.'

'Fly high, you beautiful soul. I love you, Jimmy. Fly high. Be hippy, be happy.'

His hands gave one last squeeze as he took his last breath. Jimmy's pained face softened into one that was smooth and peaceful. Just like he was sleeping.

The matron squeezed Darlene's shoulder as she walked quietly out the room and closed the door. Sobbing into the scrunched-up bed sheets beside Jimmy's resting body, Darlene reflected on their beautiful friendship.

A long while afterwards, the matron ushered her out of the room so the orderlies could do their job. Standing at the nurse's station on autopilot, she signed off as his next of kin, accepted his belongings and thanked the nurses. She smiled sadly when she saw the miniature carved marijuana leaf and wind chimes hanging off his keyring alongside the lonely safety deposit key.

CHAPTER TWO

Checking into her hotel suite nearing midnight, Darlene collapsed onto the bed in an undignified manner until the bright sunshine blinded her. Drowning her tears in the boiling hot then freezing cold shower, she dressed in Jimmy's favourite sundress and bolero and drank a very strong black coffee on the patio overlooking the sea. With her shoulders back, she tackled the day's obligations with forced composure and a heavy heart.

The post office handed her the bundle of mail and two boxes along with overflowing words of sympathy, as did the bank when she cleared out their joint safety deposit box. With the second half of the treasured painting, her travel money and Jimmy's stash of cash, plus the original manuscript and the beautifully carved, treasured wind chimes, she barely managed to get the suitcase zipper closed. She bit back a weak grin, knowing more money was stuffed up the timber tubes of the wind chimes. Jimmy preferred alternative methods of safekeeping.

Emptiness washed over her as she walked up the meandering path towards Jimmy's cottage. Tears streamed down her face when she saw his flute standing up in the hammock neatly wrapped around her hilarious pottery attempt. She didn't know if she was crying or laughing. Stepping inside his sparse but extremely tidy cottage, she changed into her gardening clothes before stashing her suitcase. Jogging up the gentle rise, she lightly dragged her fingers through the beautiful maidenhair fern growing around the base of her tree house and sighed. Jimmy had been right. The forest was reclaiming itself.

Balancing on the rocks two feet off the ground and wrapping her arms around the broad tree trunk, Darlene felt for the grooves she'd marked into the bark when she'd first bought the property fifteen years earlier, then modified when she moved back as a single woman. Jimmy was right. His more recent improvements certainly did make it easier. Without looking, she pried out the wadded bundles of opals and her treasured childhood trinkets. Originally it was her tree safe, then it became their tree safe. Nature with nature. Her and Jimmy's secret stash.

Slipping the bundles into her pants pockets, she ventured behind the tree to their organic greenhouse. The remaining carrots were growing well, lettuce not so much, but under the hydroponic tray of mixed herbs were their bags of gold nuggets. They'd made a pact that should one of them not be able to return, the other would have ownership regardless of relationship bounds. Nobody knew of the gold-bearing creek, because neither had anyone to tell. Half the secret had died with Jimmy. The other half would die when she did. Slipping the drawstring bags out of the plastic containers and into her pockets, she discarded the greenhouse foods into the forest for the wildlife.

Repositioning the iron spiral staircase around her tree, she scaled the steps with ease and burst into tears when she reached the landing. The view overlooking the Finch Hatton Gorge was as if she'd stepped back into her dream. Her childhood sketch. Her commissioned painting. A big tree house overlooking the rolling green hills disappearing into the rainforest valley where the platypus play. Pushing through the heavy timber door, she sobbed loudly when she saw the new mosquito net covering the roof hatch and natural windows. It was only as she got older that her fear of spiders and snakes had worsened. Dear Jimmy had made sure she was always without both.

Humming her childhood song, she removed the dust cover from her hammock, lay upon its brightly coloured plaited base and gazed through the canopy of the tree. This was how Darlene the Dreamer earned her nickname. As a child, she would climb a tree and lie upon its limb, staring up at the clouds, finding shapes or gazing into the deep blue sky. At night, she'd sleep on a hammock under the stars and always got into trouble for doing so.

Nine days later, she returned from town carrying Jimmy's remains in a ceramic urn. He had explicitly wished to be scattered where he fed his cherished lyrebirds. As she stepped through the makeshift pathway, the rainforest fell silent. Not even her footsteps could be heard. Breathing in the damp scent and admiring the ancient tree ferns, she followed the bright blue flash of the butterfly dance from the magnificent Ulysses. Beside the permanently full birdbath stood Jimmy's pair of pottery lyrebirds and a seat carved into a massive fallen tree trunk. Sprinkling and scattering the ashes, she prayed and talked to him as if he were around, and a string of different bird calls echoed through the secluded setting. His lyrebirds were welcoming him home. Jimmy was at peace.

Darlene mourned the loss of her only true friend and took comfort in the knowledge that he was free of pain. The night skies progressively got thicker with cloud, eventually blocking out the stars. By early morning on the last day of her rainforest seclusion, watery sunrays painted the curtain of mist with speckles of gold. It was as if the sky was weeping, not wanting her to go, yet encouraging her to leave. Her own heart was torn, but it was time. Time to say goodbye to Queensland. There was nothing left for her here, but there was a beautiful trophy some five thousand kilometres away that had her name on it.

Securing a deal with the motorhome company to return a rather elaborate vehicle to Perth within nine days for the cost of fuel plus one dollar ticked a lot of boxes. It had already been five days since she'd loaded her treasured white Jeep into the enclosed transporter, and she missed its burbling note awfully.

Admittedly, by the third day of driving, she had grown accustomed to the swivel seats, security and convenience of the motorhome on the long journey from Central Queensland to Western New South Wales. The biggest bonus was her blue suitcase. Her life was in it and was always in view on the floor of the front seat.

Looking forward to stretching her legs, she took her usual late afternoon break at Broken Hill, where her eyes nearly popped out of her head. Twice. The largest hamburger she had ever seen in her life and the shortest, roundest man with the happiest of faces, who had just clambered out of his neon-painted Peterbilt. Darlene smiled into her napkin and helplessly gawked at the driver's ageing, wobbly stomach protruding out from under a garish multicoloured hi-vis shirt. Even the perfect semi-circle of where the steering wheel had worn through looked like a smile. She discreetly observed the genuine friendship between him and several of the drivers, but there were two men he seemed to interact with more.

Inadvertently having tagged up with a Kenworth 910 and a Mack Superliner while travelling the Cobar Line and having heard them call each other *Spook* and *Tiny* over the two-way, Darlene hoped the two men were them. A twinge of envy at their mateship forced her to chew properly.

From what she could gather from listening in on their conversation, these guys regularly travelled in convoy when they drove the long haul to

Western Australia. The three of them overtook each other respectfully with the objective to change their driving view only. The wave or indicator dance for acknowledgement was the only form of communication. She never spoke on the two-way.

Without trucks, Australia stops. These folk didn't have an easy life, but their laughter was like a breath of fresh air. She certainly didn't feel unsafe being in the vicinity of the almost dozen drivers and their trucks, until the dirty-purple International prime mover pulled in. The driver's use of air brakes was excessive, and the prat hadn't dropped his dust before turning into the roadhouse. A big no-no in the country.

Through the grimy cafeteria window, she watched as the tall, spindly mobile tattoo parlour kicked each tyre and almost lovingly spit-polished a mark on the chrome bullbar. Goosebumps crawled all over her body. This was one creepy dude. Pulling her cap lower, she firmly inserted the stereo plugs into her ears but didn't turn on the music and swivelled a bit in the seat, obstructing any visual contact from the cashier's console. It was pretty obvious the creature's appearance wasn't appreciated. Almost instantly, the loud conversation coming from the trucker's restaurant dropped a few decibels. The temperature dramatically plummeted the minute the doors opened and he loped inside the driver's lounge. She slipped out unnoticed during a commotion echoing through the building and locked herself in the motorhome.

Intentionally, she was the third-last vehicle to make tracks following the sun's path and rolled out behind the familiar set of trailers. Listening to the two-way conversation, there were roadworks just over the border stalling long-haul drivers, which drastically impacted their deadlines. Occasionally, someone would say something amusing, and she'd burst out laughing. It felt good.

The instructions were to pull into the cleared area shy of the border and wait. Her congested thoughts gradually dissolved into the white lines as fatigue from the long day of driving crept in. The delay at the remote border crossing between New South Wales and South Australia was actually a blessing in disguise. After proving to the border patrol officers that she didn't have fresh lemons, potato or onions, she was able to strategically position herself a fair distance away from several other trucks but slightly ahead of her convoy buddies. Darlene double-checked the mirrors while replacing her baseball cap with a big hat and hoped nobody would take a second look at someone wearing hideously baggy clothing. She knew she'd lost weight and toned up over the last few years. The four new notches in her trusty old leather belt being the tell-tale sign. Pulling out the shirt disguised any ounce of a figure.

Feeling the temperature on the wheel hubs indicated the passenger front was a lot hotter than usual. The thorough machinery checks performed by the company's mechanics prior to her hiring the vehicle included replacement wheel bearings, but something wasn't right. She was quite capable of changing tyres and repacking bearings – which she hated doing – but wasn't keen on the red dust and certainly didn't want to attract attention.

Several other long-haul truckers had rolled in ahead of and around her. Without making obvious eye contact, she watched her convoy buddies, as well as the drivers of the shiny Western Star, cab-over Kenworth and the Stirling from the roadhouse, all talk in a group. Now sandwiched between the truckers preparing themselves for the long journey westwards, she smiled inwardly at the game of tag which had started out at Dubbo.

While checking the rear tyres of the motorhome, a loud bang brought her head up swiftly, and her right hand wrapped itself around the pistol grip of her Colt 45.

'Hey, mate.' A man's voice drifted through the dusty air. 'We're gonna be stuck here for a bit, plus there's a major threat of a dust storm. Noticed you haven't had a break since Cobar.'

She looked up as he approached and nodded in acknowledgement, then raised her hand, indicating he needn't come any closer. He was huge and knee-weakeningly handsome, with short, grey-white hair. Incredibly tall, with broad shoulders that carved down to strong hips and hands like a bear.

'Cat got your tongue, mate?' he asked, scratching at the coloured stubble on his face.

'No, it hasn't, and I don't talk to strangers. Although I will thank you for being a polite travelling companion and hope it continues.'

'You're a chick!' His voice dropped a notch as he took several steps forward. 'Lady, you shouldn't be out here on your own.'

'I have some friends with me.'

'Yeah, well, um, you're going to get smothered with this dust storm if you stay where you are. How good are you at reversing?'

She straightened up and looked at him confidently, neither of them removing their sunglasses. He had mentioned Cobar, but she wasn't sure if he was Spook or Tiny, because this man wasn't white like a ghost, nor was he small, though he was one of the drivers who'd talked to the rotund, happy man.

'I'm willing to give it a shot. What's your plan?'

He suggested she reposition her vehicle alongside his second trailer as close as possible, and his convoy buddy would tuck in beside. Thereby buffeting the lightweight vehicle from the wind and keeping her somewhat protected.

'Watch for my hand signals. We won't talk on the radio. But when I tell you to stop, you stop, and you do not leave your vehicle. The dust's a bastard, and going by history, we could be here for six hours.'

'Thank you. Say, that purple rig...'

'Stay away from it.'

'Copy that.'

'After we're done, go down two channels and keep your ears on. In a long while, listen out for three short blasts on the air horn. Pay attention after that. In the meantime, get some sleep.'

He scrutinised her appearance before swiftly pivoting on his feet. When he'd finished checking his trailers, he stopped at his middle trailer and beckoned her to hurry up and start reversing. He seemed to grow the closer she reversed. He really was a very good-looking man. Feeling reasonably comfortable with the plan, she followed his hand signals vigilantly. His thumbs-up and smirk indicated he was impressed.

Twenty minutes later, Darlene nervously watched a trailer reverse until it almost rested against the motorhome's windscreen, then she hurriedly scampered through the back and watched just as nervously as a massive chrome bullbar and bonnet filled her rear window. It was quite nerve-wracking watching a fully loaded triple road train idle alongside with barely six inches separating them.

The two-way crackled shortly afterwards. 'Rog. Staying put and bunking down. May as well update the logbooks and get some shuteye. Night, lads.'

Several other drivers concurred with the plan and signed off the same way. She covered up and ensured all the windows were tightly closed, double-checked the locks and prayed she'd survive the dusty onslaught. Within the hour, a distant rumbling coincided with swiftly darkening skies. An eerie orange hue swept overhead as it dumped a thousand million tiny sand granules. Craning her neck up the side windows, she gasped. It was like being in the tunnel of a massive, dirty wave. The curl of the wind was phenomenal as the trucks disappeared in the cloaking dust. She imagined the sand growing up the sides of the vehicle and swallowing it whole. Sand rained continuously.

Finally, exhaustion crept upon her like a hairy caterpillar. Each time she felt her eyelids droop, she'd rub her eyes roughly. It was pitch-black outside. A long time later, she awoke with a fright and her hand firmly wrapped around her 9mm Smith and Wesson underneath the pillow. In her dream, the purple prime mover had stalked her across the Nullarbor while Jimmy's words of warning echoed in her ears.

The wind had dropped, and it was eerily silent. Freshening up her appearance and disposition, she was brewing a very strong coffee when the peace was abruptly disturbed by turbos winding up and the sounds of idling trucks. She could almost feel the vibrations rippling through the thin walls. A fine layer of dust coated absolutely everything. Shaking her head feebly, she sat in the driver's seat, ready to roll. For what seemed like an eternity, three short blasts penetrated the melodic air-horns disappearing into the thick air as each driver rolled out. The two-way remained silent.

'Hey, mate, from what we can tell, you should be right to follow the lights in front of you. For the next ten clicks, travel at walking pace. Port Augusta do a good burger.'

Recognising the voice as being one of her original travelling buddies, she knew he was talking to her and depressed the talk button twice. What she wasn't sure of was how they knew she liked hamburgers.

'Reckon you should try Port Pirie.' An unfamiliar childlike voice filled the airwaves before being abruptly told to get off the channel.

Trying to rub away the sudden onset of goosebumps and peer through the filthy windscreen, she followed the lights, travelling very slowly at a respectable distance. Sighing as the early morning sun bounced off the dusty side mirrors, she thought of using the wipers when suddenly, a massive wall of water made her cry out. She had been totally oblivious to the road crew alongside the eastbound lane. Several water trucks were working their magic, and by the time there was greater distance between her and the familiar rear trailer, she could see clearly. Nobody heard her thanks, but she felt better for saying it.

Am I lonely? she asked herself and immediately dismissed the thought. Being adopted into a wonderfully loving Australian-born family hadn't left her with the desire to learn about her Norwegian heritage. It was at her eighth birthday party when her oldest brother explained why she had fair skin, wavy blonde hair and long legs while everyone else was graced with pitch-black hair, light brown eyes, olive skin and average height. None of it had mattered. She'd always felt loved, safe and happy. As she grew up, she accepted that things happened for a reason. It might have taken a while, but she did eventually.

What am I searching for, then? Was it the sea, with its white sand, turquoise waters, dolphins and whales? She'd always be Darlene the Dreamer, that was for sure, but solo competitive sports were her forte. Her consistent accuracy in nailing the bullseye developed from playing bows and arrows and cops and robbers as a youngster. Her most prized toy was the lacky band gun her dad had made for her, but her favourite was a cap gun which shot plastic darts. She just loved how it fitted perfectly in her hand. She was also a keen dart player, with several trophies under her belt, but didn't like the pub competition scene.

Pistol shooting started as a hobby. The older she got, the more eagerly she wanted to improve her personal best. Then she blindly got swept up in the arms of relationships and careers. Sex hadn't played a big part in her life, which was probably another blessing in disguise, because there weren't any children to have endured the pain of a broken family. Perhaps she had broken the cycle! Thank God for that. That thought brought about a smile. Thinking of her ex-boyfriend felt like looking into a maze of crazy arcade mirrors. His tanned skin, puppy-dog brown eyes, thick black hair and wry grin suddenly contorted into something hideous, where his ears wrapped around his head and his kissable lips disappeared into the dimple on his chin. She shuddered, giggled at the stupidity of it all then sighed heavily.

She was determined not to give into the doldrums of the wasted years and subsequent awful experience. Instead, she mentally rehearsed the familiar pistol training regime.

CHAPTER THREE

Oddly enough, Tiny – who was actually a smidgen under seven foot – had instantly felt drawn to the single traveller the first time he was overtaken. Easily passing his fully loaded triple, the motorhome travelled at a sensible speed ahead, and he couldn't help but grin when he saw the tail indicator lights do their dance. At the next overtaking lane, he watched as the vehicle overtook Spook's Kenworth 910 and smirked when his convoy buddy commented politely on the two-way. The two-button response was too coincidental for it to not have been from her. He enjoyed the game of tag and hoped it would continue.

He had deliberately encouraged Spook to call into Broken Hill, hoping they'd be followed in. His sigh of relief when the motorhome headed to the diesel bowsers was only heard by him and his four-legged travelling companion, Nova. A four-year-old black and tan spayed female kelpie with a floppy ear, two brown dots above both eyes and a permanently happy smile on her face.

He was glad the opportunity arose to interact when he watched the traveller checking the temperatures of the front hubs. There was no way her feminine outlines were obvious, so it was apparent she wasn't wanting to draw attention. He imagined Elaina, just this woman was bit taller, and had secretly been relieved that only he'd heard her firm, polite voice with its gentle lilt.

'Hey, Spook, go private.'

'Rog.'

Shortly afterwards, Tiny answered Spook's phone call.

'Hey, man, thanks for helping our traveller out back there in the dust storm...'

'Yep, no worries. What's the story, anyway?'

'Nah, best we just keep travelling the way we have.'

'You can't fool me, bloke. What's got you all paternal-like?'

'Was it that obvious?'

Spook chuckled. 'Was? It is! You're like old man emu with a wayward chick. Wait... our little buddy *is* a chick?'

'Sounded like one.'

'Keep it in your pants, dude. You've got this far in life without having sprogs to worry about. We've often wondered if you were gay or something!'

Tiny burst out laughing and said, 'Initially, I envisaged the Danish Pastry.'

'Ah. Well, she's safe and sound where we left her and sends her love. Not sure if we'll see her this time.'

'Yep.'

'Is that all you've got? Are you sure you aren't gay, Tiny?'

'Piss off, Spook! You ever see me eyeing off one of you ugly bastards?'

His laugh was loud and genuine. 'How you know this traveller is similar?'

'A lilt in her voice, but you can't fool me, buddy. You're just as curious, seeing as you suggested the burgers at Port Augusta!'

'Yep, I saw the one that got devoured. She's got a healthy appetite, anyway. At least we know she eats meat!'

Booming laughter echoed through the cabs.

'Keep the dotted line on your right, Tiny. I'm overtaking you shortly. We'll play this game of tag until she leaves our company. Right now, the little lady can watch my tail for the next few hours! Yours is getting fat!'

The line was disconnected as Spook depressed the transmit button and spoke in an amused voice, 'Kenworth overtaking Mack triple and motorhome heading west.'

'Copy that, road is clear,' Tiny replied with a chuckle and smirked as the familiar anonymous response was heard.

Spook frowned. He and Tiny had known each other for a long time. He'd always admired the big fellow's sense of humour and chivalry, and often wondered why he'd left the Special Forces. The subject had come up once and was swiftly closed down. He'd never known Tiny to have a girlfriend or girl in any port. But there was a painful secret buried deep. Of that, Spook was convinced. It was strange that Tiny felt some sort of connection to this stranger and was compelled to protect her in a dust storm. *Whatever the outcome will be, will be, but she did do a smart job on reversing. No doubt about that.*

With his own children now in their twenties and his wife reinventing herself as an interior designer, Spook simply loved driving trucks. Always had. His wife knew the perils of falling in love with a truck driver, but true to his vows, he always returned home with a pure heart. A solid foundation was what he'd given his children.

He smiled at the sweet memory of releasing the air brakes as he watched his son score the winning try of the local U-18s footy grand final. The lad had sprung up, cleared the oval's picket fence, leapt into the prime mover's cab and pulled on the air horn jubilantly. His teammates had swiftly followed suit and just about emptied the air out of the truck. That night, the two men had shared the first of many beers. A relieved sigh had escaped Spook's lips when the prodigal son announced he was going to be an optician specialising in eye diseases. Being much older than his sister, he successfully pursued that goal and was highly regarded amongst his peers in Switzerland. The improvements of technology eased the pain of the distance that separated them, but the young man had promised to bring his future bride and instant family out for a visit the following year.

His only daughter, his princess and gift from God, had asked him to be her chauffeur at her wedding. His eyes still welled up at the thought of having to share her love with another man. He'd loved her first as only a father could and constantly reminded his now son-in-law of this. A watery smile played around the corners of his mouth as he recalled the billowing white train of her wedding dress filling the cab, her angelic face, their mutual blubbering when, with linked hands, they pulled on the air horn upon arrival at their special garden church. Two years later, Spook was going to become a grandfather to twins.

He rubbed his bristly chin and picked up the two-way as he settled into being the leader of the convoy.

'You got your ears on, Tiny?'

'Rog.'

Spook couldn't contain the excitement as he blurted out, 'Looks like I'll be playing Grandfather Christmas this year.'

Tiny laughed into the mic, 'Congrats, man. You'll make an awesome granddad.'

'Thanks, mate. Twins!'

'Holy dooley, let's hope they get their mother's looks and brains.'

'Say, why don't you actually join us this year for Christmas? I'll tell the... uh... my missus not to invite any single chicks, not even her lesbian friends.'

Tiny chuckled. 'You're a tease, you bitch!'

Darlene burst out laughing. She loved the guys' sense of humour and didn't feel guilty about listening to their conversation. If they started talking strong male stuff, she'd simply turn it down, but for the last twelve hundred kilometres, they hadn't.

A sound like someone clearing their throat crackled through the speakers. It was peculiar to hear Tiny speak quietly. Almost shyly.

'Hey, Spook, I'll think about Christmas if I can bring a friend.'

'Who's being the tease now?'

'I'm serious, man.'

Spook spoke as if choosing his words carefully. 'As always, you're very welcome, and a friend of yours is a friend of mine. The dress is, as it always has been, Christmassy and classy. When I know all the details, I'll let you know. Deal?'

'Deal! When I know numbers, I'll return the favour.'

'Rog. Out.'

Wiping the tears from her eyes, the mere phrase of 'Christmassy and classy' brought back happy childhood memories for Darlene. Although the tropics teemed with humidity, everyone made an effort to look the part. Even the Christmas pyjamas! Endless thanks were given to the inventor of the air conditioner! Up until she turned eighteen, her entire extended family all celebrated Christmas together. Being the youngest by eleven years, she was blessed to have had her siblings and their growing families at every Christmas celebration. It was always so much fun. The deeply buried fond memories brought on a torrent of sobbing. She could barely see in front of her.

'Hey, mate! Keep 'em straight.'

A stern voice boomed through the speakers, forcing her to gather her wits while having a very serious word with herself. This was no time to lose control. Heaven forbid! She wasn't even halfway across the country. Darlene depressed the talk button twice in acknowledgement of the advice.

Concentrating on the good times of her life, she wondered if her own family had started thinking about Christmas. After all, it was mid-September, and the rest of her family were scattered along the coast between Brisbane and Sydney. Her happily retired parents had decided the outskirts of Coffs Harbour was halfway between their kids. Dad couldn't drive anymore, and, well, it was a lot to expect Mum to drive vast distances. Technology provided the link. Darlene was still their kid, but had preferred the serenity of the bush, rainforest or smaller beach towns, which was where she'd lived and worked for most of her adult life. Not alone. As her career grew, so did her contacts. A very reliable private charter airline and her struck up a mutually beneficial arrangement. They flew her to her functions; she promoted them loudly and widely. Then she wondered why she didn't fly to WA.

Dismissing the mind noise, she thought about another hamburger and dismissed that notion as quickly as it appeared. All this sitting was not doing her any favours. She wanted to run, ride a horse, walk through the rainforest, anything, as long as she was doing something physical.

A massive explosion caused the rear trailer of the truck in front to dance across both lanes, and she carefully swerved to miss the flying debris. Dropping her speed gradually, she hugged the far-left side of the lane.

'Spook, steady up, ol' boy, your tail's wagging. You done a tyre.'

'Bastard. Inner or outer?'

'Just coming around the RV, stand by.'

Darlene knew it was the driver's side inner rear but had no way of communicating it without revealing who she was.

'What was it? Inner driver or outer? One or two?' Tiny's question caught her attention.

She depressed the talk button once.

'Driver or passenger side? One or two?'

Darlene repeated the response.

'Copy that,' Spook replied. 'I'm not going to make Port Augusta, you roll on.'

She depressed the talk button once.

'No way, mate. Go private.'

Darlene followed the trailer lights of Spook's truck. Now she knew who was who. Although there was absolutely nothing she could do, she wasn't about to leave this convoy anytime soon. A fairly congested truck and trailer stop forced her to pull short of all the other semi-trailers and stay out of the way of inbound trucks.

'Go to forty, mate.'

It sounded like Tiny's voice, so she dialled the two-way up and listened to the days in the lives of the long-haul truckers. What a cesspit of mixed characters! Trying to decipher who was who was impossible, so she left the volume up and went through to the kitchenette. She did ten minutes of combined Pilates and yoga stretching, followed by some Tai Chi, freshened up then lay down on her bed and waited for the kettle to boil.

A cup of soup would suffice. If she kept eating burgers while driving across the country, she too would be wearing a hole in her shirts. Giggling at the thought, she stretched her back and stared at the sky through the side window.

'Hey, mate, gonna be tied up here for a bit. Same as before.'

She stopped what she was doing. *Was he talking to me? Was that Spook or Tiny?* she asked herself.

'Copy?'

Darlene lunged and responded in her normal fashion.

'Scalies on their way, boys. Get your logbooks out.'

After a massive outcry of groaning, the radio fell silent. Scalies were the road transport officers who scrutinised drivers and their logbooks and sometimes penalised the blokes for a spelling mistake. She'd heard numerous complaints from the guys who shipped the cattle and grain. Darlene knew to listen out for three short bursts of the air horn then wait for more information. She just didn't know how long to wait. Watching the two men converse at the rear of the dusty trailer, kicking at a tyre, she realised who was who. Tiny was as broad as he was tall, and Spook had a head full of white wispy hair. She giggled at the picture they painted.

Sure enough, within twenty minutes, three police patrol vehicles and four canopied utilities pulled into the westbound rest area. Thankful that she didn't have to explain her travels to anyone, she removed the magazines from her weapons and got the paperwork in order. Just in case. A blip on an airhorn brought her head up rapidly, and she watched a scalie approach Spook and Tiny. Getting fidgety, Darlene covered up the windscreen with a sun visor, donned her disguise and quietly slid open the side door. Bobbing down beside the troublesome passenger hub, she grimaced. It was still far too hot, and worse was a rather deep split in the tyre.

She challenged herself to break her twenty-minute tyre changing record.

Out of the nine men at the station who'd participated in the competition, she came third. Granted, it was by thirty seconds, but she'd held her own. And it was on the Boss Man's massive Dodge Ram without a hoist. They thought it was a hilarious challenge thrown down as a farewell party starter. Her departing gift from the station hands had been a fully charged cordless impact wrench for removing wheel nuts.

As she put her head back inside the motorhome, she heard the two-way crackle.

'Hey, mate, I repeat, gonna be a while.'

She responded in typical fashion and peered over the sun visor. Nobody was walking around their vehicles. Several drivers were visibly preoccupied with the officers of the law. She pulled down her hat even further, slipped on the gloves and flipped the front seat forward to access the necessary tools.

The amount of dust that caked the spare tyre nuts was out of this world. What felt like forever to get them undone was really only five minutes, but those minutes were critical. Two trucks had already departed without blowing their horns. They'd all been caught up in the dust storm and all had more than enough rest hours. Clearly, the men had taken that opportunity and completed their necessary paperwork. Scalies had a reputation for being prolific and ruthless. Like sharks around bleeding live bait.

Adrenaline helped lift the jack to an appropriate height, and by the time Darlene had free access to the overheating wheel hub, another truck had rolled out. Feeling particularly stressed and vulnerable, she took a deep breath and forced unacceptable doubts out of her head. Lifting the spare tyre onto the axle, she lightly did up the nuts and gave it a spin. It did not turn easily. It wasn't the bearings causing grief, but the damned brakes. She was hoping she'd never have to aquaplane; she'd be able to get away with the issue, considering the replacement tyre was in better condition. Rapidly tightening the nuts with her departing gift from the boys, the moment she began to roll the old tyre away, a cough nearby made her freeze on the spot.

'You right, mate?' a stocky, middle-aged police officer asked pleasantly as he approached.

She nodded, gave him a gloved thumbs-up. He watched as she silently hoisted and secured the old tyre to its rack, then returned the tools to their place.

'Can you speak?'

She had to do something, and instead of speaking, wrapped her dusty gloved hand around her throat and hoarsely whispered two words. 'Sore throat.'

He removed his sunglasses and scrutinised her intently. Again, she gave him the thumbs-up and stepped inside her safety zone. She was about to slide the door shut when he put his foot on the sill. She spun around immediately.

'Not so fast. You travelling alone?'

Darlene nodded her head firmly.

'No dog?'

One shake of the head.

'If I search your vehicle, will I find anything illegal?'

A shake of the head again, and she drew a question mark in the air. She bit back a smirk when he roughly tore out a piece of paper and insisted that she wrote down her answers instead. She pulled a pen from her shirt pocket and held it poised, straight faced.

'Do you have any drugs on board?'

She showed him her answer. *No.*

'Where did you come from?'

Darlene flipped up the paper like it was a scorecard. *Today, Broken Hill. Before that, Mackay, Queensland.*

He didn't smile. 'Where are you going?'

Rolling her eyes, she dutifully showed him her answer. *Perth.*

'Why?'

Now her ire was rising. More trucks had left and the two-way was quite loud. She scribbled on the paper and showed him what she wanted to know. *Why all the questions? Do I look like a criminal?*

'Your appearance is clandestine, but no. Have you had any physical interaction with any drivers?'

She shook her head vehemently.

He smirked. 'Driver's licence please, miss.' He laughed at her astonished look. 'Nice try. You got away with it from a distance... but you really shouldn't be travelling alone. Have you tagged up with any of these fellas?'

She had to smile as she showed him her affirmative answer. *Yes.*

'Which ones, and do they know where you're going?'

Sighing heavily, she knew there was no point in lying. Even though she didn't have a sore throat, she purposefully wrote down the names of Spook and Tiny and explained they were the ones dealing with the blown tyre. While he was reading it, she retrieved her driver's licence and paperwork associated with the gun licences, permit to carry and upcoming competition. When he looked up, she handed him the lot with a wry grin on her face. He compared the revolting photos with her current appearance and kept a straight face.

'Please remove your sunglasses, Darlene Adams.'

She did so, deliberately making her eyes larger than they were naturally.

Clearly trying very hard not to stare, he simply nodded before handing back her documents. She felt a slight tingle when their fingers touched but swiftly concealed all emotion.

'All's in good order, and I know those lads. You're in good company. All the same, please leave a message when you have arrived at your destination. Travel well, Ms Adams.'

He held out his hand. His look was of hopeful expectation, so she shook it as firmly as she could and smiled then nodded her head.

'Please, just be safe. There's a lot of nothing between here and there.'

In a fake but convincing hoarse voice, she whispered, 'Thank you, sir. I appreciate your discretion.'

Deputy Sergeant Troy Oscane stepped backwards and waited until he heard the distinct sound of a door being locked. His stomach felt like it was being swept into a maelstrom, and for some stupid reason, he did not want to talk to Tiny and Spook. He was even more jittery when the two scalies moved away as he approached the familiar pair of drivers.

'Sarge,' Spook greeted him politely.

'Spook, Tiny. Still Deputy, but thanks all the same. Nice to see you blokes again. I'm led to believe you've got an inconspicuous travelling companion heading to Perth. Just know she's a very capable woman.'

'Can you tell us anything else?' Tiny asked, a little bit too eagerly.

Troy looked at him closely, wondering why the interest. He'd never seen or heard about Tiny being in the company of anything except a dog, and always a kelpie. The men had known of each other long before Tiny signed up with the federal police, and Troy also knew he had been encouraged to join the Special Forces. It was a huge mystery why he was now driving freight trucks across Australia.

25

'Yeah, she's to leave a message when she reaches her destination.'

'Is she going straight there or doing the tourist thing?' Spook asked.

Troy frowned. 'What's going on?'

'Nothing untoward, sir,' Spook said firmly. 'We're already behind the deadline thanks to the blasted dust storm and cannot afford being chaperones. Our femme traveller has to run with us or go at her own speed.'

'Well, I'm not about to be the go-between, so you–'

'Sir,' Tiny interrupted, 'It's pretty obvious she doesn't want any attention from any of us blokes. Incidentally, that purple prime mover is on the road. Suspect he's en route to Port Pirie from Broken Hill.'

Not particularly impressed about being the errand boy or hearing news about his nemesis, Troy put his hands on his hips and studied the two men before him. Not once had they done anything out of the ordinary in all the years their paths had crossed. Plus, they always seemed to drop snippets of information about something not quite right. A road transport officer coughed as he approached, causing the deputy sergeant to whirl around.

'Stu?' Troy said loudly.

'We've got a job to do here, Troy. You can't have these boys' attention all the time.'

He cleared his throat noisily. 'Yep, righto. Lads, you know what you've got to do. I've got something to do too. Keep left, fellas. See you on the flipside.'

He waved over his shoulder and investigated several other trucks as he made his way towards the motorhome. Again. Troy had no real reason to find out the itinerary of the female traveller, but he could see the logic in what the men were saying. He called out his intention as he got closer to the vehicle.

'Deputy Sergeant Troy Oscane approaching motorhome.'

He amiably removed his sunglasses as he stood alongside the sliding door. Darlene had been watching the interaction and made him wait several minutes before unlocking the latch.

'I'll knock twice then open the door,' he said calmly.

She was leaning against the jamb in the same attire, except for the hat, and took his breath away.

'Ahem. Ms Adams.'

Troy admired the way her wavy blonde hair framed her naturally beautiful face and nearly lost himself in her large hazel eyes. When she raised a perfectly arched eyebrow and smirked, he realised he was fumbling with his sunglasses and felt like he was blushing.

'Um, uh, Ms Adams.' He cleared his throat again. 'You have all the wares of being a very capable woman. However, your convoy buddies are on a strict deadline to get to Perth. What does your itinerary look like?'

He didn't mean to speak so gruffly, but he was totally unnerved. It had been many years since he'd tripped over his words in the presence of a beautiful woman.

Her neutral expression didn't change, nor did she speak. Instead, she spread the road map out onto the floor. It was clear to him that Perth was the primary destination, with a couple of stops across the Nullarbor Plain. Once she was in Western Australia, Norseman to Perth was a direct route.

'I would like us to swap mobile numbers, please. Also, I will be informing Spook and Tiny that your intention is the most direct route to Perth. Do your parents know where you are?'

Darlene laughed silently. Troy badly wanted to hear her laughter. Her voice. There was something special about this woman; no wonder Tiny was intrigued. He watched as her hand flew gracefully across another piece of paper. The way she held the pen was firm, confident, yet her writing was so swift and neat. He gently took the piece of paper from her outstretched hand and read it silently.

I'm a big girl now! They know I'm travelling and mobile phone coverage isn't reliable. I'll check in with them at Ceduna. Thanks for your concern and continued discretion, Deputy Sergeant Troy Oscane. Please extend my humblest gratitude to Spook and Tiny. I'll do my best to continue being the responsible convoy buddy. By the way, I think I finally worked out which one's which LOL

His deep rumbling laugh made her smile broadly. Their eyes met, and they held each other's gaze. She respectfully broke the connection and clasped her hands together. He acknowledged the international symbol for thank you, nodded his head and stepped back into the glaring sunshine. She held up her mobile phone and tapped it.

'Ah, yes, thank you for reminding me. Here's my business card. Please send me an update of your travels. I will not share your details with anyone else, unless you want Spook or Tiny to know it?'

With her lips pursed in thought, she stared into the distance above his head. When her vision returned to the current moment in time, she smiled warmly and shook her head. She opened her mouth to speak, then rolled her eyes. He couldn't help himself and leaned in, trying not to loudly inhale her scent.

In a hoarse whisper, she said, 'Thank you, but not this time.'

'Okay, I'll let them know,' he whispered back.

This time, he did blush. It was too late. She'd seen it. This naturally beautiful woman with the long slender neck, wearing the baggiest clothes disguising what was probably the most amazing figure and absolutely nothing like the driver's licence of yesteryear. Whatever had happened from that time to now could only have been for the better. She had bloomed like a perfect English rose. Collecting his wits, he dipped his lid and walked purposefully away, desperately wanting to turn around one last time and drink in her beauty.

Darlene slid the door shut and sat heavily on the bed. Why were her hands shaking? Why was her heart racing? Was it because she'd kept up the lie about the sore throat? Why was he so damned nice? His eyes were mesmerising, and he had a great laugh. Why were Spook and Tiny so concerned about her? When his head had been so close to hers, she damned nearly kissed him. She badly needed... *No. Stop thinking like a brazen hussy. It's been far too long, and you're almost forty years old*, she admonished herself harshly. But damn, when it doesn't rain, it pours!

Flipping her attitude, she grumbled as she reactivated her phone. A bit of ESP was happening, it seemed. Listening to the voicemail from her mum brought tears to her eyes.

Cordial, sporadic phone calls had been the trend with her family for several years. Sadly, the last family catch-up hadn't been pleasant. Probably because it was too soon after the relationship breakdown and her emotions were in a mess. Everybody had voiced their opinion around the dining table about what she should do with her life. Shock horror. Single. Nearly forty. Childless. Overweight.

Not one adult family member comprehended her decision to work on a remote grain and cattle station. Only Cassie, her favourite niece, had sat and listened without speaking. Her parents, her siblings and their spouses had laughed, scoffed and laughed again. *Darlene the Dreamer* echoed in her head for a long time after she'd left the lights of the city behind her that night. She had never returned.

Replaying the telephone message, she sighed heavily. The abrupt message hadn't lost its edge, and she was in no mood to return the phone call.

Lying idly across the bed, she stared out the window. The blue sky with soft cotton-ball clouds tying themselves up into big fluffy mountains brought a smile to her face. Jimmy was having a puff with his hippy mates.

Spook glared at the back of the departing road transport officer. It was as clear as day that the black pen Spook had been using had been running out of ink and he'd only had a blue one handy. What was he supposed to do? The prat couldn't answer the question and was about to ping him with a fine when Tiny interjected. He somehow managed to talk the scaley around and avoided any further altercation.

'Simmer down, mate,' Tiny suggested quietly. 'You're about ready to explode, I reckon.'

'Effing idiot. This isn't my first trip. Great! Here comes Oscane. That's all I need.'

With Tiny's assistance, he'd replaced the trashed tyre and reconfigured the duals. They were just waiting to roll. He angrily kicked at the tyres and rechecked the straps on his freight. The female traveller had also got under his skin for some reason, and he'd never even laid eyes on her. In all the years he'd been steering a truck with sixty-plus wheels, he had only ever felt anxious twice. This was the second time.

The first was when he and Tiny broke the golden rule of interfering in another trucker's load. The scrawny driver had cleverly disguised his face with a scary Halloween mask. Little did they know they were going to save a foreign girl from being abducted. Little did they know who the maggot was. Without involving the police, an arrangement had been made, and his abductee was stowed away in Tiny's truck. Then swiftly transferred into Spook's rig in the middle of the night in the middle of nowhere and given safe haven until she'd recovered enough to stand on her own two feet. She owed them her life and had let them know that every fifth day for the last eight months. Because of her origins, beauty and sweetness, they'd nicknamed her 'Danish Pastry'.

Tiny and Oscane stood either side of him and waited patiently until he grunted, 'What's up, you pair?'

'Over to you, Sarge,' Tiny murmured.

'I can tell you that your buddy is going straight to Perth...'

'She spoke?' Tiny asked, his eyes wide open.

'No... wrote down her answers. A sore throat, apparently.'

'Oh,' was all he said.

'So, what else did she tell you?' Spook demanded.

'To thank you both and she'd do her best to keep up,' Oscane said. 'You boys need to get a wriggle on. The sun's ahead of you now.'

Troy shook both their hands firmly and bade them safe travels as he fondled the note in his trouser pocket. He'd tag along until Lincoln Gap, then he was out of his jurisdiction and looking for trouble if he hung around. By then, the purple prime mover should have been picked up.

CHAPTER FOUR

Watching dust plume around the purple engine cover as he slowed to a stop long before Wilmington gave Spider the opportunity to avoid the overarching scrutineers. The scalies who had nothing better to do. He wasn't pulling a load, but he did have a rendezvous to make and couldn't afford being delayed unnecessarily. Besides, he did not want to see his cousin. Deputy Sergeant Troy Oscane. The only uniformed cousin. The one who decided to avoid the family business. The one who just couldn't quite make it in anything he did with his life. Almost married. Almost a sergeant. Almost rich. There's being smart and there's being cunning. Simple theory of not getting caught was how this game was played.

Signal eventually came through that the scrutineers had vacated and uniformed personnel had dispersed accordingly. His run was clear. Slipping into low gear to reduce strain on the ageing engine, he traversed Horrocks Pass slowly. He had to turn right several kilometres before the main intersection of the Augusta Highway. That's where he'd collect his passengers en route to Port Pirie. Then he could get the long-awaited paint job done on his prime mover and have a holiday at the same time.

The thought of his treasured rig having a new paint job only marginally lightened his mood. He was still riled up and had scanned the channels and different frequencies constantly – after being told to get off number thirty-eight – in the hope of tracking them, but they'd fallen silent after that.

How dare they? You can talk on whatever channel you like. How dare they? Find them. Deal with them.

Shaking his head violently to dispel the angry voices, he envisaged what his passengers would look like and let his excitement grow instead. Waiting for him should be another two young women wanting to bum a lift as far as he could take them. His scheduler always organised his company, and he'd had no reason to complain so far. Spider liked Danes and Russians, but the

31

Russian girls were his favourite. They were nice and tall and didn't speak much English, plus their mouths were nice and large. Nobody missed them. He was sure of that. The only thing he didn't like was dealing with Reg Oscane. He was the go-between, not the scheduler of toys. That was the mystery man.

Spider had quite a collection to play with. Nine so far, almost one a day for a fortnight, all waiting for him in his underground cellar. He wanted fourteen by Christmas, because he was having two whole weeks off. His playpen was cool, nicely furnished and dark. He liked the darkness.

Soon he would be at home. His toys would be well rested after his uncle Max had enjoyed his holiday with them. Max was also smart and cunning. A businessman who made decisions at meetings during the day, but after hours and on weekends would coordinate cargo and keep the tobacco, happy weed and powder trade alive. People liked to smoke. Simple. The nips still grew the good stuff, were the biggest population who still smoked, and they also loved cash money. Thanks to this smart businessman uncle, a deal had been struck at the local marina. And now, that uncle was very rich.

All Spider had to do was hook up the container-loaded trailer and drop it at the nominated address wherever in the country, then return to base. From there, he'd go in the opposite direction and retrieve the empty trailer. Reg, he was only ever called Reg, only knew about the tobacco! Uncle Max was so clever. It was too easy. Great pay. No stress. And Spider had toys. He liked his toys.

Idling into the enormous shed, he made the obligatory phone call. His father. The boss.

'Hey, Reg, I'm back.'

'Yep, someone dropped off two different treats for you. A Danish pastry and an Aussie patty cake, both feisty and new to how we do things in the bush. Anyway, first there's an empty you need to collect from the west in three days, then–'

'Three days? Hell no. You said I could have more–'

'Cut the whinging, unless you want Stevo to take your share?'

Take the girls with you, go now. Then come back and play some more.

His lips curled into a sly grin. Yeah, that was a great idea.

'How's this for an idea? I'll take my two treats with me on a slow trip west.'

'I'll think about it. Max wants to give your place a makeover, anyway, but go via Pirie and swap rigs.'

'So soon?' he gasped in excitement.

'Spider, listen to me. The Purple People Eater is drawing too much attention. Why don't you take the Black Widow?'

The Black Widow? Yeah, yeah. Now's your chance to live your namesake. Do it. Do it.

'You win, Reg. I'll go to Port Pirie, swap rigs, do what I have to do and come back, pick up my goodies and head west.'

'Good lad.'

Spook led the convoy and checked his mirrors after the three short blasts on the air horn. Without fail, the motorhome rolled in between him and Tiny. He automatically went down two channels and presumed his convoy buddies would do the same. They were still several hundred kilometres east of Port Augusta and had lost another three hours. He knew he'd make Ceduna easily without another stop and put it across the airwaves.

'You got your ears on?' Spook grumbled.

'Rog,' Tiny replied instantly.

Spook was about to revert to Channel 40 when he heard two definite replies. He didn't realise he'd been holding his breath and exhaled loudly.

'Good. Listen, mate, how do you feel about pushing through to Ceduna?'

'Yep, sounds good to me.'

A split second later, the familiar two clicks were heard. Spook decided the less the single female was in public view, the better.

The harsh outback, riddled with heatwaves, gave the appearance of fluid movement. It was quite mesmerising. Comparing the South Australian remoteness to that of Queensland, Darlene didn't give a tuppence for either. Too brown. Too many signs of starved animals. Too much obvious heartache. She was hankering to see greenery and the sea. The familiar pang of missing stimulating conversation made her sniffle. Up until two years ago, her adult life had revolved around motivational speaking, event coordination and volunteering. She had to phone her parents. Alas, no coverage.

'Mack triple overtaking motorhome.' Tiny broke the radio silence.

'Clear, mate,' Spook responded.

Darlene automatically dropped her speed as she watched the gleaming, bulldog-adorned truck gently glide into the outside lane. She grinned, did the 'pull the air horn' sign out the window. He obliged the request as he overtook and tucked in neatly behind Spook. The indicator dance was dutifully performed. There was nothing she could do but look at his rear trailer for a while. It was fine with her. She was getting pulled along, and they were breaking the headwind. Being last in the convoy also gave her more opportunity to look at the changing scenery.

As drastic as the barren lands were, the abundant young green wheat and budding golden canola fields emerged as they approached the coastline. The air was heavy with a salty aroma and the sky seemed a deeper blue. Drinking in the amazing, colourful scenery, her composure returned. Two more voicemail messages chimed on her phone.

Taking the opportunity of full mobile phone coverage, she listened to the most recent frantic messages from her mother. Apparently, Cassie had decided being an au pair in the Northern Territory was good work experience, except nobody had heard from her for several days. Her silence had triggered a bit of a panic attack because Darlene hadn't phoned home for a while either.

Taking a deep breath, she let it out in one go when she answered her father's gruff greeting.

'Hi, Dad, it's me,' she responded happily.

'About time, darling. Where are you?'

'In the middle of South Australia and all's well. How are you and Mum?'

'It's nice to hear from you. Mum's a tad stressed and is resting. Cassie hasn't phoned anybody for three days, which is highly unusual. At least one of us would've heard from her. We all talk every day. Well, some of us do, anyway.'

She shook her head to dismiss the snide comment and smiled as she caught sight of a magnificent wedge-tailed eagle.

'Why did you take so long to call?'

'Dad, in some places, mobile coverage is as useless as some of the people in government. Perhaps the mobile network has fallen over where Cassie is and you're all worrying too much?'

'Not likely. Her mother's instinct cannot be argued with. Hell, neither can her grandmother's instinct. Any mother's instinct, Darlene.'

'Yep, thanks for that. You and I have a pretty solid connection, though.'

'True, although beside the point. Cassie took a posting in Alice Springs.

The last we heard, the family she's working with were taking the horses to some gymkhana thing. That's why we're so worried.'

'Where were they going?'

'Nobody knows! But you said you're in South Australia. Where?'

'Nearer to the Western Australian border than not. And no, I cannot turn around.'

'What are you doing?'

'Returning a motorhome to Perth.'

'You're what?'

'I've got my friends and contacts en route. I'm safe, I promise you. Can you send me a current photo of Cassie anyway?'

'Fat load of good that'll do when you're going in the opposite direction. We're praying she's okay. We discovered the reason she took the job so far away was because her boyfriend had ditched her. We've decided that if nobody can get hold of the family or her by tomorrow night, the police will be called.'

'That's a good idea, but why wait? There should be a rural police station at the Alice. Give them a ring. Tell them as much as you know and ask questions. Talk to someone that can do the leg work. That'll help put all your minds at ease.'

Her father's breathing was ragged. 'Yes. Yes, that is actually a good idea. Thanks for calling, pet. I'll take your love and give some to Mum.'

'Thanks. It was nice hearing your voice and talking to you. Sending lots of love, always. Keep me posted, hey?'

'Yes, pet. Bye.'

'Love you, Dad. Bye.'

He managed to choke out the sentiments before sniffling and disconnecting the call.

'Oh, Cassie, I hope your mouth didn't get you into trouble again,' she mused loudly, recalling the heated debate between her niece and a male cousin when the lass was much younger. Cassie had ruthlessly caned the lad to the point where he had hyperventilated. The smart-mouthed, glib-tongued, now-twenty-four-year-old knew from an early age the power and tone of her words could make someone blind with rage if she pushed the buttons hard enough. And she could be relentless. The cat fights at school had also been quite embarrassing. It was a momentous occasion when she graduated with a degree in childcare, in record time and without trouble. What was most surprising was her tenderness and kind disciplinary ways with young children. They all presumed the she-leopard had changed her spots.

One particular evening in a nightclub, Darlene witnessed that in fact, she had not, having to intercept a very nasty argument between Cassie and a bloke who did not appreciate her sassy lip nor her right hook. The pair had spent the next two days defending her action with the police, the bloke and the establishment. They settled on Cassie leaving town, never to return. She had kept her word.

Darlene said a silent prayer for her safe return and pleaded with her to make contact with someone in the family. Anyone. Suddenly, the gangly tattooed thing in the purple prime mover popped into Darlene's head, and she shivered violently. She was not a seer by any stretch of the imagination, but she did play her hunches. She desperately needed to find out more. Taking a punt, she dialled Deputy Sergeant Troy Oscane's number then swiftly hung up. She could not have got her voice back so soon! Doing something highly illegal and extremely unusual, she sent a text instead: *pocket call :-)*

His reply expressed disappointment because he'd hoped she'd gotten her voice back. Spook's voice jolted her back to reality.

'Hey, mate, pulling into the servo west of the town. There's a rest area behind it. Take advantage of it for a while. Next leg will be long. Same as before.'

She responded in her usual way just as her phone chimed. Expecting it to be from her father, she smiled as Cassie's photo filled her screen. Her ebony hair, almond-shaped brown eyes, button nose and ruby lips captured mid-word. Not the most flattering photo, but a naturally candid image of the pretty girl with the smart mouth.

After paying for fuel at the bowser with the gift card, Darlene utilised the smaller vehicle rest area and tucked herself as far away from everyone else as possible.

Taking the opportunity for some downtime, she did her stretching exercises and boiled the kettle. A gymkhana? This late in September? Flipping open the laptop, her fingers flew over the keyboard. Nothing. She wasn't surprised. Most outback horse races and events happened during August or early September. Darlene wasn't liking what she was feeling and sent a meaningful text to the deputy sergeant.

Hi, DS Oscane. All's well near Ceduna. Any reports of an accident or incident involving horses in the vicinity of A/Springs during the last week or so? D. Adams

Almost half an hour later, she got a negative and questioning response.

Rumours of an au pair and family en route to gymkhana. I know it's a big country!

Unusual for this time of the year.

I agree. Something's not sitting right. A niece is the au pair. Could you keep your ears out please?

It was extremely cheeky to ask, but she knew damned well eyes and ears in the rugged country either helped solve problems or got you into a lot of trouble. Someone always won and someone always lost.

It'll be easier to talk to you!

LOL

Instead of continuing the conversation and making a coffee, she hung out her washing, put on another load and took a shower before wiping away as much dust as she could. She imagined Tiny taking his shirt off, then swiftly dismissed the thought.

Troy's heart sang. The beautiful Darlene Adams had reached out to him. Now he had good reason to do some research on her and her family. She'd raised a question, and he would do his utmost to keep her informed. Seated at his paper-strewn desk with a sandwich in one hand, he realised she'd also given him the perfect excuse to stay in contact. Typing one-fingered while he ate seemed to be his way of doing his office job, because there was no way he would ever eat or drink in his patrol car. It was spotless. Reaching for his phone, he punched in the number for Dino, his contact at the cross-border mobile roaming unit.

'Troy Oscane, you're the last person I'd expect to get a call from. What's up?'

'Hey, mate, seen anything weird lately?'

'Nope. No sign of Purple People Eater. No single women, either!'

'How about a family with an au pair travelling to or from a gymkhana?'

'Nope. Wrong time of the year for that.'

'Yeah, yeah. You'll let me know if you see or hear anything, hey?'

'Yep. Is that purple rig a going concern?'

'Always.'

'You know they've expanded into pot and powder as well as tobacco?'

'Same reply as it's always been. I suspected it. Just can't prove it, but I will.'

'Yep, as is mine. Bloke, you've been on this mission ever since you joined the department. Aren't you tired of it yet?'

'Nope.'

'That's why you'll always be a deputy, buddy.'

'Yep, and I'm fine with that. Keep me posted. Thanks, bloke.'

'Ciao.'

Troy smirked. Old Dino was always on the hunt for a woman, but his easy-come-easy-go attitude with money blew any chances of a long-term relationship. The twice-mentioned topic of the purple rig was peculiar. Then Troy recalled the lads also mentioned it and they'd come through Broken Hill. Dialling the roadhouse, he announced himself and asked to be put through to the manager. While waiting, he dialled into the traffic cameras on the intersection from Horrocks Pass to the Augusta Highway. They were annoyingly offline.

'Jules here. How can I help you, sir?' a gruff woman's voice bellowed through the phone.

'Thanks, Jules. Could you run through your security tapes and describe any single prime movers in the last forty-eight hours for me, please?'

'Can tell you right now. Just the one. That bloody purple thing with the tall streaky piece of painted pelican poop kicking up a ruckus in the restaurant. Didn't drop his dust beforehand and didn't hang around afterwards. Paid cash for his fuel like he was some high roller. Gawd, he boils me blood for some reason.'

'Thanks.'

'Anytime, sir. Say, there's a burger and milkshake waiting for you.' Her husky chuckle did not warm his heart one iota.

'You never know! Bye for now.'

He disconnected the call quickly and dialled Stu's number. After the very brief greeting, he asked if they'd intercepted or seen the bothersome prime mover. The negative reply encouraged him to reach out to the highway patrol crew, and he asked them the same question. Preparing himself for the never-ending jibes and negative responses, he thanked them for keeping the roads safe and hung up.

It was a long shot, but he phoned the Alice Springs branch and was surprised when the duty officer answered. They didn't usually on pay day. He announced himself and asked to speak to the boss.

'Nuh, not today. Big mystery. Horses and family gone walkabout.'

'When?'

'Nobody sure. Big boss out looking.'

'Must be important people.'

'Very, boss. He medicine man. He been doing good stuff with sick people. Don't care about skin. Community accept him, married princess wit' two young 'uns.'

'How can I help?'

'Find 'em. We need 'em. Missus sick.'

'Your missus?'

'Nah. His. Smart-mouth white girl demanded help five day ago. Boss booked chopper. Never turn up. They drove.'

'Was white girl theirs?'

'Nah. Too old. Not from here. Her hair blacker than me, boss.'

'You do a good job, keep it up.'

'Thanks. Community very worried. Bad juju with horses gone too.'

'They special horses?'

'Yes, Boss. Other girl magic. Not good time for horses. Bad flies now. Big rain come.'

'Tell me about the young 'uns.'

'Wait. Boss back.'

Troy waited for what seemed like an eternity before he heard another voice on the phone. After introducing himself, he soon learnt his much older counterpart, Neil Chalkham, had been the OIC for almost eleven years and had never seen or heard of anything like the current situation before. The doctor was a middle-aged Kenyan who'd won over the local community and had been helping the locals for almost five years.

'Can you tell me about his family?'

'His wife's a creamy, been here for generations and of good stock. A good woman, too bad she's sick. The medevac had a priority one and got diverted. The twin boys are aged three, healthy and rowdy. Their nanny is a newcomer, has hair blacker than I've ever seen on a white woman and a particularly direct tongue. Another young woman, similarly aged, is Danish and brilliant with horses. From what I can determine, the horses and trailer have all gone too. That's about it. I'll keep you apprised. Say, what's your interest anyway?'

'Just following up on an enquiry. Thanks for your time, sir. Good luck with your search.'

'Cheers for that, DS Troy Oscane. Wait... that name's familiar. Are you Dillon's son?'

'Yes, sir, I'm proud to say I am.'

'He was a good man. A real travesty what happened to your folks. Sorry for you, real sorry for you, son. It'd be nice to have a long chat over a couple of beers or the other way around sometime.'

'That's very kind of you to say so. I would like that very much, thank you, sir. Your words mean a lot to me.'

Troy hung up very slowly. The age-old headline broadcasting the tragic deaths of his parents flashed before his eyes. *High-Ranking Police Official and Wife Amongst Many Others in Train Disaster*. He vividly recalled the day. The day he was about to sit the sergeant's exam. The superintendent had tapped him on the shoulder and indicated he needed to leave the room. What happened afterwards was a blur, but Troy Oscane would retire or die a deputy sergeant, or at least be remembered as one. Sorrowfully, the harshest of realities came when he learnt his sister and future wife were amongst the deceased.

In an instant, he became a lonely thirty-two-year-old orphan. Their funeral service had been awkward. Over a dozen grieving immediate families mourned their losses together. The rogue Oscane family dutifully attended. Only Uncle Reg spoke to Troy after the service and offered him a Havana cigar. One of his father's favourites. Troy had accepted it graciously and never cracked the seal. Sliding open his top drawer, beside his backup revolver was that very cigar.

Troy Oscane was the only surviving upstanding member of the family. Yet he still had to prove the others representing the name weren't.

CHAPTER FIVE

Spider had always admired the Black Widow. His namesake. The snub-nosed pitch-black Volvo with its ginormous sleeper cab almost radiated from under the second shed's halogen lights. He'd entered through the disguised back door. The shed-house with its secret. There were even more toys, and none of them recognised him with his now shoulder-length hair and different full-length arm tattoo sleeves. He detested needles ever since his very first tattoo, but loved them so much he'd found a way to accommodate his desire to be painted. Even his legs, but sometimes, the painted stockings got too hot.

The toys all moaned behind their taped mouths. It was clear Max had added to the collection, had fed them and ensured they were clean before he'd left. Spider could always rely on Trixie to look after them after he'd done what he had to do.

He sighed heavily and blew them all kisses before gleefully skipping up the stairs. His juvenile voice telling them to behave.

Ninety minutes later, sliding down the gears as he rumbled through the tree-lined driveway towards the massive shed, his excitement grew. He was driving the Black Widow. He wore his spiderweb tattoo sleeves proudly and looked the part with his slicked-back black hair. His new toys would love him like no tomorrow. Grinning wickedly, he announced his arrival.

'I'm back, Reg. Ready to roll.'

'Righto. Precisely nine kilometres south of Yalata, there's a track on your left. Travel for six more, hook up, go beyond the township for fifteen clicks then return to base.'

'Give me my toys,' Spider hissed.

'No. They've gone. News came in which has changed the game, Spider. A young family have more use for them.'

Rage crept out of every pore of his skin and oozed through the colourful sleeves. He could even smell it. 'That's the fourth lot you haven't given me. Do you keep them?' he growled into the two-way.

'Don't be a bloody idiot. I am not that vile. Now go and do your job.'

'You're getting soft, you old bastard.'

What are you going to do now? You can't go back to your collection. You need some company. Go find someone else. Go on. Nobody will know.

'Don't push it, Spider. I've been doing this longer than you've been out of diapers.'

'Three days to hook up still?' he said coldly.

'Yep. The fuzz are sniffing around, so don't do anything stupid and make sure you've got the right damned logbook before you leave. You hear me, Spider?'

'Out.'

When was the old bastard going to die? Stupid, greedy old man. Why was he suddenly scared of the pigs, and why be so concerned about a young family? Stupid, stupid old man.

Spider vented as he navigated his way between the trees. He suspected the pigs were looking for his favourite girl, the purple prime mover. But now being incognito in the Black Widow, he'd get through the southern coastal towns without turning any heads. He needed another toy and hoped a backpacker would magically appear. Giggling, he looked at the Halloween mask. He would wear it again if he had to.

The lights of Border Village were a very welcome sight. Darlene was absolutely exhausted. Certainly not from overexertion, but the extended hours of uninterrupted concentration. She hoped Tiny and Spook would have an eight-hour break, because she felt she definitely needed it.

'Hey, mate, welcome to a long rest. We all need to stretch our legs.' Spook's voice was particularly strained.

Dutifully, she replied in code. It wasn't surprising there had been very little conversation as they crossed the Nullarbor Plain. Not much to see, not much to say. Awful headwinds, a lot of traffic and far too many wombats and kangaroos to avoid. The scudding showers had brought the daft wildlife too close to the road. Thankfully, there hadn't been any incidents. Darlene was almost regretting not playing the tourist when she saw the signs for the helicopter whale spotting. She desperately wanted to see the Great Australian Bight.

Tucking out of the way of the unfamiliar trucks, she positioned the motorhome strategically in order to stay out of sight from curious eyes. The more she'd thought about her clandestine appearance with Spook and Tiny, the guiltier she felt. She decided she'd best introduce herself to them, considering she was so far away from Queensland and hopefully any trouble.

Now she did allow herself to think about the horrible Oliver Cady and the circumstances she'd found herself in. She claimed self-defence when she shot him. Her intentions were to clip the dust beside his ankle, but she was just far too good a shot for deliberately missing. She'd gotten sick and tired of his bullying nature and sexual advances during the three-day competition, plus the rough treatment after the presentation dinner.

She relived the circumstances without emotion. She had deliberately parked away from the crowd and had been cleaning her prized Colt 45 when he'd thrown stones at her Jeep, announcing his arrival. His drunken stagger and bulging jeans announced his intentions. That was the last warning she'd given the steroid freak. The first had followed the attempted rape after the award ceremony seven months earlier. She'd been so roughly thrown to the ground her weapon had slid out of her reach. She had to use her feet instead and kicked at his groin with all her might.

Both circumstances still played on her mind.

DS Troy Oscane accepted the anonymous call.

'Go ahead, I'm listening,' he said formally and depressed the track and trace machine.

'There are two females at Spud's joint. They're alive, rehydrated and from out of state. Don't leave them there for any longer.'

The line disconnected. There was only one common place called Spud's. The Roadhouse at Pimba. Troy cursed under his breath as he turned off the machine. The phone call wasn't long enough, which indicated the caller knew what he was doing. The voice was disguised, probably with a pen stuck in his mouth. Or a cigarette. A cigar? He rubbed his eyes. He was tired, but his gut was gnawing at his last thought. Reg Oscane? His uncle? He felt he was clutching at straws, yet he couldn't wait another moment. The only female officer available was a relative newcomer to the region, not particularly dainty and a bit of a mother hen, but came with a reputation for being a darn good cop.

Right from the beginning of the working relationship, they'd both established that their personal lives were out of bounds and neither were fond of idle chatter. The two police officers had covered one hundred and twenty of the one hundred and ninety-two kilometres in companionable silence when the satellite phone rang. Officer Bev dutifully answered, listened to the message and relayed it back to her boss.

'That was your contact from the Alice. The missing family have checked in to the Whyalla Hospital, all being treated for dehydration. The adult female is in intensive care on renal dialysis. The horses and float were found at Coober Pedy in fairly good condition and on their way back home, but that's where the nanny and backpacker went AWOL.'

Troy murmured his thanks. He hoped the nanny was Darlene's niece and he'd be able to let her know the good news. A small smile played about his lips as he thought of her. She ought to be checking in soon.

He caught his colleague looking at him curiously and felt compelled to respond.

'Just hoping like hell that we can give someone good news instead of bad.'

She just nodded her head and smiled. Joint anticipation increased the closer they got to Pimba. They certainly had a welcoming party as they pulled into the driveway. Several people were waving madly at them by the entrance to the caravan parking area beside the roadhouse. A burly man wearing socks, sandals and a khaki safari suit couldn't wait for the car to stop and tried opening the driver's door beforehand.

'Sir! Sir! I saw two women being helped to that caravan over there in the early hours of this morning.' He pointed enthusiastically behind him. 'The two blokes didn't hang around. One was in a red-stained grey four-wheel drive with NT plates. The other took off on his dirt bike. All very suspicious, if you ask me.'

By now, Troy was irate. Firstly, he did not like people in his face, and secondly, the pompous sod was waving his mobile phone around. To his relief, Officer Bev took control of the situation and swiftly confiscated the phone while she steered the man away.

'Righto, folks, move along,' she commanded naturally. 'Nothing to see here. Leave us to do our jobs now. Thank you.'

Amazingly, they did so without a fuss. Troy watched as she firmly encouraged the bloke to allow her to transfer the captured images from his phone to hers. She had the broadest grin on her face as she permanently deleted the most recent files before returning it.

'Let's go, boss. All's good here.'

She led the way to the caravan and announced herself loudly as she opened the door. The two younger women were curled up so they could see the door in a back-to-back foetal position, their hands tied and mouths gagged, staring at the officers with wide, terrified eyes. Ever so gently, they were unbound and encouraged to sit up. Whoever had left them there had also left four bottles of water in a cheap Styrofoam esky within reach. They greedily grabbed at the bottles the minute their hands were free while the police officers introduced themselves.

'Thank God you got here.' The dark-haired younger woman spoke bluntly. 'I'm Cassie; this is Asta. She's from Denmark. We insisted the doctor leave the horses and float with us and get to a hospital. His wife is terribly ill. Two Abos recognised the kids and said they'd look after the animals. They had a ute. They kept repeating that big rains are coming. Then a truckie saw our plight and offered us a ride, but we had to wait until he had a break. He said he was going back to the Alice. We had to wait around for two whole days! He thought he'd drugged us, but we knew not to drink opened bottles of anything.'

The police officers listened intently to Cassie and took notes alternately. All the while, her friend kept nodding her head.

Officer Bev asked a question which only a woman could ask. 'Were either of you touched inappropriately?'

This time, Asta spoke up. Her soft Danish accent was more pleasant to listen to.

'Um, that's awkward, but we weren't raped or anything. We don't know where we were taken to, but it was south of here. The sunlight streaming through the window gave that away. We were blindfolded, and we reckon we're north of where we were. Anyway, the truckie preferred boys, from what we witnessed...'

'Care to clarify that, miss?' Bev asked quietly.

This time Cassie spoke even more vehemently. 'Yeah. The filthy bastard from Coober Pedy made us get out of the truck each time he felt the urge. The poor lad was drugged to the eyeballs and had no concept of anything.

The mongrel called his prey "cargo" and was taking him west. His words when he thought we were asleep. Don't ask who he was talking to. We were also blindfolded.'

'Do you feel up to travelling or did you want to rest a bit longer, ladies?' Troy asked gently.

The two women shared a look and reassuringly squeezed each other's hands, but their faces were hopeful. 'Yes, we travel,' Asta said quietly.

'You'll be pleased to know the family are safe at the Whyalla Hospital, which is in South Australia. You are in Pimba, south of Coober Pedy. Incidentally, where are your valuables?'

'In Coober Pedy,' Cassie replied flatly. Her lips pulled into a thin line as a deep frown creased her brow.

Asta patted her hand. 'Cassie, we'll get them back now. They don't have to make a phone call.'

She explained that they'd left their belongings with the manager of the post office. If the girls hadn't collected them by the first week of October, a phone call would've been made to the police.

The two police officers stepped outside and exchanged concerns, both knowing it was a six-and-a-half-hour return trip from their current location to the rugged opal capital of the world.

'Boss, how about we call the post office and see if they can arrange a courier to our station? The girls can freshen up there. We'll sort something out about accommodation.'

'Good call. I'll do that. Maybe have more of a girly chat and get them ready to travel back. I want to be off the road by nightfall tonight.'

'Yes, sir.'

CHAPTER SIX

A message came through from Deputy Sergeant Troy Oscane requesting an update on her position. Darlene responded candidly with the thumbs-up emoticon and a photo of the Border Village sign followed by a string of Zs. She hadn't given him much thought and attended to her chores before collapsing. But people had other ideas, it seemed, as another message came through on her phone.

Dragging herself to an upright position, she activated her phone and couldn't believe what she was reading. Two young women were safe and in the company of a female officer overnight until something could be arranged. Her fatigue had evaporated, and she flicked a photo of Cassie through to Troy. His confirmation made her burst into tears with relief. Then the aunty instinct kicked in. She stressed the importance of the young lass contacting a family member, as they were worried sick, particularly her grandparents.

She only wants to talk to you and has never known you to lose your voice when she needed help. I can't believe she's your niece. You pair look like nothing like each other!

Darlene didn't know how to respond, so she didn't. She closed her eyes and tried to sort out her thoughts.

Spider was liking the early evening view as he crested the hill beyond Whyalla. The weather was warming up and the skirts were going to get higher. He snorted like a horse as his mouth twisted into a sly grin, his fingers wriggling around the steering wheel. Yeah, anywhere near the beach was a good hunting ground.

Taking a seat in a darkened corner of the restaurant, he drank a Pepsi while he observed the scenery. Nothing really took his fancy, but he ordered a juicy steak and vegetables. *You have to eat good to look good.* His guiding voice encouraging him not to stray off his eating habits.

And then he saw her. The waitress. The dining room lights glinting off her dangling earrings. He wondered if her belly button was pierced. He liked that. He hoped she was bringing his dinner. She was! He gasped and squirmed in delight when he saw the tattoo peeping out from around her neck. He wanted to know more. He had to have this one.

'Thank you, young lady. I like your tattoo,' he said in his politest voice.

'Ta, see you like spiders! I like snakes. We should get together sometime.' She winked cheekily.

This is the one. Steal her away after dinner. You know you want to. You have to. You're lonely.

'So, spider charmer, when does your shift finish?'

'Ooh, snake catcher, in about three hours.'

'I'll wait.'

'Cool. Meet me by the timber shelter. Enjoy your meal.'

She rolled her eyes as she turned around! He wished he'd never seen that. He hated that.

Darlene had just sat down with her cup of soup and lightly traced over Jimmy's name on his manuscript when her mobile phone chimed with a message from an unknown number.

This is Officer Bev... your niece, who does not mince her words, needs to hear a familiar voice. She's here with her friend. Only us three women are at my private residence. Can you talk now?

Sighing and smirking, Darlene practised speaking in a forced whisper before dialling the number.

'Thank you for phoning, Ms Adams, I'll put her on...'

'Can I ask you something first, please, Officer Bev?'

'Of course.'

'Strictly between you and me... um, tell me, has she phoned her grandparents yet?'

'Of course, and no, she wants to talk to you first.'

'Okay, thank you for being there.'

She listened to the phone being handed over then Cassie's familiar tone.

'Aunty Darlene, thank you. I knew you'd talk to me. We've had a horrid time. First, we had to do a rush trip from some godforsaken hole in the desert, then the horse float bearings got too hot. They're prized horses, see. Then the Abos took them back and we got left behind. Inadvertently. We went exploring–'

'Cassie, Cassie, slow down. Have you been hurt in any way?'

'Only our eyes.'

Darlene gasped. 'Your eyes? What happened.'

Her niece's relieved giggle turned into a great belly laugh, which caused a domino effect from her audience.

'Nothing. It's what we saw, then what we had to do! We'll never be able to unsee certain things, but we've become the best of friends.'

'Phew! I'm relieved, Cas...'

'I have a friend, Aunt Darlene,' she said in a much gentler voice. 'I finally have a real friend. I mean, one my age. You're my friend too.'

'That's sweet, thank you. I'll always be your friend. I'm happier knowing you have a friend your own age as well. Tell me something, how do you feel about talking about what happened to you both?'

'Yeah, we're ready to talk. Officer Bev said she'd have to record the conversation but would only pay attention to anything that the police would find interesting. By the way, we're safe here. She's letting us stay out of sight.'

'That's very kind of her. Be nice and polite, now,' Darlene said with a chuckle.

Cassie responded with a sassy chortle, then progressively, her voice quivered as she described the recent events in her somewhat sheltered life.

'I jumped at the chance to escape a bit of smothering back home almost a year ago and ended up working for a black doctor and his local creamy wife. They needed an au pair for their twin boys. Anyway, I'd met Asta on the bus on the way over, who's been looking for her friend but had run out of money. We wrangled a deal with the doctor so we could both pay our way. Asta's a natural with horses. Aunty Darlene, they even won the local race! It was a tie, so now the horses are famous and treated like royalty.'

She took a shaky breath.

'Um, I told my parents we were going to a gymkhana so they didn't worry. We knew the mother was sick. She'd progressively gotten worse, but the medevac never happened, so we hitched up the horses and were headed to Adelaide. It's one hour less than Darwin by car. Us two entertained the boys, but when we got to Coober Pedy, everyone was hot and bothered and we were all concerned about the horses. So Asta and I said we'd stay behind and look after them. The priority really was the mother. She's the princess or something of importance in the community. Anyway, two ringers recognised us and they said they'd care for the animals. They were awfully concerned about their mother-aunty.

'Asta and I got sucked in with the history of opals. Asta's a pretty switched-on chick and has done a lot of backpacking through Europe. Being pay day, the cop shop's usually unattended, so we decided to go to the post office. They took pity on us, particularly as they knew of the doctor and his family, and took us in for the night. The next day, we hit the roadhouse looking for a ride down to Adelaide or back to Alice Springs. We got one, but had to wait for him, so we went back to the post office, described the truck and driver and asked if they'd take care of our belongings, with instructions to phone the cops if they hadn't heard from us within a week.'

Cassie's bravado had started to falter. A few more sniffles entered the conversation, even though the two other women comforted her while encouraging her to talk things out.

'The truck itself was a faded blue and had a separate bunk in the back, which was painted a dirty yellow. It was an old truck, rough as guts. He was a vile bastard, not only in his behaviour but his looks. Black rings under his eyes, chunky rings on every finger, just plain evil looking, and thankfully for us, preferred boys. Yeuch, we both almost vomit each time we think about what happened up there. That poor kid was drugged to his eyeballs. We had to get out whenever the dirty, dirty faggot had the urge. When we were travelling, us two hunkered down in the corner of the bunk, away from wherever the males slept. Aunty Darlene, it's dreadful. I don't reckon the lad were older than eleven.'

'You haven't had any water. Feel like a break, Cassie?'

'Nope. I mean, no thanks. Asta is teaching me to speak more feminine, but occasionally I slip and the language spews out of me like a bilge pump. Oh yeah, I haven't had a punch-up since we saw each other last.'

'Phew! Sounds like you're learning the art of how to behave appropriately in mixed company. Great stuff. Now, keep practising talking more feminine to me, if you're up to it?'

'Yeah, yes, thanks, I'm right to go. We never drank from the open bottles. We had to wait a couple of days, then we were blindfolded. There was a lot of hush-hush chat on the phone. We knew we were headed south because we could feel the heat of the sun as it rose. We always sat on the passenger side. Then... then... oh, Aunt Darlene, I don't know how to say this except bluntly... so brace yourself. We ended up in some sort of shed. It was massive. But if we didn't perform a lesbian act, the old man where we got dropped off threatened to have his way with us. But we never saw him get out from behind his desk. We had to learn quickly. Um, I think I'm bi. Asta's really good!'

'Cassie, let's stay focused, shall we?'

In a little voice, she asked, 'Are you ashamed of me?'

'Of course not! I'm relieved, actually. Heavens, we do what we have to do to survive, and you can always talk to me. Don't you ever forget that.'

That was when the floodgates opened, and Cassie bawled into the phone. Her words were incoherent for a while until she composed herself.

'You'd know about that too, Aunty Darlene. Holy sh... I think all my pain just came out then. I never cried after my boyfriend dumped me. Wow, I feel like a new person! Knew it'd help talking to you. Thank you.'

'We should all be very grateful right about now.'

'Hell yeah. Anyway, the old man really didn't care about us, except he made sure we had access to the bathroom. He even gave us towels and let us use the laundry. He didn't hurt us in any way. Couldn't cook for shite, but the water bottles were never opened when he left them by the door. I don't think he's a very well man, his coughing was dreadful. We could hear big dogs, then a truck idling for a while and the sound of voices, but couldn't make out the conversation. Then the truck drove out. Sometime later, another one drove in. Same deal, a conversation then left, but this time a lot quicker.

'At some ungodly hour, we were blindfolded and gagged before being helped into a vehicle. It stunk of cigars, but the seats were comfortable in the back and the aircon was on. Asta and I have talked about it since, and we both agree we were heading north, because it felt like it was in reverse to the way we came from Coober Pedy, which was a long straight, then we hung left, up a hill, then left.

'Time passes strangely when you can't see, so we have no idea how long we drove for. We were carried one by one into a caravan and made to lie on the floor. We heard voices and a motorbike. Anyway, it was dark when he removed the blindfold, but he did speak gruffly. Gave us some old person advice and told us not to move. He'd send someone to help us.'

'What was the old person advice?'

'Women shouldn't be travelling alone in the outback. There's a lot of nothing between here and there.'

Darlene nearly fell off the bed. That's exactly what Deputy Sergeant Troy Oscane had said. She gathered her wits and asked quietly, 'Cassie, who found you?'

'Officer Bev and her boss, DS Troy Oscane. Um, he said you'd contacted him?'

Darlene brought Cassie up to date on her most recent adventure, much to her niece's enthusiastic interest.

'Can we go with you? Please?'

'Sorry, ladies, but how about on my way back? What do you reckon about surprising the oldies for New Year's, and maybe we do something for Christmas?'

'You promise?'

'Yes. Pester your friendly constabularies and do everything you can to be useful but not in the way. Make finding Asta's friend a mission in the safe environs, if Officer Bev can put up with you pair.'

'I'll ask.'

Darlene smiled at the animated conversation going on in the background. The squeals of delight were answer enough.

'Officer Bev said she'd be happy to. She's a great cook. We're going to learn heaps and have a lot of fun too.'

'Cassie, dear Cassie, now you have to promise me something.'

'What?'

'Please ask Officer Bev if you can make two more phone calls and talk to Granny and Granddad first. They're frail and sick with worry. Granddad reached out to me. Let them know that you're safe and in good hands. You don't have to explain anything, just assure them nothing bad happened to you. Please. They need to know. Tell them you met a friend of mine and everything's going to be okay. You're just waiting for your belongings to be returned to you, you still have a job to complete and you'll be home after Christmas. Then call your folks and stay in regular contact, like every Sunday night.'

'Christmas? That's three months away!'

'Exactly.'

'Will you get me and Asta home?'

'Yes, yes, I will.'

'Promise?'

'I promise. Now are you going to promise me?'

'Yes, I promise, and I have witnesses. Thanks, Aunt Darlene. I gotta go, kitchen duties, but first I gotta make two phone calls.'

They both rung off amid a flurry of sniffles. From a completely different number, she received a message. *I have been known as the mother hen, Ms Adams. I promise you that this pair will not be let out of my sight for the interim! Thank you for calling.*

Darlene took a deep breath. She felt a bit perplexed that the advice was the same as she'd received, practically word for word. Then wondered if it was a typical bushy term. Spook and Tiny would know. Plucking up a lot of courage, she decided to leave her hair in a ponytail and leave the hat behind. The only additions to her attire were her waist-wallet and Smith and Wesson 9mm in her baggy cardigan jacket. Reaching for the two-way, she depressed the transmit button twice, hoping she wasn't going to wake them if she approached their camp. Shining her high-lumen torchlight through the same pocket as her friend, she swept the beam across her path. She could hear two men's voices as she walked between the rear trailers, then a low growl.

In an instant, the men were up on their feet.

'Oi, who's there?' one of them bellowed gruffly as the growling got louder.

'Two-button response,' she said, followed by a stifled giggle.

She let the kelpie sniff her feet and hands before meeting the men in between the middle trailers. The LED lights cast a soft hue as she clicked off the torch.

With an outstretched hand and clear voice, she said, 'How do you do, I'm Darlene Adams. Your convoy buddy.'

She felt like a dwarf even though she was tall for a woman. Both men introduced themselves with polite, firm handshakes, and the three of them all spoke at once then laughed with ease.

'Have you had dinner, ma'am?' Spook asked.

'I have, thank you, and please call me Darlene when it's just us three and pooch. I'd prefer to continue communicating the way we have while we're driving, if that's okay with you guys.'

'Yes, of course,' Tiny adamantly replied. 'Um, why are you out here, all alone?'

Darlene grinned. 'Simply transferring a motorhome to Perth en route to a very important function.'

'We're led to believe you have some friends with you?' Spook asked gently.

'Yes, I have one with me right now, actually.'

The knowing chuckles were warm and genuine.

'You see, Tiny, this lady's all over it! You've got nothing to worry about!' Spook said and lightly punched the big man on his shoulder.

And just like that, the banter started. It was as if they'd all known each other for a lifetime. Darlene hadn't felt so comfortable in others' company for so long she felt like singing from the rooftops. Spook was like a kind uncle, and Tiny, well, he emitted an aura of warmth and security. She felt herself wanting to stand near him, but his pooch made sure she didn't. They continued ribbing each other while having hearty conversations, but it was getting late. She covered her mouth to conceal a massive yawn.

'I'll have to bid you goodnight, gentlemen. Thank you so much.'

'I'll escort you back to your wagon, li'l lady,' Spook said in his best cowboy drawl.

'You, old man, should be getting some shuteye. Allow this knight in shining armour! Come, my fair lady!' Tiny drew himself up to his absolute full height, as did his pooch.

'Not gonna argue with you, big fella. Darlene, it's been a pleasure being in your company. We roll in seven hours. Will you be okay with that?'

She wrapped both hands around Spook's outstretched one. 'Absolutely, no need for the three short blasts this time. Thank you so much for looking out for me, Spook.'

'Right. Night, you lot. Tiny, you need your beauty sleep, mate.' His deep chuckle echoed into the cool night air.

She easily fell into step with Tiny while the pooch walked in between. Darlene felt alive with the natural chemistry that seemed to simmer hotter the longer she was in his company.

'Tiny, I must thank you for everything as well.'

'It's the least I could do. Just wish we could put your vehicle in one of our trailers. We'd feel better.'

She let the suggestion settle over her and actually liked the thought of it too, but caught herself slipping back into complacency.

'Two things... is that why you travel with pooch, and is the next stretch dangerous?'

He explained that his kelpie was the granddaughter of his original dog, so the bond was particularly strong, plus she'd never had to learn how to share. Then assured Darlene the only dangerous components which lay ahead were more kangaroos and the throttle jockeys. In comfortable silence, they leaned backwards against the bonnet of the motorhome, gazing at the rhinestone-studded night sky.

'Do you make a wish when you see a shooting star?' Tiny suddenly asked.

'Of course!' she replied automatically.

The silence was warm. Reluctantly, Darlene moved towards the door and sighed softly.

'Thank you. I bid you a good night and will happily follow the leader when we roll.'

'Can I phone you, please, Elai... I mean, Darlene?'

She looked up at him with a peculiar frown. 'How about I give you my number when we get to Perth? Deal?'

He clasped her hand firmly, but his thumb had a mind of its own and gently stroked her wrist. She was rooted to the spot. When he spoke, his voice was thick with emotion.

'Deal. Good night.'

'Night,' she whispered.

They stared at each other for a long time and both jumped when Tiny's mobile phone blared. Their embarrassed laughter raised a notch when he read out Spook's message.

It is WAY past your bedtime!

'Best we listen to our elders.' Tiny winked and held open the door.

She grinned, ruffled the kelpie's head and ever so lightly rested her other hand against Tiny's warm cheek. Her thumb automatically caressed his lips.

'See you in Perth, Tiny. Good night.'

Tiny practically floated back to his truck. Why did he almost call her Elaina? His hand kept returning to his cheek, and he couldn't stop rubbing his lips. He could still feel the pressure of her soft hand. He swore quietly and shook his head. Then he had a mild panic attack. Did she know Elaina? Would they talk?

He flopped down on his bunk and sighed heavily. It'd been a long time since he'd ridden the emotional roller-coaster. Nova, his kelpie, sulked on her bed.

CHAPTER SEVEN

After dinner, Spider waited patiently by the timber shelter. She was the one. It was almost midnight when she finally appeared. Her black apron slung casually over her shoulder, revealing a particularly short skirt and tight top. The Doc Marten boots complimented her shapely legs, particularly when he dragged his eyes slowly up the outline of a tattooed snake wrapping around her knee and continuing upwards. It disappeared under her clothes, then reappeared above her right breast and curled around her shoulder. Its head just nuzzling under her neck.

'You did wait!' she said excitedly.

'Yeah. Why did you roll your eyes at me?' Spider said coldly.

'Not at you, at the customer behind you. He pinched me bum while I was serving you.'

'You want me to sort him out?'

'Nah, but I reckon you can sort me out, you snake charmer!'

Her giggle was like tinkling glass of a chandelier.

This is the one. Be nice.

'You up for a drive?'

'Yep, but I need to be back here tomorrow night. Gotta pay the rent, buddy.'

'Don't we all. Come on, let's fly this chicken coop. We got some miles to cover!'

'We can't go far—'

Her eyes opened wide as he shoved something into her mouth and forced her to climb into the cab. He liked what he saw immensely. His spider wriggled. His guiding voice shouted harshly. *Not yet. Be patient. Go where it's nice and dark.*

Forcing her to drink from a spiked bottle of Pepsi, he swallowed a No-Doze then slipped the Black Widow into gear and quietly rolled out of the empty carpark. He never asked her name. He didn't need to know any of their real names. He named them what he wanted to call them, and just liked to play with them and keep them all to himself as much as he could. But they had to play with him too and not try to escape or they got hurt. He didn't like hurting them initially, but then he discovered he liked the way they shied away when he waved his thingy at them. When it stood out in front of him, his knew his spider face looked very threatening. He had seen it. In the mirror.

His passenger flaked out against the window until he dragged her onto his lap. Spider knew a quiet road which would see them far away from city lights by the time the sun rose. She was not going to make her shift at the restaurant. Ever.

A sly curl of his lips made his silver tooth reflect the lights off the dashboard as he leaned forwards and turned off the GPS. The only guide he needed was his mind from now on. Three days to cover a nine-hour drive. Pure bliss.

As Darlene laid her head on the pillow, she thought of Tiny and slipped into a peaceful slumber. It felt like she'd no sooner shut her eyes than she sat bolt upright. The creepy prime mover had shattered her dreams. The faceless driver was yelling at her that he was also adopted, so why couldn't she love him too? She'd only had five and a half hours of solid sleep and was too spooked to consider getting any more.

Activating her mobile phone, she read the two messages. One was from her parents, expressing their relief that Cassie had contacted them. The second was from Cassie herself, with a really nice selfie of the three women seated at the dining room table. Instantly, she could tell her niece was in sober company. The woman fondly referred to as Officer Bev was a solid woman with kind eyes. Her sigh of relief was louder than expected.

Cooking herself a hearty bacon and egg roll, with melted cheese and BBQ sauce, she took what was left of the frozen Sara Lee chocolate cake and slipped it into the fridge. With a full belly and a large coffee, she settled in for the next leg of the arduous journey.

Spook loved the roads through to Norseman. Wide, plenty of overtaking room and plenty of pull-off areas, all sensibly designed. The large spaces easily accommodated cars and grey nomads without interfering with triple trailers or the drivers. He'd picked up on the instant chemistry between Darlene Adams and Tiny and doubted she even realised how intoxicating her company was.

Then he recalled the natural attraction Tiny had with the similarly beautiful Elaina. Spook badly wanted to see Tiny happy and settled down.

They both knew he drove the long haul to pass the time and not for an income. The smallest piece of personal information the big fella had ever shared was his life-changing inheritance. The circumstances behind it were the saddest. That was all Tiny had told him, which had left Spook guessing. Then he wondered how much Oscane had seen of Ms Adams, and smirked. He hoped the two bachelors would be vying for her attention. Watching as his convoy buddies exchanged places, Tiny tucking in behind him, he dialled his number.

'Morning, Tiny. Did you get any sleep?'

'Morning, Spook. Some!'

Their laughter was loud.

Spook wolf-whistled and said, 'Hey, she looks similar to Elaina but more beautiful! How is that possible? Anyway, the newborns will have put paid to a restaurant, and I'm going to suggest us grandparents host Christmas. A great way to christen the new shed if it's raining. What say you?'

'We'll see, mate. Both women are stunning, no arguments there.'

'Sarge had a chat too.'

'Yeah, I've been wondering about that. Plus, this one said she'd see us in Perth and that's where we'll swap numbers. Do you reckon she knows of Elaina?'

'Worry about what you do know. Besides, he's over a thousand clicks behind us now!'

'Good advice. Say, ask a question on the two-way where we hear a two-button response!'

They drowned out each other's laughter as they hung up.

Spook took on the challenge and had woken up thinking about the chocolate cake his wife always made for him when he got home. Picking up the handset, he waited until the truck going in the opposite direction had disappeared.

'Morning, mate, trust you slept well.'

As expected, the two-button response was instant, then Tiny answered positively as well.

'Sure did. You?'

'Absolutely. Do we all like chocolate cake?'

'Hell yeah!' Tiny blurted out.

If a two-button response could be made loud, he reckoned Darlene could do it.

'Anybody got any?'

Tiny remained silent, but her response kissed the air like an angel.

Spook's broad grin must have come through in his voice. 'We're pulling up at Balladonia whether you like it or not!'

Tiny's rumbling laughter through the speakers was exactly what he expected and what Darlene needed to hear.

Darlene shook her head but couldn't wipe the grin off her face. She suspected the men had had a conversation, then rolled her eyes as her mobile phone registered Deputy Sergeant Troy Oscane's incoming call. No point in pretending about the sore throat any longer.

'Morning,' she said quietly.

'Oh, choice! You've got your voice back. Nice to hear it, Ms Adams, and a good morning it is. Great news about your niece and her friend, and I just wanted to bring you up to speed. I'll do the talking. Wouldn't want you to end up losing your voice again.'

'Thank you, sir.'

'Officer Bev has taken the girls under her wing. I believe you'll be taking them home for Christmas, which lends me to believe you'll be in the west for longer than I'd hoped. Anyway, they'll be in good company. Both are running parallel on a mission. The Danish girl has filed a missing person's report on her friend, and your niece is hassling to become an officer of the law and focus on either internal border patrol or chasing down sexual predators. She's sure lippy and feisty, yet has got the brain capacity to absorb new things quickly. She'd make a good detective, in my view.'

'Scary!'

'Yeah! Good cop bad cop in one person.'

They both laughed.

'Listen, their belongings will arrive here at the station, then the girls will be doing some shopping. Officer Bev's fashion doesn't cut it, but she's happy to pick up the orders locally. Now, I have some questions for you, Ms Adams.'

'You've got an interesting time ahead of you, sir. Thank you for what you're doing and going to be putting up with. I'll happily contribute to the additional expenses incurred. Fire away with your questions. We'll talk until the signal drops out...'

'Good. I recall you saying you came through Broken Hill and presume you were there the same time as Spook and Tiny, am I correct?'

'Yes.'

'Did you see any prime movers without trailers?'

She shivered. 'Yes. Just one. A hideous purple one at the roadhouse.'

'Can you describe the driver?'

She almost dry retched and drank half the bottle of water she had beside her.

'Are you okay?' Troy asked, his voice rife with concern.

'Yes, yes, I am, thanks. The thought of that gangly mobile tattoo parlour makes my skin crawl and stomach tighten. There's something creepy about the whole thing. I've had nightmares since.'

Troy fell silent. After a long pause, he said, 'Help me understand what they were about, please.'

'When my dad informed me about Cassie, instantly the purple prime mover popped into my head. I hate it when it happens.'

'It's happened before? These images popping into your head?'

'Yeah. I'm not a psychic or anything, but I do go with my gut. I don't know what it is about this purple rig, except there's something not right and there's no way they would have been in the same place. Nobody can cover that much distance. So, he couldn't have had anything to do with the girls'... what... abduction or safe return? Even that's sus... somebody must have found out about the doctor and his wife. How are they doing, by the way?'

'Hmm, I'm inclined to agree with you on all counts. I hope to have an update on the family soon. But have you seen the rig again? Apart from in the nightmares?'

'No. I have a question for you.'

There was no response. Signal was lost. Dropping back a couple of gears, the Madura Pass was torture for the heavy trucks around her. Spook suggested she take the lead through to the Balladonia roadhouse. A huge sigh of relief escaped her lips. She'd be running on the smell of an oily rag by then. It was just as well she'd crammed so much fuel into the tank at the last stop, including draining the jerry cans. The headwinds were a killer on fuel consumption. Transmitting in the usual affirmative manner, she finally chugged past Spook's fifty-plus-metre-long vehicle and did the indicator dance. The loud blast on the air horn made her squeal in fright. She hung her hand out the window and waved while calling him a rather rude name, grinning.

Darlene kept Spook within sight, which retained the two-way coverage.

'Hey, mate, whoever gets there first, fuel up, park up and boil the billy.'

She replied appropriately. A broader smile creeping across her face.

DS Oscane was like a cat on a hot tin roof and driving his officer mad.

'Dammit, man. Stop pacing. Sounds to me that the woman is very capable of looking after herself,' Bev said bluntly.

'She had a question for me!'

'Well, it's not going to be about a ticket to the Policeman's Ball, is it? Think about getting some fresh air, and while you're at it, grab some smoko. The petty cash tin's been topped up!'

Troy spun on his heel to say something smart, but he was looking at the woman furiously punching numbers into the telephone. He'd never seen her face so contorted with anxiety.

CHAPTER EIGHT

Spider awoke feeling quite ordinary and alone. He flew into an enraged panic. The sun was beating in through the skylight. *Has she run away? Didn't you lock the doors? Where are the keys? How far could she have got? What's Reg going to say?* He banged the side of his head with an open hand, trying to dispel the confused voices.

He recalled how they'd played for hours and continued for a while after he turned onto Highway B90. Another favourite out-of-the-way short cut. Snake Girl had fallen asleep with her head on his lap by the time he parked in the darkened rest area north of Cummins, and obligingly let him have his way with her when he moved her to the bunk. But where was she now? He discovered her panties, then one Doc Marten, and frowned. Why would it be on the bed? He never ever allowed shoes on any furniture. He angrily threw it into the cab and heard a groan.

Scrambling through, there she was, curled up on the floor in front of the passenger seat. Her make-up smeared her face. Her eyes were bloodshot but wide open, and her mouth had something stuck in it. Where were her hands? He raked her semi-naked body with his eyes and felt his spider growing bigger. She was shaking her head mournfully and whimpering and sniffling and rolling her shoulders. Then he remembered! He'd tied her hands behind her back because he didn't want her to play with his hair. What was in her mouth? *Think! You must have put it in there. Yes, you do. Remember? Her sock!* That was punishment for standing on the bunk with shoes on. Then he immediately felt bad because he had put her on the bed. That was his fault. His spider shrunk in shame. *No, no, no. Stay strong. Tell her you're sorry. Make her feel better.*

He slowly crawled into the cab, talking in a hushed voice, trying to soothe her nerves. Ever so gently, he removed the sock, telling her how sorry he was the whole time. She didn't have a chance to scream. His spider was growing nicely in her face. He kept telling her how big and beautiful her eyes were and he needed to see the whole snake now that it was daylight. He held her head to stop it shaking from side to side. Then he yelped and slapped her hard across the head.

'Why did you bite my spider?' he hissed. 'Why? Why? Why? That was not nice. Now come here. You need to be punished for that.'

He roughly dragged her from her squashed-up position and forced her into the bunk. He put his hand over her mouth, turned her around and spanked her with her own boot before flinging her on her back. She cried out in fear and kicked hard, revealing the snake curling around her upper thigh. *Naughty snake. Time to come out to play.* Spider's lip twisted into a cruel sneer as he caught both her legs. Clasping her ankles together in one large bony hand, he reached for a bottle of Pepsi. Loosening the cap, he knelt beside her and forced her head up.

'Time for you to have some breakfast, that's a good girl. Drink up. You don't want to die. I don't want you to die.'

With the kettle boiled and chocolate cake ready to be served, Darlene had just finished converting the bed into two bench seats when she heard the kelpie yap nearby. Her grin was broad when she opened the door.

'Welcome to my temporary abode! Come in, there's enough room, and please bring pooch in too.'

She noticed both men were wearing double pluggers and insisted they keep them on. All of a sudden, the motorhome felt like a cramped disco cubicle.

'Darlene,' Tiny said quietly, 'I think it's time you officially met Nova.'

At the sound of her name, Nova sat on his foot and eyeballed the new female. Her tail wagging slowly from side to side. Taking the lead, Darlene extended her hand downwards and commanded Nova to shake. She eventually did, after thoroughly sniffing the outstretched hand, then promptly jumped up on the seat beside her competitor.

'You've been accepted into our little circle!' Spook said with a grin before helping himself to the cake.

'Care to tell us about yourself?' Tiny asked cautiously.

She lightly shrugged her shoulders and said, 'Not much to tell, really. Single, childless and on my way to win a couple more trophies.'

'Trophies?' The men responded in unison.

Darlene burst out laughing. 'Yes. I shoot competitively.'

'And accurately, by the sounds of it!' Spook said with a suitably impressed smirk on his face.

The three shared small talk about hobbies without delving into anyone's personal life, until she looked squarely at them both and asked the burning question.

'Guys, is the saying *"There's a lot of nothing between here and there"* a common one in this neck of the woods?'

They looked at each other and shook their heads.

'Not really common,' Spook said. 'Only bloke that we've heard say it frequently is the Sarge on the way to Port Augusta. You met him...'

'Oh! DS Troy Oscane?'

'Yep, that's him.' Tiny spoke candidly. 'He's been doing his job long enough and good enough to be a sergeant, that's why we call him that. To his face, too. Every single time.'

'Is that often?'

'Almost once a week for a very long time,' Spook answered.

'Wow! You sure do know this road like the back of your hands!'

'Yeah, are you exhausted yet?'

'I take my hat off you to you fellows for doing all this driving, that's for sure. It's pretty fatiguing, but I'll be right. I'm on a mission and a deadline, but would love to do the tourist thing at least once in my life, I fear it mightn't be this time. My niece... um... I promised my niece I'd pick her and her Danish friend up on my way back east and surprise the oldies for the...'

The men were looking at her intently. She blushed. 'I've said too much, please excuse me. I feel it's been forever since I've had a conversation!'

'Oh, I reckon I speak for Tiny here, but we could listen to you talk all day,' Spook said kindly. 'Your voice is like music to our ears!'

The laughter was genuine. But time was ticking on. Tiny automatically rinsed the coffee cups after encouraging Nova off the seat while Spook happily divided the rest of the cake between the three of them and offered a suggestion.

'All going well, we've got about one day's drive left of this trip, folks. I propose we hang a right at Norseman and rest up at Coolgardie for several hours. Darlene, we have a large shed on the outskirts of Perth which will easily accommodate your vehicle. We can have more of a chat then, if you're happy with that?'

'Is that where you usually pull up before dropping trailers and the like?'

'Yes. We have our own dongas.'

She looked from one to the other while contemplating the offer. The expressions on their faces were hopeful. Smirking, she put them out of their misery and happily accepted.

'Good,' Spook said. 'Then we can continue with our conversation about Oscane.'

'Unless we swap phone numbers now and chat on the way?' Tiny suggested a little too enthusiastically.

She winked. 'Then we'd have nothing to talk about when we got to your shed!'

Cassie hated seeing Asta cry. It had been over six months since there'd been any trace of the missing friend. Last known place of work was a pub at Port Lincoln. The security cameras didn't hold records from that long ago. Bev had also torn her hair out exhausting all channels of assistance and was just as upset. Fuelling Cassie's determination to help catch the deviants, she came up with an idea and wanted her aunt's opinion. She dialled Darlene's number as she walked outside and looked towards the Sterling Ranges. Such a daunting country, no matter if you were a stranger or native. Cursing when the phone went to message bank, she sought out DS Oscane, knocking on his door loudly. She waited for him to approve a visit before entering his office. Walking in with her shoulders back and head raised, she knew she could work her charm to her advantage.

'Cassie? What can I do for you?'

'Sir, Officer Bev continues to be a tremendous pillar of strength. Is there any way I can be useful here at your station? I really want to contribute somehow by reducing the scarily growing list of missing persons.'

She felt quite comfortable being scrutinised by a future boss, having deliberately ordered corporate clothes for such occasions. Her youthful figure brimmed with confidence.

'As the officer in charge of this station, I do have authority to hire a civilian for administration duties. There's a whack of filing that's long overdue. Let me have a chat with Officer Bev, okay?'

'Today?'

'You are eager.'

'Yes, I am, sir. I am of the belief that someone goes missing every day, which means heartache for families.'

'The pay won't be much, you understand,' Oscane said firmly.

'I need to start contributing to the living expenses. It's unfair that Officer Bev has all the outgoings.'

'How's Asta coping?'

'She's distraught and frustrated. I can encourage her to pitch in if you'll allow us two to work together. As she's a foreigner, how about some sort of traineeship under me? I do have a Cert III in Business.'

'As well as a Cert IV in Childcare? You were busy after school.'

'I had the best influencer for self-improvement.'

He grinned. He was pretty confident a certain Darlene Adams had a lot to do with this young woman's determination.

'I'll get back to you by the end of the day, Cassie. In the meantime, ask Jan, the receptionist, for two employment forms. You can start filling in the blanks to the best of your knowledge.'

Cassie could hardly contain her excitement. 'Thank you ever so much, Deputy Sergeant Oscane. We won't let you down.'

'I have a feeling you won't deliberately. Please shut the door behind you.'

Cassie's grin brought her brown eyes to life as they glimmered with tears. 'Thank you, sir, thank you.'

She skipped down the hallway, planted a kiss on Officer Bev's cheek and squeezed her shoulder excitedly on the way to the front office. With the paperwork clutched tightly in her hands, she raced to where Asta was moping around the front courtyard. Hugging her tightly and wiping the tears away, Cassie animatedly explained how their lives were on the up.

Little did the girls know, the local courier watched the interaction as he retrieved the delivery from the back of his van. He liked what he saw of this pair and could imagine the fun they'd have together. It was Stevo's last delivery for the day, and it was his turn to tend to the flock. Trixie was running an errand for Max, which gave Stevo all afternoon and night to play.

He subconsciously rubbed his hands with glee, then scowled as he watched the two females skip back inside the police station. Then he grinned. Maybe they had brothers.

Reg Oscane growled at the message bank tone for the twentieth time. His mood getting broodier each time. Spider could not be traced, which meant two things. He had turned off his GPS tracker and had taken a side road. Reg bellowed in rage, the corrugated walls echoed his sentiments. Punching in the numbers for the blokes in the opal fields, he impatiently drummed his fingers on the desk.

'Finally!' he boomed through the phone. 'Any of you pricks seen or heard from Spider?'

'Nuh. He shouldn't be up this ways, not in that purple rig. Too many eyes.'

'It's having a facelift. Besides, he's in the Black Widow.'

'You're kidding? Reg, you're either getting stupid or soft in your old age. That was foolish.'

'Actually, it wasn't, and cut the insults. Let me know if you hear from him, bucko.'

'Yep. Go and have a pappy nap, you old bastard.'

Angrily crushing the cigar into the overflowing ashtray, Reg resolved to give Spider until nightfall to make contact. Staring at the road map filling the wall, he tried to think like the deviant son but shook his head despairingly. Where in the hell did he come from? With a sad smile, Reg remembered Spider's mother had freaked out when he came home at the age of fourteen and happily walked around swinging his tattooed spider for all the world to see. Oddly enough, that was the last time he'd ever had anything to do with needles. By the time the boy had become a man, he had tattoo body stockings and sleeves coming out of his closet.

Reg's wife and partner in crime of twenty-three years, Ruby, died in her sleep. A blessing that she was never a witness to the depraved mind of her oldest boy, Graham, or Spider, as he called himself from an early age. Stevo, their other son, was lazy and loved to take advantage of his brother. He was always on the hunt for extra cash, smoke and easy prey.

The elaborate franchise Reg Oscane had developed over the years of distributing merchandise – that the law objected to, which was tobacco – was quite a testament to his discretion, cunning delegation and perseverance. Almost untouchable, but not without caution. It'd be either his sons or the crooked Max that sunk him. Reg was fully aware his uniform-wearing nephew held onto his suspicions like a bub on a tit, yet proof had eluded him for a very long time.

Spider updated the fake logbook while his captive slept securely bound in his bunk. They'd take another short cut and head for the coast. He imagined adding a mermaid's tail to his new toy and building a sandcastle for her to curl around. What a lovely holiday, and nobody knew where he was. *Reg needs to know. You have to tell Reg.*

Scowling at his reflection in the mirror, he turned on his mobile phone, dutifully sent a brief message that his trip was going well but coverage was poor and swiftly turned it off. His scowl turned to a lopsided grin as his spider moved again.

Reg jumped as his phone blared with the incoming message, cursing loudly. His attempt to have a conversation was futile. The Yalata pick-up had been compromised. Spider had to return to base for fear of drawing too much attention. A drug raid on the outskirts of Ceduna had Reg spooked.

Cassie didn't know what had gotten into her. From the tremendous elation, she'd turned into a complete and utter bitch and caused mayhem at the local pub. Sitting in the day-lockup with her head on her knees and back to the barred door, big hot elephant tears rolled down her cheeks and plopped onto the concrete floor nosily. She didn't want anyone to see her crying.

'You've got some explaining to do, young lady.' DS Oscane spoke dangerously quietly. 'Start talking.'

'I hate my life,' she moaned.

'That is not acceptable. Try again.'

Rage boiled up and exploded out of her mouth. 'Yes. I snapped. Yes, I hit the bastard in the pub. He drugged Asta then cornered me in the bathroom. Nobody has the right to manhandle me or hurt my friend. What else was I going to do? Cop a beating? Get raped? I want to see Asta. NOW.'

'She is in hospital and recovering well. Nothing happened to her, thanks to the barmaid. But you? You have undone all the good you did. Officer Bev cannot have her career jeopardised by an unruly tenant, Cassie. Perhaps you ought to think about being useful with your time down in Whyalla? Or go home?'

'Home? I can't do that. My parents wouldn't understand...'

'How about your aunt?'

'That's different,' she muttered.

Troy smirked. Sliding the cordless phone onto the floor just inside the cell, he chuckled softly.

'Cassie, you have so much to look forward to and experiences to learn from. Don't throw it all away. From the little I know of your aunt, she's a tremendous inspiration. You need to make one phone call. Choose wisely.'

Cassie thought long and hard about her situation. She had a horrible feeling something would have happened to Asta if she hadn't intervened. Both she and Asta shared the same miserable suspicion about the missing friend. Drugged, raped and probably dead. Nobody had seen her for over six months. Her bank account was untouched and her mobile phone untraceable.

Tears welled up in Cassie's eyes when she thought about the doctor's situation. It was far worse than hers could ever be. His wife was probably dying, and they had two mischievous, adorable sons. Cassie had neglected her responsibility, several of them, actually, and admitted it loudly as she stood up and turned around. Oscane's words rang in her head. One phone call. Choose wisely.

Please answer, please answer, she prayed to the ringing tone.

'Cassie! How is my wayward niece?'

'I'm okay, my wayward aunt. Where are you now?'

'Happy to say about four hours from Perth, where I'll pull up for a night. What about you?'

'I'm... I'm in a jail cell, Aunty Darlene.'

'Whoopsies, you haven't wasted any time! So, how hard did you punch this bloke?'

They both giggled.

'I kneed this one in the nuts instead. The horrible vision of the filthy bastard in the truck just popped into my head and I felt caged in, so I dragged Asta to the pub with me. After a few beers, I felt like a game of pool. We're both pretty good. Anyway, we were minding our own business when this nicely dressed, good-looking man – even though his face was pockmarked – approached us and offered to play the winner. You know what I'm like with that sort of challenge. Asta downed her beer and, well, lost the game.

'After that, I pretty much owned the table then deliberately sunk the black. I wanted a rematch. Asta had been giggling and yawning, and I wasn't getting jealous, but something wasn't gelling. So, I was stalling for time. She was fawning all over him or his friend, whichever one wasn't up, which was most unusual. Asta doesn't behave like that. Then I realised, after the next beer she downed like it was water, the bastard had drugged her. I didn't touch the beer he bought me.

'When she went into the bathroom, another man blocked my path and tried to entertain me. He was older, but I had to help Asta. This same arsehole had been bragging about how he was a candidate in the upcoming local election and a fairly big-time shipping magnate and was looking for some company. Eventually, I squeezed between him and someone else then dashed into the bathroom. Asta was lying under the hand dryer. The next thing, the first bloke steps out of the cubicle closest to her; he was in the ladies! Dirty pervert. Anyway, he looked in the mirror and turned towards me like he was going to catch me into his arms.

'I stopped, feigned a swoon and waited until he held my wrists. I swear to you, Aunty Darlene, I swung my hip like I was possessed and drove my knee into his groin so bloody hard I've been limping ever since.'

'So has he, by the sounds of it. Good job. But why are you in jail?'

'Probably for my safety. Asta's still in hospital. I snapped and turned into a complete bitch to everyone here. I'm so pissed off. There are so many women, girls and boys missing in this vast country. It's really scary. We're only just realising how close we came to being a statistic and how lucky we are that some cigar-smoking old fart couldn't get it up.'

'I can keep an eye out on my travels if that helps you two. Perhaps Asta has a photo of her friend?'

'Yeah, yeah, that'd be great. I'll ask. But... but I feel really bad about the doctor and his family. They're down in Whyalla, not even an hour away, and I haven't let them know we're okay, let alone found out how they all are and if I could be more useful there. I'm not even a police cadet. DS Oscane has been so kind and also thought doing some filing might ease my impatience, or whatever it is.'

'Did you end up getting your belongings from Coober Pedy?'

'Yeah! Thank God everything was there. We've been contributing to expenses so haven't been totally rude. Officer Bev has been fantastic, but Aunty Darlene, I think she's worried about someone too. She doesn't talk about her personal life, yet is a great listener. Like a big sponge that holds everything in.'

'What do you think you should do now, Cassie?'

'See if Asta is happy to stay here then reach out to the doctor in Whyalla. If he's still there, his sons would be quite the handful in hospital and I really ought to be fulfilling my end of the bargain. I pray he is, because I really don't like Alice Springs, but if I have to go back up there, at least I'll save face once in my life.'

'That sounds very grown up! I wish I had your wisdom twenty years ago.' Darlene laughed wildly. 'But then, I wouldn't have had the best two years, plus the most amazing trip this last week of my life. So maybe I don't!'

After a long pause, Cassie said quietly, 'Do you remember that painting you gave me for my thirteenth birthday?'

'The one with the green hills rolling into a valley overlooking a rainforest?'

'Yes! You remember it perfectly.'

'Of course I do,' she replied softly.

'It's still on my bedroom wall, and it's the wallpaper on my phone. But I've always wanted to know why it sort of just stops and has "one slash two" above the artist's signature. It is half of a panoramic?'

'Almost. The artist was commissioned to continue the painting of the same scene. I've got the second half. We're somehow connected, you and I. I don't know how, but we are, and that's why you got that one. Kiddo, I might drop out soon, I'm going up a range. It's been fantastic hearing from you. Thank you. You know what you need to do, my girl. You always have tried to save the world, but you have to be kind to yourself first. You always have to be kind to yourself before that kindness can be expressed to others. Try and remember that, okay?'

'I'll try. Please can I phone you soon?' Cassie asked as the tears tumbled down her face again.

'Yes. I would like that very much.'

Troy Oscane had never felt so guilty in his life for eavesdropping on an inmate's phone call. The picture the beautiful Darlene had described filled his own mind with peace and tranquillity. Absolutely everything about the woman was captivating. But the description of the truck driver didn't sit right. He was dead.

Troy automatically searched the archives for the particular trucking incident and wrote up a brief report. Flagging it on his system with a red question mark would be a reminder to talk to Tiny when the situation was right. He sent a meeting request to Bev for the following morning, then made a phone call to the Whyalla hospital.

CHAPTER NINE

Officer Bev smoothed down her trousers, fastened the middle button of her jacket and entered the local café. She knew her appearance could be friendly yet intimidating at the same time, but her matronly manner had won over the staff. They had her order ready and waiting.

'Local elections coming up, ma'am,' Tommy, the freckle-faced, brace-wearing teenager, said enthusiastically.

'That's right, Tommy. May the right candidate win! Thanks for the order, I'll settle up the tab.'

'No need! A pay forward did.'

'Well, then, I'll do the same. Will twenty dollars cover it?'

'Sure will, cheers for that.'

Her pleasant smile swiftly changed into a frown as she walked across the road back to the police station. A pay forward? An irregularity in the small town. More so as there hadn't been any strange vehicles hanging around and the café was typically empty for the late morning.

The strange message she'd received very early that morning had unsettled her steely resolve. *Is Milly back home?* Milly, her daughter, hadn't been home for six years. Bev didn't respond straight away. She never had answered questions immediately. Anywhere up to eight hours was the usual time lapse.

Using her shoulder to push through the door, she nodded to Jan as she walked past.

'Officer Bev, a fax came through from Coffin Bay. It's been scanned and e-mailed to you as an attachment. Your little helper would make a good detective if she could cool her temper!'

'Thanks, Jan. I'll be sure to address it after the meeting with our boss.'

Her mind was churning over the concept that perhaps the Danish girl had been seen. Backpackers seemed to be drawn to the coast, no matter the season. She was still frowning as she entered her boss's office.

'Something on your mind, Bev?'

'Yes, sir. But let's attend to the hot croissants first! Say, you ever heard of pay forward in this town?'

He looked at her steadily. 'It's not uncommon, but something I've never experienced or participated in. Why?'

'Oh, this is all pay forward. I did the same for twenty bucks.'

'Put the receipt in petty cash and take what is yours,' he said before taking a huge mouthful of the buttery melt-in-the-mouth ham and cheese croissant. 'There's something weighing on your mind, Bev. I hope you know you can confide in me as a friend and colleague.'

'The girls!'

Troy smirked and handed her the information he'd obtained from the hospital. The woman would be in hospital for quite a while, then they'd arrange to have in-home dialysis care. The doctor flew three times a week back to the Alice to perform his role and tend to the horses as best he could, while the boys were in desperate need of their au pair. At present, they had a live-in carer at a unit at the hospital. The urgency of improving that particular situation was paramount.

'How is Asta?' Troy asked between mouthfuls.

'I heard from the hospital she's grateful and bored. Wants to go home but needs money first. How's Cassie?'

'Angry ant, frustrated and conflicted. I think she knows she's not fulfilling an obligation.'

'Yeah, I sensed that. She's trying to save everyone but ignores herself. Not good. Incidentally, any update on the purple prime mover?'

'No. Like it's disappeared off the face of the earth. Bloody annoying, that's for sure.'

'Wanna take a trip to see your uncle?'

Troy looked at his colleague closely. His eyes traced every line, wrinkle and sunspot that adorned her strong face. Her brown eyes were pools of mystery and kindness, yet her teeth had cosmetic work that showed every time she smiled. Which wasn't enough.

'Tell me more of your thought process, Officer Bev,' he encouraged formally.

'That drug bust near Ceduna has had a ripple effect through the short-haul drivers, according to my source at Main Roads. There seem to be a lot more courier vans than semis doing the Nullarbor run. But nobody has seen the ominous purple prime mover.'

'What else?'

'My daughter, Milly.' Bev showed her boss the phone message. 'She hasn't been home for six years. We haven't had a conversation for longer than that. Went feral after her father walked out, then left in the middle of the night and waited on tables in another town. Her flatmate discreetly lets me know of her well-being regularly. That message came in very early this morning. Milly's shifts are every night. That way, she has the house to herself during the day. I usually don't respond straight away. But now I am getting concerned.'

'You think the Oscane enterprise has got something to do with it?'

'Something's not gelling, boss. The purple prime mover at Broken Hill, then nothing. Wilmington to Port Pirie is just a stone's throw, and someone mentioned burgers at Port Pirie. I don't know. I could be barking up the wrong tree, but something isn't sitting right.'

'Okay, first things first. You'll know when and how to respond to the message. Let's transfer Asta and Cassie to Whyalla. Jan's got a relation down that way who might need a farmhand. After we get the girls settled, you and I'll go on a road trip. Sound like a plan?'

'Why are you so kind to me?' Bev blurted out.

Her question caught him off guard. He bit back a smirk and could feel the heat from a blush creeping over his face. 'You're a good woman and good cop. Plus, I like being in your company.'

She grinned. 'Likewise. We've got work to do, boss. Which problem child would you like to take on?'

'I'll take Asta!'

They both laughed as they walked out of the office. Troy stopped off at Jan's desk, explained the situation then made his way to the hospital. He hadn't stopped thinking about Darlene Adams, but suddenly, each time he did, he saw Bev's smiling face. He was long overdue for a holiday.

Bev read her e-mail and tried to slow down her racing heartbeat. There had been a Danish girl learning to be a lifesaver earlier in the year with aspirations of hitchhiking to WA. The picture was of a beautiful young woman filling out her swimming costume like a model, sporting a grin from ear to ear, holding a certificate and what looked like a pamphlet for dolphins. She sent it through to her boss. He was dealing with Asta!

'Hi, Cassie,' Bev called as she unlocked the noisy door to the cells. 'Feel like a change of scenery?'

'Officer Bev! I am so sorry for my behaviour, please forgive me. Yes. These four walls are more suffocating than my overbearing family.'

'Without family, you have nothing. Always remember that, my dear. Now come along, we have important things to discuss. Let's go and see Asta at the hospital.'

The two girls embraced each other like long lost friends. Each cooing over the other, ensuring neither was hurt. Asta gently cupped Cassie's face.

'Cassie, DS Oscane has something he needs us girls to do. It's very important to their jobs, but it means we can't stay here. Do you want to know more?' Asta asked in a manner that was without doubt demanding a positive response.

'First, I need to apologise to you all,' Cassie said humbly. 'My guilty conscience has kicked me in the backside. Please forgive me for my recent behaviour. I would like to do anything I can to be useful, and yes, Asta, I want to know more.'

Asta happily explained the transfer that would be taking place that afternoon, after which Cassie threw her arms around each officer gratefully.

'Thank you, thank you. I don't know how you did it, but thank you.'

'Uh, firstly, do either of you ladies recognise this woman?'

Asta ripped the phone out of Troy's hand. 'Yes! Yes! That's Elaina, where is she?'

'There's a possibility she is in Western Australia–'

'That's where my aunt is!' Cassie burst out. 'She said she'd help as much as she could. Send it to her, DS Oscane.'

'Oh? You've spoken to her recently, then?' he asked.

Cassie's face reddened like a beetroot. 'Yes, sir. That was my phone call. I will phone my parents again when we get to Whyalla.'

'Actually, Cassie, you should phone them sooner than that,' Bev insisted. 'Or at least your grandparents. You need to constantly assure them you are safe. Otherwise, you're just being cruel.'

Cassie burst into tears. 'I didn't get a word in last time, and now I don't know what to say.'

Bev gathered the girl into her arms and held her while she cried her heart out, then shuffled over to Asta and held both as their wails softened to sniffles.

Troy quietly left the room, shielding his wet eyes as best he could. Nobody had held him when he sobbed with grief. He hadn't been comforted for so long. He hadn't been jealous of anything, until that moment. Then he thought about Bev's own personal dilemma, wiped his eyes and walked back into the room.

'Ladies, let's all group hug and officially call it the start of a tremendous friendship.'

The look on Bev's face melted his heart as the four of them bit back their own personal tears of grief, relief or joy.

Tiny did the indicator dance as he led the convoy. He'd desperately wanted to find out if Darlene knew Elaina when they'd pulled up outside of Southern Cross, but she was as coy as a small antelope. Neither man saw her during their delayed stopover. The familiar two-button communique was the only form of contact since they'd left Norseman. He had been in his own world and was guilty of not contributing to much of the brief two-way conversations.

They were on the home run now. Dialling Spook's number, he lightened up his mood before his mate answered.

'Yeah, Tiny, what's up?'

'Hey, man, how're you travelling?'

'Good. Looking forward to some fresh air! Say, when we get to the shed, let's tuck the little lady away from our dongas so she doesn't feel conscious about what she's got to do?'

'Yeah, yeah, that's a good idea. How long do you want to pull up for?'

'Steady on there, chap, we can't keep her here forever!'

'I meant–'

'I'm stirring you! We offload our trailers tomorrow; have a few days' rest, then see about a return load. My daughter has gone into early labour so is in hospital. When I get back, I'll probably call it for the year with long hauls.'

'You need a buddy to come back with you?'

'Always, mate.'

'Rog.'

'We'll see what our little pistol-packing mama is up to. Might be able to hook up somewhere again.'

'Yep.'

'I'll lead the way. We're not far from our second home now.'

'Rog.'

Spook grinned as he spoke into the two-way. 'Hey, mate, not far now. I'll lead the way, so just follow me in, then we can stretch our legs and go from there.'

The familiar two-way response made his grin broaden, then he burst out laughing at Tiny's response.

'Fresh air at long lasssst.'

Darlene chuckled loudly and nodded her head. She was inclined to agree with them both. Deputy Sergeant Troy Oscane was calling her, and she answered immediately.

'Sir, hello to you. Is everyone okay?'

'Ma'am, hello. This is Officer Bev, and yes, they are. I hope you're travelling well?'

'Oh! Pardon me. Hello, Officer Bev. Yes, thanks, all's well here. Just shy of the Swan River!'

'Good. Forgive the officialism of my call, but I've scheduled a conference call with your niece, her parents and her grandparents. Is that acceptable?'

'May I have a quick word with Cassie first, please?'

She heard scuffles and the phone being moved before Cassie spoke. 'Hi, Aunty Darlene. I'm okay, Asta's okay. We are all okay! What's up?'

'Are you sure you need me on this hook-up?'

'Well, yeah. My grandparents are your parents, you know.'

'Don't be sassy with me, young lady. I'll smack your ass again when I pick you up for New Year, and you can buy the carton of beer too.'

'Deal, but only the first carton for Christmas.'

They both laughed.

'Righto, please tell Officer Bev to go ahead.'

Shortly thereafter, Darlene was listening to several people babbling over each other as soon as they were aware who they were talking to. She didn't need to speak. She listened to the fluctuating emotional responses and brimmed with pure delight when Cassie announced her and Asta's schedule for the next few months totally uninterrupted. The way she worded it canned all doubt and ridicule. She had suddenly grown up. Only when there was silence did Darlene join in the conversation.

'G'day, everyone, I'm well and in a hilly area east of Perth after the most amazing trip. I'll be playing here for a couple of months and hopefully getting my hands on a few more trophies.'

'When do we see you, dear?'

'Hello, Dad, you sound well. I'm aiming for New Year. What're you doing for Christmas?'

'Heavens, child, it's not even October! It would be nice if we could have it here with everyone. Just like the olden days, before we all got older!'

'That's a nice idea, Mum. Maybe continue the *Christmassy and classy* theme until New Year's?'

'We'll see. Cassie, tell us more about this doctor and his family.'

Darlene chuckled under her breath. 'Folks, I'm in and out of coverage here. Love you all. Bye for now.'

Cassie was the only one who responded before being swept away in the tide of relentless questions. Darlene disconnected the call. Nothing had changed. She'd have her own conversation with her parents another time.

Several minutes later, her phone rang again.

'Hello?'

'This time it is DS Troy Oscane. The girls won a bet, hence the call from my colleague. Ms Adams, I'm going to send you a picture of a Danish girl, a friend of Asta's who went missing over six months ago. Her name is Elaina, and we got a lead that she may be in WA, possibly involved in surf lifesaving. It's a long shot, but...'

'What did you say her name was?'

'Elaina.'

'Got it. By all means, I'm happy to help. If you're sending the same image to your colleagues over here, would you mind letting them know of our... um... our... gosh, I'm not usually lost for words. Care to help me here?'

'I like to hear you stammer. You're more human!'

After sharing in a hearty laugh, Troy saved her any further embarrassment. 'I'll let them know of the connection, yes. Good luck with the shooting competition, Ms Adams.'

'Thank you. All the best.'

They hung up simultaneously.

A frown creased her flawless forehead. *A popular name, it seems.*

Jan's relation had come up with a proposal which everyone accepted. She would put Asta up during the week, working on the property as a helping hand in the kitchen and in the horse yards. On the weekends, Asta was to volunteer at the Whyalla hospital and travel by bus. Cassie and Asta hugged tightly and promised they'd talk regularly and see each other on the weekends.

The doctor was most relieved to see Cassie. He welcomed the two police officers graciously and explained his wife was sleeping. She would have been overjoyed to meet them. He ushered them into the tiny unit, where the twins were sitting wide-eyed in front of a television. Cassie immediately grabbed the remote, turned it off and sat on the floor cross-legged in front of them. They squealed excitedly and waddled over to her. Their chubby arms wrapped around her neck and body. She gracefully stood up, holding each boy on her hips. Bev happily accepted a nurse and cuddle from the boys, one at a time.

Troy stepped outside, the doctor at his heels.

'Boss, you have a sad story hidden inside you. Time you let it out.'

'Yeah, one day,' Troy said as he squeezed his eyes shut, forcing out the memories of almost adopting two children. They had to be married first. It was the second hardest day of his life when he went back to the orphanage.

Neither police officer spoke on the return drive to their station. Each lost in their own thoughts. Eventually, Bev broke the silence.

'Sir, that was quite a seamless process. Thank you! I feel better knowing they're where they're meant to be.'

'For sure. We can get on with our jobs now.'

'I've been thinking about that. How about I do a bit of undercover and sniff around the trucking side of things? I'd pass as a female trucker, except without tattoos.'

'No way! That's just looking for trouble.'

'What? You reckon some pipsqueak is going to drug me, throw me in their truck and have their way with me? I think not.'

They burst out laughing at the mere idea of it.

'Let's sniff around together, then acquire some assistance that doesn't have a familiar presence. It's a little town. People talk. Besides, I think our perp's network is greater than we allow ourselves to believe. You've got more pressing things to deal with. Where would you like to start with your daughter's peculiar behaviour?'

For the first time in a long while, the woman's strict posture slackened, and she threw her arms up in the air helplessly. She was at a loss.

'She lives in Port Lincoln and works at a food joint at night-time. That's all I know. Her friend, Amy, who'd lost her mother at an early age, befriended me and coincidentally met my Milly through singing lessons. That was when we lived in the Adelaide Hills. My oldest is off overseas playing on aircraft carriers. There's eleven years difference between Clive and Milly. Long story short, I lost my mojo when I came home to an empty house with divorce papers and dust circles on what was left of the furniture. Milly had just finished high school and was getting ready for the graduation formal. Her father was meant to have the father-daughter dance.'

Bev sighed, staring out the window.

'He never turned up. She blamed me, trashed her dress after the achievement awards, bailed from the choir, got a job hairdressing then waiting on tables, dyed her hair all sorts of colours, got piercings and a tattoo. A bloody snake of all things. Eventually, and without word, left the Hills. By that time, I was divorced. Then, out of the blue, six years ago, I get a text message from an unknown number. Amy had sneaked my details from Milly's phone and kept me discreetly and appropriately informed of her well-being ever since. No secrets revealed, no juicy stuff, just letting me know every now and then that my daughter was keeping well, still the wild child, but earning a dollar and paying her way.'

'Bev, maybe we should be concentrating on your daughter. We'll reach out to the west for the Danish girl, what say you?'

'I'd like to grill Reg Oscane first. I reckon he had something to do with the safe return of this pair. They both talk about cigars. Not cigarettes. Cigars. He's the only man I know around here that puffs on a big fat Havana cigar every time he trundles through town in that big Chevy. How the hell does he drive it when he's in a wheelchair?'

'Yeah, it's been a mystery for a long time. Okay. We'll do it your way. I'll take a back seat on the interview process.'

'I get it, boss. It can't be easy for you.'

'It's not. But there is a man in the Alice I would like to have a beer with someday. He knew my father.'

Officer Bev suddenly gasped. 'Oh, my. Oh, sir, please excuse my ignorance. It didn't even click. Chief Inspector Dillon... God, that was your father. Please forgive me and accept my belated, sincere condolences.'

Troy lightly patted her hand. 'Thank you. Sincerely, thank you. It wasn't easy in the early days, sure hasn't gotten any easier with time, but it is nice to...'

She enclosed his hand in between both of hers and squeezed. 'You needed that hug this morning just as much as I did.'

They had chased the sun the whole day and beat it before it settled over the ocean's horizon. Its shadows painted the long streaky clouds a deep orange. Darlene had seen some sheds in her life, but never as large as this one. It could easily house five trucks and their three trailers. The massive yard was fenced with barbed wire housing several cordoned-off dongas. The fake green grass was a nice touch and quite pleasing to the eye. She followed Spook's hand signals and parked under the only shady tree, out of sight from the road and far enough away from their quarters. Disembarking, her grin was as broad as her convoy buddies', and she shook their hands happily.

'Gentlemen, thank you for everything. I don't have any ice-cold beers, but I do have a whack of good frozen steak. Don't know about you, but now I'm looking forward to a meal of both. They'll take too long to defrost. Is there a decent food joint around here?'

'We'd happily accompany you to the pub up the road,' Spook said kindly. 'It's quiet, and there's a nice beer garden. You'd pass as my daughter's friend.'

'Okay, done. My shout for the lot, and no arguments. How much time do I have before you'd be ready to go and the pub stops cooking?'

She observed the men's looks of surprise.

'Um, this is all new to us!' Tiny said, fidgeting with is fingers. 'Tell you what, let's order for eight o'clock. That'll give us a little over an hour.'

'Brilliant idea, mate!' Spook slapped him on his back, 'Let's get cracking, I'm famished. Three medium-to-rare?'

'Nailed it. With pepper sauce and a loaded potato, please,' Darlene called over her shoulder.

Spider kept looking at his toy. She was beginning to get stinky, and he didn't like it. He had to wait until it was really dark before he could get her outside and wash her. He needed a bath too, but she was really, really stinky.

Spider held his nose and blew out his mouth. The moon wasn't coming out to play again tonight, and he was happy with that. But he wasn't happy because of the wrong turn he took. He did the calculations and would have fuel up at Ceduna.

He giggled when he saw the next town he would stop at. Piednippie on the way to Streaky Bay. *Piednippie, where you can play with your snakie hippie in the nudie.* His giggle abruptly changed into a growl when she wriggled and moved around. Why did it take so long to get dark?

Troy and Bev rolled into the massive trucking yard just outside of Wilmington after dark and were met with three snarling chained up Rottweilers. Their shadows made them look larger than they were in the vehicle's headlights and under the halogen spotlights flooding the yard.

Bev immediately got out of the car. 'Reg Oscane, get out here and give your dogs some water!' she bellowed as loudly as she could. Even her boss sat up and took notice. 'Their chains do not reach the water bowl. That is cruelty to animals. Get out here now, you hear me?'

Troy stood at the front of the patrol 4WD, one hand on his gun, the other casually by his side. One almighty yell from behind them silenced the yard.

'What's got you all wound up, Officer Bev?' Reg Oscane asked calmly, appearing out of nowhere. His body remarkably upright even though age crept over him like a greying, tattered rag.

'Your dogs haven't got water. How dare you?'

'You came out all this way to check on these mutts?'

'I will take them off you if you cannot look after them. They have souls. Remember that. Now, you and I need to have a chat. My boss here is going to stand by and catch anything you drop. Get it?'

'You doing his dirty work?'

'Absolutely not. I am doing my job. Now, where is this purple prime mover and both of your sons? Spider and Stevo?'

'What's it to you?'

'A lot, actually. There are some young women missing and a drug raid that's sent cats amongst the pigeons. Prove to me you have no knowledge on any of the above.'

'No women missing that I know of, unless someone didn't act on the information provided.'

'Not those women. But others.'

'I've let more go than have been kept. I'm getting too old for any more of that crap, ma'am.'

'Yet you still have plenty of trucks, shipments to deliver and employees willing to do your bidding.'

'If me workers want a floozy, well, they want a floozy. As long as they do their job, I'm just like any other boss.'

The large man rolled his wheelchair past them and towards the dogs. He nimbly unlatched their linked chains from the pole and pulled them towards their water buckets, a plume of heady cigar smoke trailing behind him.

'See, Officer Bev? They know what's best for them as well.'

'Do you, Reg Oscane? Do your sons?'

'Neither of my sons have been north of the border for the last month.'

'Yet the purple prime mover was seen drifting through Broken Hill and causing quite the commotion. You knew that?'

'Ain't no tittle-tattlers in my books. We done here? These boys might enjoy a bit of pork for dinner tonight if you're hanging around.'

'Where is the purple prime mover?' Bev demanded.

'Unserviceable right about now. We done?' The old man shook the dogs' chains, causing them to growl and snarl at each other.

'For the time being.'

Reg watched the police vehicle slowly traverse out the driveway with disdain then wheeled up the ramp into the house, his three dogs trotting beside him. He sneered as he pulled the pork chops out of the fridge and tossed one to each dog. He'd been losing his appetite and couldn't handle the smell of bacon anymore. He suspected cancer, but there was no way in hell he was going to the doctors. They hadn't helped his wife when she needed it. He just prayed he'd go out the way she did.

His bloody sons were going to drive him into an early grave. He knew that. Now he couldn't reach Stevo, although he suspected where he was. Playing with Spider's toys. Dialling Max's number, Reg absentmindedly fingered the barrel of the shotgun lying on the table.

'Ship's not in for another week, mate,' Max said.

'Yeah, that's fine. You seen those little sprogs of mine?'

'Ol' Stevo was describing two fillies playing around the cop station the other day. I nearly had one. A real pretty thing, but her bitch of a friend got me in the nuts. I couldn't believe I lost them both! But Spider? Not since he scored a loose baggie off me, two days ago.'

'Spider was meant to pick up a backload west of Ceduna...'

'That's recently been busted...'

'Yep, and now I can't get in contact with the little bastard. He was going to take three days to get there. I can't reach him to get him to turn around.'

'Send Stevo out. I need some more playtime after hours. This election run is doing my head in.'

'Can't. The Purple People Eater is getting a paint job, so Spider took the Black Widow—'

'You damn crazy fool, Reg! Send Stevo in his courier van, then. Hell, it ain't even decaled. How he gets business is anyone's guess. You getting old, man. How about I come see you tomorrow? You could donate to my election promise of cleaning up the highways by getting rid of rogue drivers.'

'You're an idiot, Max.'

'Takes the heat off you and our sideline, buddy.'

Darlene had changed three times in less than ten minutes. Her favourite mauve and white wrap dress wasn't right for a pub dinner, yet jeans and a t-shirt felt too casual. Eventually, she settled on her white knee-length denim skirt with her white and yellow hanky-hem blouse. Her tan wedge sandals accentuated her toned calves. Why did she feel she had to dress to impress? They knew she was a woman under all the baggy clothing. But for some reason, the flutter in her stomach reminded her of going on a date. The three of them had clicked instantly. The fleeting urge to kiss the deputy sergeant was a very distant memory. Tiny had occupied her thoughts ever since they talked about making a wish on a shooting star.

The men's reaction was not what she had expected. They stared and stared, looked at each other and stared again.

'Too dressy?' she asked.

'Hell no,' they replied in unison.

The awkwardness dissolved into laughter. 'Reckon we're in safe company tonight, Tiny... you got a friend with you, Darlene?'

'Naturally.'

Tiny held the door open for her as she sat in the front seat of the Holden Statesman then folded himself into the backseat. Spook was happily revving the V8 engine, grinning like a teenager.

'Darlene, Tiny and I've been talking, and it feels like we've known you for a long time. It's like we just clicked. We've got to stay in touch – what say you?'

'Yeah, I'd really like that too. I did promise you we'd swap contact details. May as well do that now if you're happy to, guys?'

'Hell yeah!' The laughter was as loud as it was genuine.

Spook led the way into the perfectly lit beer garden, each holding their second ice-cold beer. The first ones hadn't touched sides. No sooner had they sat than their steaks were brought to the table. They devoured the perfectly cooked meals in companionable silence; it was only when they all picked at the centre bowl of chips that conversation fired up.

'When and where's home, Darlene?' Spook asked.

'I don't actually have one, but one day, it'll be where the rolling green hills disappear into the horizon.' *And maybe where the platypus play.*

'Really? I thought you'd be a beach bum.'

'I was. Too much maintenance living by the sea. What about you guys?'

Tiny answered while Spook drank. 'Bathurst area when I'm at home, Esk in South East Queensland when I'm not, or when I'm waiting to hook up with Spook!'

'And then we meet at Bourke. I'm at Scone. By the way, that's where Christmas is this year.'

Darlene held Tiny's gaze but couldn't disguise the blush.

'I'll get us another beer.' Spook chuckled.

They gazed into each other's eyes across the table with silly grins dancing across their mouths.

'How's this going to work, Tiny?'

Coughing quietly, Tiny finally said, 'Not sure, actually. Is it short or long barrel, this competition you're attending?'

'Ha. You shoot?'

'Been known to.'

'Would like to see that sometime. But right now, how good are you at tracking down lost Danish girls?'

'What?' both men asked as Spook handed them their beers and retook his seat.

She showed them the picture on her phone and sat back. Spook kept looking at Tiny, back to the photo then back at Tiny.

'Okay, I'm no fool. Spill it.' Darlene spoke softly.

'She looks like she could be a relation of yours!' Spook said and quickly drank his beer.

She studied them closely and shook her head. 'No, no, guys. I can sense you're not telling me something, so spill.'

Tiny took a long sip of his beer, swallowed hard and in a quiet voice said, 'Told you to be wary of that purple prime mover for a reason, Darlene. Her name is Elaina. We saved her sweet sorry Danish arse from disappearing for good. She's over here, with a new phone, and trying to nail the sicko all by herself. How do you know of her?'

Darlene explained the mysterious discovery of her niece and Cassie's Danish friend, who was looking for her own missing friend. She didn't want to talk about the deputy sergeant, but the nagging question came up.

'There's a lot of nothing between here and there. Why'd you ask that?' Spook read the play easily.

'Because my niece said that was the advice the cigar-smoking old man gave them.'

'That old bastard still alive, Tiny?' Spook asked and lowered his eyes.

'Yep, still in a wheelchair.' He replied practically in a whisper.

Darlene suddenly shivered. Swiftly changing the subject, she tapped the picture of the missing girl. 'Can you get a message to her, please?'

'Sure,' Tiny said quietly.

'Oh. Is she your girlfriend?'

'Ah, no, um, not really. Her name is Elaina, and is on a personal mission. She's the cat's mother!'

'So, could you please stress the importance of her informing her parents and the deputy sergeant of her whereabouts? It's cruel not to let anybody know…

unavoidable, since she's... alive. From what I can gather, her best friend is over here trying to find her and nearly disappeared herself. There's some sort of connection. I don't know what it is, but now we're all involved. I'm aiming for a satisfying outcome. Care to join me?' Darlene smirked.

'Doing what?' Spook asked as he drained his beer.

Darlene shrugged and winked. 'Taking out the trash and partying like crazy during the festive season!'

Tiny roared with laughter. 'Taking out the trash! I love it. Yeah, there are some maggots that need taking out, alright. Another beer?'

'No, thanks. I'd really love a coffee and something sweet,' she said with a smile.

Spook answered for Tiny. 'We know just the place, and Nova will be getting lonely.'

CHAPTER TEN

Ever so gently, Spider scooped up his stinky bundle of fun and held her until she could slide down the truck steps and lean against his legs. He liked the idea of letting his hands do the exploring, but then he got a whiff. *Pooh. Too stinky. Use the water. Slowly. But you need to see what you're doing.*

Carefully unwinding the blanket then unbinding her hands, he firmly clasped one large hand around her thin wrists. Talking in a melodic way while he removed the gag, he watched as the LED lights under the chassis lit up the ground but the ones around the mirrors cast a soft light on their bodies. Catching her when she almost fell to the ground, he caressed the snake's head.

'Don't do anything stupid, pretty Snake Girl, or my spider will hurt you worse than you tried to hurt it. Just play nicely and we'll get along fine. We're going to go to the seaside soon, and you can be my mermaid during the day. Play nicely.'

'Please, Spider, I need some food and water,' she whispered hoarsely. 'I'll play nicely, but I'm weak. Have you got any real food?'

Yeah, feed her. Fun needs energy.

'Oh me, oh my. I had forgotten how nice you sound. Yes, but first we need to bathe, then I'll cook us up something to eat.'

'Thank you.'

Milly kept on praying that someone was missing her. The snake tattoo was an expression of the restricted grief that had consumed her when her father just left without saying goodbye. But she had never felt so ashamed of unfairly neglecting to stay in contact with her mother as she did now. Did she stay in the police force? Was she even alive? Then Milly admonished herself severely. How the hell could she have been so reckless after a shift? Regret washed over her like a tidal wave, but as she tumbled to the ground, revenge was slowly boiling inside of her. Never had her body been violated in such a contemptuous manner, but she'd bide her time. She knew every detail about this creep and longed for the day where she could pick up her pencils and put him down on paper.

She was going to survive this ordeal. He was not.

Bev had thoroughly enjoyed spending a lot of time with her boss. However, she detested the fact that his uncle was the biggest rogue out, who was cunning enough to avoid being arrested.

She paced her office in frustration. Amy in Port Lincoln couldn't shed any light on the situation, either, but had filed a missing person's report at the local police station. The café didn't have security cameras in the public carpark. It was getting late, and the investigation board was as blank as it was an hour earlier. Throwing her arms up in the air, Bev yanked open the door just as her boss was about to knock. Their eyes met and the world stood still for a second.

'Care to have a change of scenery, Bev?'

'Yes. Yes, I do. Let's go back to my place.'

'I'll go home and freshen up.'

'Do that at my place. Come, let's go.'

She giggled then and grabbed his hand. They were always the last to leave the station and, in typical fashion, left through the back door. Troy pulled her into his arms as soon as they stepped on the lamplit path and kissed her hard. She returned it with the same amount of vigour. Their tongues nervously exploring each other's mouths. Breathing heavily, they pulled apart and grinned like a pair of naughty teenagers. Gripping each other's hands, they walked briskly until they were inside Bev's kitchen. He showered while she reheated the lasagne and set the table. She showered while he made a salad.

They were drawn to each other like magnets. Each filled with desire, desperate to end the years of loneliness. They made love. Slowly. Passionately. Urgently. Tenderly.

The delicious aroma of freshly brewed coffee filled the air as Spook escorted Darlene to their outdoor kitchen with Nova bounding happily ahead. Tiny had insisted on preparing the after-dinner aperitif and had disappeared inside the enclosed kitchenette.

'At this stage, we could be in town until mid-week, Darlene. What are your plans?'

'I'd like to deliver the motorhome tomorrow and pick up the bonus, which I want to share with you guys. Then I'll head into town, localise myself and find somewhere to stay for a couple of days. You men have things to do – I don't want to be in your road. But promise me we'll see each other before you head back.'

'Oh, that's a guarantee! Where will you stay?'

'I'd prefer a hotel suite that overlooks the water. After a little while, I'll make tracks to Bunbury. That's near where the shooting competition is being held, and I need to familiarise myself with the wind and climate, as well as get some practice in.'

'After that?'

'I want to swim with the dolphins and go exploring, then pick up a casual job during the harvest somewhere.'

'Nobody back home waiting for you?'

'Nope.'

It wasn't the first time she'd thought of Jimmy, but it was the first time Darlene had really thought about where home once was, and she didn't dwell on it. That chapter was closed. She'd well and truly moved on.

'It'd be awesome if you could encourage Tiny to join us for Christmas, but you will promise to stay in touch, won't you?'

'That's a bit presumptuous! Why me?' She chuckled and blushed at the same time. 'Of course I'm going to stay in touch, and Spook, I truly hope all goes well with the birth of your grandchildren.'

'Yeah, didn't think I was old enough to be a granddad!'

'Remain young at heart and you'll never feel old.'

Tiny was pleased with his efforts. The crepes looked as professional as he had anticipated. It had been a while since he'd made them, but his pastry chef skills hadn't let him down. He'd been craving crepes, and Darlene's outfit had oddly been the inspiration. Tiny felt nervous, though. Elaina had been the last woman he'd spent time with. He still wondered if his now forty-six years were too old for anybody.

Although the veil of bad memories had gradually gotten heavier, subsequently blurring the vivid images, he could still hear the blast that blew his lover and unit into smithereens. The haunting memory of him returning to the armoured vehicle at the wrong moment would last a lifetime. They were meant to follow him back out of the alleyway. They didn't. They died. Everyone died. The whole apartment had collapsed. But Tiny survived. No amount of praying recovered any living soul.

He squeezed his eyes shut, cupped his hands over his ears and blew out through his mouth, envisaging the dust and grief disappearing into thin air. He sensed Spook before he heard him.

'I'm right, bloke, take a seat. Will be with you both shortly.'

'Sounds good. Smells awesome, mate.'

Darlene couldn't sit still. She'd been treated like a VIP since before dinner and felt she had to contribute something to the last course. Whatever Tiny had been cooking in the indoor kitchen had filled the air with sweet delicate undertones of lemon. She had never smelt anything so delectable in her life. Then she remembered the bottle of tawny port and smiled at the memory of the lead ringer waiting for her at the creek crossing. She'd often discovered him dozing under the eaves of the laundry with a shotgun across his lap when the mustering was on. He wasn't the most intelligent, but by golly, he could ride a horse, and he was fiercely protective of her virtue. She respected him for that; he respected her for her shooting ability.

The men were waiting expectantly and grinned broadly as she placed the port on the table. She only had eyes for the impeccably rolled lemon crepes.

'My, oh my. This just gets better! Tiny, those look and smell delicious.'

'Yep, they sure do. Please don't wait. They're best eaten straight away.'

Conversation stopped, and groans mixed with light sounds of lip-smacking. It was only when the last of the coffee was drained that conversation and laughter rippled through the shed.

'Heaven. Absolute heaven on a plate. You're a man of hidden talents, it seems.'

'Thanks! Ordinarily, I'd insist we drink port out of the appropriate sipper. However, we're not at my place...'

'That's alright, mate. Any objections if we use the coffee cups, Darlene, Tiny?'

'None from me,' she said, and slid the bottle towards Spook.

'I'll do that, mate. You're the man of the hour!' Tiny reached for the bottle and cracked the lid.

'Best not make it a big one. We've got to register zero by ten tomorrow morning. Darlene, we need to drop our trailers off, and we'll be gone several hours. We don't want you to feel you've been locked in; would you be up for breakfast, say, seven o'clock?'

'When you say "up for breakfast", I'm happy to cook. I've got more than enough steak and bacon with me. In fact, there'll be enough to last you guys for the next week, so please don't buy any!'

'Don't you eat eggs?' Spook asked as he stared into his port.

'Sure I do.' Suddenly, she stood up and said, 'Let's toast to our good health, newfound friendship and everlasting laughter.'

Both men joined her, and they clinked coffee cups together.

'And to eggs,' they said in unison and burst out laughing.

Bev placed the mugs of coffee on the bedside table and smiled tenderly down at Troy before kissing his forehead. His hands shot out from under the doona and dragged her back onto the bed. They giggled and snuggled together before plumping up each other's pillows and settling back with their coffees. Watching the burnt orange glow gradually creep towards the horizon, they sat in silence as the day came alive in front of their eyes. Their fingers entwined.

'Feel like a road trip to Port Lincoln, Bev?' Troy whispered.

The tears she'd been withholding slowly slid down her cheeks. She couldn't speak straight away. She could still feel his warm mouth upon hers, his solid body pressed against her matronly build. Her heart was aching for her daughter but revelling in the aftermath of the passionate night. Letting him take her cup out of her hands, she raked her eyes over his kind face, down his tanned throat, and smiled as she wove her fingers in his greying chest hairs.

'When?'

'After I've kissed this angel good morning, again.'

Milly longed to be back in her own bed. She hated being cooped up with no fresh air. She hated not being able to talk, let alone sing. She hated this fake-tattooed creep and hated spiders even more. One in particular was going to wither up and die a painful death.

She wished she knew someone with a gun. She'd shoot this spider to hell. Plucking up the courage to have a conversation, she pandered to the psychopath's interest in her snake. She nudged him gently with her chin, her constant mumbling forcing him to eventually pull over and undo her bounds. 'Shall I keep calling you Spider or snake charmer?' Milly asked while rubbing her reddened wrists.

'Just call me Spider. I don't want to know your name, but you have to let your snake get some sunshine. Will you be a good girl for me? We have to get to the sea, so you have to play nicely while I drive. Remember, it's daylight, so if I tell you to get in the sleeper cab, do not argue with me. I don't want to hurt you, but I can and I will.'

'Yes, Spider. I can't wait to see the sandcastle you build for me.'

He patted the edge of her seat. 'Trace the outline of your snake, and we'll see how long it takes for the sun to arrive.'

'Which beach should we play on, Spider?'

'Not telling. But we can only play for a little while. Then I have to go to work.'

Milly stopped fidgeting with her snake and pouted. 'Are you going to leave me behind?'

'No way. I'll take you home with me. My home, where I can keep you and your snake real safe.'

'Am I in danger, Spider?'

'No more questions. Play.'

Darlene had slept like a baby and dreamt of being in Tiny's arms. She could almost feel them and lazily stretched and smiled. Rolling onto her stomach, she was disappointed to discover she was alone, but she could see his donga and the shadow moving around inside. Daylight was making its presence swiftly known, and cooking for three people was a darn sight easier than cooking for fifteen, yet she had to get cracking.

Dressed in her long summery floral jumpsuit and sandals with her hair tied back in a French braid, she familiarised herself with the well-appointed outdoor kitchen. The steak, bacon and sausages had defrosted perfectly overnight. Loving the sound of the click-click to fire up the gas cooktop, she giggled softly. It always reminded her of camping. Something she desperately wanted to do again. With Tiny. He'd be nice to camp with. She'd feel safe, that was for sure.

Reluctantly pushing the daydreaming aside, she got on with the job at hand. Dicing up what was left of the defrosted baked potatoes and vacuum-sealed bags of mushrooms, tomatoes and shallots, she sprinkled the last of the withered parsley and chilli over the top and let everything sauté in the melted herb butter over a very low heat. She'd been craving parmesan toast since she'd left the outback Queensland station and was going to have it come hell or high water with breakfast that morning.

Exactly fifteen minutes before seven o'clock, the aroma of sizzling steak, sausages and bacon, mingled with whatever else had been cooking for a while, wafted up Spook's nose. He knew Darlene would have taken the initiative and wasn't going to interfere. But dammit, he didn't want to fill out the Santa suit so early.

Tiny's message of *she'd make someone a good wife one day* made him stifle a loud laugh.

His reply of *Someone? Are you sure you're not gay?* received no reply.

Darlene's timing was to perfection, naturally. The kettle had just boiled, the juice was poured and the parmesan toast perfectly coloured. Nova's wet nose on her ankles made her laugh loudly. Turning around, she grinned at her two new best friends and served up the feast.

'Morning, gentlemen. Hope you're hungry, or... hope we can burn this off today!'

'What are you doing tomorrow, young lady?' Spook asked with a grin from ear to ear. 'This looks fit for a king.'

'Two kings, mate!' Tiny said.

Darlene nearly fell into his eyes. The big green-blue pools of unadulterated admiration weakened her knees. Blushing profusely, she had nowhere to go, nowhere to hide, and looked at Spook for inspiration.

He simply winked. 'Let's devour this here fine spread of culinary delights. We've got a lot to get through today. Darlene, follow me in the Statesman to the motorhome place, then I'll drop you off so you can localise yourself. How about a late lunch and go from there?'

'Sounds fabulous!'

'Spook, we should see where our Danish Pastry is too!' Tiny grinned liked a Cheshire cat.

Darlene looked at him quizzically then laughed politely when she realised who he was referring to.

Cassie worked on a two-and-a-half hour time difference between her and her aunt. Even though daylight savings time hadn't kicked in, it just made her feel closer. But she desperately needed to talk to her. The twins were having their midmorning nap, and the doctor was doing his rounds. Asta was mad keen on going exploring on the weekend along the coastline to where her friend had last been seen. Cassie couldn't wait any longer and said a silent prayer to the ringing tone.

'Morning, Cassie, I've got my hands full of dust, dirt and whatnot. Thought you'd like to know that! Seriously, how are you? I never got to ask you the other day.'

'Hi, Aunty Darlene. Health-wise, I'm very well, thanks. Settling in okay, too. I feel better doing what I'm supposed to be doing, but I still have this hankering to help find Asta's friend and all the others that are missing. Do you know there are at least fifteen in the last two months that have just disappeared off the face of the earth? All here. All in South Australia. It's a vast spread of land, but that's a lot of sad folk waiting for word. What's worse is they're not all from Australia. Anyway, Asta's coming through this weekend and wants to go to the joint where her friend was last seen. I don't want her to go alone, but she's persistent. I feel I should phone Officer Bev and ask her if she could get the weekend off. What do you reckon I should do?'

'Go with your gut. Make that phone call and talk it through with her. Being Thursday, it might be enough time to get something planned. Cassie, let me know if you need some funds to contribute to expenses and if you owe any money. I can do a transfer right now or tonight; see, I'll be heading into town soon, attending to some business.'

'You would? What business?'

'Of course! Do your maths and let me know.'

'What business, Aunt Darlene? Did that prick with the busted ankle contact the police after all?'

'You were never to speak of that again, Cassie.' She spoke sternly. 'No. I'm returning the motorhome, then window-shopping for several hours before meeting some friends. Okay?'

'Whoops, sorry. Money talk now – I've already checked out how much this is going to cost us. Hell, this joint's expensive, and Asta and I do have an IOU.'

'How much?'

'Eight hundred bucks for two nights' accommodation, plus budget meals and the bus fares, and five hundred for Officer Bev. I haven't saved that much.'

'Are you still going to buy me a carton of beer for New Year?'

'Yes, and pay you back at Christmas time!'

'You're on. Flick me through your bank details before you phone Officer Bev. That way, you can talk to her with confidence should money matters arise.'

'Love you, Aunt Darlene. Thank you.'

'Love you too, kiddo. Be sensible, please.'

'Will do. I'll phone you Sunday night as well. Bye.'

Darlene's natural high from the appreciative comments about breakfast and the plan for the day was boosted by hearing her favourite niece's voice. Forcibly trying to bury the horrid thoughts of Oliver Cady, she tucked the phone in her pocket and swivelled around on her haunches as a shadow approached. Tiny blocked out the sun perfectly.

'Can I be useful at all?' he asked politely.

'Tiny, you guys really need to get hold of your Elaina. This weekend, my niece and her Danish friend are going to where she was last seen in South Australia. Just a reminder, Cassie, who is my niece, and Asta, the Danish friend, almost became statistics, and I will not let it happen a second time if I can help it.'

With that, Darlene spun back around on her haunches and went back to checking the hose connections. She so easily could have put Cassie ahead of her life, but for how many more years should her own life come second? Damn him. That jerk! Damn her ex-boyfriend. How dare he?

She suddenly wondered if she had trust issues. She shouldn't have spoken like that to Tiny. She felt vulnerable and just wanted to be swept up in his big strong arms. To be held. To be loved. To be appreciated. Her phone chimed loudly, causing her to shriek, and in an instant Nova was by her side. So was Tiny. His huge hand engulfed hers. He pulled her into his embrace as he helped her up. With his lips pressed against her hair, he murmured words of comfort and encouragement.

'You don't always have to be the toughie. Doesn't mean you're any less strong, but you're allowed to be vulnerable. You're a woman, for heaven's sake.'

She leaned into him with all her weight and sighed softly.

'I don't know what happened to you, but you can forget all about that now. Please, Darlene, we're your friends.'

'First, you have to tell your Elaina to check in with her friends, or at least the police. I beg of you, it's critical. It's urgent, Tiny. Please.'

'I'll go and talk to Spook.'

Watching the interaction through the office window, Spook couldn't help but smile. These two were nicely suited to each other as far as he was concerned. He pretended to have his nose buried in his invoice book when Tiny knocked and entered the office. He ignored the frustrated look on the big man's face.

'You about ready to roll?' Spook asked.

'Mate, we got ourselves a situation. Elaina has to volunteer her well-being, else others are going to be put in danger. Namely, Darlene's niece and Asta, Elaina's best friend. When do you think the two birds should talk?'

'She's not due to make contact for another day, but leave it with me. See if you can get a picture of Asta. That might be the tipping point. Our Danish Pastry has been talking about going home before she outstays her welcome here. I can take her with me, drop her off at a rendezvous with Sarge and shut the book on that chapter. It might be hard for you, but you'll have to work that out. To be honest, Tiny, I'll be glad when we're not her surrogate guardians. It's getting harder each time with the tax man. Can't keep on donating without getting receipts... you get my drift?'

'Yeah, I do. Okay, I'll go and let Darlene know.'

'Cheers for that. Listen, we roll in an hour. I'm willing to bet our Pretty One will be ready to leave at the same time, but just double-check. Thanks.'

'Pretty One? Our Pretty One?'

'Yeah, it's a great code name! We've already got a Danish Pastry. Can't have two.'

'Copy that,' Tiny said and quietly shut the door behind him.

Tiny threw Nova's ball as he walked towards the motorhome, whistling a happy tune, but suddenly fell silent and stopped short when he heard her raised voice. He knew he shouldn't hang around, but he couldn't help himself. He hid behind the tree and listened to the one-sided emotional conversation.

'Thanks, Dad. No. I don't want a telephone interview, and definitely don't give him or anybody my number. No! I'm participating at the shooting comp over here. I am not coming back any sooner. No.'

A pause, then a muffled angry bellow.

'A what? A DVO? On me? That bastard bullied me the whole time at the Queensland State Finals, tried to rape me before that, then thought he could corner me and damage my vehicle. I aimed for the dirt beside his ankle, but for the first time that day, I missed the target. Did you hear me? You and Mum weren't even interested if I won or lost that day.'

A long pause.

'He said what? You're kidding. When did he phone you?'

Tiny could hear Darlene stomping up and down the motorhome.

'That's crap. Please block his number after you've sent it to me. I'll return serve. I'll report him to the Rifle Association. The bastard. How dare he? How dare he try and tarnish my name?'

Tiny's heart twisted when he heard her burst into tears. He hated hearing women cry. Then he wished he had walked away and not heard any more. But it was too late.

'Seeing as dirty laundry is being aired, let's clear the elephant out of the room once and for all.' Her voice was tight. 'It's been getting stale over the last few years. Why did you and Mum resent me for the relationship breakdown? It was like you blamed me.'

A pause.

'Kids? Married? Oh, come on. He wasn't home long enough, and when he was, there wasn't any loving, I can tell you... my career? What? I was successful in my own right, earning a buck and paying my way. Bloody hell, Dad! But let's get back to answering your question, shall we? Dammit, I knew none of you listened to what I was telling you... nor to what the callous bastard said when he handed me the settlement cheque. No. All you did was ask questions and jump to conclusions. The whole lot of you. Why?'

When she spoke again, her voice changed from indignation to expressing the obvious pent-up hurt that had been eating her alive for far too long.

'Yes. A settlement cheque, that's what I said. A fat *goodbye, have a good life* de facto settlement cheque. Okay?' A long pause. 'No. How the hell should I have reacted? Perform a happy dance after being told I bored him? What man says that, anyway?'

Tiny nearly barged in when she coughed and spluttered, like she was choking.

'Thanks... yes, an honest man. Yep. Great empathy there. Anyway, time's a-ticking, and I've got business to attend to. Thanks for the heads-up. I'll see how I can nail more than one target this time. Send through the numbers straight away, please. Thanks for calling, Dad, but I will not be late. Love you both. Bye.'

Tiny silently walked away with a burden of guilt for eavesdropping.

Milly memorised the pin code to Spider's mobile phone and the GPS but wished she'd never seen the angry scowl contort his face as he flicked through the list of missed calls and text messages. Using it to her advantage, she started bawling as soon as she recognised the outskirts of the sleepy town of Haslam. They were on the way to Smoky Bay. She loved this part of SA. She had loved it. Not anymore. She had to survive so this prick didn't. Knowing full well the service station was beyond the town, she wailed even louder when the police cars went in the opposite direction.

Spider rolled into the roadhouse, trying hard not to lose control of himself. The snake girl had gotten herself all worked up, and he didn't know what to do. *Stop her from crying. Buy her an ice cream. Do something!*

'Are you hungry?'

'Hungry?' Milly screamed at him. 'I haven't had a decent bath or sufficient water, and I need to go to the toilet. I'm sick of these restraints. If you want to be my friend, you have to be nice to me too. Do you still want to be my friend, Spider?'

Yes! Yes. You want her as a friend. You like her. You like her snake.

'Yes, I want to be your friend. You can't leave the Black Widow. You're naked. How about I let you phone home, say you're on a holiday and you'll be back soon? Will that make you feel better?'

Just then, Spider's mobile rang. He stabbed angrily at the answer button then held the phone tightly against his ear.

'Yes, Reg. I'm nearly there... What? No, I can't turn around. I haven't got there yet.'

'I'll scream if you don't let me talk,' Milly said loudly.

'What? No, that's my friend. She was being funny.'

'Spider, give me that phone now,' Milly commanded.

She's really mad. Her snake is even angry. Look, its scales! All scrunched up. Don't look. Look. Don't look. Look.

Spider growled angrily and thrust the phone into her hands before revealing his growing spider.

Milly recoiled and timidly spoke into the phone.

'Hello, I'm Spider's PL assistant. We'll be back in a day or two, just on a holiday.' Then, in a girly singsong voice, 'I'm going to be his mermaid and he's going to build me a sandcastle and we'll be smokie in the nudie.'

Spider giggled. 'Smokie in the nudie.'

They sang it together. *Yeah. Sing it. You're on holiday. Yay!*

Reg spoke very quietly into the phone. 'I'll get you help. Put the freak back on.'

Milly sang the silly words loudly as she handed Spider the phone and made loud hissing noises.

'Stop that, Snake Girl,' he growled before grabbing the phone.

'Why do I have to turn around now, Reg? What about the trailer?' Spider whined.

'Spider, listen carefully. Dangerous people are up ahead. You need to come home now. Have you got fuel?'

'I'll be getting some when we hang up. But I want to take my friend to the sea.'

'I'm dying, Spider. I need you to come home. Stevo and Max need you too.'

Milly watched as Spider rubbed his eyes and banged the side of his head.

Reg dying? No. No. He's not allowed to. Stevo and Max need you. Wow. Reg's dying. What are you going to do?

'No, no, no. You're not allowed to die. Mamma died before she said goodbye. Please wait, Reg. Can you wait? Please?'

'I'll try, lad. Why don't you bring your new friend home with you? Then we can all go to the beach. Will you do that for me, Spider? Will you?'

Milly tried to push herself against the corner of the truck to get far away from the cruel look that came over Spider's face. She gasped with horror when she saw what had revealed itself between his legs.

'Get in the sleeper, Snake Girl.' A completely different voice came from Spider. 'You will wait there.'

Get fuel first. Then leave. Then play. Then go to the sea. Then go to Reg. Get fuel first. Don't touch her snake yet.

'Reg, I'll get fuel first. You'll know when I get home.'

Run away. Go to WA. You'll see them another day. Be free.

Milly let him grab her hand and shove her into the sleeper. She knew what to do. Wrap herself up in the sheet, sit on the floor and be quiet.

She heard the doors slam then lock. Cursing under her breath, she realised he'd taken the phone and turned off the GPS. She prayed that whoever Reg was, he'd have the decency to do the right thing.

Officer Bev and DS Troy Oscane were ushered into the renal floor of the Whyalla Hospital. The sorry sight of the varying ages of those in care tore at their heartstrings. They knocked quietly on the door of the suite where Cassie was reading to the twins while they lay beside their mother. Both women looked up and smiled, but it was the twins who scrambled up on their legs and put their arms up in the air. The two police officers took one each and gave them a cuddle as Cassie gently helped their mother to sit upright.

'You been good to me. For that, I thank you,' the ailing woman said. 'When I get home, you come and visit. We look after you. We adopt you, just like I want to adopt Asta. But she got other plans. People go missing all the time. My people and yours. My husband back in two days. Maybe you see him?'

Her breath got shorter as she laid her head back on the pillow. Cassie held a glass to her mouth and helped her drink, stroking her hand gently. The mother patted the bed and held out her hands for her children. They gurgled happily and lay down quietly beside her. Their hands linked together across her skinny legs.

'You go for a walk with your friends. We be fine,' she mumbled.

'Thank you, Mother-Aunty. I'll bring you some flowers,' Cassie said quietly.

She threw her arms around Officer Bev the minute the elevator doors closed and hugged her tightly, then shook Troy's hand.

'This is a wonderful surprise! We were only talking to each other this morning, and suddenly you're here! Are you staying overnight? Is this a working holiday? You look great in your civvy clothes.'

She fell silent as the doors opened into a very busy canteen. The three walked through the hospital gardens towards the bench under the glorious fig tree, each lost in their own thoughts. Bev grinned at the gentle dig in her ribs from her boss.

'Cassie, the research you did has given us some hope for locating Asta's friend. It's also given us a lead we're investigating down at Port Lincoln. You indicated you both had the weekend off... I hope you're being honest with me about that... Anyway, we'd rather you and Asta didn't join us on this occasion, so how about you two girls go and relax at Cowell? When you think about it, you've had quite the harrowing time!'

'Oh, Officer Bev.' Cassie burst into tears. 'It feels like it. I'm so tired. I haven't been sleeping. As much as I desperately want to help Asta, our hands are tied. We don't know how to do investigations. We don't even know anyone in this part of the country except you two lovely people.'

'Do you think Asta would like a quiet weekend by the sea?' Bev asked. 'Cowell is a really pretty place, particularly at this time of the year.'

'Shall we call and ask her? She's still using the phone you kindly gave her.'

'Yes, let's do that,' Troy said. 'In fact, I will.'

'Phew,' both the two women said together and giggled.

They watched as he walked away, dialling numbers into his phone.

'How are you really, Cassie?'

'I am okay. Truly, I am, Officer Bev. I just don't know why I'm not sleeping. It's not the twins – they're angels when it comes to bedtime.'

'Do you reckon you're homesick?'

She laughed crazily. 'Homesick? Me? I don't miss the smothering.'

'What do you miss?'

Big elephant tears erupted and spilled down her ruddy cheeks. 'Mum and Dad. Hearing their voices is nice, but I miss seeing their faces. Smelling Mum's talcum powder and the timber oils Dad uses in the shed.'

'Believe me, Cassie, no matter how old you are, you will always miss your folks.' *And your kids.*

They hugged each other tightly and both sniffled quietly.

Troy fist-pumped the air in jubilation. He was going to have Bev to himself the entire weekend. It had been a very long time since he'd looked forward to anything. Although they'd be doing police work, they'd also be sharing in each other's company. He silently prayed they'd have a lead on her daughter to reduce any sadness and the growing anxiety.

'Well, looks like Cowell is going to have the pleasure of two lovely young ladies. Cassie, no pubs and no brawls this time, please!' He chuckled as he approached.

They stood up together, with Bev ending up in the middle.

'No way! We're going to relax. Um, thank you both so very much for everything.'

'We'll walk you back to your post, young lady, then we must be on our way.' Bev patted the younger woman's shoulder lightly, while squeezing her boss's hand.

Reg Oscane released his three Rottweilers as Max stepped out of his late-model 4WD. He watched as the dogs happily bounded around him before gently taking their large marrow bones. Oddly enough, they didn't smash them as ferociously as they usually did, plopping them by Reg's wheelchair and returning to their recently dug hollows under the porch.

'How you doin', Reg?'

'Feeling my age, mate. Not sure if I'll see Christmas, actually. Coughing up a fair bit of blood.'

'You'll be here this Christmas, and probably the next, just like you were last Christmas. You've been saying this every time the weather heats up for the last three years!'

'Yeah, but I'm feeling tired. The boys have gone rogue.'

'What do you want to do with them?'

'Let's go inside. Getting too bright out here.' Reg wheeled his chair back inside.

Max swiftly opened all the windows. 'Hell, man, I never needed to take up smoking!'

'Easier to shift the shit, hey?'

They both laughed as they each cracked the top off a stubby.

'Checked in on the prime mover. Why grey?'

'Spider's choice. He said it'd blend into the road.'

'Bumps up the insurance cost a hell of a lot!' Max thumbed his chin.

'It comes out of his annual salary; silly prick has no idea about business. Stevo's as slack as a line with no sinker.'

'Trixie's worried about two of the girls. One's not eating properly, and the other one might be up the duff. That's a problem.'

'For who? You?'

'Nah, I always wear a rubber. Dunno 'bout the lads, though.'

'Humph. Just let them go. Blindfold the lot, transport them in the middle of the night and drop them off in a dark carpark with plenty of water and fresh towels.'

'You have got old and soft, Reg!'

'Nah, I've never liked what you do with women. Listen. They're someone's kids. Who knows if their parents have died from a broken heart, or committed suicide from grief. How long has the playroom been growing? Six, seven, eight months?'

'You really don't know, do you?'

Reg slammed down his empty stubby and gripped Max's wrist roughly.

'You will go down for this shit. The boys are slippery but not stupid. Why throw away everything you've got? For what? Some pussy? Grow up.'

'Years, Reg. It's been growing for years. Spider has his stash, and Stevo and I like the same assortments. We just add to them when we want to.'

'How many years?'

Max grinned smugly and stood up. Reg swung the shotgun up from alongside his leg and cocked it. Max froze.

'Bullshit. You gonna kill me, old man? Then what? How you gonna clean it up? Trixie? She won't come out here, she hasn't for years.'

'How many women have you got stashed, Max?'

'Over two weeks' worth of variety...'

'You're a sick man. They're someone's mother, wife, daughter... that's damn cruel.'

'Yeah, and some are sons and brothers. Their–'

'I will pull this trigger if you describe any more. Get out. Get out and never come back. You're despicable, just like those two sprogs. I don't even know that they're mine.'

Max laughed coldly as he walked backwards out of the kitchen and down the ramp. Reg spat the end of a freshly unwrapped cigar in his general direction, flicked his fingers, and instantly the three Rottweilers sat in front of his crippled legs.

'Mr Reg Oscane,' Max said with forced pleasantness, 'thank you for your support in my election campaign for reducing the amount of rogue truck drivers.'

His toothy grin didn't reach his eyes as he continued with his vindictive spiel. 'Be it said, without me, your tobacco and weed business would have failed a very long time ago and you'd have been dead a lot earlier.'

'You did the drugs part, you bastard. That was never, ever the plan. I detest drugs and despicable behaviour towards women. You knew that a hell of a long time ago, too. Now, you best leave, Max. You come back here, and you die where you stand.'

Reg pulled the trigger. The dirt kicked up around the front of the shiny 4WD. At the same time, the hollow cartridges fell down beside the worn-down rubber wheels of his chair.

'Not if I kill you first, you soft old bastard,' Max yelled as he slammed the door and broadsided his way down the driveway.

Max was seething. He should have told Reg about Spider and Stevo. They weren't Reg's sons. They were his. He punched the steering wheel in frustration and thought about his first trophy. His first love. Ruby. He'd drugged her and kept her for himself, then he wanted more and more but didn't have the right hiding place or courage. Then he did the stupidest thing he'd ever done in his life. Introduced Ruby to Reg. It was impossible to deny the love they had for each other. It was impossible to deny she still craved Max's loving. Ruby had shown him the DNA report each time. Each time, they had celebrated while Reg was away in Queensland. Max swore to look out for the lads while the fool raised and paid for them until the day he or Ruby died. She died too soon. It was Reg who should have died.

Resentment is a powerful thing. It fed Max's ambition to be powerful. To control. To build the secure playhouse, the creative shed. To increase his captives. To ship the assortment of tobacco, weed and powder. To use his best friend. To guide the local shire to achieve his goals. For the last seventeen years, it had worked. Now, there was another contender in his electoral division. The campaign had started earlier than usual. Max had the money, the contacts, the wherewithal. His contender had foreign investment, an ear inside the state government and was twenty years younger. And a woman.

Reg kept seeing the look on Max's face when he voiced his doubt about his sons. He couldn't comprehend their sick behaviour. Reg had treated his own mother like a queen, just like he'd seen his father treat her. That was how to treat women. Not badly. Not shamefully, and certainly not humiliatingly. He hadn't been able to understand where the two lads had gotten their depravity from, until Max had opened his ugly mouth. That was when the penny dropped.

Tears welled up in Reg's eyes when he thought about his Ruby. He had adored her and was so proud when he was told he was going to become a father. Twice. Shaking his head, he took the tattered photo album down from the bookshelf and flicked through the dusty memories. The boys had grown up watching Reg cherish his wife, their mother, but it all changed when she died. Spider had left home at sixteen, and eventually, Stevo moved in with him. They only came home when they wanted something, or when Reg had a job for them. Stevo's loose lips after too many beers brought Reg's attention to the debauchery the boys got up to. Neither one mentioned Max, their surrogate uncle. His best friend. No. His former best friend.

Coughing harshly into a clean handkerchief, Reg battled to catch his breath. He wiped the blood-stained spittle off his mouth and threw the linen into the bin.

I'll be seeing you again soon, Mother. Forgive me my ignorance and blindness.

Spider had to ditch the Black Widow. It was far too conspicuous along the coastal highway. He had to decide to go to Yalata or phone Stevo. Either way, they needed a car and to keep driving westwards. He had enough money stashed in his bag to last six weeks. By then, the heat would be off him and Snake Girl, and he'd sneak back home. All undercover like. *Yeah. Do that. Go now. Play later. Build a sandcastle on a different beach. Far away. Go now. Play later.*

He'd found a clean shirt and tracksuit bottoms and helped Snake Girl get dressed. Eventually. She had behaved nicely and nobody and no creature got hurt. He liked when she played nicely. He liked that very much.

Looking over at the sleeping toy, he knew she wouldn't wake up for several hours after the last drink of Pepsi.

CHAPTER ELEVEN

Feeling oddly carefree after returning the burdensome motorhome, Darlene followed the curved pathways through the magnificent Kings Park, wheeling her life in a trusty blue suitcase. Hugging almost every large tree she passed, drinking in the peace and tranquillity and lush green grass, she was so tempted to do grass angels and giggled at the inner child just busting to break free. Instead, she made her way to the Botanical Café and ordered an iced chocolate. While devouring the delicious treat, she referred to Spook's mud map. He'd scrawled the name of the shopping mall, the taxi ramp and then, in very neat writing, the rendezvous for a late lunch. '*The Island at Elizabeth Quay.*' It all sounded very fancy. When she had asked Spook why the choice of location, he'd said it was like being on a secluded island on an island and laughed when he opened his car door. That was when she saw the smart casual trousers, collared shirt and dress shoes.

She looked down at the outfit she'd worn at breakfast. They were to meet at 2:30 p.m. That was in three hours. Hailing the first taxi, she made him take her to Portmans. The only shop for her annual dose of retail therapy. As soon as they pulled up, the dress hanging in the window had her name on it. A high-necked, bare-shouldered, pleated dress with pink ombre and turquoise-coloured waves. She liked the pink clutch and matching strappy heels too. Darlene pressed a fifty-dollar note firmly into the driver's hand, encouraging him to wait.

One and a half hours later, she alighted from the taxi outside the Double Tree Hotel with her freshly laundered outfit and matching set of lingerie, appropriately covered, hanging off the handle of her suitcase. The aged concierge smiled as she breezed past him, then she booked a premier room with a view of the Swan River for one week. During casual conversation, the assistant manager waived the short-notice fee when he learnt she was relaxing before the upcoming pistol shooting competition. He was one of the judges. His kind, twinkling eyes swept over her appearance and told her he looked forward to seeing her take on the competition. As he escorted her to the elevator, he mentioned the complimentary carpark available in the lock-up garage underneath the building and how to configure the security safe in her room.

After freshening up and revelling in a decent sized shower, she styled her hair simply, so it caressed her bare shoulders. She was feeling a million bucks, and it was high time she had a bit of fun. With her smile reflecting the shimmery waters of the Swan River, Darlene was ready to take on the world. *Right, Tiny, best bring your A game*, she thought. Grinning mischievously, she waited in the foyer of the hotel for her prearranged taxi.

Spook recognised her the minute she stepped out of the cab. She was ten minutes early and looked stunning. Tiny was already waiting for them inside at the table overlooking the Swan, missing out on the beautiful vision Spook was enjoying all by himself. He simply loved naturally beautiful woman. No fake tans, no fake hair. Just like the women in his family. He watched her admiring the trees, the sky, stopping and listening to the birds before taking in the incredible interlocking octagonal building with its arched windows. Getting her bearings, she turned around slowly and looked directly at him. He walked towards her, mirroring her grin.

'You are a sight for sore eyes, Darlene.'

'Oh, Spook, thank you. I couldn't resist it!' She twirled around, the pleats opening and closing like a pretty flower. Kissing him lightly on the cheek, she said, 'How's your daughter and bubs?'

He rested her hand on his arm in a fatherly way and chuckled. 'They're all doing well. I have been seconded into finishing the nursery two days after I get home!'

'Nice! You'll have time to wash your truck first!'

'That was the condition. Come along, Tiny's waiting for us.'

'Oh, he's early!'

'If he's late, there's something wrong. In all the years I've known him, he has never been late, never let me down and never forgotten anything. I trust him with my life, and he's one hell of a best mate, that I can tell you.'

'How long have you known him, Spook?'

'Feels like all my life. I think I've spent more time in his company, driving our trucks, than I have my own family. They love him to bits. You hungry?'

'Yes, and thirsty!'

Darlene saw him the moment she walked through the door. He filled the room. The sea rushed in her ears, her heart raced and she felt the blush rise from her breasts and flush her face. Her eyes raked over the crisp white shirt snugly hugging his broad chest. She easily imagined her hands undoing the buttons. They held each other's gaze. The world stopped.

They smiled and met halfway across the room. He took her hands gently and kissed her on the cheek.

'You are exquisite, Darlene. Thank you for being here.'

'You took the words out of my mouth, Tiny.'

He ushered them to the best table in the restaurant. With glasses in hand, they saluted their friendship and the glorious view. Darlene just loved the way the gentlemen waited until the lady sat before taking their seats.

Officer Bev studied the footage of the external security cameras while her boss interviewed the staff. Nobody had seen Milly after she finished her shift at 11:15 p.m. The corner of a prime mover with a sleeper cab was captured as it drove in at 6:43 p.m., with only its coupling visible to 9:08 p.m. It was impossible to tell what make or model it was, and disappointingly, no other camera angle provided any further information. Even more annoyingly, the internal cameras were more focused on the integrity of the staff than of their patrons.

Troy excused himself and stepped outside as he answered his phone.

'Old man?'

'Nephew, we need to talk.'

'Now isn't a good time. I'm conducting an investigation.' Troy frowned and rubbed his forehead.

'Listen, lad, I think I'm going to be meeting up with your pa soon, but I gotta tell you something. Spider is in the Black Widow. A black Volvo with a sleeper cab heading west.'

'Are you sending me on a wild goose chase, Uncle Reg?'

'No. I have never done that, and nor will I.'

Troy listened to his uncle coughing, spluttering and gagging before his rattly voice was back in his ear.

'I'm dying, boy. Spider has got a girl with him. Oh, shit. Max is back. He's a sick, twisted bastard. Nail him when you get a chance.'

The phone went dead. Troy called him back, but it went straight to message bank. He saw Bev walk towards him with two paper bags and bottles of fruit juice. The look on her face was utter dejection.

'Who was that?'

'My dying uncle. A black Volvo with a sleeper cab should be our focus, not the purple rig. I've got to make a phone call later on, but tell me what you found.'

'Absolutely nothing. Bloody useless security setup,' she grumbled. 'Amy's going out of her mind with worry, plus Milly never took her phone to work. Apparently, the boss was very militant about mobile phones. It was turned off. That's why we couldn't track it.'

She paused to take a breath, looked up and smiled. 'Here comes Amy now. She wants to meet you.'

A pretty, auburn-haired, petite young woman walked confidently towards them with a warm smile. She hugged Bev first then extended her hand to Troy.

'Afternoon, sir. I'm Amy, a friend of Bev and Milly's. May I sit?'

'Of course! Nice to meet you, Amy. Tell us about Milly, please.' Troy sat back and studied the two women as they conversed.

'She's a little underweight, yet has the most beautiful singing voice. Bev, she never stopped singing. That's why she took the night shift – so she could sing during the day. Our neighbour thought she'd died and gone to heaven when Milly moved in. She loves jazz, and well, you know Milly's voice... it's smooth like fine whisky and thick like melted chocolate.'

Amy reached over and squeezed Bev's hand. 'It's important you know that. I believe Milly will understand when she finds out that I've been in touch with you all these years. Yes, I know I'm talking about her in the present tense, because I believe she's still alive. She doesn't back down when something's important to her. Yeah, she's done drugs... no needles or amphetamines, mainly pot, and is vigilant on making sure her drinks aren't spiked. But...' Amy wiped her eyes. 'We haven't been out together for ages, so I don't really know what she does after her shift. I never hear her come home, but I peek in on her before I leave for work.'

'What do you do for a living, Amy?' Bev asked.

'All sorts of things! I volunteer in the mornings at Meals on Wheels, do an aged care degree at uni and am a cashier at the servo. But I'm on placement at the moment at the local palliative care during the day only. I hoped to see Milly for dinner the other night, but I got called into work.'

'You haven't noticed any unusual trucks or single prime movers at the servo or getting around town?' Troy asked.

'No. We don't get many at the one I'm at. It's too small.'

'Amy, please let me pay Milly's part of the rent, at least until we find her and bring her home,' Bev said.

Tears welled up in both women's eyes.

'She'll come home. She'll be livid, but she'll come home, Bev. I know that. I feel it's a bit rude to ask you for help, though.'

'It's the least I can do. Tell you what, how about I write a cheque out to the real estate to cover the next four months' rent? That way, you can focus on what you do and what you can do, okay?'

'I'll pay you back. I swear on my mother's grave.'

Amy threw her arms around Bev and buried her face into her shoulder and wept. Eventually, she composed herself, graciously accepted Troy's handkerchief and gripped Bev's hand tightly.

'Milly is so lucky to have you as her mother, and I'm lucky to have you as my second one. We have to stay strong together. If there's anything else I can do, or if I hear of anything, I'll let you know. But I'm sorry, I have to run. I won't be late for work. I'll text you the real estate's details. Thank you so much.'

Troy watched as Amy kissed Bev on her cheek. She turned to him and smiled.

'You're a nice man. Look after this beautiful woman.' She kissed his cheek before running through the park.

'We should adopt her,' he heard himself say.

'We'll have to get married.'

'Let's find Milly first,' they said in unison then had their lunch in silence.

Checking she was still breathing, he heard her moan as he prodded the bundle. Spider thought she'd be thirsty but she kept on sleeping. They were in an old siding off the highway and out of sight, listening to the static of the scanning two-way. He absolutely had to ditch the truck for a car. Punching in Stevo's number, his long bony fingers wriggled around the steering wheel while waiting for him to answer.

'Spider, dude,' Stevo drawled lazily. 'These toys are awesome, man. You on your way?'

'No, man, I'm out Woop Woop. Hey, what's the go with me having to turn around?'

'Dunno. Whaddya want anyway?'

'A car. I need a car. Got any contacts at Penong?' Spider spoke gruffly.

'Shit, yeah. I forgot, big bust out by Ceduna, so watch out for the pigs. Go see Bluey. There's a side road past the hotel. Hang a left at the blue letterbox. Take another left – last time it was graded. There's a big shed. Tell him I sent ya. Hope you got something you can trade.'

'Trade? Like what?'

'Guess! He's like Uncle Max and me. You know. Boys? Girls?'

'Sicko. What else does he like?'

'How much cash on ya?'

'Enough.'

'Give him two K. Any pills or pot?'

'Yep.'

'He likes pot. Now, I got me a toy to play with. See ya.'

Angrily replacing the mobile into its holder, he roughly shook Milly's shoulder. 'Snake Girl, wake up.'

She flopped about on the seat and moaned, then licked her lips. 'Water. I need water. Please, Spider.' Her eyes never opened, so he made her sip some more Pepsi. She fell back against the window frame.

Fifty minutes later, he'd partly reversed the truck into a small space in a massive, very congested shed. 'Hey, Bluey!' he called out. 'Stevo sent me. Got some goodies for you. I've got to pick up a car for him.'

'Oi, what goodies?'

Spider turned around and stared at the little man with red hair holding a sawn-off shotgun.

'How about some pot?' Spider asked pleasantly.

'That it?'

'Nah, he said to give you the two K he owes you.'

'Stupid bastard only owes me fifteen hundred bucks, but I'll take it. Can't remember what car, but!'

'Don't matter. Give me one with the most fuel. I got to meet him at Border Village. It's about five hours from here, isn't it?'

'Yeah, but take your time. There's activity happening out there, and mind the pigs, roos and wombats!'

'Here you go,' Spider said as he handed him the half bag of pot.

Spider opened the passenger door to the truck and caught Milly as she tumbled into his arms. Talking softly to her, he carried her to the yellow Ford Focus, balancing her on his knee as he opened the door. Bluey leaned in from the driver's side and helped her sit up.

'She's a sleepy one. Pretty, but sleepy.'

'Yeah, did a lot of driving. Say, you don't have any girls' clothing around here, do you? She ran away and hasn't got much.'

'Might. There's a bag or two in the shed. Can I play while you go look?'

Spider looked at him with such ferocity he scrambled out of the car backwards and yelled over his shoulder, 'I'll bring it. Wait there.'

Nobody touches Snake Girl. Play nicely. You have to leave. Ditch your phone. Ditch the GPS. Lock Black Widow. Lose the keys.

The seatbelt held his toy nicely against the seat. Spider raced back to the truck as quickly as his gangly legs let him and removed any evidence. He searched frantically for her boots, loopy earrings and blanket, then remembered he'd already ditched them in the boondocks. He disconnected the GPS, cut the ignition wires and ripped the SIM card out of the phone. *Hurry up. You have to leave.*

'Here. Take these,' Bluey said excitedly. 'They're all girly stuff. There's a brush in there. She needs to brush her hair. It's untidy. Got some water bottles too.'

'Ta.' Spider stuffed the bag in behind the driver's seat. He looked at the unopened bottles of water and grinned. Putting them by the bare feet of his mumbling passenger, Spider folded himself into the little car, tossed Bluey a wad of money and waved madly.

'Have a blast,' he yelled out as he sped down the driveway.

He was chasing the sun.

Troy opened the front door of their secluded abode and gently ushered Bev inside. Her eyes were as wide as her mouth was agape. The sea views overlooking the bay were extraordinary.

'Why? Why so... so... far away from everything?' she whispered.

'Because I figured we both deserved an environment of simplicity.'

He let her take control as he watched her undo the buttons of her shirt, then his. He responded to her passionate, demanding kiss and gave in to her dominance.

Darlene grinned at the two standing men as she retook her seat at the table and helped Tiny push her chair in. They'd feasted on several share plates and sampled several boutique beers throughout the afternoon, and all were enjoying the long shadows.

'Whereabouts are you staying?' Spook asked casually.

'I've booked at the Hilton, and it comes with a carpark. Don't think you pair are bailing without me seeing you off! When is that, anyway?'

'Monday, at this stage,' Spook replied apprehensively.

She watched the two men communicate silently while she sipped her beer. This wasn't her party. This wasn't even in her plan. But she was loving every second of it.

Tiny swallowed hard after a long sip of beer and said, 'I'm free tomorrow morning but have errands to run later in the day, so Spook can be your chauffeur or chaperone if you like. How about I meet you at the hotel early tomorrow, help familiarise you with a few of the key roads and landmarks?'

'Are you offering to buy me breakfast, Tiny?' The question came out of Darlene's mouth before she realised it, and she laughed and blushed profusely.

'Would rather cook,' he stated without hesitation.

Spook said heartily, 'Great idea! I'll pick you up, then take you back to enjoy Tiny's breakfast. We can go from there. What do you reckon about that?'

She fell into Tiny's gorgeous eyes and nodded until she found her voice. 'That sounds like a marvellous idea. Wouldn't it be wonderful if we could treat the time we've got together as a type of holiday? It's sure started off beautifully!'

'I'll drink to that!' Spook said.

'Let's go and have dessert somewhere quiet, gentlemen?'

The noise was getting louder by the minute as corporate personnel filled the restaurant. Spook called the waiter over, who discreetly slipped the folder between him and Tiny. Darlene desperately wanted to pay her way, but respected the chivalrous behaviour of her company.

The gentle lapping of the waves was a blissful reprieve from the noisy environment as they ambled along the boardwalk in comfortable silence, Darlene in the middle of the two men. Further along the path, they found the culprit disturbing the peace with its occasional *Greensleeves* jingle blaring into the night air. A soft-serve ice cream van. Laughing like three big kids, they waited in turn before finding the nearest park bench and eating their ice cream sundaes.

Tiny talked about Nova and the pet resort she stayed at while they were in Perth. It was so important to him and her that she had dog company before the long trip back. He reluctantly explained that his grandmother's health had taken a turn for the worse and he felt it only right that he go and see her. She had raised him when his parents had died in a car accident. But he and his eccentric cousin were the only surviving members of the family. While the staff operated the B&B, his gran did her best to keep up the tradition of her famous fresh bread and scones.

'Was she your inspiration, Tiny?' Darlene asked softly.

'Yes. Granny taught me the fundamentals of how to treat dough, and I couldn't get enough.'

'What about you, Darlene? Who taught you to cook the way you do?' Spook asked before noisily slurping ice cream out of the bottom of the cup.

'I had to learn pretty damn quickly. Believe me, breakfast for three is a walk in the park and an absolute pleasure! Cooking for fifteen is a challenge. Being organised comes naturally, and I soon discovered multiplying quantities does too!'

'You cooked for that many at once?' Tiny asked and handed her a clean handkerchief. 'Like, in a café or something?'

'Thanks. Only these last two years... on a remote cattle and grain farm. In an earlier life, I was a motivational speaker and event coordinator.'

'Wow!'

She laughed. 'Yeah. Bit like that.'

'How'd you get into shooting?' Spook asked with a peculiar grin.

'Individual sports as a kid, just got better and better.'

'Ever think about long-barrel comp?'

'Listen to you talk the lingo, Tiny! You said you'd been known to shoot, care to share?'

'Another time, perhaps.'

Spook barely shook his head when he caught her eye.

Darlene averted any awkwardness by saying, 'Surely. I've used a dart gun but not sure if I could handle the kick of a proper rifle. Do they kick like they make them out to do in the movies?'

'Some do, some don't,' Tiny replied levelly. 'We can give you a try if you like.'

'Let me think about it! Can't afford not to win this competition around the corner!'

Spook stifled a yawn, which set off a chain reaction. The day had caught up with them. Confirming the arrangements for the morning, they walked with Darlene and in gentlemanly fashion said goodnight to her inside the hotel foyer.

'Water. I need water,' Milly begged. 'Please, Spider.'

'Here you go. Look, you can undo the cap yourself, and we're in a car now. We'll be pulling up soon, and you can find some clothes in the back. Told you we were going on a holiday.'

Yeah. Be nice. Be friendly. She plays nicer then. Play time soon.

Milly couldn't see anything. There were no streetlights, just strings of trailer lights. The road had been straight for ages, and it was pitch-black outside when she craned her neck up the window. The button to open it and the door handle were inoperable, but the air conditioner worked. She laid the seat back and stretched out and instantly regretted it. A large, clammy hand fondled her upper thigh.

'Do you want to do it under the stars, Spider? There's nobody around, just my snake and your spider. Do you?' *And when I find something sharp, it's going to cut two things. Your dick and your throat.*

'That'd be fun. In a little while. We drive for a bit longer.'

'Are we going home?'

'Not yet. Mermaids and sandcastles first. Have some more water. Sleep. I don't care, just stop asking questions.'

Deputy Sergeant Troy Oscane's work phone rang just after 6 a.m.

'Hey, boss, it's Deputy Carl. Sorry to bother you. We just got back from a disturbance out at Wilmington then got a call to check on some dogs that had pulled down a beast out by Swinden. Three dingos and a feral goat, but we could hear some dogs howling by that rundown old farm with a massive shed and decided to check it out. An old man had fallen out of his wheelchair. Feisty old bastard, but the dogs were chained up. He reckoned he'd been lying there since sundown after falling out of his chair trying to fill up the dogs' water dishes. We're sus on that. Anyway, they're clearly all fond of each other, hydrated and upright. He's okay, just needs to drink more water, and flatly refused to go to a hospital. He insisted we got a message to you, but only after we were on the way back to the station.'

'I'm listening.'

'A Danish girl got taken from Port Lincoln a while back. The link is strong.'

'What link? Is that it?'

'That's all he kept saying. He wasn't delusional, but he made us repeat it word for word several times until he was satisfied that we could remember it.'

'Okay. What about the dogs?'

'As soon as he was upright, he didn't want any more help. We watched as he filled their water dishes, made them sit, then waited until we were on our way back to the vehicle before wheeling over to them and unclipping their chains.'

'And?'

'Bellowed for us to leave his premises before he let them loose.'

'Thanks, Carl. Leave it with me.'

Troy cursed under his breath and checked to see if Bev was still sleeping soundly. She was. He quietly slid open the massive glass door and stepped onto the patio and shivered. Sending a global text to his two trucking buddies, Spook and Tiny, he hoped they'd be able to respond in a timely fashion.

Hey lads. Any word on the grapevine about a Dane girl anywhere in the last twelve months being picked up from Port Lincoln? There's a matter close to home which may be connected. Keep an eye out for black Volvo with sleeper cab. Approach with caution. BTW did D. Adams arrive safely in Perth? Haven't heard.

He quietly slid in beside Bev's warmth and nuzzled her neck.

'Who was that?' she asked sleepily.

'Shh. Just an update on a cold case. Go back to sleep. The sun's not even up yet.'

He planted soft kisses on her bare back and continued to do so until she rolled over and faced him. A dreamy, sleepy smile lit up her face. Troy had fallen deeply in love with Bev.

Spook rubbed his eyes and read the message again. He sighed heavily and saw the diffused light from Tiny's donga. He'd also been woken up by the same text. They met at the table, steaming cups of coffee in hand, faces glum, and sat down noisily.

'Didn't hear from Elaina yesterday, did we?' Tiny asked quietly.

'Nope. Man, I can't wait to retire,' Spook moaned. 'I'm at the point where this is my last run home from the west. You can have this place, or we sell it. What do you want to do, mate?'

'Get my head straight!'

The men laughed hysterically then drank their coffees in silence until they felt more awake.

'Spook, follow up on that mining mob that wanted to lease the yard a while back. They may have struck gold and are in the market to buy.' Tiny's strained voice gave away his concern.

'That's a great idea. I will do that, but what's really going on?'

'I received a message from my gran last night. Her body is tired, and what she'd really like for her birthday is one where she can reflect on her eighty-eight years. So, she's going to accept her eccentric nephew's offer for the B&B and retire.'

'Where does that leave you?'

'Comfortable in my decision that I'll bring her back home to the outer hills of Bathurst. She'll love it there. I'll get a carer in, and they can have the chalet and unit overlooking the valley.'

'You'll be welcome to join us for Christmas if Granny's up for a road trip.'

'Thanks, mate. It'll give her something to look forward to.'

'Grand bloody central this morning,' Spook grumbled as he reached for the vibrating phone.

He read the message then slid it over to Tiny.

Hi Uncle Spook. I'm well and not going home just yet. Anyway hope be working in Albany for harvest. Hope you and the not-so-little one are happy and well. PS. sorry message is day late. E X

Tiny chuckled. 'Over to you, Uncle Spook.'

'I don't know what to write. Can you do it?'

'Sure, how does this sound?' Tiny swiftly typed a response and showed Spook.

Hi our sweet Danish Pastry, always nice to hear from you and your news. We're both well. Listen, your best friend Asta is over here looking for you. She nearly got abducted but also got saved. You have to let her know you are okay. It is critical because other girls have gone missing and their parents are sick with worry. The nice police man and woman looking after Asta need to hear from you. Please E, it's super important. US X

Spook shrugged, grinned and sent the message on its way. Almost instantly, his phone rang.

'Oh, Uncle Spook, you know she's been on my mind so much lately. I love it here, though. Where is she?'

'Elaina, she's safe and in South Australia. She was travelling with an Aussie and looking for you when they got abducted then rescued. The Aussie is a lady friend's niece. So, you see now how important it is they hear from you?'

'Yes, yes. Does this lady live over here?'

'She's on holiday here.'

'When do you men have to drive?'

'Soon.'

'Can I meet this lady, please?'

'Is something wrong, Elaina?'

'No, but it'd be nice to talk to another woman.'

Spook and Tiny looked at each other as if they were warding off a witch. Women's business was strictly out of bounds for them.

'Uh, yeah. We're seeing her for breakfast, can I give her your number?'

'Yes, yes. Let the nice policeman and woman know, but don't tell Asta just yet, okay?'

'We won't, but you have to by the end of the day. And your parents, Elaina. They need to know.'

'Okay, Uncle Spook. Can I talk to the not-so-little one, please?'

'Sure, I'll put him on.'

Tiny took the phone from him, took it off speaker, got up and made another round of coffee.

'Elaina,' he said in a gentle voice. 'How are you?'

'Going well, thanks. Miss you heaps.'

'Likewise. Please stay safe and keep in touch.'

'Yes, I will, I promise. Can we see each other?'

'Not this time... either. Why don't you try and get back east for Christmas?'

'That does sound nice. We see each other then?'

'Yes.'

'Good. Please put Uncle Spook back on. Bye, gorgeous man.'

'Bye, my sweet Danish Pastry.'

With the phone back on speaker, he put it and coffee in front of Spook.

'Thanks, Uncle Spook. I have to go now. The bus is taking me to Albany. We talk soon. Thank you forever.'

'Keep in touch and be sensible, Elaina. Bye for now.'

The call had already been disconnected.

'Mate, I'm tired. I love my truck, but I love my family more. Reckon I need to spend more time with them and watch my family's family grow. I'm going to retire. Happy?'

'I've only been driving the long haul to make sure you keep 'em straight. Hell yeah, I'm happy!'

They had a damned good laugh. Tiny suddenly stopped, stared at Spook and admitted he'd eavesdropped on Darlene's conversation. After he'd repeated it, Spook pursed his lips and rubbed his chin pensively.

'Leave it with me, mate. I'll have a conversation when I pick her up.'

'Speaking of which, we'd better get a move on. You reckon eggs benedict will be good enough?'

'Awesome, I've been dreaming of that since we left home! Hey, I'll let Sarge know that our convoy buddy is safe and well.'

'Cheers, mate. See you in a little while with our Pretty One.'

'You want some flowers?' Spook asked with a grin and dodged the cupful of water coming his way.

Darlene emerged from the bubble bath smelling of lavender and feeling extremely playful. It was going to be a delightful day. No pressure, no driving, just good food and great company. Her sunflower-print maxi-dress with its cheeky slit just above the knee replicated her mood. Styling her hair in a side-swept ponytail complimented it. She couldn't get Tiny out of her head but did admit he kept his emotions close to his chest.

Troy listened with bated breath to Spook's account of Elaina's discovery and Darlene's well-being. He didn't realise he'd been holding the phone so tightly until pins and needles took over his fingers. Swapping hands, he paced the verandah as he described Bev's daughter's disappearance and the information his uncle had shared. But he hadn't followed through enough. His uncle's words continuously rang in his ears, yet he concentrated on what Spook was saying.

'Mate,' Spook said sternly, 'I'll let Tiny know about the situation, but Elaina calls her own shots. Do not disclose it to her friend. You need to accept that. She's on a personal mission.'

'When is Ms Adams returning?'

'That's another woman who calls her own shots. Literally!'

'Please keep in contact with her. Cassie, her niece, worships the ground she walks on.'

'Will do. We'll talk a bit later on, mate. Take care and all the best. Will let you know when we're in your jurisdiction.'

Troy jogged back inside the unit and swept Bev into his arms. Sharing the good news about Elaina ignited their confidence that Milly was also going to be found.

'Amy agrees with your sentiment that she's strong-willed, Bev. She'll probably be on a personal vendetta afterwards, so we'll tread carefully all the way.'

'If she doesn't kill the bastard, I certainly will!'

Troy rocked her gently and plastered soft kisses all over head, murmuring positive thoughts into her sweet-smelling hair. All the while thinking about what he'd like to do with the sick bastard if Tiny didn't get hold of him first.

'Bev, I've got to make one more phone call,' he said as he suddenly broke the embrace and stepped outside.

His mind racing a million miles an hour, he vaguely heard something about morning tea. Dialling Reg's number, he took a deep breath.

'Nephew... bit early, isn't it?'

'You okay?'

'Yeah.'

'How'd you know Spider had a girl with him?'

'I spoke with her.'

'Care to tell?'

'About time you asked me that. Hope it's not too late...'

'Don't turn this on me, Uncle Reg. Just don't. Now, best talk to me like I'm someone you actually respect.'

'Troy, you have to understand something first. I do what I do because I'm good at it. My minions keep my hands clean. You do what you're good at, but sometimes you get your hands dirty. It's all part of the job. Now, listen carefully. You know very little about your family, and we both know there's one man alive I respect above all others, and that's Tiny. It took a big man to return my stepbrother's dog tags. You never even turned up to my Ruby's funeral. At least I pitched up at your old man's. Strange, isn't it? Tiny turned up to my wife's but not to your father's. Ever wonder why?'

'As much as I'd love to reminisce and discover more about these family mysteries, I have urgent matters to attend to. Let's get back to who is in the truck with Spider and where he was going, shall we?'

'Righto. Shit. Max is calling again. He's a full-on deviant...'

'I'll deal with him, I swear. Please talk to me, Uncle Reg. It's a matter of life and death.'

'Yeah, I'm getting very familiar with that. She said something like being a PL assistant...'

'A what?'

'PL assistant, and stop interrupting me, else I'll forget or get confused. She sorta sang what sounded like 'smokie in the nudie', then I thought I heard Spider say something about a snake. That's all I got. Wait. She said mermaids and sandcastles and being on holidays. Yeah. That was it.'

'Tell me what you think.'

'Sounds like Spider is travelling along the coast westwards with an abducted girl and a snake. You gonna pay me to do your job?'

'Did you talk to her?'

'Yeah. I told her I'd get her help.'

'Did this bust at Ceduna affect your business?'

'Did you really get the other girls?'

'Yes, thank you. Answer the question about the Ceduna drug bust.'

'Good. One more thing, nephew... get Tiny to drop me a line before I die.'

Troy stared at the blank screen. Who owed who the biggest favour, and why didn't Reg answer the question about Ceduna?

The call had long been disconnected when he heard Bev's voice.

Spider wriggled uncomfortably in the seat and shifted his wallet. He'd reluctantly given his driver's licence to the cashier before they were allowed to refuel and avoided any details being recorded when he slipped him an extra $100 cash. He really missed the elevation of a big truck but liked the manoeuvrability of a little car. Particularly when they could park close to the edge and look down on the Great Australian Bight. It was like some ginormous sea monster had taken a huge bite out of the sandstone cliffs centuries earlier. Even Snake Girl had smiled for the first time since he'd picked her up. It was an awesome sight. The fleeting thought of pushing her into the churning deep blue sea far below then diving in to save her had resurfaced. Then he remembered the bag of lollies and dragged her back to the car.

'Snake Girl, want some lollies?' He waved the bag in front of her blank, pallid face.

Lollies! Lollies! Play nicely. Smile. Eat some lollies. She can't talk, you gagged her. You eat the lollies. Get clean. Drink Pepsi. Play.

Eventually, darkness gave them cover to leave the vehicle. He held her tight and snuck into the showers at Border Village when everyone was asleep, and now, they were both nice and clean. *She used a lot of soap. Must like soap. She brushed her hair. Looks pretty. Time to play soon.* Grinning slyly, he helped her adjust the tight-fitting top and rested his hand gently across her mouth when she yawned loudly.

'You should always cover your mouth, Snake Girl. A spider could crawl inside!'

Spider laughed and laughed at his funny joke and squirmed when he felt his spider waking up. He made sure she couldn't run away or talk any more until they were back inside the little car.

'Tell me where we're going, please, Spider.' She managed to speak through her swollen lips and dry mouth.

'No. But I need to earn some money to pay for fuel and food. You're going to have to hide and be quiet. I will tie you up if you don't.'

'Phone a friend. I bet you have some nearby,' she mumbled.

Yeah. A friend. Phone Max. He'll know. Don't phone Reg. He's angry with you. Phone Max.

'You're my friend, Snake Girl, and I can have you as close to me as I want. Now, be quiet, play nicely. I'm going to use that payphone over there.'

Spider wrenched her hand from her lap and made her grip his spider.

'You *will* play nicely,' he hissed vehemently.

Milly shot daggers at his back while he stabbed at the keypad of the public phone. She knew he'd locked her inside with barely a five-millimetre air gap. The diffused glow of the streetlight afforded her enough light to sneak a look inside the glove box. There she discovered a shotgun casing, a couple of faded receipts and a fragment of a crayon. Retrieving what she could and pretending to be leaning forward and sneezing when Spider turned around, she managed to get it closed before he walked around to her side of the car. He shoved his pelvis against the window. She looked away, swallowing the bile that rapidly rose up her throat. He was going to die a very slow, painful death.

Trying to not cry out in fright when he banged the roof of the car, she looked through the window and right at him behind the glass. Rage contorted his face.

'I've been sneezing,' she yelled. 'Should I have sprayed the window?'

He thumped the roof again, unlocked her door and ripped it open. Crouching down to her height, he shoved his face into hers. He took a deep breath and a growling spiel spewed out of his mouth.

'Don't you ever shout at me again. I will tear you to shreds. I want to keep you, so go back to who you were when I first met you and you can stay. But... and a big but, if you do anything like that again, I swear on Ruby Oscane's grave you will not see another moon rising. You might feel the difference between night and day, but not for long. Say yes. Then we drive together and forget this ever happened.'

'Yes.'

Milly shuddered with the force of the door being slammed and committed the name 'Ruby Oscane' to memory. With a temper gradually increasing to a slow boil, she watched his gangly body skitter around the car then fold back into the driver's seat. That's when the tears fell. She begged Spider to forgive her. She pleaded with him to let her have some water. She'd even have more Pepsi if he wanted, but only if she could have something to eat as well. Then, just as swiftly as the tears started, they stopped when he shoved a bottle of water into her hand. She drank the contents in one go, drank half a bottle of the opened Pepsi and passed out.

Darlene tried desperately to keep her emotions in check while she waited for Spook to walk into the hotel lobby. Their earlier casual conversation over the phone about being in trouble with the law had unnerved her, and she'd helplessly broken down when she described how close she came to being raped, then the consequences of shattering the ankle of Oliver Cady. Afterwards, she had composed herself sufficiently, but her emotions were further twisted knowing that Elaina now needed a female friend and wanted to talk before reaching out to her best friend in South Australia. Then there was Tiny. She hadn't been able to get him out of her mind. Even in her dreams. She had never desired someone so badly. And he was cooking breakfast! Gazing mindlessly out the floor-to-ceiling window, she concentrated on her breathing and almost jumped out of her skin when she heard her name being called softly.

Spook liked to talk when he had company in the car and painted a beautiful picture of his home in Scone. Its north-facing aspect provided a magnificent view of the distant hilly ranges, with a crystal-clear creek running through the south-eastern corner. The jacaranda-lined driveway, jasmine shrubbery fence line, lush green grass and several grazing paddocks for horses and cattle were easy to envisage.

'Gosh, it does sound beautiful,' she said.

'I'm not being biased here, Darlene, but my daughter is brilliant at pottery. She's planning on having her own studio where she can have her babies with her while she gets her hands dirty. Her mother's words!'

'Spook, I'm not looking forward to Monday!' she blurted out and nervously smoothed down her dress. 'Pardon me. I want to hear more about your daughter and your family, but do you guys have to leave so soon?'

'Yeah, we're a bit torn as well. We're needed back home and feel bad about leaving you with a problem child. We won't discuss this over breakfast, but later today I will be talking to Sarge. Reckon he can get that DVO squashed on some grounds.'

'Nice thought, thanks, but it's in a different state. Queensland's not in his jurisdiction, and the DVO is state specific. We weren't in a relationship... that's how stupid the jerk is.'

'Point taken. Take an AVO out on the bloke, or at least get the ball rolling. If he's in the Shooter's Association, drop a casual complaint. Besides, you might be returning a missing Danish girl, which would put you in good stead for a positive character assessment, and they'll drop any charges.'

'You have got to be kidding me! What are you getting me into?'

'Nothing you can't handle. Of that, I'm sure. Just make sure you win that shooting competition, hey? I'd love you to meet my family and join us for Christmas!'

'Thank you for your kind offer! I need to earn a buck too.'

'Yeah, there's plenty of work around if you want it. Go to Albany, meet

Elaina and see if you can get a casual job during harvest. It's good pay. Bloody hard work, long hours, and they'll give you a bright yellow shirt if you're lucky. Better still, work for a farmer. Less BS, not as high pay, still bloody hard work and long hours, but you'll be safer than mixing it with a bunch of truckers. They're not all like Tiny and I and several others we know. Granted, a vast majority are terrific fellas working their butts off to feed their families, but as in every industry and walk of life, there are always a few maggots. Read the play like you've done and you'll be fine. I'll be checking in regularly.'

'And now you want me to sit down, enjoy a no doubt scrumptious feast and pretend I've got nothing on my mind. Is that how you see breakfast playing out, Spook? I suppose the weather is going to get hotter, too?'

She couldn't resist grinning at his belly rumbling chuckle. 'Yep, it's going to get hotter! Ahh, we so enjoy being in your company – just as much as you enjoy being in ours, I reckon!'

Recognising the massive tree which cast its glorious shadow over the yard, a smile played about her lips.

'We're here!' Spook announced eagerly. 'How do you like your eggs, Darlene?'

'So far, unfertilised.' She burst into laughter, with Spook's loud guffawing disturbing a flock of galahs on the side of the driveway.

The cloud of pink and grey caught the breath in her throat as she craned her neck up the windscreen to watch the colourful dance.

'You'd get on well with my daughter,' he said as he parked the car. 'Hope you like eggs benedict!'

'Do I ever! Haven't had it for yonks.'

Their eyes met, and the laughter was instantaneous.

Tiny hung up the phone and chewed his bottom lip. Sarge's cryptic message ate at his nervous excitement. He'd dreamt of the two women being one and was sure he'd smelt a delicate perfume when he got up in the middle of the night to look for shooting stars. What was it with these women who looked so alike, didn't know each other, yet liked shooting stars? Swearing under his breath at the smell of burning toast, he swiftly removed it from the toaster just as Spook drove in.

'Good morning!' she said as he opened the door for her.

'Morning, Darlene.' He lightly kissed her on the cheek as she stood up.

127

'I'll look after the toast, Tiny. Seems like our timing was perfect.'

Tiny escorted her to the table and gently pushed her chair in closer as she sat.

'And you made the hollandaise sauce.' She giggled and squeezed his spare hand as he placed the perfectly presented eggs benedict in front of her.

Uncannily, they all ate at the same pace and put their cutlery together in perfect synchronisation. Essential compliments to the chef were extended as the table was cleared and the coffee put on to brew.

'Do you always bring your suitcase around with you?' Spook asked casually as he wheeled it towards her.

'Yes. Just in case,' she replied.

'Of what?' Tiny said.

'Just in case. Would you like to see the winning weapon?' she asked hopefully and unlatched her suitcase.

'Ah, yeah, okay,' he said with forced enthusiasm.

She carefully slid back the barrel bolt of the mahogany box and opened the lid, revealing royal blue satin padding her gleaming Colt 45 with its shiny cobalt finish.

'Classy,' Spook said quietly.

'I'll go and make the coffee.' Tiny spun on his heels and practically jogged back to the kitchen.

'Did I do something wrong?' she whispered.

'No, just bad memories. You'll have to be patient. Don't talk about the exhilaration of shooting too much. In fact, let's not discuss it at all. Best put your toys away now. He's gonna stir the ceramic off the mugs if we don't hurry up!'

'Hey, the coffee's poured, you two!' Tiny's bellow echoed through the shed. 'Sorry, that was louder than anticipated!'

Small talk about the weather ensued, with contingency plans for dinner being discussed in great detail. None of them wanted a stuffy restaurant, and Saturday night wasn't the best for a quiet dinner at a pub. A movie was out of the question.

'What about ten-pin bowling?' Darlene suggested.

The guffaws were loud.

'Food, woman, we'll need food! Snacks aren't going to fill this beautiful body!' Spook leaned back and patted his podgy granddad tummy.

She didn't want to make it awkward for anybody and bit her lip about room service, but could see the logic of the men staying in town for the night.

'Leave it with me!' She winked at them both, forcing all doubtful thoughts out of her mind.

All three phones rang at the same time and at different volumes. Their groans were unanimous. But the ringtone jam session with a mixture of Bluegrass, AC/DC and Chopin was hilarious.

'I'd better take this,' Spook said and excused himself from the table.

'Looks like I'd better as well,' Tiny said, looking at her expectantly.

Darlene nodded, excused herself and walked swiftly to the big tree. Not wanting any telephone call to put a dampener on her happy disposition and still drooling at the memory of the perfectly poached eggs and delicious sauce, she let her phone ring out and stared up the trunk. Hearing the strains of Chopin's *Nocturne in E Flat* again, she gave in to the curiosity. It was from a landline in South Australia, again. Presuming it to be Cassie, she answered it happily and was surprised it wasn't her wayward niece.

'Morning, Ms Adams, it's Officer Bev. I trust this isn't an inconvenient time?'

'Hi, it's fine. Everyone okay?'

'Yes and no. Your niece and friend are behaving – just thought you'd like to know they're spending the weekend together at Cowell. My boss and I are further south in Port Lincoln.'

'That's nice to know. What was the other reason, Officer Bev?'

Bev's voice lost its formality and wavered instead.

'I... I know you're aware of the Danish girl who went missing several months ago. Well... this is hard... but my daughter has gone missing. It seems as if Port Lincoln could be a hot spot–'

'Oh, no. I am sorry to hear that. What an awful time for you. I'm relieved you have company around for support.'

'Ta, it helps.'

'I interrupted you, please continue.'

'I'm led to believe you're in WA for a while. I know it's an expansive state, but with harvest coming up, a lot of bulk haulage truckers head over that way for work. We're looking for a black Volvo with a sleeper cab. My daughter's name is Milly, a wild child with a snake tattoo. I never knew where it started, but its head rests near her neck.'

Darlene leaned against the tree trunk and listened quietly to Bev describing the estranged relationship, as well as her conviction that her daughter was still alive, with a very heavy heart.

'How can I be useful over here?'

'I've always believed that the wider the word is spread in obscure circles, the easier a villain can be caught. That theory has never let me down in almost thirty years of being a policewoman.'

'Obscure circles?' She chuckled gently.

'From how my boss and your niece describe you, you can be ambiguous yet accurate in your intentions. Discretion is vitally important to me as well, so I get your drift.'

'Thanks for the vote of confidence. I'll save your contact details but feel it is better if we communicate via text messages, so please send me the number. Do you agree?'

'Absolutely. Thanks for your time, Ms Adams. Enjoy your stay in WA, and I look forward to meeting you. Your niece speaks very highly of you.'

'As she does of you, Officer Bev. I'm sure our paths will cross. Have a lovely day, and feed the positive vibes that you're feeling.'

Milly awoke with a stiff neck, a swollen tongue and perspiration dripping off her. Only the driver's window was open, with Spider snoring his ugly head off. She studied every detail of his face. She would sketch it at the first opportunity, then shoot it until there was nothing left. If she had a gun.

She finished another bottle of water and wondered how long she'd been asleep and where they were. The whole landscape was different. Shrubby, scrubby little trees, paddocks of green grain for as far as her eye could see. She had to escape. She had to get word to Amy. She had to see her mum.

Big hot tears trickled down her cheeks as she silently begged for forgiveness. She hadn't meant to blame or take out her angry grief on her mother, but she was the only one around. Milly still had no idea where her father had gone, or even if he was alive. She just wanted one chance to ask him one question. *Why?* She wanted one more chance to tell her mum one word. *Sorry.*

Darlene watched as the two men conferred at the table. Spook was such a dear man, naturally paternal and genuine. Dreading Monday, she waved at them from the end of the shed and, noting that their in-depth conversation had finished, walked towards the table as Tiny stood up.

'Another coffee?' Tiny called out over his shoulder.

'Yes, please, if we've got time,' she said, frowning at his back. Something had happened, she knew it. She felt it. It was like the air had suddenly turned to lead.

'Uh...' Spook looked at her, completely perplexed. 'Come sit. We... um... Aw, hell.'

'What's happened? You look awfully pale, Spook.'

'Our holiday party has been cut short,' Tiny said in a tone which begged no questions as he put the coffees on the table, sat down heavily and grabbed Darlene's hands. 'I'll be piggybacking Spook's rig on a flatbed, and we'll be driving straight through, two-up. No backload. It's critical we get back east as quickly as possible, and this is the only way. The trailers stay here, but our rigs are ours.'

Fighting back tears, Darlene did ask one question. 'When are you going?'

Spook's voice was barely audible. 'Midday tomorrow. We're so sorry, Darlene.'

Swallowing hard, she took a deep breath and wrestled one hand free to wipe away the tears welling up in her eyes.

'Promise me you'll stay in touch?' she whispered.

'We want to go and pick up Elaina and bring you both with us!' Tiny stated.

'I can't!'

'We know. We get it,' Spook said kindly. 'We also know that you're quite capable of looking after yourself.'

She sat up straight, pulled herself together and gave them a watery smile. They were right. She could.

'But you are going to pick up Elaina?'

'No, we won't have time. We're going to leave that one with you.'

'Thanks, I think. Right, let's sort this morning out... it sounds simpler. I'm fairly adept at volunteering my time, so if I can be useful, please let me know.'

'Thank you,' Spook said as he breathed a loud sigh of relief. 'We are going to need an extra pair of hands.'

She listened carefully to the detailed list of errands and obligations the men had to complete in a very short space of time and opted for the lightweight but necessary items. The washing up and cooking easy-to-heat meals and generally having the run of the yard while they attended to business.

131

'You haven't mentioned Nova... is she okay, Tiny?' Darlene asked with wide eyes.

'Yes, she's fine. I was thinking we all go and pick her up later on this arvo, and have fish and chips by the sea.'

'Absolutely wonderful. Can we swim too?' she asked without suppressing her excitement.

'Uh, suppose so. Nova loves the sea. You swim?'

'Love water, yes, but the sea where I lived in FNQ was either tainted with crocs or stingers, so the pool was it for relaxing and cooling off!'

He handed her the key to the gate. 'If we're not back by two o'clock and you're ready to roll, let us know, lock up behind you and we'll meet you at your hotel, say, five o'clock. Sound good?'

'Sounds great! Thanks, Tiny.'

'You'll be right with a cab?' Spook asked.

'Of course. I've got one on auto-dial!'

'Why does that not surprise me?'

They all sat back and studied each other, grinning at their own personal thoughts.

Darlene couldn't ask for better non-judgemental, terrifically supportive people in her life. And she intended being in theirs one way or the other. Secretly, she was looking forward to Christmas and hoped Tiny would ask her to join him. But she'd have to wait. There was a lot to do between then and now. She shivered when she thought of the similar phrase DS Oscane and Cassie had said, then rubbed away the goosebumps of those who had gone missing.

'Please can I have Elaina's contact details?' she asked as she collected the cups.

Spook confirmed the message had been sent just before answering his phone. 'Bullshit! No way.' He coughed and spluttered and almost jogged to his donga.

Tiny and Darlene looked at each other in amazement.

'Did you get to see his face?' she asked.

'No, but he didn't sound angry, so that's a relief! Wonder if he's already become a grandfather?'

'He'd make a wonderful one, that's for sure.'

'Yeah. Yeah, he would.'

Darlene looked at Tiny's crestfallen face and lightly put her hand on his arm. 'Are you okay?'

His broad shoulders dropped as he sighed heavily. 'My paternal grandmother is getting old. She wants to retire and see her days out in a quiet place. I owe it to her. She's all I have left that I can really call family.'

She stretched and ever so gently kissed the edge of his lips and whispered, 'Best you go and do what you need to do, Tiny. We're old enough to start minimising regrets.'

He hugged her and stepped back quickly. 'I have so much to tell you. But I've got to call someone.'

Darlene stared at his back as he stormed towards the office.

Troy's scowl deepened as he pressed the phone against his ear.

'Tiny, what's the story with you and Reg Oscane?' he barked. 'I have to know. He's dying and insisted you phone him before it happens. He's a scoundrel but blows wind up your dot, like you're his hero or something.'

'It's not really any of your business, because the connection is his late wife's family. How bad is he?'

'Bad. Have you spoken with Ms Adams about my colleague's missing daughter?'

'No. I don't intend to, either. She's not a cop.'

'Does she know about this Elaina?'

'Yes.'

Troy sighed heavily. When he eventually spoke, he sounded quite defeated. 'I'm going to talk to you like a brother, not for advice, but to get your views on something. I can't see the wood for the trees. I'm falling in love with an employee and am almost ready to retire. But I have to do something first. Tiny, please hear me out. My uncle, like my father, was always gallant, chivalrous and respectful of woman. You went to Ruby Oscane's funeral... was he sad?'

'Mortified, more like it.'

'Who else turned up?'

'Hell, Troy, this was a bloody long time ago. I've had a lot of sad losses in my life, too, don't forget. Where's this all going, anyway?'

'Yeah, we both got ripped off when it came to love and longevity with our parents. I know and fully comprehend that pain. But, please, can you remember anything that didn't sit right? Always thought you should have been a detective instead of a Special Forces operative.'

'Those days are over. Just left with bad memories and living nightmares.'

'Mate, they'll fade. The sounds and images will eventually, too.'

'Yeah... Righto, it's about time you knew, because I doubt Reg knows, or if he does, would admit it to anybody. He'd probably take one other person who has the same knowledge with him to the grave. Brace yourself, bucko.'

They both took in a deep breath at the same time.

'Go for it, Tiny. I'm all ears.'

'You talked about Dillon and Reg being respectful to women. They were. Your father was a man of integrity and probably the most ethical person alive at that time, yet it's crazy how members of a family can be so alike in some ways and poles apart in others. I was in a hot zone overseas when news of your family tragedy reached my unit. Okay? Just so you know that. Now listen. Ruby had another life before she moved to South Australia. She and Max were... um... together... before he introduced her to your uncle. Max, Spider and Stevo were at Ruby's funeral but stood to the side of Reg. Sorry, man, but they're not your cousins by blood.'

Troy staggered and fell heavily onto the swing-seat, slamming it against the patio railing.

'Max? The councillor? Uncle Reg keeps referring to him as deranged, a sicko...'

'Troy!' Tiny barked. 'What information have you got on Spider or Stevo?'

'Stuff-all. The purple rig is off the road. A girl with a snake tattoo is missing, and nobody has seen a black Volvo with a sleeper before or after the recent drug raid at Ceduna.'

'That's wide-open country from there onwards. Both those bastards are slimy enough to have changed vehicles. You checked with the Border Village?'

'I know how to do my job, Tiny, but with everything going on, it hadn't occurred to follow up with the servos heading west. Bloody hell, they could be anywhere in WA by now.'

'We'll spread the word amongst our community, but I'm not making any promises.'

'Righto, best you phone Uncle Reg. Not sure how long he'll be around for. Max seems to be threatening him and his dogs.'

'What are you doing about it?'

'Working on a missing person's case at the hot spot of Port Lincoln. That's where Elaina disappeared, but you already know that. Why'd you keep it from me, bloke?'

'Mate, it's a long story for another time. Best you go and sort out what you can back in your own jurisdiction. The rest will fall into place. Gotta go... thanks for the message. Catch ya.'

Bev read the report inside the cabin, while her boss rocked furiously on the swing-seat with the phone glued to his ear. She was pretty sure he was onto his fourth phone call in about fifteen minutes. They'd agreed that over the weekend, they would work the case for four hours straight, then have the rest of the day off.

She sighed heavily and looked at her watch. Two hours to go before knocking off. The trace on Spider's phone indicated he'd definitely been zigzagging westwards through the back blocks of the Eyre Peninsula. Then all indications of his whereabouts disappeared. Their colleagues who had conducted the bust at Ceduna hadn't seen a black Volvo. Bev prayed loudly to her Milly, pleading with her to stay alive and do what she had to in order to do so. As much as it broke her heart to think about the torture her daughter would have to endure, she affirmed they would be able to work through the trauma together.

Tiny shook his head and stared blankly at the calendar dates of October. Gran's eighty-eighth birthday was the day after the anniversary of the tragic accident that killed his folks. For the first time in many years, they would be in each other's company. He smiled sadly at the thought but changed his tune when he found himself dialling her number.

'Sonny! This is a wonderful surprise. How's the west treating you this time?'

'Just dandy, thanks, Gran. Say, what would you like for your birthday?'

'Ooh, what I have wished for many years. To share my cake with you!'

'Yum! Your special chocolate cake?'

'No. I was going to show you how to make it. Your eccentric distant cousin–'

'Your late stepsister's mother's husband's adopted son's son, son of a–'

'Yes, that one, and not necessarily in that order. It's easier to describe him the way I did, young man. Anyway, he's had all the legal paperwork completed and is pushing hard to have the B&B and staff out of here by the end of October. Rotten, greedy, airy-fairy sod!'

'Hmm, I see.'

'That's not why you called, was it?'

'No, Granny. Many years ago, I had the inglorious task of handing a man his late stepbrother's dog tags.'

'Yes, I recall. Reg... is he still alive?'

'I believe so. Where's the connection? His nephew is doing an honest day's work but is quite perplexed about a current situation.'

'Oh, Sonny, you've always had a way with words. His nephew followed his father's footsteps and is now feeling obligated to help out a wayward uncle. Am I correct?'

'Yes.'

Tiny listened as his gran explained the twisted connection between the two families. Her mother had taken in two older siblings who wouldn't believe they were siblings, but they took on the family's surname along with their own. This pair had three children by the time they were in their early twenties. All 'touched in the head' in one way or the other. Granny and her two real brothers would have nothing to do with the extended family as soon as their revolting incestuous behaviour was revealed. Her real brothers took her and put her into a convent before they went to war. By that stage, their mother had died and the father hadn't been seen for many years. One of the offspring from the incestuous family had a son out of wedlock, who was put up for adoption. His name was Daniel Woolbury Jackson. The parents of Dillon and Reg adopted the boy, who extended his name to Daniel Woolbury Jackson Oscane when he joined the Army.

'Woolbury? But that was Great Uncle Rupert's surname. Your maiden name.'

'Yes, pure coincidence. He admitted he'd read the name on a cotton gin somewhere and liked it. Anyway, Daniel was Reg's stepbrother. My maiden name was dead and buried when I married my dearly departed beloved. The surname and bloodline Woolbury are also long since dead, thankfully.'

'This family history lesson ends right here, Granny. Okay?'

'Suits me. Now describe those rolling green hills around your home to give me something to think about, please. These white-washed walls are full of abstract art, which I find awfully confusing.'

Troy eventually walked back inside the cosy unit to find Bev making paper aeroplanes with the e-mailed printouts.

'I'm officially off duty. There's nothing we can do, Troy. Either you keep pacing or rocking with the phone glued to your ear, or we do something else.'

'Talk to me, Bev.'

'We have a bloody good weekend, or we pack up and go back to the office. I suspect you've got pressing needs up there, and we've got stuff-all down here.'

'Reckon we can turn off to the world for a little while?'

She ripped off her work shirt and grinned. 'There's only one gun I want in my world for a long while.'

Snapping wide awake, Spider fought disorientation from lack of food and the sun in his eyes. His Snake Girl was curled up in the front seat with her back to him, revealing her bare waistline. Smiling evilly, he turned the key and slowly drove down the graded road. They had another forty kilometres of dirt road before getting to Max's contact. There, he would work the harvest, and she would be waiting for him to return every night, locked away in his own personal caravan. She'd cook and clean and stay out of sight. *Keep her. She will be good. Another one to your collection. Christmas will be fun. Max won't be there.*

They'll all be yours. All. Of. Them.

Darlene wasn't surprised by the mini grocery store and appliance shop at her convenience, given Tiny could easily be a chef. Spying the two slow cookers and the pressure cooker, she knew exactly what meals would be on the menu. Deftly preparing the corned beef, Hawaiian chicken and beef and bacon stew, she battled to keep her mind on the job at hand. She'd waved as they'd driven out of the yard. A melancholy sigh escaped her lips. It just wasn't meant to be this time around, but she was grateful the meat wasn't going to waste.

She grabbed a chair and went and sat under the big tree. Dialling Elaina's number, she had no preconceived notion about the forthcoming conversation and smiled when she heard the coy, lilting Danish accent.

'Hello, Elaina. I'm Darlene, a friend of–'

'Uncle Spook and gorgeous... I mean, the not-so-little one.'

'Yes, that's right. Tell me more about this harvest gig. I'll be looking for some casual work in a couple of weeks.'

'Oh, I don't even know if I get a job. Albany expecting bumper harvest, and many people want to be by the sea. But I'm desperate for money. I have to see friends before Christmas and I want to stay but miss my family. Here I am dribbling, please excuse.'

'That's okay, you need to talk. I gather Spook explained to you who I was?'

'Yes. Yes. Asta's friend's aunty. My English not best. I love Asta, we are best friends, but she wanted country, I wanted beach. We laughed, cried, favel... um... said goodbye. I hitchhiked the way down the coast without problem. A great way to see this flipping huge country, but not the smartest. Even got to swim at famous Bondi Beach. Then got casual job being a runner for a parcel man, got really fit, too, then picked different vegetables before being in Adelaide. Ah, those churches. So beautiful. Historical architecture, also my passion.

'Then life changed. I saved little boy from the surf. It was far too cold for them to be swimming, but Asians have no idea, too many drown. Anyway, thumbed a lift to Port Pirie, had amazing burger, befriended older man. Actually, he was nice man, in beginning. He popular, too, but I... um... uncomfortable with younger male company always around him. Very icky. Left and caught a ferry across to Cowell, hitchhiked to Port Lincoln, did lifesaving course, got really good and played on the beaches across to Coffin Bay and back.

'I remember talking to some guys, went to party, but only drank water... own water bottle. The next thing, it's blacker than oil, hard to breathe, my hands tied up, my shoes gone and everything I was wearing stinky or wet. I had lost my phone and purse. I just pray to the gods that Asta has my passport. I been trying to find... um, how you say, *sindssyg*... um... freak, yes... freak who took me. None of the truckies have helped me, but it's harvest time. I learnt lots come here for money.

'I not know where Uncle Spook and not-so-little one saved me. Somewhere in memory very loud angry words, some beating noise like drum then a bang. Not like gunshot, but like big heavy door. Hard to explain. Then I heard kind older man telling me everything going to be okay. He carried me like baby. There was giant man shaking fist at whining man wearing scary mask. That popped in head yesterday. Then I see the sun, my hands free, still wrapped up in this horrid scratchy blanket, but I could see giant man driving truck. I'll remember forever what I heard coming from telephone speaker. I put it in my memory. Would you like to hear, Darlene?'

'Yes, Elaina. Yes, I would.'

'Mate, we'll get her to our shed, give her time, space and earn her trust. We

don't know who she is, where she came from, but the bastard that took her will get his dues. I swear on my mother's grave. Then giant man driving truck say, *Yep, that's exactly what's going to happen.'*

Darlene shivered and envisioned the purple rig and gangly creep. 'Oh, those words are so important and the ones you have to keep in your memory, even though you went through an awful ordeal. How blessed are you that you were saved by two wonderful men!'

'Exactly. I'm grateful forever, and I'm glad you're our friend. I need female one. When can we meet?'

'Initially, we'll stay in touch. I've got a commitment next week then could be available after that. Let's save each other's numbers. Promise me?'

'Yes. We will. Promise. Thank you for phoning, Darlene. I look forward meeting you.'

'Likewise. Keep being sensible, and next time, tell me about the harvest work, please. I might need a job too!'

They shared a quiet laugh before hanging up.

CHAPTER TWELVE

Morose Monday. Toying with the catch on her suitcase while waiting for the taxi to reunite her with her hugely missed Jeep, Darlene's large sunglasses disguised her reddened eyes. They were as puffy as a bullfrog, and she wasn't feeling as sorry for herself, yet the simple blue shift dress was as plain as she felt. Saying farewell to Spook and Tiny and Nova had broken her heart, and all the grief she'd stored up had poured out when she'd gotten back to her hotel suite. She had cried all night. Although she had cleverly disguised her croaky voice when Cassie made contact and shared the great news about Elaina, Darlene couldn't disguise her loneliness. It was unfathomable. The tears threatened to spill again as she fondled the delicate dolphin bracelet Tiny had affectionately clasped to her wrist. Taking a deep breath, she stifled a sad chuckle. She didn't even know their real names!

By lunchtime, she finally admitted to herself just how much she'd missed a V8 and navigated her way back to the hotel for one last night. She didn't care if there was a penalty for checking out early. There was nothing left to keep her interested in the city skyline, and Bunbury was calling for two reasons. The challenging competition at the nearby shooting range was going to be her biggest yet. Entering the action match, field pistol and target pistol – the relation to America's bullseye discipline – she needed some serious practice. But first, a swim with the dolphins was definitely on the cards. The Discovery Centre would be her playground for the next few days.

Milly watched as Spider peeled off his tattooed sleeves, attached the wig to his head and slipped on fake glasses. The uniform the bearded man had given him fitted well. He almost looked like a respectable creature.

'I'll be working to keep you safe and fed, Snake Girl. You have to stay inside here and keep things clean and tidy. Then, in the near future, we go home, rich and happy.'

'Can I give you a shopping list, please? There are things a woman needs.'

What? Who does she think you are?

Spider took one large step and pressed his face against hers. 'I am not your servant.'

She pressed hers harder against his and hissed, 'Nor am I yours, but it seems you have a sex slave. The least you can do is get me some toiletries. I dislike being dirty, and I will not be humiliated any further. Do. You. Hear. Me?'

Milly almost headbutted him with the last four words and scurried out his way when he stood up and raised his fist.

'Don't you ever–'

'You hit me, Spider, and that's it. I will kill myself. You will be so alone you'll want to kill yourself too. Instead, be kind to me and I will do your cooking and cleaning. I will need fresh air at night-time and hope that you and I can eat dinner outside. Fair trade?'

No. Don't die. Mamma died. Reg is dying. I don't want Snake Girl to die. Do the shopping. She is a human.

Spider sat down heavily with his hands between his knees like a naughty boy. 'I don't like it when you're angry with me. But you are my favourite toy. Yes. Give me your list. I will get the shopping done. Even the women's stuff you need. I know. You're a human.'

That's a good boy. She is a human. Be nice and she plays nicely. You know that now. You're a working man again. Cash. Pot. Pills. Food. Pepsi.

Giggling at the thought of how much they enjoyed the Pepsi, he suddenly scowled. In a threatening voice, he said, 'Be nice to me and I'll be nice to you. Hurry up. I have to go to work soon, Snake Girl.'

Milly hurriedly wrote out the shopping list on the back of an old receipt she'd found in between the cushions. Memorising the peculiar name Jacup, she folded it up and handed it to the outstretched bony hand.

'Be careful when you wash my sleeves. They'd better not shrink, or they'll end up around your neck, Snake Girl.'

'Have a good day at work, Spider. See you at dinnertime.'

And may you die a very slow, painful death when I get the chance.

Driving into Bunbury, Darlene felt claustrophobic and nibbled at her bottom lip. Her adventurous spirit baulked until she pulled up outside the B&B

overlooking the bay. Right across the road, the turquoise waters teemed with playful dolphins. She knew why she was deliberating. The nagging messages from her father about the DVO and a damn journalist. After checking in, she paid a visit to the local police station.

She wasn't into name-dropping. However, a certain Deputy Sergeant Troy Oscane made for a strong referee when she informed the duty officer about her current situation and the unfair order placed against her from a fellow competitor in the eastern state. Similar to Spook's advice, the officer encouraged her to have a conversation with the local president and secretary of the Shooter's Association about her plight and return the e-mailed form with as much detail as she could.

Upon returning to her secluded room, she ticked off her to-do list. Satisfied with the confirmed visit to the shooting range the following afternoon, Darlene grinned. Her appointment was after the judges' meeting. It was all just too easy. Feeling confident, she phoned the journalist, introduced herself and left a very brief message.

Two hours later, she was in her element, blowing kisses to Jimmy in heaven, in between swimming, like the dolphins that surrounded her in the shallows, without a care in the world. She was free.

Spook had to shake Tiny awake after they'd pulled into the border check stop. He let the big man have his space and stepped down onto the heat-warped bitumen. The road transport officers were doing their retentive checks, but it was the police watching their dogs intently that caught his attention. He didn't recognise any of the blokes, but a familiar long-haul driver acknowledged him and waddled over. His girth protruded over his belt, but his round, happy face made everyone smile.

'Peachie, you've got a new shirt!'

'Yeah, Spook. Me favourite finally gave up the ghost. Problem with your rig?'

'No. Saving on fuel.'

They shared a good laugh and waited for Tiny to emerge before having a truckers' chat. They stood facing the other rigs, observing the interaction with the authorities.

'Word has it there's a rogue in a black Volvo,' Peachie explained. 'A bust at Ceduna brought out a lot of cockroaches, but a few dirtbags slipped through the cracks. Bastards like that give us guys a bad name. I'm beginning to wonder if all the headache and bullshit we've got to go through is worth it.'

'Yeah, tell us about it. Last time we saw you was Broken Hill. How'd the Queensland run treat you?'

'Good, thanks. Glad I kept ahead of that dust storm!'

'Yeah, we copped it. You see that purple prime mover?' Tiny asked.

'Nope, others haven't either. Let's hope that dirtbag fell over the edge somewhere. You want me to do anything if I see a black Volvo?'

'Let Spook know, please. You doing the harvest again, Peachie?'

'Sure am. Love the south-west, and scored a contract running to Albany this time. My timing should be just about perfect.'

'Nice. Any other uniforms closer to Port?' Spook asked.

'Augusta? Nah, aside from Oscane and co. They're a good bunch there. Pirie... man, that place gives me the creeps – yeah, several. Believe that's where that purple rig was last seen. These scalies out this far can be a bit ordinary. Looks like I'm up. See ya, fellas. Keep 'em straight and stay in touch.'

'Yeah, mate, you too. Keep your eyes peeled for us.'

'Always.'

The three men shook hands heartily.

Tiny yawned and helped Nova down for a walk. She obediently followed his commands and ignored the handsome Belgian Malinois and beagles roaming around the other stationary trucks.

'Spook, wasn't there something dodgy going on in the back blocks of Penong years ago?'

'At the old wrecking yard? Yeah, but the boys in blue were all over it like a fat kid eating a cream bun.'

'Oh, I could kill for one of those right now!'

'Yeah, actually, I could too. Any of your contacts doing training out this way, Tiny? It'd be the perfect location for clandestine recces or delivering a cream bun.'

'Ha! You sniffing a rat there?'

'Kinda. The dusty middle-of-nowhere hole popped into my head as we pulled in. Looking at all this activity, something's up. There are a lot more cops and dogs than normal. Might as well heat up one of those scrumptious meals. We're going to be here a while, and we're more than half a day behind schedule.'

'You wanted to sign that contract before we left, Spook. So that's on you.'

'Yep. Reckon it was worth it, too. With your share, you can retire early and roll in those green hills yodelling like a Swiss Alp avalanche.'

'Funny bastard, eh? Get your books ready, here comes the grizzly.'

A rather small, solid state border officer with a lot of facial hair approached the two men arrogantly. With his head, he indicated to Nova. 'Best put your dog back inside.'

Tiny swore quietly under his breath before placing Nova on the floor by the driver's door, leaving it open. Commanding her to stay, he casually leaned against the doorjamb and studied the man's regimented behaviour.

'I'm not here to look at your logbooks, but to fill you in on some information you may not know. You must be the ones DS Oscane calls Spook and Tiny. Correct?'

'Yes, that's us,' Spook answered.

'Believe you're his eyes?'

Tiny responded automatically to the way he spoke and pulled himself up to full height. 'Senior Sergeant...?'

'Duckworth. I was in a former life. At ease, lad. Consider me a colleague of Oscane's. I'm from Ceduna.'

'Then you have our attention, sir.'

'Good. I like no-nonsense people.'

Tiny and Spook listened carefully to the same information Troy and Peachie had shared. Spook offered up the dash cam footage for the last fifteen hours, which was refused.

'Is there a description of the suspected driver or drivers?' Tiny asked.

'No, most of the usual suspects have been accounted for and tagged accordingly. Men, you know what to look for and who to call. I'll be on my way then. Nice knowing you.'

'Likewise, sir.'

Spook and Tiny looked at each other with the same level of dismay.

'You're thinking of that scrawny weasel and Elaina, aren't you, Spook?'

'Yep. This reeks of him.'

'I've got a telephone call to make. Excuse me, please.'

'Give her my love, Tiny.'

Spook's rumbling chuckle rang in Tiny's ears as he settled back in the bunk. He desperately wanted to hear her voice, but it wasn't the right time or place. Sighing heavily, he dialled Reg Oscane. A frail old man's voice shook him to the core.

'Sir?'

'Tiny? Is that you?'

'Yes, sir. Are you alright?'

'No. Son, I'm dying. Coughing up blood, and I'm tired. Tired of all the bloody BS, the lies, the abhorrent behaviour of who I thought were my sons. Now I know they aren't mine. Never bloody were. But I still loved Ruby.'

Reg coughed, spluttered and gasped for air.

'Do you want me to call an ambulance for you, sir?'

'No,' he wheezed loudly, 'I'll die by my own hand if I must, but it's my dogs that I worry about. Bloody Max keeps threatening them, so I don't let them off their chain to eat the bones he brings them. Not anymore. Something they've done for the last eight years either here or at the shed! I can't kill them, son. I'm not cruel like that, and I definitely don't want Spider or Stevo to have anything to do with them, either. Who knows what the filthy bastards would do? They're all sickos.'

'I got your message, sir.'

'Thanks for calling and listening. My nephew acted upon a tip and rescued two girls a while back. What I want you to do is take your buddies and go do some night-time tracking out near Penong. Stevo turned up whacked out of his brain and started rambling about Spider, the Black Widow and Bluey. There's a girl with him. I reckon they've headed to the west...'

The following coughing fit was horrendous. Tiny felt absolutely helpless.

'Please let me phone an ambulance or Troy. Please. I have to do something for you in return.'

'Son, I've always called you that because that's who you are to me. Never acknowledge my last name in any correspondence. Give my regards to your amazing grandmother and never speak of her maiden name. I always admired her, please tell her that. She'll have an envelope addressed for your attention only. I haven't written a will. They can kill themselves over it for all I care. Save my dogs, please, and the girls. They're at a house... they... have... have to be found... and saved. There's a house full of them in Port...'

'Sir... Sir?'

'Get Troy. Get him here ASAP, son. Save... my dogs... the girls...'

Tiny lunged into the cab and ripped Spook's mobile off the holder. He frowned when he saw a recent call from Troy and redialled.

'Spook? So soon?'

'It's Tiny. I did what you asked, but you've got to get up to Reg's now. He's in a really bad way. He talked about a house full of girls in Port and said to save his dogs then faded away, coughing his lungs out. I'm stuck at the border. You have to do this. Please.'

'On my way, mate. We'll need to have a chat sometime. But which Port? Pirie? Augusta? Flinders? That's three in this bloody state that I can think of straight up.'

'Don't know. Get your arse up there now and save those dogs first.'

Reluctantly disconnecting both calls, Tiny hoped the cigar-smoking old man in the wheelchair lived to see another day. He peered out through the blind covering the window and noticed Spook and several scalies scrutinising the bundle of logbooks. Thanking him silently, Tiny retrieved his secret-issue silver slimline phone and made one more call. He smiled at the fond greeting of his call-sign from a former life.

'Lima Bravo. How nice it is in the sunshine!'

'Tango Mike, as it is in the moonlight!' Tiny automatically looked skywards, knowing Overwatch was out there somewhere.

'What can we do for you, boss?'

'Haven't been that for a while.'

'Always will be in our eyes. Spill. Time's a-spinning up here.'

'Roger. Any feet on the ground in the mouth of the south of Oz?'

'Can be.'

'Copy that. Any eyes in the sky west of the oysters or between Papa and Yankee?'

'Can be.'

'Seeking a midnight arachnid with a slippery hand.'

'Singular?'

'Negative.'

'Copy. Will keep you apprised.'

'Roger. Out.'

Tiny slipped the phone back into his pocket. The phone nobody ever laid eyes on.

Troy led the way up the driveway, the ambulance almost kissing his boot lid with only the lights flashing. Bev slowed down her breathing as she reached for the loudhailer. The scene in front of them was eerie. Expecting to be met by three snarling, bloodthirsty Rottweilers, there was nothing except chains clinking softly against the rotting timber panels of the porch.

'Reg Oscane. It's the police. I am approaching.' Troy spoke into the mouthpiece with his hand resting on his Glock, then indicated for the ambulance crew to stay put.

Officer Bev stood behind the open passenger door, her steady hands aiming the tranquilliser gun at the front door. A low growl came from nowhere, then a whimper, as one bloodied dog crawled out from under the porch. Instinctively, Bev lowered her weapon to the ground, got down on her haunches and duck-waddled towards the dog.

'What the hell are you doing?' Troy said as he followed her and placed the tranquilliser gun beside her ankle.

'What I know best, boss. Treating injured animals.'

'That's not the answer I was expecting, but go ahead.' He walked closer to the house as a second dog crawled out from under the porch.

'Talk to him gently,' Bev said.

'Nice dog. Where's your master?' he mumbled, then yelled, 'Reg Oscane, where the hell are you?'

A murderous howl came from behind them. They pivoted on their heels as the dog launched. In one motion, Bev swept up the gun and put a dart in its neck just as Troy caught it. The other dogs snarled and snapped, but watched with deathly cold eyes as he very gently laid the suddenly weakened dog on the ground. Its coat stained with moist blotches.

'Dammit, Officer Bev. You trying to knock out an elephant or something?'

'No, boss. That's not his blood.'

'Dog squad's on their way, boss,' the deputy constable called out.

'Deal with these and stay put, Bev.'

Troy jogged to where the dog had come from and discovered his uncle staring at him wide-eyed, gagged and barely breathing. His broad, arthritic hands zip-tied together tightly. Activating his shoulder speaker, Troy summonsed the paramedics as he carefully unwrapped the bloodied cloth from Reg's mouth.

'Friggin' hell, mate.'

'My... my dogs?' Reg managed to gasp.

Snipping through the nylon ties, Troy rubbed the old man's wrists gently to increase circulation. 'All alive. Officer Bev's taking care of them.'

'Good... she... have them...'

'We'll see about that. Now, stop talking and let me make sure you aren't bleeding anywhere else.'

'Max... Stevo... done me over. They... trashed my...'

'Uncle Reg, please stop talking.'

'You have to... listen...'

The paramedics battled with him and the oxygen mask.

'Troy... listen... ple... please...' His imploring eyes were wet with tears, but his grip was vice-like.

'Take in some oxygen for one minute, then we'll talk.'

'No time...'

Troy put his ear close to his uncle's mouth and listened.

'Sickos booby-trapped my house... couldn't find... anything... they won't... the cash... somewhere else. Nothing... worth saving... separated me... from... my dogs... bastards...'

A gurgling coughing fit heightened the urgency of getting Reg to a hospital.

'Wait...' He clutched Troy's hand. 'House... in Port... shed... go...'

'Which port? Pirie? Augusta? Which one, Reg?'

Troy felt the pressure gradually release as a single tear made its way down the grooves of the old man's withered face.

'Keep him alive,' Troy demanded and raced out.

'Bev! Stop! Don't move,' he yelled. 'Booby trap–'

'I have to save the dogs!'

Troy swore under his breath and retrieved the half-eaten sausage roll from her patrol car. He had been enjoying it until Tiny phoned.

'Stay here.' He placed it in her hand. 'That house is booby-trapped. I need you to stay here until the dog squad arrives, then meet me back at the station. I have to do something.'

'You cannot leave, Troy. I'll have these dogs eating out of my hand shortly.

Get the guys to run your errand until we can get there. Now, move away from me. You're intimidating the dogs.'

He reeled backwards at her stern instruction and dialled the station.

'Jan, broadcast this to all units and stations via telephone. No radio talk. Go unmarked. Wherever there is a place that starts with "port", search for a house that backs onto or is attached to a large shed. Do not enter. Recce mission only. Also, get the bomb squad to my location. Copy?'

'Yes, sir. Actioning now.'

Reg smiled behind the oxygen mask while the paramedics made sure he was comfortable. He knew he could rely on Tiny. Resting his hands on the dog tags hanging around his neck, he was happy knowing when it was time to meet the Maker, he would die a pauper with a relatively clean conscience. The bloodline would be eliminated, the rogues would be nailed, and Tiny and Troy would be very rich men.

Sunshine, saltwater swimming, dolphin interaction, and sand between the toes were exactly the things Darlene had needed to calm her inner self. After leaving the coast, she felt poised, confident and glad she'd changed accommodation venue.

The exclusive chalet tucked up in the hills not far from the shooting range was the ideal place for her mental preparation. She had discovered it after the pleasant, informal meet-and-greet with the judges and her own successful meeting at the shooting range.

The officials of the Shooter's Association also reported Cady to the police for inappropriate behaviour. It was voted unanimously that his registration for all competitions nationwide be declined for three years effective immediately. Additionally, his registered weapons would be confiscated, and the DVO he took out on her was in the process of being deemed null and void.

She desperately wanted to tell Spook, but the impression she got from their very brief conversation was he had extremely pressing matters to contend with. She knew when to mind her own business and when to get on with her life.

After four days of a strict, self-imposed training regime and pistol practice, Darlene prepared her weapons for the pre-shoot scrutiny.

It was the first day of the two-day shooting competition, and she was ready. She always wore her custom-tailored royal blue pants, short-sleeved jacket, soft-leather ankle boots and sunshine-yellow blouse on the first day. Her confidence clothes. They made her feel ten feet tall and bulletproof. She was relieved she didn't have to rely on the stretch fabric as much this time around and felt quite at ease with how the trousers hung from her hips. Brimming with confidence after a long day of very accurate shooting, she collapsed into a dreamless sleep.

The second day, she looked just as smart in denim, but that outfit didn't need to be dry-cleaned. Who she didn't expect to hear from that morning was the journalist, Gavin Milne.

'You're a difficult lady to reach, Ms Adams.' His nasally voice annoyed her instantly.

'I'm a very private person, Mr Milne. I have quite the day ahead of me, so please make it brief.'

'I know exactly what you'll be doing today. I wish you all the best. Your marksmanship is of keen interest, and I would love the opportunity for a face-to-face interview.'

'Why?'

'My magazine needs a fresh face.'

'Your magazine?'

'Yes. I will not disclose too much just yet, but be assured it's not in competition with the existing magazines.'

'I am not a model; you know that, don't you?'

His laugh oozed confidence. 'You can be who you are in my books. I don't purely target the masculinity of weapon artistry.'

'Weapon artistry? You sure have a way with words, Mr Milne,' Darlene mused.

'I propose we strike a deal. If you come second in any of the disciplines today, I have first dibs on an interview at a designated location.'

'And if I don't?'

'You get to call the shots... pardon the pun! You name the time and the place. We can enjoy each other's company for about an hour over lunch in a nice quiet restaurant.'

'Either way, you're getting what you want.'

'That's right. Good day, and I wish you straight shooting.'

Arrogant prick. She shook her head in disbelief. Why on earth would someone want to interview her, anyway? There were other pistol shooters in the country equal to if not better than her, she knew that.

Shoving everything else out of her mind, she was determined to get her hands on this particular trophy. Her dream for nearly twenty-five years. Giggling quietly while deactivating the phone, she visualised every projectile she'd handled in her life nailing the bullseye. Long may it continue.

Milly battled to handle the long sunny days. It was as if the sun set, then five minutes later, it was daylight again. She realised she was in Western Australia. The variety of trucks that trundled past the caravan were amazing. She still wasn't sure which one the creep was driving, but whoever the farmer was had a hell of a lot of grain.

Enjoying not being drugged or molested for almost fourteen hours a day, with the established domestic routine relatively simple, she practised her singing. Initially, she sang into the cupboard in case someone heard her, although she was nowhere near foot traffic, but as her confidence grew, so did the strength in her voice. Singing and drawing, her two passions in life. Both frustratingly restricted. She hadn't dared ask for pencils or paper in the shopping list but, for the first time in her life, gave thanks for dust. Living near the silos was the only advantage to her current situation.

Crunching footsteps warned her of someone approaching the caravan. She hadn't heard a truck pull up, even though the freak usually parked his where she could only see trailers. He was unusually early, too. Three loud knocks rattled the aged structure.

'You decent?'

'Yes,' she called out and rolled her eyes.

Milly seated herself behind the little table in the spick and span caravan and waited patiently with gritted teeth. The lock rattled, and she braced herself when another man's muffled voice mingled with Spider's.

'Right, coming in.'

The creep entered first, then a much smaller, but very solid older man followed him.

'Do you want a job?' he asked her. His bushy greying eyebrows danced quizzically as he took in her modest appearance.

'I would like to earn a living, yes. Could you tell me what the job entails, please?' Milly always spoke politely to a prospective employer. She'd learnt that manners opened the door wider than experience sometimes. Someone can always learn a job; they can never undo rudeness.

'If you're willing to stand in the sun all day operating an auger to load the trucks, you'll get paid in cash. You will wear a fly veil under a large hat and proper clothing, and I'll show you the ropes. Eventually, I'll get another person in to help. It's going to be a bumper harvest, so expect long hours and one day off in every thirteen. Interested?'

'Yes. I am, thank you.'

'Any questions?'

'A couple, mister. Can we keep living here, can we get groceries delivered and please, please can the ablutions and air conditioner be brought up to current standards?'

He smirked, and his eyes came alive. He didn't take them off her as he spoke to her captor.

'You got a live one here, mate. I like her.'

'She's mine. I don't share.'

'Settle down. You're not going to have time to get it up anyway. Right, girl. You start in two days, very early in the morning. Exactly four o'clock. You got boots? Long trousers? Hat?'

Milly shook her head forlornly.

He frowned. 'What have you got?'

'She ran away from a horrible situation and doesn't have much. How can we fix this?' Spider demanded.

The man shrugged. 'You work it out. You're going to town to deliver a load – take her with you. Let her get some appropriate clothes, stock up on groceries and essentials and whatever else she needs; you've been paid in advance. If you want some advice, be a better man and they'll stick around longer.'

The man looked at Milly again and nodded. 'Yes and no to the first two questions. I'll see what I can do about the other. Four a.m. by the tallest silo, two sunrises from now.' He tilted his head towards Spider. 'He can collect and deliver the groceries.'

Biting back a smirk, she replied politely, 'Thank you, mister. Four a.m. by the tallest silo, two sunrises from now.'

Milly barely managed to contain her excitement and watched as the creep glared at her threateningly. Then thought, *What a weird way of saying when I start a job.*

'Be ready in one hour,' Spider hissed as he shut the door loudly and locked it.

She rushed over to the door and shoved her ear up against it, hoping to hear a conversation.

'You don't have to lock it. Nobody's going to come sniffing.'

'I protect what's mine. Thank you for improving our living quarters – I get very angry when I don't feel clean after using the bathroom.'

'You're a strange critter.'

'Don't push it.'

'Yeah, no wonder Max was happy to send you cross-country.'

'Where's town?'

'Albany. An overnighter. Thought the girl could do with a change of scenery.'

'The real reason?' Spider challenged.

A sudden loud thump against the door made her clasp her hand over her mouth, but she stayed rooted to the spot. Unable to hear the rest of the conversation, she silently returned to her seat behind the table. Fifty-six minutes and counting.

Spider looked across at his passenger. 'You're actually smiling, Snake Girl,' he said smugly.

'Of course! We're in a truck again,' Milly replied and stuck her head out the window, desperately trying not to scream.

'Don't do that! It's a long drive. I have to be completely straight, or we both will end up somewhere we don't want to be. You have to hide in the bunk while I'm dropping off the load, then we'll find the shops for you. Snake Girl, you do not want to do anything silly.'

'Spider,' she said in a gentler voice, 'do you think we could get a motel room for the night? Maybe one with its own bathroom?'

'Yeah, I would like that too. We'll see. Now...' He grabbed her hand and pressed it against his stirring spider. 'Play time.'

Officer Bev couldn't stop pacing the office and stretching the telephone cord to its maximum, waiting to talk with her boss, who was at the hospital visiting his rogue uncle. He'd been lying on his deathbed, eking out non-related snippets of information between bouts of delirium, which Troy had passed on. The forensics didn't have any information for her, but one glimmer of hope was the black Volvo had been found. Well, the remains of it, anyway. How the explosion had occurred was a big mystery, and she was not privy to any of the information.

Jan swept in with files and coffees and squeezed her hand reassuringly. Studying the investigation board for the hundredth time, Bev plastered question marks all over the highway from Port Augusta to Border Village. Stevo hadn't been found; nor could they trace his phone. Every house with a shed attached or near it in Port Augusta, Port Lincoln and Port Pirie had been searched to no avail. Max was conveniently unavailable, as was locating him via his mobile phone.

'DS Oscane speaking.'

'It's me, boss. I'm not high enough up the food chain for information, it's too early for forensics and...' She pulled herself together. It felt strange referring to her lover as 'boss', but they had agreed to practice professionalism when they were wearing the uniform. 'Has our patient coughed up any useful information?'

'No, Bev. He probably won't make it through the night. How'd you go with the dogs?'

'I'm keeping them.'

'Pardon?'

'I'm keeping them. I'm going to use them to sniff out Max. One of the marrow bones had been laced with heroine. The old man was onto it. Incidentally, when can we enter the house and shed?'

'We're going to have to wait. A higher priority has resources stretched. As far as I know, the place has been cordoned off and we're running with security patrols.'

'Dammit. I feel so helpless.'

'Looking after three dogs is going to take up a lot of your time. Take the rest of the week off, get to know them and learn to trust each other. A scent just doesn't disappear out of their memory quickly.'

She cupped her hand over the phone and whispered, 'Stay with me?'

'I'll be there tonight.'

Tiny laid the opened envelope on the hospital bed and clasped his grandmother's hand gently. 'How long have you been the keeper of this information, Granny?'

'Oh, long enough to know when to give it to you.'

'You're a cagey old bird. The doctor indicated you should be right to travel in a few days; where would you like to go first?'

'I would like to see Spook and his family. But right now, you need to go and do something. I won't have you sitting here waiting on me for one more day. Before you go, give the old rogue a message from me, please. Tell him not to wait, I'm in no hurry. Now, go on, scoot!'

'Something you need to tell me, Gran?'

'No, Sonny. Not today. We'll have plenty of time together.'

Kissing her on the forehead, he smiled gratefully at the nurse before closing the door softly.

No sooner was he in the vehicle than he phoned Troy.

'Tiny. He's still alive. Something you need to tell me?'

'That's good. Only have a message for the old man. Is he up for a phone call?'

'He's rallied this last hour. Don't know if it's his last hoorah, but I'm surprisingly happy to have the old bastard hang around for a bit longer. You hear the news?'

'The other girl been found?'

'No. But the two other suspects are also MIA.'

'Can we do this another time, please?'

'Yep... stand by.' There was a pause. 'Okay, here he is... apparently, I have to leave the room. Un-bloody-believable, you pair.'

'Son, so good to hear from you. Don't interrupt, I've got a good deal of breath to use up. Some excitement, hey! I hear there were several missed targets, but sure made a beautiful mess. Thank you. Say, anybody find a yellow Ford Focus? There's about thirty kilos of white powder in the spare tyre well. It was Max's insurance. Straight from Stevo's inebriated mouth a while back. Enough of that now. Listen carefully, please. I'm not long for this earth. How's your gran?'

'Hello, sir. Word travels fast! More trickle feed, you old codger? Thank you for your generosity, the letters and the map. I'll ensure your nephew receives his correspondence. By the way, Gran's getting better each day, thank you. And with greater thanks to you, she'll be well taken care of. Incidentally, she says to tell you not to wait and that she's in no hurry.'

Reg's rasping laugh was the sweetest sound Tiny had heard coming out the old man's mouth for a very long time.

'Ahh, that's what I wanted to hear. Love is such a peculiar word. Maybe you should have heard it more often. Find that one who sits happily by your side then live out your days with her. You deserve it, son. You deserve it.'

'Sir, I think I have.'

'Bring her home... Until we meet again.'

'Wait... please...' Tiny bit back the building tears.

'No. We don't need to say those words. We've got them etched... Here comes my nephew, he needs to hear a few things and will be going in the opposite direction. Go on, skedaddle. You've got things to do, people to see and plans to make.'

'Yes, sir. Thank you for being in my life.'

'I thank you, son.'

Tiny waited until the call had been disconnected before sighing heavily and wiping his eyes. Reg Oscane had squirrelled away some of his wealth and converted a lot of it into properties surrounding Tiny's rural home near the Bathurst tablelands and, oddly, somewhere west of Mackay near the rainforest. The map was military grade. There was a lot of cash in the envelope, too. Yet Reg's strict instructions were to only give his surviving nephew his rightful correspondence after the old man had passed away. Tiny wasn't looking forward to visiting South Australia any time soon.

Reaching for his slimline phone, he made another phone call and looked skywards, anticipating the usual greeting.

'Lima Bravo. How nice it is in the sunshine!'

Tiny didn't keep the smile out of his voice. 'Tango Mike, as it is in the moonlight! You did well.'

'We enjoyed the fireworks. Any other adventures for us?'

'Funny you should ask... looking for a yellow Ford Focus.'

'Ooh, sounds enticing. Any prominent features?'

'A few bricks in the spare wheel well. There's a max payload.'

'Copy that. How do the damsels flourish?'

'In the west, promisingly. In the east, there's a mystery beholden, because *beford* is not a word!'

There was a lag in the conversation, with Tiny's attempted humour lost in the atmosphere.

'Time frame tight. Will do our best.'

'Wouldn't expect anything else. Out.'

Driving towards the soon-to-be-closed magnificent B&B, he was not looking forward to packing up his grandmother's cherished belongings. She'd already marked everything the furniture removalists were to take with a blue dot. Yellow-dotted items were to stay, and white-dotted items were to go to the antique merchant. Unless there was something specific Tiny felt he should keep. He immediately envisaged all the Queen Anne furniture he'd grown up with and the glorious bedroom suite. Never before or since had he seen such an exquisite dressing table. The deep mahogany, aged over the generations, and the gold-gilded trifold mirror. With qualms of becoming a hoarder, he'd fight tooth and nail to keep them.

Spider almost burst into tears when he saw the ocean view as they crested the last hill into Albany. A melancholy wave swept over him. He slammed his fist into the steering wheel, and his passenger shrieked awake, which did not improve his mood.

'I have to make a phone call,' he growled. 'Keep a lookout for a telephone box, Snake Girl.'

'Use the mobile the boss man gave you.'

His left hand latched onto her wrist tightly. 'Do not tell me what to do. I tell you. If you want to survive this trip, do as I say. Now, find me a telephone box.'

Rage exploded out of Milly's mouth. 'What the hell?' Then she looked closely at his face and softened her voice instantly. 'Are you okay, Spider? You look... sad. Talk to me.'

Yeah. Talk. You miss Reg. He might be alive. Where is Max? Where is Stevo? Nobody can contact you. You're lonely. Yeah. Talk. She's nice. She plays nicely when she's happy. Talk. Talk. Talk.

A strangled scream ripped out of Spider as he suddenly swung off the bitumen, bounced onto the graded strip and shuddered to a noisy halt. Blasts of air horns and car hooters and torrents of abuse echoed past the truck and three trailers. Milly turned down the two-way, undid her seatbelt and pulled the now-sobbing Spider into her embrace. *I should kill you and put us both out of our misery, you sick bastard*, she thought. Instead, she comforted him as if he were a child, trying ever so hard not to dislodge the stupidly attached wig.

'I miss them,' he whimpered. 'They might all be dead, and it might all be my fault.'

'Talk to me,' she said in an encouraging voice.

'I can't. You're not supposed to know anything. I didn't even want you to be working in case you got seen.'

'Nobody's going to recognise me. I'll be all covered up. And I don't know anybody except you.'

'We have to find a telephone box.'

'Okay, let's think. A post office, maybe?'

He pulled back, smiled an almost tender smile, which did not reach his eyes. 'Be nice when we're in the street together. Or else.'

She sat back swiftly. 'Yes, Spider.'

Three hours later, with the now-empty trailers and prime mover parked in the allocated parking area, they awkwardly walked the five kilometres into town. It was almost four o'clock in the afternoon when Milly stopped outside a second-hand clothing shop and tugged at Spider's hand.

'Not yet,' he said angrily. 'I have to make a phone call. It'll be nearly night-time there. Come on.' And he dragged her roughly away.

Across the road, Peachie had just pushed his very full trolley out of the grocery store. He didn't like what he saw and yelled across the street.

'Hey! Don't do that.'

Everybody looked at him, except the lanky bloke who was either deaf or deliberately ignorant. The girl with him craned her neck but was swiftly blocked from doing anything except toe the line.

Peachie grunted in frustration and pushed the trolley in the opposite direction. 'Why did he look so familiar?' he mused loudly. The people around him either raised their eyebrows, frowned or pretended nothing happened. It was harvest time. A very busy season. For the next two and a half months, having a break was only ever going to happen if there was a storm or a total harvest ban. And that was caused by everyone's greatest fear. Excessive heat, lightning, then fire.

Absentmindedly, Peachie didn't look ahead as he rounded the corner and nearly ploughed his trolley into a group of backpackers.

'Sorry, folks,' he said cheerily, doffed his cap and waited until they'd stepped around him so he could get to his hired motorhome. Home base while he was in the west. He listened to the different accents as they milled around the bus stop and he stocked his vehicle.

'Mister, do you know we can get work in harvest?' a twenty-something-year-old lad with a foreign accent asked him.

'Work visas are useful, but if not, there might be some farmers who'll take you on. The post office or pubs are good places to find out, but you've left your run a little late. Some places further north are already delivering their loads to port.'

'Can you give us names, please, sir?' a pretty girl asked with a Danish accent.

'No, sorry. I'm from the east but usually do harvest further north of here.'

'East?' the same girl asked. 'Like South Australia?'

'I drive through there, yeah. Why?'

'Oh, I want to get back there.'

'Don't you go hitchhiking, now, young lady. A lot of us are good men, but...'

'Yes. I know.'

Their eyes met. Peachie noticed her bottom lip trembling.

'Maybe we see each other again? Thank you, mister.'

Her friends were pulling her away. 'Come, Elaina, let's go and see if we can get you some work. We just want to party. We worked all year, and we want you to stay longer.'

The girl named Elaina turned around several times and waved. Peachie returned her waves and chewed the inside of his lip. *Something's awry. I'll have to keep my ears open*, he thought, then promptly eyed off his chunk of thick-cut rib eye steak.

Flicking angrily through the dogeared notepad, Spider dialled Stevo's number. Also to no avail. Max's hadn't even gone to message bank. Reg's mobile was disconnected, and the landline had rung twice then stopped. His last hope was to phone Bluey. He toyed with Snake Girl's hair while he leaned against the booth of the telephone box, waiting for the call to be answered.

'Yes?'

'Hi, I'm looking for Bluey.'

'Spider? Is that you? You stupid bastard. What are you doing phoning me on this number?'

'Max? Max! Why are you answering Bluey's phone? Yours didn't even–'

'Shut up and listen. Reg's almost dead. Everything's turned to shit. You need to get back here and deal with a few things. Where the hell are you, and where the hell is my car?'

'Your car? I'm confused. Please don't shout at me, Max. You know I don't like it. Where's Stevo?'

'Playing with our toys and keeping his head down. Now, Graham Oscane, where is my car?'

'Don't you ever call me that. You have no right to call me that. Only my mamma called me that.'

'I'm your father, Graham. It's time you and Stevo knew the truth. I need you to come and pick up your papa. There are things in my car I need. We'll then pick up Stevo and go on the big boat. You remember that big boat? How's that sound?'

Reg is your father. How can Max be too? Who are you? Who is Graham? You are Spider. The keeper of the girls. The lonely one. The one far away from home. The lost one. Spider. Graham. Spider. Graham. Spider.

'Make it stop!' he yelled into the handpiece and slammed it down.

Sliding down the glass, he dragged Snake Girl down with him, her neck twisted at an ugly angle. In a strangled voice, she said, 'Spider, I'm your friend. Let's play nicely together. Please stop hurting me. That's not fair.'

Go shopping. Find a room. Get clean. Have fun. Sleep. Have fun. Sleep. Have fun.

Slowly wrapping his large hands around her arm, he stood up. Pressing his awakening spider into her, he whispered, 'Let's go, before my spider comes out to play.'

Milly looked around hopefully as they stepped out of the cramped space, onto the footpath. The police station was across the road. She'd never make it without losing a tonne of hair. The crick in her neck had given her an instant headache, and the creep still had her ponytail wrapped around his hand. The weight of his gangly arm on her shoulder was not helping.

'There,' she said bravely. 'There's that second-hand clothing shop. I only need a few clothes because I wash ours regularly, Sp–'

His draped arm curled around her neck. 'Do not say my name.'

He thrust her into the shop and tailed her through the racks, blocked the path when she stepped into the change rooms and looked threateningly at her the entire time their eyes met. Milly was terrified. *He's more than psycho, he's bordering schizo.* She fumbled getting in and out of the clothes, angrily swiping at her tears. Sniffing loudly and choking back a sob, she cowered against the back wall when he barged into the open cubicle.

'What is wrong now?' he hissed.

'I'm hungry and I'm scared,' she whispered. 'What did I do wrong?'

'Wasn't you. Just hurry up. We have to find somewhere to stay tonight. I have to think, and you have to be quiet.'

Leaving as many strands of hair as she could on the clothes that didn't fit, Milly gathered up the bundle of baggy long-sleeve shirts, scarves and jeans. She eyed off two pairs of work boots and sat down on the chair to try them on. Bending forwards, she managed to remove the shotgun shell in the hip-band of her panties and slip it into the wrong-sized boot. Closing her eyes, she prayed someone would find the hidden note.

'Hurry up.' A loud hiss in her ear made her jump.

Pretending her finger was stuck in the boot, she flinched as she turned to look at him. 'You did hurt my neck, remember? I'll try the other pair, won't be long.'

'Don't care. Just hurry up. We've been in here too long.'

Shoving the ill-fitting pair to the back of the rack, she did up the laces on the second pair and stood up. They fitted okay. She sat back down and wore the horrid flat shoes from someone else who probably wasn't alive anymore.

When she looked up, she noticed he'd put on a hat and pulled it downwards. He thrust one on her head as she gathered up the clothes and boots.

'How much do you need?' Spider growled.

'Forty dollars, please. I'll pay you back as soon as I get paid.'

'You don't get paid. I do.'

She knew better than to continue the conversation, particularly in a public place. Standing silently together with their heads lowered as the cashier stuffed the clothes into one bag, Spider's hand alternated between unclenched and clenched beside her right thigh.

'Thank you, we're running late. I've tallied up it already, ma'am. It's forty dollars neat.' Milly adjusted her blouse by her neck, and pressed two twenty-dollar notes into the woman's hands without looking at her face. 'Thank you. Okay, we can go now.'

He shadowed her as they walked outside. 'Don't ever think you can escape, Snake Girl,' he warned quietly. 'You are mine.'

Milly raced to the nearest rubbish bin, clutched at her stomach and dry retched, then burst into tears.

'Oh, yuck!' Spider stared at her.

The shop assistant ran out with a bottle of water and thrust it into Milly's hands, 'Here you go, you looked a bit washed out. The heat is going to get worse for the next few days. Best you find somewhere cool to rest for a while.'

Milly groaned her thanks and did her best to wash her face and clean off the spittle.

'You got sick, why?' Spider hissed.

'I'm hungry, silly. You promised me a decent meal, a decent bath and a decent bed.' She glared at him daringly. *For the first time in my life, I am grateful for my period. You are going to die, Spider. You. Are. Going. To. Die.*

She smiled wanly and nodded to the motel sign down the street, thanking the gods for the cramps she got before her cycle began. They and the clots had been getting worse the last four months, and she'd just put it down to put it down to stress, but she'd never dry retched before.

Deputy Sergeant Troy Oscane closed his uncle's eyes, whispered a prayer and begged the good Lord to forgive the old rogue's ways and allow him to rest in peace. He took it upon himself to cover the bony frame with the sheet and help the orderly transfer the body to the morgue. The minute he stepped out of the elevator, Officer Bev rushed over to him.

'Boss, I am sorry for your loss, but there was an explosion at Reg's yard. Kris, the patrolling security officer, is being operated on as we speak. They're removing the shrapnel, but the place was blown to smithereens. There's nothing standing.'

'When? When did this happen?'

'Almost three hours ago. Kris heard the phone in the shed ring twice. About five minutes later, he'd just patrolled the yard between the house and the shed when it went up. The shed first, then the house.'

Troy's first thought was of Tiny for the precision, then he swiftly dismissed it. Tiny hadn't even been in the state when Reg had told him the house was booby-trapped. What the hell did they use?

'Why? It was all meant to be cordoned off. Forensics?'

'Still too hot to go in, boss. The firies are working their magic.' Bev steered Troy towards the coffee machines near the seating area. Encouraging him to sit, she kissed him lightly on his cheek, squeezed his shoulder and went to get them drinks.

She observed him from a distance. His stony face and upright posture keeping his emotions in check. Gently pushing the coffee and opened chocolate bar into his hands, her eyes welled up when she saw his. The pained expression tore at her heart. All the pent-up grief was threatening to break its barriers.

His coffee didn't even touch sides. 'I need to make a phone call and wait for Kris to get out of surgery. Has his wife been contacted?'

'Not yet, boss. She's two days away from having their first baby.'

'Bloody hell. Listen, Officer Bev, thanks for being here. I'll be fine. I'll meet you in PIC.'

Troy turned and headed towards the exit. The full force of the last thirty-odd years almost causing him to stumble as he pushed through the heavy doors. Walking automatically towards his vehicle, he dialled Tiny's number.

'He's gone, mate,' he heard himself say. 'Reg Oscane passed away a little while ago. Thought you needed to know.'

'I'm sorry, Troy. Sorry you had to be there alone and sorry for your loss. I'm dealing with my gran's circumstances at the moment, but...'

'You've been an orphan for a lot longer than me, Tiny, but now I really am alone. Is it right to fall in love with someone else after someone you love dies?'

'A wise man would have said that it was.'

Troy chuckled sombrely. 'Yeah, no doubt. What do I do now? Nobody's going to come to his funeral. Besides, he wanted a cremation. Max and scum have crawled under the rocks they spewed out from. Do I try and find them? Shall I just make it a private cremation? Do you and I work out where to scatter his ashes?'

'How about you catch your breath and take bereavement leave? Sign over your role to the appropriate personnel, get your house in order and seriously think about retiring. In my opinion, the man never wanted the limelight. Why change it now?'

There was a long pause before Troy spoke. 'Thanks, Tiny. That actually makes a lot of sense. By the way, we need to have that drink sometime. Just you and me.'

'Let me know of the arrangements, and I'll do my best.'

'Yep. You always do.'

Tiny thumbed his stubbly chin. He was sad, and not sad. The old rogue had been suffering for a very long time, but he was sad for Troy. Looking at the envelope on the old rolltop desk, he knew Troy would be able to retire and live with the woman he'd fallen in love with, with no regrets. Guessing she was in her late fifties as well, there was nothing wrong with loving someone for the second half of one's life. But he would have to hand-deliver the correspondence. That was part of the old man's instructions.

He grinned at the incoming call. 'Hey, Spook, how goes it with you?'

'All well, thanks. You heard from our Danish Pastry?'

'No. Not since we left, and you're her uncle, not me! Hopefully she made it to Albany. Let's not get ourselves worked up just yet, hey?'

'Wasn't that where Peachie was heading?'

'Yeah, I think so. How uncanny!'

'Wonder if he could do some sniffing for us?'

'Why there, Spook?'

'We did say we'd ask around, and we know for sure Peachie will tell us first.'

'Yeah, true that. You follow up with him, please, I've got a bit on my plate.' Tiny coughed quietly. 'Listen, mate, don't mean to be the bearer of sad news, but the old rogue passed away...'

'Oh, hell. Sorry, man.'

'Yeah, thanks.'

A respectful silence passed, then Tiny said, 'Gran's coming out of hospital soon, and I'll be taking her home, but she wants to see you all first. We could be there in time for her birthday. I've already sent one truck with her nominated furniture; another one goes tomorrow with the antiques I'm not giving up. But, Spook, there are two old rocking cradles, like the ones you see in the old black and white movies... um... do you think your daughter and son-in-law would appreciate them?'

'That's huge. Send through a picture and I'll ask for you. But, mate, you're young enough to make babies... you wouldn't keep them?'

'I can always borrow them back.'

They were still laughing when they hung up.

Several hours later, pushing the doors closed on the B&B for the last time was heart-wrenching for Tiny. More so because Granny didn't want to be around when it happened. The eccentric distant cousin was conspicuous in his absence, although he had furnished the staff with a tremendous farewell dinner and lucrative bonus. Sitting at the ornate bar, losing himself in the smooth port, Tiny thought about phoning Darlene. Before he could, Spook called again.

'Hey! You miss me, don't you, Spook?'

'Always. We've just got back from the hospital – the kids would love those cradles and are happy to share them when needed! By the way, did you tell Reg about the dames in the west?'

'Not in detail...'

'And Granny?'

'Sort of.'

'Humph. Speaking of the dear lady, the girls in my family have said they'd love to see her and suggested she should have company for her birthday. Not just yours. Can you take a slow trip down to home and bring the cradles with you? We'll look after the cake. I'm hoping my daughter will be able to leave the hospital. If not, we'll work something out.'

'I'll put it to her in the morning. A chapter has just closed in her life, and I suspect she'll be mad keen to get the hell out of Queensland for a while!'

'Keep us in the loop. We've got plenty of room.'

'Thanks, mate. Hey, what would be the most comfortable vehicle for an elderly lady to travel in?'

'A Mercedes. The doors open really wide, they're a good height off the ground, they look flash... and Tiny?'

'Yes?'

'Buy a white one. The insurance is a killer for any other colour.'

'Thanks. Will keep you posted. Night, Spook.'

'Oh, one more thing, mate... talk to Granny.' Then Spook disconnected the call before Tiny could say anything else.

CHAPTER THIRTEEN

everal days after taking out the National Pistol Shooting Titles, Darlene was still relishing in her victorious win. She'd slayed her competition in all disciplines and picked up the cash prize for consistency. The impressive gold-plated pistol mounted in front of a titanium bullseye was the trophy she'd had her heart set on, and she was overjoyed to hold it aloft. With her name emblazoned on a shield at the base, she had willingly left it at the shooting range and accepted the miniature version for her collection. She had deliberately kept a low profile at the well-attended and very pleasant award ceremony.

Nobody had phoned her, nor had she phoned anybody. Celebrating by herself wasn't an uncommon experience, and she maintained her tradition. A day of pampering, including a long massage, then several days of doing nothing but relaxing, reading, running and sleeping. Except Donnybrook didn't really have what she needed, and breakfast had repeatedly been disappointing. Plus, she had to meet up with the journalist. Whereabouts was entirely her decision. Flicking lazily through websites, she kept being drawn to a town called Denmark. *How ironic*, she mused and thought about Elaina, promptly dialled her number and continued browsing for appropriate accommodation.

A very tearful voice answered the phone. 'Oh, Darlene. Thank you for calling. I've got no credit on my phone and I can't work at the big harvest places and I can't go home and I'm late in sending message to Uncle Spook and–'

'Elaina, slow down,' she interrupted kindly and firmly. 'Where are you?'

'At the backpackers in Albany. I used all my money to have somewhere safe to sleep. I've been trying to find somewhere a farmer pays cash who doesn't care who works there as long as they work. It's a very big harvest this season. But I cannot find information.'

'Please be careful about those sorts of arrangements.'

'I'll be fine. That's how I got as far as I did before I got drugged. My memory is slowly coming back, too. He was tall, lanky, gangly, like a skinny oversized orangutan. Bet I'd recognise him if I saw him.'

'And then?'

'Wish Uncle Spook and my gorgeous... um... not-so-little one were here to sort him out.'

Darlene bit back a laugh. She'd do the same if she feared for her safety.

'Listen, I'll pay the credit on your phone. How long can you stay in Albany for?'

'I have no place to sleep Monday night.'

'Okay. We'll meet that morning. While you're waiting for me to get there, please find a nice place to eat lunch, one where you and I can have a nice chat without too many nosey parkers.'

Elaina giggled. 'Are you famous?'

'No, but I am having a meeting with a journalist and would like you to be near me, but not at the table, during the interview. We can come up with a plan afterwards. Sound fair?'

'I thank you forever too, Darlene. We stay in touch, yes?'

'That's your responsibility now – your phone is recharged. I look forward to meeting you. Take care.'

By the end of the conversation, Darlene knew exactly where she would be spending an extended pampering session. She made the necessary phone call and packed her suitcase. She would be arriving in Denmark in time for a roast lunch and an icy cold beer. Niggling doubt about the journalist, Gavin Milne, was not going to dissuade her from enjoying her retreat, so she dialled his number.

'Ms Adams, to what do I owe this pleasure so soon?'

'I have been unable to find your magazine or any reviews on your journalistic talents. I am not a fan of deception. Who are you really, and what do you want?'

His quiet chortle admitted guilt. 'You got me. Okay, I'll confess. I'm an environmentalist and horticulturalist and abhor cruelty to animals but don't like feral animals. In other words, quite a confused individual.'

'Carry on.'

'I've been a keen shooter myself in the past for veterinarians and farmers, but since having a family, I've... grown up, for want of a better description.'

'And you think I'm different?'

'Definitely not. Your consistency is exactly what I'm looking for. Have you ever shot a long barrel with a tranquilliser?'

'Yes.'

'Excellent.'

'Mr Milne, Albany will be the destination next Monday. I will inform you of the location that morning. Does that suit you?'

'I'll be there with bells on. Thank you very much. Good day.'

Nodding in satisfaction that her doubts had been squashed, she thought no more of the conversation and followed the signs towards the ocean in the south. Tuning into the national news on the radio, she nearly drove off the road in shock when they reported on a horrific incident between Yalata and Penong.

Apparently, a truck had exploded, and several vehicles were also destroyed, along with a massive hydroponic and methamphetamine lab. In a nearby parkland, Forensics had found decomposing human remains as well as skeletal remains. A complete media ban was in force until further notice. Goosebumps spread over her body. With trembling hands, she dialled Tiny's number.

'Hello, Darlene.' His voice was hushed. 'I'm in a hospital room with my gran, so I can't talk for too long. Spook's okay, home safe, and his daughter is in hospital but all three are in good health. I have to go. I... uh... have you... did you nail the bullseye?'

She fought back tears. 'Oh, Tiny, I'm sorry to hear that. I'll be praying your gran makes a swift recovery. Yes! Yes, I nailed all of them. You should see the trophy!'

'Thanks. I knew you would. Congrats! It's quite a prestigious title you've earned, and yes, I did my homework. It's awesome. Darlene, have you seen Elaina? Oh... I've got to go.'

Tiny hung up. Into the dead air, Darlene sang, 'I think I love you; I hope you love me too, and what is Elaina to you?'

The exclusive retreat was exactly what she had been expecting. After the amazing lunch and complete disassociation from technology, the extended afternoon pampering session lent itself to an early night.

Milly had stayed true to her ethics of being on time, dressing appropriately and doing the best she could at her job. But the heat was beginning to be oppressive. It had gradually gotten hotter over the last two days, and the previous night was the first she had been by herself. Although locked in, she had relished being alone and sang her heart out either side of painful cramps. The clots had been the worst she'd ever experienced. She found herself hating Spider even more, because when she'd finally plucked up the courage to go a female doctor, she foolishly got abducted.

Adeptly switching augers under the watchful eye of the boss, she started to load the eighteenth trailer of the morning. Counting rigs wasn't satisfying enough for her. The greater the number, the higher the tonnage, the better the pay. Any wastage came out of a harvest bonus. She rolled the truck forward with the expected hand movements, stopped him short, screamed and clutched at her stomach. Collapsing to her knees, she stayed doubled over and breathed slowly.

'Driver, stay in your truck.' Her boss's voice boomed through the two-way speaker.

'You pregnant, girl?' A growl came from behind her shortly afterwards.

'Hell no. Just girly problems.' She pulled her shirt down in an attempt to cover her trousers and swore under her breath as the blush turned her face magenta. Bravely, she said, 'They only got this bad a few months ago, and as you can see, I'm not pregnant.'

'Jesus H. Christ. You got to get that seen to,' he said as he wrapped a hi-vis vest around her waist, scooped her up and carried her around the back of the truck. 'I will not have you humiliated. Aren't you girls meant to have annual checks or something?'

'You're a man. How do you know of such things?' She flinched as another cramp took her breath away.

'I grew up with two sisters, and I have three daughters. This is not normal.' He supported her as he unlocked the caravan. 'I'll send my wife over with some stuff. Don't worry about the grain, I'll sort it. With this heat, won't surprise me if we have a harvest ban in an hour or so.'

Milly smiled meekly. 'Thank you. Please don't tell him. He'll be angry if he knows there'll be a mess.'

The look of utter disdain that crossed the man's face was somewhat reassuring.

'I'll stall him. He'll have to be stationary if it's a total ban.'

'Thank you.'

'Do what you've got to do. Sorry about the air conditioning. I'll fetch my wife, but I've got to lock the door.'

Milly just shrugged. 'Yep.'

As soon as the door was closed, she fell into the shower and undressed under the tepid water. The tears fell, and she sobbed loudly. 'Mum,' she murmured into the water, 'Mum, I need you. Please be alive.'

Lying on soft green grass beside the crystal-clear brook, Darlene stretched out to kiss Tiny. Their lips had just touched when the strangest bird started singing. Its orchestral notes peeled out Chopin's *Nocturne in E Flat*, and she watched Tiny's gorgeous face evaporate in front of her eyes. Groaning, she desperately tried to get back to the tender moment, but the damn phone did not let up. It was the last day of her retreat. She had been so relaxed until the phone rang for the first time in three days. Rubbing her eyes and pouting, she blinked and was wide awake.

'Elaina! My goodness, it's early–'

'Darlene.' Her voice was a panicked whisper. 'He's here... I've seen him...'

'Who? Where are you?'

'The orangutan. I'm still in Albany. Please tell me you're coming here today? Please...'

'Yes, yes, I am arriving there this morning. Where are you right now?'

'Still at backpackers. I'm not going with my friends – they're all going fishing or something. I've lied and said I wasn't feeling well. He was here. Can you hurry, please?'

'Why phone me now? So early in the morning?'

'Because it's the first time I've been on my own. My friends, they party, we share room. Gee, it is hot.'

Darlene frowned. She didn't really know this girl, but she was upholding a promise she'd made to Spook and Tiny.

'Stay where you are and keep your mobile fully charged and switched on. I will let you know when I'm there. I'll come inside and ask for you. Promise you'll stay there until I do?'

'Yes. Yes, I promise. Thank you forever. Please hurry.'

Darlene shivered. She had a horrible feeling the orangutan was the one she thought of as the gangly mobile tattoo parlour. She'd keep a vigilant eye out for the purple prime mover from hereon. Making a hurried decision, she phoned reception and extended her stay for another week with an adjoining room for an international cousin. Taking the pending heatwave warning on board, she showered and dressed appropriately in her white cotton sundress. With her prize possessions packed alongside some clothes, she threw in an extra set just in case. Just in case. It was always just in case. Ever since she was nineteen. It was always an overnight bag with an extra set of clothes and a towel, just in case.

The quantity and length of the grain trucks on the road was astonishing, as were the size of the paddocks. But the heat was absolutely dreadful. Some fields of canola brightened up the world with their brilliant yellow and painted quite the picture against the backdrop of green wheat. With the air conditioner turned up a notch, Darlene smiled broadly when she saw the magnificent splendour of the sea. All the pretty colours filled her heart with so much joy, she almost forgot the reason why she was in Albany.

Finding the backpacker accommodation was easy. Finding a carpark wasn't. Parking outside the post office, she wheeled her suitcase down the hill. Entering the reception was relatively pleasant, but the manners of the person behind the window weren't.

'Yes?'

'Never mind, I'll make a phone call instead.'

Stepping back outside, onto the footpath, she dialled Elaina's number.

'Where are you?' she asked urgently.

'Downstairs, outside. It's bloody hot, care to get a move on?'

'Isn't it! Down soon.'

Several minutes later, a tall, bronzed, blonde-haired beauty with a delicate nose, a full mouth and blue eyes timidly stepped outside, her backpack snugly wrapped around her front. The women caught each other's eye and smiled.

'Darlene?'

'Yes, Elaina.'

She was almost flung backwards with the strength of the hug. 'You're so beautiful, thank you. Uncle Spook wants a photo.' Then Elaina looked around nervously. 'We need to go. Harvest ban has been called, and truck men will make their way to town to shop, drink or look to having good time.'

They walked briskly back up the hill. 'You've learnt quite a bit of Aussie and harvest speak, haven't you? Your English is improving, too.'

'I listen to people talk but want to work and have been reading on the 'net.

See, fires are every farmer's biggest fear around harvest time. And with heat, tiniest spark can destroy paddocks quickly.'

Darlene explained that her suitcase travelled on the floor of the front seat and was always in sight.

'It's your call, but I'm not a taxi, so you will not be sitting in the back. Adjust the seat, or rest your feet on it. Now, food time. I don't know about you, but I'm thinking of pancakes. Should we find a café?'

'Yes please. The Emu Café is a little out of the way, and maybe everybody stay at home, except the cook and waitress!'

Seated in the cool building with their luggage beside their feet, Elaina took selfies with the sea in the background. They took several until they were both happy with the photos and giggled like teenagers the whole time. Spook's message to Darlene made her eyes water: *Thank you so much. We miss you and love your cooking. Come home for Christmas.*

Given the heat and few patrons, the owner was quite happy for the two women to use the establishment for most of the day. They positioned themselves out of the way and settled into a shaded back table which gave them a good view of the park overlooking the sea, directly under the air conditioning vent. Darlene sent the address to Gavin Milne to meet her at midday.

Milly moaned as a solid knock rapped on the caravan door. She'd done her best to clean up, but it was going to take more than handwashing. The last cramp had brought her down to the floor, and she hadn't moved.

'It's your boss and his wife, coming in.'

She heard the question very clearly. 'Why is this door locked, Bo?'

'Hon, you know not to question my environment, as I don't question yours.'

'True, but this isn't normal.'

'You ain't seen nothing.'

'Good God!' the older woman exclaimed as they entered and rushed over to Milly. 'Bo, I need more towels. While the ban is on, get your arse into gear and bring this accommodation into the current century. She'll die in this caravan, and she needs a damned washing machine. Grab the spare dryer too, and sort out the wet room. Get going!'

Milly felt a cool towel being pressed to her perspiration-drenched forehead. 'Thank you. I don't mean to cause trouble.'

'You're the girl working the augers... heard nothing but good reports, and you're still here. Not many last two days. Can you cook?'

'I can. Been a waitress for several years longer, though.'

'Hmm. I believe we're not to swap names, but geez, that's one hell of a tattoo. Nearly freaked me out!'

'Sorry.'

Milly assisted in being sat up and tried to help clean the latest mess. Before she left for her shift, she'd spread newspapers and shopping catalogues all over the floor as a precaution. They needed most of them.

'Girl, this is too much. You been this heavy ever since you started?'

'It's gotten worse these last four months. That should be the end of it. Generally, the biggest clot is like the grand finale.' Milly smiled feebly. 'And it is day five. That part is normal. And consistent.'

'When did you last have a smear?'

'Two years ago. Haven't been active for three, until... until...'

Milly flinched when the woman put her fingers under her chin and lifted her face. 'You here on your own accord?'

'Ma'am, I need the money.'

'That's not what I asked.'

She was about to get her answer when Bo opened the door and turned away. 'Sorry, should have knocked.'

'No worries. Clever man, thanks for bringing the old birthing towels from the shed. Girl, these towels are the only ones that are laundered professionally. My prize sheep, you see...'

'Gosh, I'm honoured. Are you sure, ma'am?' she asked, and cried out in agony.

'I'll get going,' Bo said. 'Um, hope you're okay. You're a good worker.'

'Thanks, boss. Sorry about any trouble,' Milly managed to say while doubled over.

He grunted and shut the door quietly.

'I fear you'll get into trouble if I say too much. Can we see how this all plays out?' Milly pleaded with the woman while trying to sit up properly. 'I have to find my mum and want to be home by Christmas. Please?'

'There's a fighting spirit in you. Have it your way. We might not do things strictly by the books, but we....' She paused and pursed her lips.

'Thank you, ma'am.'

Milly sighed inwardly when the older woman helped her with the towels then opened and closed the cupboard doors.

'Why do you have a tub of dust?'

'I like to draw and will find anything I can to do it.'

'Don't see any drawings.'

'You won't, usually. I reuse the dust. I draw or sketch, wish my picture alive or dead depending on my mood, then scoop it back into its container until the next opportunity.'

'What do you draw?'

'Landscapes. Pretty things, mainly.'

'Mainly?'

Milly blushed profusely and lowered her head.

'I'll hang around here until the men get back. They were meant to have these quarters done last month, but harvest kicked off early.'

Milly poured two cups of iced tea, which they drank in companionable silence. The sound of a very slow tractor and several men's voices brought the older woman to her feet. Thanking her again as the woman closed the caravan door behind herself, Milly peered through the little windows and watched in fascination as four men and the boss positioned a donga opposite the caravan under the direction of his wife. Her commanding stature was not to be argued with, but her maternal side was that of a nurse.

Twenty minutes later, Milly was being shown how to use the washing machine while the box air conditioner was being changed out. The men made themselves scarce except for the boss. He moved the tractor out of sight.

'Ma'am, when I get some money, may I please pay for the laundering of your special towels?' Milly asked politely.

'Ever seen a prize stud ram?'

'No. I would like to, though.'

A squawk over her two-way made the older woman rush over to the tractor. 'Do your chores then whatever else inside,' she yelled as she caught up with her husband. 'The day's over. Stay cool and hydrated.'

'Yes, ma'am. Thank you very much,' Milly called as loudly as she could and peered around the edge of the donga to catch the last of their wave.

DS Troy Oscane switched off the pre-recorded interview and watched as Kris awkwardly took the vase of flowers off the table and stood up. His face wasn't showing any sign of the explosion, but he had several patched-up wounds across his back and chest.

'Sir, I confirm my statement. I'm glad you waited until my wife had been admitted before telling her the news. Reckon that's what stopped my son from being born early! She swore at me. You know that? She really swore, then smiled and told me how much she loved me when we heard the baby cry. Then we cried. We get to go home as a family today. I am eternally grateful for whoever was watching over me.'

'Kris, any man can become a father, but it takes a special man to become a dad. Congratulations to you and your wife.'

'Thank you. I think I'll consider getting out of the security patrol business.'

'You'll know what's best for you. Take care, young man. All the best.' Troy looked at the incoming call and excused himself politely as he shook Kris's hand.

'Officer Bev, how goes it with you today?' He held open the door, nodding respectfully at the beaming father.

'Are you in your vehicle?'

'No, on my way to it now.'

'I'll wait.'

Troy jogged to where it was parked, flung open the door and pulled it shut as quietly as he could. After fumbling and muttering under his breath, he finally had the seatbelt on and the Bluetooth connected. 'Okay, I'm good to go.'

'I've got good and bad news,' she replied quietly.

'I'm listening.' Troy braced himself as he drove out of the hospital grounds. He was a good hour away and prayed it wasn't devastating news about Milly.

'I'm at home, so we can talk freely. Forensics got back to me. No evidence of any of the remains being Milly's, but still no sign of her, either.'

'We have to keep positive, Bev.'

'Yeah, I know. Time's flying by, but it's dragging, too. Incidentally, Amy would like to come see us. She suggested we meet halfway so she can meet Cassie and Asta as well. Feels like we've got an instant family, Troy!'

'And they're all toilet trained,' he said, laughing hysterically.

'You're weird. Think about when. Love you, miss you. Your workload is increasing, best you get home... I mean, back to the station soon.'

He'd just passed the intersection of Lincoln Gap when he shivered. Once upon a time, the sensation would be a sign that his uncle would phone. A premonition of sorts, which usually left Troy emotionally torn. Today, all he could do was pat the urn of ashes. 'Is this where you'd like to be scattered, Reg Oscane? Here? Why?'

His frown deepened the further away he drove, and he decided to contact Tiny. He might have a solution. Swearing quietly while listening to his voicemail, Troy just hung up. What was the point? There wasn't one, he reminded himself.

A tall, distinguished, middle-aged man wearing what one could only describe as nautical casual clothing strolled into the Emu Café at 11:50 a.m. and looked around for a suitable table. Elaina politely nodded and went back to looking at her phone. She sent a text to Darlene: *think your meeting man is here.*

Without turning around, Darlene stood up and made her way to the restrooms. After hearing Elaina's recount of the gangly unpleasant character and the most recent sighting of him, but without tattoos, she was keen to know more about the job offer. Standing behind the artificial-greenery-covered trellis, she watched the man's behaviour. Neatly stacking the cutlery onto the placemat before moving the pile aside. The loud snaps of his briefcase as he opened and closed it. The careful placing of the manilla folder onto the table before resting his elbows on top and pitching his fingertips together. Methodical and calculating. Who was interviewing who, anyway?

Elaina knew to remain where she was. They'd chosen the tables specifically so they could see the front door but were obscured and one table apart. Winking at Elaina as she reached for the suitcase, Darlene wheeled it towards the table where Gavin Milne was seated.

'Mr Milne?'

In an instant, he was up on his feet. 'Ms Adams! You've blossomed.'

'Pardon?'

'The last time I saw you was four years ago on the other side of the country. You've...'

'Lost weight?' she supplied with a grin.

'Well, yes. You look fabulous! Allow me to introduce myself. Gavin Milne. It's a pleasure to finally meet you.'

She shook his hand firmly and looked at the table he'd rearranged. He pulled out a chair for her and waited until she was seated before he followed suit. Something didn't feel right. Warning bells went off immediately.

They ordered lunch; he a seafood platter and a beer, she a Szechuan calamari salad and the house special. A strawberry and mint iced tea. Polite conversation with polite laughter ensued during the meal, then it was straight to business.

'Congrats on your recent trophies. I read that you whopped the competition!'

'Thank you. I must say it was more challenging than I anticipated, and I did have a lot of fun.'

'When would you try the long barrel?'

'Not sure. Definitely won't be in this heat!' Darlene laughed politely, but her mind was racing. She and Elaina were staying up the road for several more days. If she could find suitable work for her Danish cohort, it'd free up some shooting time at the range. She was definitely keen to give it a go, particularly as she might... just might...

'Ms Adams, hello?'

She jumped as she focused on a waving hand in front of her face.

'Oh! Pardon me... you were saying?' Blushing profusely, she manoeuvred the straw into her mouth, took a long sip of her refilled glass, then discreetly blew it back. She hadn't ordered another drink. Pushing the glass away, she eyeballed her companion.

'Not thirsty?' He looked at her steadily.

'Not stupid, either. What are you playing at, Gavin Milne?' she asked quietly. 'I thought I made it quite clear I did not like deception. That was your last shot at any further consideration of continuing this conversation.'

'Well, you passed the smarts test, Darlene Adams. This is what I want you to consider.'

He flicked open the folder, spread out several sheets of paper containing typed notes and foolscap-coloured maps and sat back. She scan-read the bullet points and correlated them with different sections which had been outlined with a solid black pen. Two regions had bright pink crosses scattered throughout. Research was being undertaken on unusual levels of toxicity in feral goat excrement resulting in a high death rate of ground-feeding finches. The greater concern was the goats getting into the stubble the sheep ate post-harvest.

'That's where I'd like your expertise, Ms Adams. Work with us to track the goats. You tranquillise them; we remove them and transport them back to the laboratory. You don't need to be involved once they're down. Then you go to the next area. Do the same, and so on.'

'How far behind will the removalists be? You can't afford them dehydrating.'

'You know something about animals?' he challenged.

'Enough to know that if they're tranquillised and unattended for too long, they dehydrate, die an awful death then explode. Not on my watch. You can leave right now if that is your method.' Darlene sat back, retrieved the napkin off her lap and folded it neatly before returning it to beside the empty plate.

'We're not monsters.'

'Just making sure. There are some very nasty, cruel people out there. They ought to have the shot as well.' Her hand flew to her mouth in embarrassment.

'Ah, the DVO...'

'We're done here. You've spoken out of turn on something that is not your business and that you have no knowledge about. You may leave. Goodbye.'

'I apologise. You are correct. Some ought to be shot.'

They had a stare-down, which Darlene knew he would lose.

He eventually rubbed his eyes, but not before they turned to steel. 'Should have guessed I'd never outstare a crack shot like you. Please accept my apologies. Have a read, I'm going to stretch my legs for about half an hour.'

'You should add on another fifteen minutes,' she replied, highly annoyed.

Totally unimpressed, she watched him stand up, nod and turn to walk towards the door, just as a very short, round older man entered the café. His eyes swept the interior and rested lightly on Elaina before settling on Darlene. His already happy smile broadened.

'Never in a million years!' He waddled over to the table, effortlessly avoided Milne and extended his plump hand. 'Darlene Adams, the finest pistol shooter in the country. It's my pleasure. My friends call me Peachie, probably because I always am.'

She returned his vivacious mood with one of her own dazzling smiles and happily shook his hand.

'You know this woman?' Milne asked bemusedly.

'I know of her, and it would be in your best interest to refer to her more politely. Particularly when you are in my company, lad. Weren't you going somewhere?'

'Uh, yes. But I'll be back, Ms Adams. Half an... I mean... three quarters of an hour.'

They watched him close the door behind him and walk with his back erect and fists clenched beside his thighs.

'Thank you, Peachie. Gosh, your timing was impeccable. Are you an avid shooter yourself?'

'No, but you are my granddaughter's idol! She modelled herself off you with archery and has just started on the handgun discipline.'

The second Gavin Milne was out of sight, Elaina rushed over and threw her arms around Peachie.

'Hey, settle, petal, we only had a brief chat the other day, and yes, I waved, but I am not your teddy bear!' Peachie chuckled and gently pried her hands off his shoulders.

'Elaina, please,' Darlene encouraged firmly.

'But, Darlene, this lovely man might be able to help me get work,' she whined. 'Please excuse. I'll go back to my table, but Mister Peachie, please can you help me get work? Can we talk later, when that man comes back?'

'Yes, we can. I'll come and sit at your table then, okay?'

'Thank you. Sorry.'

Peachie refocused on Darlene. 'You are a sight for sore eyes. Spook and Tiny will send their love, but they didn't tell me exactly who you were!'

Tears filled her eyes. 'It was you! At Broken Hill! I remember seeing you get out of that massive Peterbilt wearing a holey shirt. I nearly cried when I saw the way you men greeted each other. You really do a tough job. Know that I appreciate you, Peachie.'

He chuckled and looked a tad embarrassed. 'Holey shirt! I like you even more, and if you were there when they got caught up in the dust storm after that, then yes, that was me.'

They had only moved the paperwork when the waitress came over and put a fresh bottle of chilled water and clean glasses on their table. 'Sir, the kitchen will be closing in half an hour. I can recommend the Szechuan calamari salad.'

'So can I.' Darlene smiled warmly.

They both murmured their thanks, and Peachie did the honours of pouring the water.

'I'm not too keen on that bloke,' he said. 'Something's off... Mind if I take a look?'

'Be my guest,' she said, and opened the folder.

Peachie gently indicated with his head at Elaina. 'Is that...?'

'A friend, yes. Consider me her guardian on behalf of Spook and Tiny.'

His eyes widened while wispy eyebrows chased his receding hairline. 'She's the Danish Pastry?'

'Yes.'

While Peachie ate, he encouraged her to talk freely about Milne's offer. Darlene cautiously explained what the job prospect entailed, then described Elaina's orangutan and his similarity to the mobile tattoo parlour.

'They're one and the same,' Peachie said quietly. 'You need to be careful. I think it's best us three have a chat afterwards. I do know of several farmers up north who need workers. Don't quite do things by the books but are good people all the same.'

Suddenly, Peachie paused with his laden fork just millimetres away from the cavernous void. He painstakingly lowered it and replaced it on the plate then stared wide-eyed at her.

'That bastard is here with another girl,' he murmured just loud enough for Darlene to hear. 'I saw him the other day.'

Her stomach recoiled as the hair stood up on the back of her neck and arms. That was it. Her mind was made up – she was taking the job. She discreetly put her finger up to her lips.

'Keep eating, Peachie. I'm going to have a very enthusiastic conversation when this bloke returns. Are you happy to join Elaina while I discuss a few details?'

'That would be more appropriate. I'll do my best to get her work where I may have the opportunity of seeing her regularly, for everyone's peace of mind. When this is over, it'd also be appropriate if you took her home.'

'That's fair. Thank you. By the way, are you devising a plan?' She winked slyly.

'I reckon it's a mirror of the one you are. Spook will have my guts for garters... and who knows what Tiny would do, if anything...'

'Those wonderful men have enough on their plates back home. We've got this.'

Gavin Milne entered the café and arrogantly sat at their table. 'I feel as if I've been ambushed, Ms Adams,' he said evenly.

'Pure coincidence, Mr Milne. I have it on good authority that I should consider your initial proposal. Could you indicate which areas we'd be concentrating on, as well as the duration and living conditions, in order for me to make an informed decision?'

'You haven't asked about the remuneration.'

'I expect you to provide that information freely if you're wanting me to do this job, else we call it quits right now.'

'You're a tough nut to crack behind your beauty, that's for sure. Definitely not one to mess with.'

'That's correct. You were saying about the remuneration, Mr Milne?'

The bowl of ice cream never got a chance to melt as she listened to the lucrative, interesting contract. The only catch: it would stretch into late December. Milne made one phone call and confirmed they were to meet at a shooting range half an hour north of Albany in four days. There, she would get to experience long-barrel disciplines and moving targets. Her accuracy would determine if she could do the job. A firm handshake was enough to end the meeting.

'Wouldn't mind a photo of us three,' Peachie suddenly suggested from the nearby table opposite to Elaina's.

Darlene looked at him like he was crazy then read the play. 'What a great idea! I'll sit in the middle.' Catching Elaina's eye, she said loudly, 'Excuse me, miss, would you mind taking a photo?'

Elaina took three photos using Peachie's mobile, smiled coyly as she handed it back to him and returned to her table. Darlene remained seated as Milne nodded once before smiling coldly at Peachie. He then loudly announced his departure to all and sundry in the café. Almost everyone sighed in relief. His whining, nasally voice was over the top. She watched him walk between hers and another vehicle in the carpark before crossing the road and driving off in a black 4WD Landcruiser wagon, not liking the feeling she got.

Peachie had won over the owner and encouraged them to close at their normal time but, after the generous tip, agreed the three patrons could stay for an extra hour. Elaina listened intently to what the harvest jobs entailed. The majority were outdoors. Secretly, Peachie was concerned about her looks and really didn't want her out in the paddocks with the lads. They didn't need too many distractions, particularly when long days and nights were a huge thing to factor in.

The way Peachie described the grain-classifying process at some of the satellite sites made Darlene wish she'd acted on the game earlier or was twenty years younger. She would have loved to have experienced a grain harvest in the west. With the promise of phone calls and enquiries being made that afternoon, Peachie swore he'd let them know accordingly. He'd do his utmost to be Elaina's chaperone, but she had to be sensible if she was to be left on her own.

'I would be terrified that orangutan would turn up, recognise me and then...'

She was clearly experiencing post-trauma as her breath faltered, her beautiful blue eyes filled with tears and her hands shook like she had Parkinson's disease. Peachie handled the situation and soothed her fears with ease. Eventually, Elaina was calm enough to stand and walk on her own. They thanked the owners profusely, and Darlene tipped them generously for the second time, before Peachie escorted his two dames to the heatwave-rippling Jeep. Walking around it, she couldn't find anything untoward. They all groaned and fanned themselves waiting for the interior to cool down.

'Expect a dry thunderstorm later on, ladies. Have you got far to travel, Darlene?'

'Not really, about forty minutes or so.' She clutched Peachie's hand and hugged him as best she could. 'Thank you for turning up when you did, thank you for being here and thank you, thank you, for being you!'

'Aww, shucks!' He chuckled loudly. 'We'll stay in touch.'

Elaina threw her arms around him again. 'Thank you, Mr Peachie!'

'Easy up on the old man, Elaina! I got your number from Darlene, so do your best to have good sleeps, keep up with water intake and eat properly. When you work the harvest, your whole diet and body clock get a shakeup. Best you prepare accordingly. Bye, ladies, take care.'

Their farewells echoed across the hazy street. Not too many people were out and about, and it took them just under half an hour to park in her allocated space at the retreat.

'No ways, Darlene. I can't stay here?'

'Why not? It's Denmark, not quite your home, but shush, because it is a retreat where people come to relax. And that, my girl, is exactly what we're going to do for a few days. We've got a self-contained unit, too. Come on, hope you got swimmers in that backpack. The pool's cool and covered!'

'We should do another selfie...'

'We should not.'

They smothered their giggles and hurriedly entered the blissfully cool reception area.

Peachie scratched his head and twitched his lips. His eagle eyes were on stalks. He was going to help nail the bastard once and for all. He wished he'd paid more attention to the number plate on the black 4WD and was definitely going to find out more about this Gavin Milne. The way his eyes turned to steel, the clenched fists and stiff back emitted unbridled jealousy. Jealousy led to threats.

Dialling Spook's number, Peachie left a message. 'Hey, mate, following up as requested. The two damsels are flourishing. Pass it on.'

He then sent the best of the three photos to Spook and stood by for the barrage of questions.

Tiny ignored his phone and ran his hand lovingly over the sleek exterior of the Mercedes. He'd asked the doctor to keep his gran in for one more day while he took care of some business. Buying a new car was the kind of business he could get used to. The salesmen and women fell over themselves to ensure his interest was maintained. It was the reclining rear seats that almost sealed the deal. Although, there was a lot of glass, and summer was already making its presence known. He chortled at the silly-sized taillights and was disappointed in the GLS's overall lack of style.

As he strolled casually towards the S-Class Saloon, the rear seat with the leg rest struck a chord. Granny could recline in the front or the back, whichever took her fancy. The driver's seat was extremely comfortable. The doors opened wide enough, and it was a very classy looking vehicle with great lines. He immediately thought of Elaina and Darlene and tried to push them to the back of his mind. Again. It had been getting so difficult to do. He easily envisaged Nova in her travel harness doing nose-art on the windows and smiled a little sad smile. How he missed his dog. Spook had sent him photos every day of her playing with his two border collies, but there was a massive void when she wasn't around.

Negotiations were tough, but the dealership only had the previous model available in white, and it had all the requirements Tiny needed and wanted. Grinning like a teenager, he drove it off the showroom floor there and then.

After parking his new asset in the secure lock-up garage at the hospital, he breezed into Granny's room wearing the same grin. She was sitting in her night attire; her hair had been combed, and she looked happy and relaxed.

'Sonny, you're just in time for dessert! Look what these lovely people have done for me.' She waved her hand elegantly at the two beautifully iced mini cupcakes, each with delicate edible roses adorning the top.

'They look amazing. Only the best for the best, Granny.' He bent down, kissed her gently on her forehead and pressed the set of keys into her hand. 'Happy birthday to you for tomorrow.'

Tears welled up in her eyes. 'You scallywag. I wondered why the doctor sheepishly said I could only go home tomorrow. Ooh, a new car. Thank you. I can't wait to see it. Let's go and have a look now.'

The duty nurse had been hovering around, as per Tiny's request, and walked in at just the right moment.

. 'Sir, there's twenty minutes remaining for the visiting hours. Perhaps a stroll through the hallway, given this fine lady is going home tomorrow?' The nurse winked playfully.

Granny clapped her hands together, releasing the inner child, making both her surrogate son and the nurse laugh loudly. Together, they helped mobilise the elderly lady into a wheelchair and took a stroll down to the carpark.

'I'll wait by the lifts, sir, but please, don't be too long. It's getting late, and we get busy upstairs from here on.'

The excited laugh echoed and mingled with the sounds of unbridled delight. Tiny couldn't get the smile off his face and silently thanked Reg Oscane for the opportunity to go shopping so quickly. It was the old rogue's parting gift to the woman he'd idolised all his life.

During the long drive back to the almost empty B&B, Tiny realised it was the first day in practically his entire life he hadn't felt so terribly sad.

Their anticipated arrival at Scone late the following day should top off Granny's birthday beautifully. Apparently, a light and hearty supper was on the menu, but everything revolved around how she had fared on her journey. They had a three-day stopover, then half a day's journey to his little piece of paradise. He was secretly looking forward to going home. He had some serious thinking to do, and strolling through his established garden with Nova by his side was the only way to do it satisfactorily.

Gripping his mobile, Spider paced the motel room in frustration as he listened to his boss telling him exactly what a total harvest ban entailed. Nobody could fetch him from Albany, for they were all taking the opportunity to rest up until they got the go-ahead to start up again, which was exactly what his boss expected Spider to do.

'How boring. I need food. Where's my girl?'

Yeah. Who's playing with her? Is she still there? Run away. Go back to your toys. Max and Stevo are having too much fun.

Spider slapped his head to quieten the voice. 'Pardon? I didn't hear you.'

'I said, your girl is where you left her. Go and buy something to eat. You're as tight as a fish's butthole, according to Max...'

'Max? Have you been speaking with him?'

'Not recently. Now listen, we're in for a ripper storm, which will determine how we're set for tomorrow. Keep your phone on and expect my call at 6 a.m. Got it?'

'Can I have some fun?'

'Be sober, no drugs, and don't do anything stupid. Oh, yeah, that reminds me... where are the plates to that yellow car?'

'Hidden.' Spider disconnected the call.

The yellow car? Hidden plates. Why? Who knows? Go play. It's boring. I'm bored. Let's go find some toys. You can't sleep. No drugs. Boohoo. Go home.

'Stop talking!' he screamed into the pillow.

The wall of heat hit him the moment he stepped out of the cheap room at the pub. But he was hungry, and his spider was bored. Venturing into the bar room, he was disappointed to find it almost empty. The barmaid was old enough to be his grandmother. When she smiled, her toothless mouth stopped his spider's wriggling instantly.

Run away. Go home. Boring.

'Pepsi, please,' he said politely.

'Cola or something else, boy.'

'Pepsi, please.'

She looked at him and grinned again. 'None in today. Maybe tomorrow. How about some cold water? It's very hot outside.'

'No, thank you. Do you have any meals?'

'Go next door, they might still have the cook plate on.'

'Might?'

'You're not from around here, are you?' She looked past his angry eyes. 'No matter. Stay here, I'll find you something.'

Boring. Phone Max. Find a friend.

He walked around the dimly lit bar and put his head out the door. The same telephone box was across the road. Loping towards it, he looked hungrily at a noisy group of people as they entered the backpackers.

Ooh. Go there. They look like fun.

Dialling Max's new number, which was Bluey's old one, he listened to the giggles and rowdy laughter coming from the building.

Yay. Play time. Let's go and play.

'Who's this?' An angry voice spoke into the receiver.

'Me. Spider. Why are you angry with me, Max?'

'Not only you. The whole world. Reckon Reg's dead by now, mate. He wasn't in good shape, and you didn't make it home in time to say goodbye. Whatchya gonna do now? I've got all the toys and Stevo. All you've got is my yellow car.'

'I don't have it anymore. I parked it up and hid the plates. Too bad, so sad.'

Reg's dead? No. No. No. No goodbye. Nothing. Go home. Get the girls. Run away. Snake Girl? Leave her. Take her. Leave her. Take...

'Just stop talking,' he hissed and slammed the phone down with such force he cracked the handpiece.

Drawing attention from the rowdy group by the entrance, he waved casually and skulked towards them. The girls shrieked and ran away. The boys stared at him and blocked his path.

'Place is full. Go back to where you came from.'

Leave. You don't want to play. Leave. Reg's dead.

Spider found himself back in the darkened corner of the pub, tracing water droplets down the glass of cola and picking at some hot chips drowned in gravy. He was all alone now. He was free. He could find out what was so important about Max's yellow car. His spider was asleep. Even thinking about Snake Girl didn't wake it up. No playing tonight.

CHAPTER FOURTEEN

Milly was dressed and ready to go to work with greater pep in her step. She swung open the door to the caravan confidently and was hit with the oppressive heat. The predicted storm had dissipated but left the air horribly heavy. At precisely 4:00 a.m., she stood by the augers and watched a slow-moving light approach. There was no sound accompanying it. Then she realised it was a bicycle. She hadn't ridden one since...

A familiar woman's voice called out.

'Morning. Harvest ban continues. Some farms north and to the east were hit, but we seemed to have dodged a bullet. So far, anyway. Thought you'd like some things to draw with.'

Milly accepted the bag graciously. 'Thank you. But...'

'Your companion is still stuck in Albany and will be until about nightfall, I reckon. If you want some female company, follow this road for twenty minutes by foot and you'll see my studio. No biggie if you don't. I'm fine with my own company too. You feeling better today?'

'Much better, thanks to you. I didn't realise how relieving good air conditioning can be!'

'You need to phone anyone?'

'Um, not yet, thanks.'

'Righto. Well, relax while you can. It'll be full-on when we get going.'

Milly watched as the older woman gracefully pedalled away. She left the bag on the table and went exploring in the nearby sheds. Carefully lifting up corners of tarps, she discovered all sorts of different farming implements, rows of whisky barrels, heaps of plastic chairs and very old vehicles. The shed furthest away from the caravan housed two motorbikes, a big old truck, more plastic chairs and one yellow car. She was sure it was the same car she'd woken up in, before being blindfolded and carried somewhere, only to open her eyes to discover she was inside a caravan. The only door that wasn't locked was the boot. Inside were dirty blankets, kids' toys, unfamiliar shoes and pretty sandals. The spare tyre looked unusually high.

'You there, girl?'

She smothered a shriek at the sound of the distant voice and quietly pushed the lid closed before creeping around the back of the shed. Milly raced past the first two rows of the recently harvested paddock.

'Over here! The sunrise is amazing,' she called out breathlessly.

'Thought you'd be drawing.'

Her boss stood at the edge, holding up the cloth bag she'd left on the table. She walked towards him briskly with her fingers crossed in her pockets. 'I visualise the scene first, imprint it in my memory and draw from that. Not sure if it's the right way to do things, but I'm self-taught and it works.'

'Humph, shouldn't explore too far. Got a message for you.' He didn't offer her the drawing bag but showed her his phone instead: *Snake Girl, am in town. Am lonely, my spider is lonely. Just you wait until I get back there.*

Milly nearly dry retched and murmured, 'Thank you, boss.' In her mind, she was pleading him to make the creep go away, or help her help him die.

'Yep. I expected that reaction. In about two or three weeks, we're going to trial you in the kitchen. Harvest will be in full swing by then, and my missus will need a hand until we're finished for the season. Interested?'

'You bet I am! Thank you very much for your kindness and consideration.'

'Yeah, well, your personal life isn't any of my business, but I figure a change is as good as a holiday. You'll be staying in your own donga by the kitchen. No visitors.'

Milly barely contained her excitement and relief. 'Mister, I will not let you down.'

He smiled then. 'Thought as much. Your caravan is this way – can't have you wandering around out here. Will come and fetch you if we're kicking off again. I won't be locking the door, but suggest you do from the inside.'

'Yes, boss.'

Chatting happily about the similarity in landscapes at the bottom half of the vast continent, Milly described the cereal grain crops and sheep farming that dominated the farming sectors around Port Lincoln. Feral goats were an ongoing problem, according to her regular customers at the restaurant where she worked.

'Um, used to work. I work for you now,' she said bravely.

'So it seems. You will be paid by my missus when you're helping her. Here's your drawing stuff.'

Clutching it tightly, she grinned. 'Please thank your wife again for me.'

He nodded and held the caravan door open for her. Milly dutifully pulled it closed and locked it from the inside, calling out her thanks merrily. She waited until the sounds of his crunching footsteps had disappeared and broke into song: *Summertime*. Her vocal exercise emulating Sarah Vaughan and her incredible jazz voice. Milly's inspiration. She sang her heart out, affirming her life was going to turn around for the better. She was going to be home for Christmas.

'Happy birthday to you, dear Granny, happy birthday to you!'

Spook and his wife had made a great fuss over the dear elderly lady, showering her with practical homemade gifts of biscuits, fudge and potpourri bags. Topping it off was a video hook-up with the soon-to-be-parents at the hospital. The early supper was a delightful spread of light foods accompanied by a spiked fruity punch. With the backdrop of the rolling green hills and a magnificent bright orange sunset, and with three dogs by her feet, Granny raised her glass.

'You are all so wonderful, thank you for making my day so special. I feel as if I've spent a day in a luxury jet. My bones don't ache, I'm not stiff, and having a selection of seats... no, chairs, they're chairs with built-in massage functions – certainly helped, and Sonny made sure I was comfortable every kilometre of the way. Mind you, I am looking forward to walking around for a few days!'

Plans were afoot for exploring the property and surrounding hills in a horse-drawn carriage during the next few days, which reminded Granny of her youth. She happily shared stories of getting to and from school in the back of an ox-drawn cart. Her mother and grandmother having to cross creeks with their petticoats and dresses either around their ears or getting caught up in the swirls made by the wheels. The schoolkids thinking it was great fun, only realising as they got older the awful trials and tribulations the old folk went through. The torrential rains would swell the creeks, oft making them impassable. There would be logs, bovines and other horrid things caught up in the raging rivers. But either side of summer and the wet season, it was the best time of year, because the mozzies were less and the humidity had dropped off. That was when the rainforests and running streams were the best backyard a kid could have.

'Where was this fascinating place, Granny? I never knew any of this!' Tiny said in awe.

'Finch Hatton Gorge, up in Queensland. Amazing place. When I was a lot older, I worked for several very rich people in their hideaway retreats throughout the area.'

'Would you revisit it? Because the way you've described it, now I want to see these rainforests,' Spook said, his eyes all dreamy.

'Yes, actually, I would. You should see it again too. Last time wasn't much of a sightseeing trip. But I think you forgot to spike everyone's glass of punch, looking at your glassy eyes. It's not always paradise.'

'Hey?' Tiny asked, confused. 'You been there, Spook?'

'Donkey's years ago, mate. Too many weekends since then to recall everything.'

'We'll go in the winter. I hate mozzies,' Spook's daughter chipped in from the hospital. 'And, Dad, you can spike my punch in a couple of years.'

Not surprisingly, the party continued for several hours.

When Spook retrieved the bottle of tawny port from behind the bar, Tiny looked at him solemnly.

'You looked at your phone recently, mate?' Spook asked as he poured a sipper.

'No, I haven't. That's right, it chimed when I was at the car yard. Thanks.' He pulled it out of his pocket. 'Oh! It's from you... What? Where's Elaina? Who the hell is that, and who the hell took the photo?'

'Ask Peachie. Better still, phone Darlene, mate. They're three hours behind.'

Tiny downed his drink, smiled and took Nova for a walk. He had to see her in person to say what he wanted to say. Conversations over the telephone weren't going to cut it. She would be bringing Elaina home for Christmas. That would make a lovely gift for everyone, him more than anybody.

Staring into the fading colours of the sunset, he wondered about the whereabouts of this gorge that Granny had been speaking of, Spook's familiarity with the area and its correlation with the property from Reg Oscane. In sheer frustration, he lay on the grass, staring into the moonless night with Nova by his feet. He'd sleep out and hopefully awaken with a clearer head.

Quietly putting the cutlery together on their breakfast plates, the two women sat back and sighed in satisfaction. The traditional English breakfast was devoured with great gusto seated on the patio overlooking the manicured garden. Their colourful swimming towels hung over the railings, waving in the light breeze. Darlene had been building up to having a heartfelt conversation with Elaina for several days, but the timing just hadn't seemed right. She'd hoped the very early start to their day would encourage it.

The following day, she'd be going to the shooting range, and she did not want Elaina anywhere near it. Even though her nerves and confidence had improved dramatically after the regular reiki and Tai Chi sessions, she slipped into a jittery state too often. Darlene was about to say something when Elaina's phone rang.

'Fingers crossed it's Peachie,' she said excitedly and raced inside.

Her giggles, squeals of delight and effusive words of gratitude could only mean good news. Darlene quietly stacked the plates, took them into the kitchen and brewed a coffee.

Shoving the phone into her hands, Elaina jumped up and down excitedly. 'It's Peachie, he wants to have word with you. Please don't hang up – I want to talk after, but first, I use laundry. I might have job!'

'Morning, Peachie. Harvest back on?'

'Morning, Darlene. Yes, going great guns. Listen, there's a satellite site which employs girls to cook for their crew day and night. They have their own quarters, and no visitors are allowed. I quote, "They're there to work and not entertain", and I thought of Elaina. Can we meet early tomorrow morning outside Cranbrook, which is about a hundred k's north of Albany?'

'That's huge! Thanks, man. She can cook a fantastic breakfast, that's for sure! Uh, yeah. You name the time.'

'Six o'clock, please. I've been hailed to cart grain to a receival bin in the area. The farmer uses other drivers for the Albany run and needs an experienced bloke for quick turnarounds. I've got fifteen harvests under my belt. I meet him today to sort stuff out.'

'I gather you'll be at his farm regularly, then?'

'Yes. If we don't have any more delays due to weather or breakdowns, we'll be wrapped up by mid-December. A record-breaking harvest, this one. Just the way I like them. When they drag out, it's not as cost-effective, if you get my drift.'

'I sure do. This sounds like a terrific opportunity. I'll put Elaina back on, and we'll see you in the morning. What channel do I call you on if there isn't phone coverage?'

'The same one you're familiar with. Thanks, Darlene. See you then. Incidentally, make sure Elaina has sufficient supplies for two months. She won't be having much free time to go shopping. They're a long way out.'

'Will do, thanks. Here she is...' And Darlene handed the phone back to the excited young woman.

Closing the door to her room, Darlene pulled apart her handguns and cleaned them. Again. Seeing a text from Peachie made her grin. He was scheming!

Darlene, envisage those maps re feral goats. Section 8. We'll be in that area. See what you can do! We'll keep in touch via text.

A soft knock on the door interrupted her reply. 'Won't be a moment, Elaina.'

Covering the bits and pieces on her bed with the pretty light green bedspread, she opened the door just enough so they could see each other.

'I phone Uncle Spook and explain,' Elaina said. 'Then, we go shopping today, please? I pay you back, Darlene.'

'Go and make your calls, I'll wash up shortly. And, Elaina' – she gently clasped the younger woman's wrist – 'thanks for the amazing breakfast.'

Watching her skip down the hallway put an extra zing in Darlene's day. Things were going to work out. She needed to make a phone call as well and closed the door. After sending her reply to Peachie, she dialled the number.

'This is Officer Bev. How can I help you?'

'It's Darlene Adams calling. Apologies for the intrusion... is now a good time?'

'Yes, actually, it is. How are you?'

The two women covered the usual pleasantries and small talk then approached the subject in question.

'How are you coping?'

'There hasn't been any word of my daughter, but some families have had closure with a recent discovery. I believe the Danish girl made contact. That was a good news day. As a matter of fact, I'll be meeting my daughter's best friend, Amy, as well as Cassie and Asta, for lunch today. It'd be nice if we could do a video call or something. Put faces to names and build our own network. How does that sound?'

'Like a marvellous idea. I think we can start calling each other by our names now, so please call me Darlene. I'll be sure to have tissues!'

'Likewise. There's a two-and-a-half-hour time difference... does 11:00 a.m. your time work?'

'That's perfect.'

'Should we make it a surprise?'

Bev's warm chuckle brought tears to her eyes.

'Yes, let's do that. I'll make sure Elaina is away from the table when I accept your call, then we can take it from there. I look forward to seeing you and sharing in your company. Thanks for answering my call, Bev.'

'The pleasure was all mine, Darlene. Talk soon.'

They hung up simultaneously. Swiftly rebuilding her treasured pistols and securely storing them away, she met Elaina in the kitchen washing up the last of the plates. Her smile was broad, and her eyes shone. Yes. A good day indeed.

Her mind drifted to Tiny, and she smiled, frowned that he didn't leave a message then smiled again. She didn't have to try too hard to feel his embrace or imagine the tingling sensation of the tender farewell kiss, even if it was on the cheek. Somehow, she'd have to see him again.

Shrugging off the melancholy thoughts, she smoothed down her favourite mauve and white wrap dress and wrote out a shopping list.

Troy pulled Bev back into his embrace. He'd announced his plan to retire the night before and was on leave for two whole weeks. The three Rottweilers had been dropped off at the dog retreat and obedience centre on the way to Cowell, giving everyone a break for three days. Troy was having the day to himself while the four women in his life were familiarising themselves over an extended lunch. He'd received positive reviews from Cassie and Asta's employers and was relieved that everyone was hoping to be with their respective families for Christmas.

He prayed Milly would be home by then so he could finalise the plans to have his own ready-made family. He had discreetly returned to Port Lincoln and had a confidential discussion with Amy. She'd thrown her arms around him and burst into tears. Feeling welcomed and loved had been the nicest thing that had happened to her for a very long time, and she'd jumped at the chance to be in his family.

With confident hand signals, Milly rolled the truckie away from the auger, then swept up the minor spillage around the area to meet the strict hygiene requirements. The bony arm and large hand hanging out the window of the oncoming truck chilled her to the bone and made her sick to her stomach.

'Snake Girl. I've missed you. Let's run away.'

'No, Spider. We're working. Roll on until you're signalled to stop. Then please follow my hand signals until I've filled the last trailer, and move ahead out of the way, so the next truck can come in behind. He's waiting already. We're on strict time schedules.'

'Aww, let's play,' he whined. 'I was too tired last night, but now I'm not.'

A booming voice over the two-way speaker made Milly smile. 'Oi, get a move on. We're not here to muck around. Time's money, and I don't like wasting either. Move.'

Spider growled into the two-way, 'Don't ever speak to me like that again.'

'Or what?'

Milly turned off the two-way and tapped her wrist. 'Please, Spider, let's earn our money.'

'It's all mine, Snake Girl. Don't you ever forget that.'

Grinding the gears and kangaroo-hopping the bulky vehicle, he stopped at the marked area and opened the door, then swiftly shut it, ground the gears again and kept rolling until his third trailer was past the refill point.

'He giving you a hard time, girl?' the boss asked as he walked past.

'Not anymore, thank you.'

'That's right. Switch your two-way back on, I'm relocating him to my other farm. He'll be back in a week.'

'You're a legend, boss.'

Milly turned her head and grinned broadly behind the fly veil as she brought the next truck forwards. She had to find a way to repay these kind people.

Granny, ever cautious about outstaying her welcome, had offered to treat their gracious hosts to breakfast as a last hoorah of her ongoing birthday celebrations. The slightly tearful farewells were quickly replaced by happy tears with the news that the soon-to-be-mother was fit enough to be released from hospital.

'Please join us for Christmas, Granny,' Spook said enthusiastically. 'It's going to be a most joyous one.'

'Sonny?' She looked at Tiny approvingly.

'Can't see why not! Thanks, Spook. Your home will already have expanding walls – please let us consider alternative accommodation.'

'We'll make a plan. Right, you pair, on your way. Safe travels, and stay in touch. Thanks for breakfast, Granny. I'm speaking on behalf of my darling wife. She's too emotional to talk right now.'

Maureen's hug was words enough for Granny, who returned the embrace with as much strength as she could muster. The women did exchange quiet words of gratitude for the financial gifts that came with the beautiful cradles. A surprise for everyone at the right time.

With Nova in her travelling harness and already snuggled into her bed, Tiny ensured Granny's reclining seat was the optimum temperature and the strains of her favourite music filled the interior. She sighed happily; all was almost right in her world. It was her Sonny who she wanted to see settled and happy.

'Let's go home, Sonny. It's been a long time coming. Even Nova is looking forward to it. Like her, I'll sleep away the hours, but please wake me half an hour out. I'd like to see the grand entrance.'

Tiny chuckled. 'It's not much, but it is home.'

He too loved the area and admired the scenery as they descended the Great Dividing Range with its gullies, ridges and amazing flora two hours later. The cloudless day painted the distant hills a deep mauve, which shimmered in the balmy heat. Nova barked softly; her tail thumped the seat, waking up the lightly snoring elderly lady.

'Afternoon, Gran. We're forty minutes out. Nova's nose for home hasn't lost its touch. Please have a drink, there's one beside you.'

'Perfect timing!'

A quiet gasp came from the back seat as they rounded the last knoll before climbing the gently rising concrete driveway. His rose garden was flourishing, as were the orchids in the trees. It was obvious his landscape garden contractors had also worked their magic in keeping his lawn perfectly manicured.

'Home sweet home. Welcome.'

'Oh, Sonny, it's beautiful.' Granny sniffled. 'I already feel at home, thank you.'

The first thing Nova did when she was released was roll around and scratch her back, yapping happily. It was obvious she'd missed the lush green lawn too. Tiny almost did grass angels himself. Taking a deep breath of the clean, warm mountainous air, he steadied his beloved grandmother as she manoeuvred herself out of the car. Holding onto him tightly, she led him to the views she wanted to see. At every spot, she told him it would make a perfect place for a proposal.

'You haven't even met her yet, Gran. Let's not jump the gun!'

'Going by Spook's account, there shouldn't be any worries, and age has no barriers where love is concerned,' she replied, laughing heartily.

Back at the retreat, the two women were a pair of giggling Gerties for the rest of the afternoon. There had been tears, laughter and mingled conversations, and an automatic bond had formed between the six women. Phone numbers were exchanged, and the call had been reluctantly disconnected.

Seated in the restaurant, finishing an early dinner and watching the sun slip slowly behind the hilly vista, Elaina presented Darlene with an IOU.

'I cannot thank you enough and promise to send messages. I will find ways to pay you back and will not let you down. It is time to think about going home, but first I want to see Asta, and for her to meet Uncle Spook and the not-so-little one. It would be wonderful if we could all have Christmas together, don't you think?'

'All that is up to you, and we'll just have to see about Christmas. But you've got a big day ahead, and we've got an early morning start.' Darlene pushed back her chair, slipped the unopened note into her handbag and stood up, grinning. 'Nearly bedtime, young lady. Set your alarm for 4:00 a.m.'

Darlene tossed and turned. Snakes, rifles, goats, purple rigs and mobile tattoo parlours interrupted visions of a classy Christmas with new friends and families. When the alarm rudely disturbed what felt like a minute's peace, she stretched out to hit the unusually harsh-sounding tones and shrieked loudly as a small spider ran across her hand. She flew out of bed. She hated spiders. She hated snakes. But then thought perhaps she hated spiders more.

Elaina was as nervous as Darlene was jumpy. Conversation was intermittent, and thankfully, Elaina fell asleep ten minutes into the trip. Peachie had messaged her with a short cut reducing the journey, thereby bringing forward the meeting time by almost an hour. He promised he'd have breakfast waiting for them.

Bev's daughter with the snake tattoo, goats to be tranquillised and Elaina's fear of the man she said abducted her made for a very busy mind. Darlene's temperament was erring on the edge of stroppy. She hoped she had the shooting range to herself before Milne arrived. Target practice was great therapy.

Turning off the Albany Highway, Darlene shook Elaina awake. They were on time, and Peachie was leaning against his motorhome. He greeted them with a small nod and handed them each a very strong, sweet coffee. They drank in silence and watched the sun burn through the fog. Heavy dewdrops glistened on the leaves as the smell of bacon filled the air. Long after they'd disposed of the paper plates, Peachie pulled out a map and spread it on the bonnet of the Jeep.

'Ladies, I'm not much of a talker until I've had my second coffee and something to eat. Good morning, and your timing is impeccable. This is where we're headed, Elaina.'

Pointing to a highlighted area north-east of the South Coast Highway, he explained the enormity of the farms. An arrangement had also been struck with the farmer that he would bring out the prospective employee for one week's trial. Darlene had been nominated as Elaina's next of kin and primary contact. It was fortuitous that the potential goat contract put her roughly in the same area. She looked at Peachie above Elaina's head and raised her eyebrows questioningly.

'The weather forecast is in our favour,' he said with a wink. 'We're all hoping to finish this harvest uninterrupted, which means the massive sheep industry will be putting their livestock out to eat the stubble. Feral goats are second on the list of dread. Fire is always first.'

She nodded and winked. 'Got it, thanks for clearing that up.'

Transferring several grocery bags, an esky and a large suitcase into the back of Peachie's motorhome, Elaina squeezed Darlene's hands. 'We talk soon. I promise. But know that I will be busy, so we message. If I need to really talk, please can I just phone?'

'Of course you can. I will always try to take your call, but remember, mobile coverage might be hit and miss out here. There. Here! When you meet the farmer's wife, please describe who I am in such a fashion that she knows to phone me in the first instance. Promise?'

'Yes, I promise.'

Darlene's mobile chimed as Peachie hurried up the farewell.

'Thanks for breakfast and that coffee, Peachie. Reckon I'll do well today!'

'Reckon you always do, Darlene Adams. By the way, my granddaughter is so jealous!'

Laughing together with hugs all round, they departed in opposite directions. She pulled over to check the message: *You and I will stay in touch. S & T are on my back LOL*

She burst out laughing then sighed. She really missed being in the company of Spook and Tiny.

Rapid-shooting fifty bullets and tearing up the moving targets using her Colt 45 was exhilarating. Particularly as Darlene had the range to herself. She repeated the therapy with her second-best friend. Her Smith and Wesson. She was aware other visitors would be arriving for a private session one hour before she was to meet with Milne, so she fired off several more rounds, nailing the bullseye each time. After stripping, cleaning and rebuilding her weapons, she took the opportunity to familiarise herself with pulling down and rebuilding a borrowed rifle while the other private session was underway. Observing their stance, she rehearsed then perfected the position necessary to fire accurately. Nodding in self-satisfaction, she discreetly moved away from the live-firing area.

Typically, Milne was early. Typically, Darlene was waiting, seated casually with her back to the tin wall and the rifle in its case, watching the competition long-barrel shooters practice. In all the years she'd been participating in her preferred disciplines, she had never stopped to watch others. Fascinated by the different techniques and styles, her interest levels reached a phenomenally high level.

'See anything you like, Ms Adams?' Gavin Milne asked quietly.

'Morning, Mr Milne. Yes, actually. Everything. Before I fire off any bullets, please tell me the name of the tranquillising drug and dosage that I will be using.'

'Should you get the job,' he retorted.

They looked at each other steadily. His gaze wavered first. 'I learnt my lesson on that one. We like to use acepromazine, that much I can tell you. The vet that travels with us prepares the darts.'

She accepted the information and listened intently to the exercises she was to complete. To replicate the environment, she had to fire five shots from a .22 Long Rifle using her experience in reading the wind and without the use of benches initially. This was to be repeated over distances ranging from five hundred metres up to two thousand metres in varying increments. This much, she knew, was standard competition rules. Although the actual weapon she would be using was a specifically designed injection rifle, having confidence in a .22 would put her in good stead. Darlene was excited to use the telescopic sight.

Peachie's new boss, Bo, sized him up while enjoying a cigarette, leaning against the tray of a well-used Landcruiser ute. Elaina introduced herself confidently and took the previously issued advice of listening and not speaking on board. After a brief chat on the two-way, they watched as the tell-tale plume of a moving vehicle came from the bottom of the paddock. This time, a red-stained Landcruiser station wagon arrived, and a solid older woman with kind eyes stepped out. Elaina immediately liked her and shook the extended hand as firmly as it was offered.

'Ma'am.' Peachie introduced himself with all the charm he could muster.

'Your nickname suits you,' she said with a raspy chuckle. 'Us girls will be off. Get your things, Elaina, and I'll give you a quick tour before you settle in. You'll start your shift at midday.'

Peachie nodded reassuringly to Elaina. While the layout of the land was being explained to him, Elaina deftly transferred her gear to the back of her new boss's vehicle.

'We don't often use our names in front of our employees, Elaina, so when it's just us girls in the kitchen, you call me Jody. Otherwise, just call me boss or ma'am.'

During the induction, Jody showed Elaina the gleaming professional kitchen. Jody was a chef by trade and wouldn't settle for anything except commercial-grade ovens, cook plates, tools of the trade and stainless-steel benches. The job entailed preparing, cooking, packaging and cleaning up after daily cooking expeditions of a varied menu. All the groceries were supplied.

If a new meal or sweet was going to be introduced, Jody would make the decision depending on the case put forward. She was happy with change as long as it had merit and was cost-effective. Aprons, gloves and hairnets were supplied and were to be worn. Laundry was the responsibility of the staff member, as was working out their own routine of standard housekeeping with the communal girls-only ablutions and appropriately fitted out laundry. A one-week trial was agreed upon. By the time Elaina had decided which room in the donga was hers, Jody had Darlene's contact details keyed into her phone.

'Okay, you know where the kitchen is and what I expect you to wear. See you at midday.'

'Thank you very much for opportunity, boss. I will do my best to learn from you and not let you down.'

Jody cocked her head. That was a very familiar saying. She'd taken an instant shine to the pretty girl with a funny way of speaking, impeccable manners and a desire to work. Best she had a word with her husband; the girl in the caravan might be starting sooner than anticipated.

Granny found her Sonny and Nova in the rose garden and watched the interaction with a tender smile. She had seen him grow from a troubled youngster into a wonderfully kind, brave man. His intelligence retrieval, strategic and marksmanship skill taking him away for years in dangerous territory. As sad as it was that he lost his unit in the awful explosion, she was relieved her plan had worked and he'd found a familiar soul in Spook.

Many years earlier, her confidant and soulmate, Reg Oscane, had followed through on his word and set up the initial meet with Alan White, aka Spook. Although no one had expected it to be so dramatic. A truck accident on the return leg to New South Wales after carting explosives to a mine site in Central Queensland had Reg pinned for hours. Granny had been talking to him while he'd been driving. The two-way channel set up could reach fifty square miles, with the aerial having a love affair with lightning on more than one occasion. The pair had been reminiscing about the early days playing in the rainforest with the other kids – all of whom had long since passed – when the front steering arm of the old International gave out as he crossed an old timber bridge. Granny had put out an emergency call. Spook had answered and stayed until the paramedics removed the severely injured man from his truck.

Unbeknown to Spook, Reg's stepbrother was in the same hotspot region of Afghanistan where her Sonny was stationed. The stepbrother, one never spoken about in mixed company, was a distant cousin to Spook's mother-in-law.

Granny's dearest school friend, Roslyn. A field nurse for an allied service, who had sent several encrypted telegrams informing Granny of perilously close warfare involving known soldiers. During the incursions, Granny thought it would be wise to have a private circle of contacts for support for whomever needed it the most. As it turned out, they all needed it at one stage or the other.

The dog tags of the stepbrother weren't the only ones her Sonny returned to their grieving loved ones. Roslyn's was the other set. By the time Tiny had left Special Ops, young in age yet old in experience, the bond between him and Spook had formed like concrete. Granny had been automatically welcomed into the fold several years later, while Reg kept doing what he was good at: making and dispersing money illegally and freely. The ownership of the B&B was only hers until she decided to retire. Then it was up to her to negotiate the proceeds so nobody would want for anything and no questions would be asked. Her late forbidden love, Reg Oscane, had made sure it would be an easy process.

Nova saw her first and bounded over to her, barking happily. She greeted the gentle-natured dog with the same happiness and strolled over to Sonny. He handed her a beautiful bouquet of perfumed roses, almost every colour of the rainbow, and smiled.

'Afternoon, Granny. Isn't it a great day to be alive?'

'Sonny, with you, every day is! These are extraordinary.' She buried her nose into the perfect blooms.

'I suppose you're going to tell me this is a good place to propose?' he asked with the mirth of a cheeky young boy.

'You'll know who, where and when! Now come along. I've been playing in your amazing kitchen.'

'I thought I could smell something delicious, and please do use everything as if it were your own! It's your home. But you must tell me, is your chalet spacious enough? Do you need anything?'

'It's ideal, and the verandah is perfect. But I have been thinking about something. Could we adopt an older dog? Nova needs a teacher, and she also needs to know how to be a dog. I was thinking a similar-sized breed, if not smaller, but not one that's going to cark it in six months. Not even I could handle that! Nova has to come too – she's got to choose her sister.'

Walking on the soft grass between the avenues of roses with his wonderful grandmother was a dream Tiny had had when he first planted them. Almost a decade ago. Now that it had come to fruition, he would do anything to keep her alive for a lot longer.

'I think that's a marvellous idea. Let's go and see what we can find over a cup of tea and whatever culinary delight you've created.'

'Oh, just my chocolate cake. I've missed it too,' she said with a mischievous giggle.

Milne and several other participants at the shooting range were in awe of Darlene's ability to strip down a weapon, clean it and rebuild it without fault, and weren't shy in staring. Not only had her ninety-nine-per-cent bullseye accuracy stopped them in their tracks, but being in her company was captivating. They hadn't realised who she was until she'd introduced herself to the lead marksman hosting the mock-competition shoot. A former SAS sniper. Although his eyes were haunted, his penetrating look of admiration was unquestionable during their conversation.

'I'd recruit you right now if you were available. Please call me Radar. I'm forming a team for the Olympics.'

He slipped her his card as he shook her hand, nodded formally and rounded up his team of admirers.

'How's that for an inspiration, guys?'

'Sir, yes, sir.'

Darlene smirked at the regimented response. Boy, did she have some thinking to do. Former SAS crack shot. Handy man to know. She was thinking of how she'd be able to rope him into taking out the creep who haunted her mind and dreams, purely because he hurt a girl that she had become a guardian to and may have possibly abducted a new friend's daughter.

'Ms Adams... come in, Ms Adams.' Milne persistently called out her name.

'Oh, pardon me. I was still in target mode.'

'I have a report to submit. May I contact you at noon tomorrow?'

'Yes, that'll be fine.'

'I would rather you consider my offer above all others. From what I've seen today, I want you on my team.'

'Thank you.' She returned the rifle to its casing and zipped it up confidently. 'Talk to you tomorrow. Good day.'

Her face was aching by the time she pulled the handbrake back at the retreat. She was still smiling as she unlocked the door to her suite. With her systematic routine decided on, she set about cleaning her weapons, playing with the telescopic sight and unpacking her suitcase. Then she'd have a beer, take a spa and a massage, and think about dinner. If only she could be with Tiny. He'd be in trouble. Instead, she sent him a message: *Hi Tiny, all's well. I have two job offers and E has secured a job. Hope you're all well there. D X*

Yeah, one kiss should do it, she thought and promptly took the top off an ice-cold beer.

Milly was absolutely exhausted. She'd collapsed into bed after putting away her laundry and hadn't even bothered to defrost a meal. Something wasn't right, even with the extra vitamins she'd been taking. Adding a slice of lemon to her water bottle, she drank over two litres and fell fast asleep. Screaming herself awake several hours later, the light was still on, but the two-way was squawking with calls for assistance. One of the night-loaders had foolishly got his foot caught shoving grain down the tube. The auger had just about ground it off completely. She opened her caravan door, but it was swiftly pushed shut.

'You just stay inside and lock your door, please. We don't need any other onlookers. Ambulance is on its way. Why were you screaming?'

'Just a shooting pain in my head, boss, but nothing like what's happening out there.'

Milly desperately tried to drown out the cries of pain by wrapping pillows about her head, until an eerie silence fell when he'd either passed out or been helped to pass out and the vehicles drove away. Milly presumed she was low on iron and boiled everything green she had in the fridge. The bulkiest of the lot were the kale and spinach while they were raw. They cooked down to nothing, and she ate the bland vegetable mix, cooled down the liquid and drank it. If it worked for Popeye, she hoped it'd work for her.

She couldn't sleep. She had to find a way to let Amy know she was okay. She'd written Amy's number out so many times in the dust, she could shut her eyes and see the digits. The shooting pain behind her right ear caused her to cry out.

'Oi! What's going on in there?' came a female's voice through the door. 'You should be alone in there, girl.'

Groaning loudly, she stumbled towards the door. 'I am alone. It feels like someone's stabbing my head from the inside.'

'You have to unlock the door right now.'

'Only you can come in, please.'

'That's correct.'

Milly fumbled with the lock, trying to hold her head to one side. Fighting back tears, she murmured, 'What's wrong with me? I'm so tired and feel so weak, and now there's this horrid pain. I've never been this sick, and I've never taken a day off in my whole life.'

A firm hand guided her to the edge of the bed. 'Tell me what you've been eating, drinking and taking.'

She dutifully described the past week's menu of healthy meals, the abundance of frozen fruit and copious amounts of water, including the sliced lemon, her most recent concoction of iron intake and a boost of vitamins.

'I have never used drugs, until they were forced upon me, but that hasn't been since...'

'Where have you been filling your water bottles from?'

'The rainwater tank behind the caravan. I didn't think the tap by the sheds was a good idea.'

'You been sniffing around there?'

'Curiosity got the better of me early the other morning after you left, yes. But then I watched the most amazing sunrise. The boss sprung me.'

'Girl, don't you be going to areas that have nothing to do with you. One rule of the farm is to do your job and mind your own business. Break that and you're history. Now, do not drink anything else tonight and try and sleep. You're not running a fever or anything, and your tongue isn't swollen. May be too much sun. Not sure. Either way, I believe I'm going to need you working for me sooner than later. Start at your post in the morning as per usual. I'll catch up with you during the day.'

Milly thanked the boss's wife and heard her acknowledge the door being locked from the inside before crawling into bed. She prayed silently. *Please let me wake up, God. I need to find my mother.*

CHAPTER FIFTEEN

Returning to the station, soon-to-be-retired Deputy Sergeant Troy Oscane was welcomed with an exciting breakthrough. A Port Pirie security officer had called in a peculiar maze of blocked and locked alleys upon attending a call-out at a small convenience store. The discovery was escalated to the police. After they had sent up a drone, it was discovered several sheds were concealed within the exterior concrete walls of a large commercial building. The height of the sheds was particularly unusual for a non-industrial area and conveniently hidden by elevated billboard advertising.

'Sir, they're setting up a bust for 5:00 a.m. tomorrow. Your counterpart down there is expecting your call,' Jan said and handed him a coffee.

By the time the OIC, Sergeant Paul Meyer, answered the call, Troy had a plan in mind.

'Hey, mate, DS Troy Oscane here. Just wondered if I could be of any assistance. Have three canines here that belonged to the late Reg Oscane...'

'Sorry for your loss, Troy. I'd heard the old man had passed.'

'Thanks, Sarge. We can talk about him another time. Listen, I've got a strong suspicion Max Chandler is involved in this.'

'The councillor? You're kidding me. He secured that massive deal at the marina years ago and boosted employment rates.'

'One and the same. Anyway, the dogs' current handler is an experienced officer of mine and she's been looking after them.'

'The more the merrier, I say. Just what do you expect to find?'

'A freshly painted prime mover, for one... and humans.'

'Trafficking?'

'Sex slaves.'

'Bastard.'

'Yep.'

'Can you get your officer, two additional personnel and the dogs down here by twenty-two hundred hours?'

'Yes, sir. I'll make the necessary arrangements right away.'

'Good. Uh, Troy, I'd rather you sat out on this one. Come down after lunch. Tell your crew there's a driveway to the right of the station, take it and park around the back. Come unmarked.'

'Copy that. Twenty-two hundred hours.'

Calling an instant meeting with Bev and his two oldest constables, Troy briefed them on what was to be expected for the next twenty-four hours. Automatically and as expected, Bev recommended that the three spend the rest of the day interacting with the Rottweilers and sleeping when they did. They'd be the dogs' handlers on-call and on site. With everyone in agreement, they'd reconvene at the station at 2000 hours sharp. Bev didn't leave the office and shut the door.

'Troy, I'm going to insist we wear tactical gear when we go in. I don't expect these perps to be heavily armed, but I'm not going to take any chances.'

'Good. Please just be damned careful, Bev. Take back-up weapons as well. I need you all to get home, and I need you to keep me apprised of the situation. If it's awkward, get Sergeant Meyer to make contact.'

Their eyes conveyed their love for each other.

'I'll see you with your crew later on this evening. Take my 4WD, please.'

She smirked. 'I was going to ask you for the keys!'

A knock on the door prevented the conversation from continuing. Bev opened it, turned and caught the airborne bundle of car keys. 'Thanks, boss. We'll see you tonight, twenty hundred hours sharp.'

Troy took the opportunity of a quiet office to return several phone calls. His senior counterpart at the Alice was the first one on the list. He had to keep himself busy for a long time.

'Sir, I'm back in the office today. What can I do for you?'

'Thanks for calling me back, Oscane. A while back, you collected two girls from Coober Pedy, yes?'

'That's correct.'

'My lot recently picked up a young fella almost deranged, meandering through the scrub near the western border. A couple of ringers found him. About twelve, half-caste. He's recovering in hospital, had to go through one hell of a detox session, but the nightmares? In all my years of active service, I don't believe I've seen what this kid's experienced or suffered.'

'Any family?'

'He can't recall. Although, he's quite coherent at times, repeatedly talks about a big rig, ugly beast, some sisters having to leave the cab then blanks out. Troy, his eyes are pained. I don't know how else to describe it, but the poor little blighter has the eyes of an old war veteran who survived the cruellest of prison camps.'

'Geez, that's one hell of a comparison.'

'I've seen eyes like that. Grew up with my granddad...'

'I am sorry for you. That wouldn't have been easy for anybody.'

'No, it wasn't, but it was certainly memorable. Listen, I'm sending down a sketch of the truck. Can I leave it up to you to see if anybody recognises it?'

'I can do my best. Have a bit going on over the next thirty-six hours.'

'Delegate, Deputy Sergeant. You have to learn to delegate.'

'Yes, sir. Thanks for the timely reminder. By all means, send it through, and I'll action it accordingly. One of my colleagues will get back to you at the earliest opportunity.'

'Appreciate that. By the way, I'm seriously considering retiring and leaving the dust bowl for some salty air.'

'I'll congratulate you now, sir, and thank you for your contribution. We have many things in common. I'll race you!'

'What? You thinking of doing the same?'

'Absolutely!'

'Okay. The first one to retire buys the other a drink. Done?'

'Deal.'

Troy respectfully waited until the senior officer had hung up before doing the same. Jan knocked on the door, waving a printout, then darted back out to attend to the ringing telephone. Using his personal mobile, he took a photo of the sketch-artist's impression of the truck in question for future reference, attached a note to the original document then left it in Jan's tray. Emptying the carton of taped telephone calls onto his desk, he finally found the one Bev had made of Cassie's initial conversation with her aunt. Shoving it hastily into the recorder, he replayed it, re-recorded it as a .WAV file and e-mailed the relevant information to his counterpart. Immediately, a reply was received with a short response: *The race has begun!*

Milly had finished sweeping and shovelling the spilled grain around her area and unscrewed the cap of the sparkling mineral water. Putting it to her lips, her eyes welled up with tears. She had nearly cried with joy when she opened the caravan door several hours earlier and a carton of the stuff was on the step with a note telling her to drink as much as she could, without being uncomfortable doing her job. It was her first opportunity to have a break.

The grain had been transferred to the out-load silos with sufficient quantity for another thirty trailers. As she annotated the approximate tonnage on the clipboard and initialled beside the transfer, her two-way crackled to life, announcing a series of trucks rolling into the yard. She was ready and waiting. The boss man and his wife pulled up simultaneously from opposite directions.

Laughing loudly and waving with each hand, she looked between the pair of them and said, 'Is this an ambush?'

Their genuine amusement buoyed her disposition. She'd been feeling a bit stronger, but the prolonged dizzy spell during the night had been very scary. The husband-and-wife team conferred privately on their mobile phones. Milly watched as her male boss nodded to her and smiled, then promptly drove away. His wife stepped out of her vehicle and approached Milly.

'This is what's going to happen. You're being relegated to me as my employee. I know there are trucks coming through shortly – how quickly can you pack your stuff?'

'Very quickly, ma'am. The laundry is up to date, and I don't have a lot of belongings, as you saw. More food than anything.'

'Right. Off you go, and pack swiftly. Take your vitamins but leave the rest. The driver is returning tonight. You'll be with me until the end of harvest. Go now. The replacement doesn't need to see you. I'll reposition my car, and the trucks will also block all visual to your accommodation.'

'Yes, ma'am. Thank you. Will you please thank your husband for me? I'll work out a way to repay you both.'

She smiled and said kindly, 'Run along, now. I'll wait for you in the car.'

On the way to the main house, Jody explicitly described the food preparation role she was expecting Milly to fulfil. She'd work the midnight to midday shift, as the other shift was already covered. This would free up Jody to run her business in the manner it was designed to be. Milly was to share the donga with one other woman, with the strictest of rules. No visitors. No parties. No loud noise. Milly sighed loudly with relief and didn't miss Jody's grin.

'You will have twenty-four hours off in one block every five days, but I'm afraid you're farm-bound. There's a covered courtyard strictly for my kitchen staff to enjoy. Feel free to pull out any weeds and grow what you like, as long as it's legal. But you plant it, you tend to it. If it's still alive when harvest is finished...'

'I will leave it for you,' Milly said.

They exchanged a look of understanding. Jody explained the wet room consisted of two ensuites either side of the laundry. She had no intention of hiring another girl for the harvest and made no bones about hoping the two would work well together. They would all meet three times a week to resolve any issues and discuss improvements. Jody explained she wanted her kitchen to be the role model for the other farms providing satellite sites for the grower's co-op. Jody parked outside the dongas and left the engine idling. The air conditioning was beautiful.

'May I ask what the other girl's name is?'

'Funny! She asked what yours was, so I'll tell you exactly what I told her. You can wait until you meet each other. Which will be in about forty minutes. By the way, what is your name?'

'Milly...'

'Short for Millicent?'

Blushing profusely and failing to prevent her eyes from welling up, she nodded. 'Yes, but I haven't been called that for a very long time.'

'It's okay, Milly. I'm not about to go back in time. Off you go – choose your room, unpack, and when you meet your colleague, you girls can work out the rest of your living quarters. Freshen up. There's a new uniform which should fit you, including an apron and bandana, on the kitchen bench. I took a guess at the shoes. They're new. We'll make a plan if they don't fit. See you in the kitchen.'

'Yes, ma'am. Thank you so much.'

Their smiles mirrored the genuine happiness they conveyed to each other. Milly collected her meagre belongings and stepped inside the bright, clean, cool donga. Pretty sunflowers, although artificial, stood proudly in the corner, in a tall vase full of coloured glass pebbles. The chairs were hardy, retro and all different colours. Automatically understanding the closed door was not hers to enter, she chose the one on the other side of the middle room. Privacy was so important to Milly. The sliding mirrored wardrobe was the first she'd ever seen of its kind, and the king-size single covered in a pastel floral doona was extremely comfortable. She felt spoilt for the first time in her adult life and horribly alone because she couldn't share her discoveries with anyone.

The checked pants and grey shirt fitted nicely, but the shoes were a tad big. Stuffing papers into the toes was the quickest fix she could come up. Neatly pulling her hair into a bun, she slipped on the hair net and felt like she was back in the restaurant at home, except this apron was full-bodied. She tied a clean scarf around her neck. Suddenly, she was embarrassed by her tattoo.

Striding confidently towards the kitchen, she knocked on the heavy door before pushing it open. Leaning against and closing it at the same time, she stared at the stainless-steel benches, the free space, the wall of fridges and upright freezers, the series of ovens and the largest hot plate known to man and grinned. Now this was a kitchen!

'You're early, as expected. I see it meets with your approval, young lady?' Jody stepped out from the pantry with a beautiful and tall woman behind her.

The two grinned at each other as they walked with their hands extended. 'Hi, I'm Elaina. How'd you get your hair so neat?'

'Hi, I'm Milly. I'll show you sometime. Love your accent!'

'And I'm Jody, in our kitchen only. Anywhere else, I am ma'am or boss. Pleased to have you both in my company. We have a lot to do. Meat sauce for the spaghetti takes a lot of preparation. Milly, I'll leave that with you. The recipe is in the folder. Behind me is the pantry. Everything you need is in a logical place. You'll be on for two hours, then go and organise yourself. You'll be back here at 11:30 p.m. You pair will be like ships in the night, but you will have the opportunity to natter in your free time.'

Jody handed Milly the three-kilogram bag of onions and guided her to her workbench.

'Hope you don't cry like I do when I cut those things!' Elaina called out with a giggle.

'Not if you put a bowl of water in front of them.'

'Crap. Why didn't you start last week?'

The three ladies had a good laugh, then got stuck into the job at hand like it was an automatic transition. Jody had never felt so relieved in her life. *This might just work*, she told herself.

Wrapping a towel around herself after a swim, Darlene grinned as she read the text from Cassie: *Counting the days to Christmas... wherever! XX*. Replying automatically, she typed: *So am I XX*. Feeling quite enthusiastic about the time leading up to it, too, she video-called her parents and put them on speaker.

'You do care!' Her mother spoke quickly. 'Nice to hear from you, Darlene. Are you well?'

'I've never stopped caring, Mum. Yes, thanks, how are you? Dad?'

After the obligatory pleasantries, she listened to the endless complaints about how busy everyone was, as well as so far away, and how Christmas couldn't come quick enough. The weekly calls from Cassie were the highlight, but they were both desperate to find a new hobby. Golf was becoming a chore, and the buggy was getting expensive to repair.

'How about lawn bowls? I remember as a kid, you guys were always playing carpet bowls with your friends. It sounded so much fun. I'm willing to bet there's a sports club nearby. Go out for lunch today, check it out. You're free agents, please yourselves. Live!'

'You are full of ideas!'

'Dad! They're good ideas. If I was your age and without commitments, I'd hardly be home. It's not as if you still have acres of land to maintain.'

'You don't have a home, Darlene.'

The blunt reminder made her scoff lightly. 'Sure, I do, Mum. Wherever I lay my head. Then I'll know where I want to be.'

'Are you still chasing those darn platypus and dreaming away the days?'

Tears welled up in her eyes. 'You have no idea, but yes, still Darlene the Dreamer and not about to change. Just getting wiser the more I grow up.'

'Oh, wait there... the postie has stopped by.'

'Nice! Hope it's everything you've been waiting for. I must fly, too. Have a great day. Love you both, bye.'

'Yes, bye, thanks for calling.'

Her mother's voice faded away, then a long pause.

'You still there, pet?'

'Sure, Dad, but I have a meeting at midday I need to prepare for and don't want to hold you up, either.'

'I long for the day where you and I can sit down and have an uninterrupted conversation.'

'Same here. It'll come. What's been decided for New Year's Day?'

'Can't talk about it right now, take care. Love you lots.'

Darlene was staring at the blank screen. They hadn't accepted the video call. Feeling a tad deflated, she dove into the pool and managed eight more laps. The sun lounge was so tempting, as was the fruit punch on offer. Shoving all thoughts of everything and everyone out of her mind, she switched off her phone and meditated for twenty minutes.

The delicate wind chimes hanging underneath the big umbrella played their melody as a gentle breeze brought the heavenly scent of jasmine with it. Having the entire area to herself, she idled away the time watching the silent clock on the wall tick away until almost midday then reactivated the phone. She had a few questions of her own, and if they weren't satisfactorily answered, she'd decline Milne's job offer and find something else to do.

Gavin Milne badly wanted to be in Darlene Adam's company on a permanent basis. He had kicked himself ever since leaving the café that he hadn't tagged her vehicle. It was the only one in the carpark with Queensland number plates. The woman had gotten under his skin, in his mind, and he was determined to have her work for him. Side by side for at least nine weeks. He'd push the relationship boundary hard and fast in his usual manner. But this time, he was going to succeed. He liked strong women who played games. So far, she was his favourite.

A sly grin formed as he dialled her number. Engaged? What in the hell? Every thirty seconds, he hit redial, only to hear the engaged signal. Thumping the desk harder each time, he was about to explode when he finally got through at 11:59 a.m.

'I've been trying to reach you for ages,' he shouted into the telephone.

'And you've finally succeeded.'

Her calm, quick retort caught him completely unaware and shut him up instantly. Fuming inside, he tried to recover with humour.

'I just wanted to be early, Ms Adams.'

'You are, almost by a minute. Can we begin the meeting, please? I've got quite a busy schedule this afternoon.'

He imagined her wearing white linen slacks with a navy-blue camisole and matching white silky blouse and stilettos. Getting hard at the thought, he rubbed himself and coughed.

'Uh... of course. I'd like to offer you a three-month contract, to be reviewed after six weeks. Your accommodation will be attached to my mobile quarters, a cook will provide the meals and you will travel with me in my vehicle. There will be night shoots, and we will have every eighth day off for essentials and a bit of R and R.'

'Carry on.'

'You'll be paid for every hit, deducted for every miss unless the dart is recovered. With your accuracy levels, I've increased the remuneration and anticipate you'll be earning about two grand a day. That's a pretty penny for a pretty lady in a pretty remote area!'

He laughed at his own joke and was annoyed when he didn't hear hers.

'I don't particularly like the accommodation arrangements. I travel alone. I sleep alone. I eat alone. I shoot alone.'

'Not happening.'

'Find someone else then. Goodbye.' She hung up.

His hand smashed down on the table with such force, his cat shrieked as it flew off the table and dived through the ground-floor office window. *How dare she? Where is she staying? Did she say where she was staying? Nobody refuses me like that and gets away with it. Nobody.* Milne furiously redialled Darlene's number, and she answered just as it was about to go to message bank.

'Yes?'

'I think there's been a misunderstanding. You will take this job. I need you to take this job. I've already committed thousands of dollars to get this research project underway. I am relying on you–'

'You assumed I would take it, Mr Milne. Your third mistake. Others were not discussing the arrangements with me, then expecting me to accept said arrangements willingly. I politely decline this offer and would prefer it if you did not contact me again. For the last time, goodbye.'

'You bitch,' he screamed into the phone, 'You absolute conniving bitch. Do you know who I am?'

'Yes, I do. A very rude man who has just made it onto my B list. Gavin Milne, I formally advise you that our phone conversations have been recorded. Have a good day.'

The mobile phone shattered into a million pieces as it slammed against the wall, along with just about every item on his desk. When he finally caught his breath, he stabbed at the keypad on his laptop and entered the digits into his illegally acquired track and trace software. Her number was untraceable. He flew into a violent rage and drove his fist through the external monitor attached to his laptop.

He had to find her. He would return to Albany and ask questions. That fat truck driver. He'd find him and grill him until he was charred.

Perth to Albany was a bloody long way to go, and he was in no mood to drive that distance. Snorting his relaxant, he cranked up the volume of the grunge music, lay down on the plush carpet behind his desk and admired himself in the ceiling mirror. He didn't care the thumping bass would drive his neighbour mad.

Darlene's face was flushed. She'd been yelled at and called much ruder names before but never with such vehemence. She removed the SIM card from the phone, slipped it into her sunglasses case and returned to her suite. Oh, how she wished she was tucked away in her sleepy little rainforest. Robotically showering and changing into her baggy clothes, she grabbed the big hat off its post and went into town.

Purchasing two cheap mobile phones, a blue and a black one, then adding sufficient credit to both using the prepaid options, she found a telephone booth inside the post office. What a novelty! It had been years since she'd used one. Dialling Peachie's number, she prayed it wasn't inconvenient.

'Have you got the wrong number?' Peachie answered.

Almost in a whisper, she said, 'Oh, hi, Peachie. It's Darlene Adams. Um... things went awry with Milne. Hence the change of number. Please don't ever have anything to do with him. I actually think he's dangerous.'

'Tell me all about it. I've got several trucks in front of me, and I couldn't think of a better way to pass the time! But first, promise me you are nowhere near him and you are okay.'

She assured him of her well-being, described the cute little telephone booth and her unsuspecting attire. He congratulated her on deactivating her mobile. He would do the honours and contact Spook and Tiny for her without disclosing the situation, instead saying she was out of range with the harvest and the old phone didn't have coverage. It was easier to get a new number. Neither wanted to highlight their scheming. Elaina needed to hear from her directly, as did several others. They were in agreement with that.

'What happened at the shooting range?'

'Oh, I think I'm liking the long barrel more and more now.'

Chuckling deeply, Peachie asked, 'So, what are you going to do?'

'A former SAS guy was recruiting candidates for an Olympic team at the same time. He offered me a job. I'll tee up a chat soon... at the range.'

'Pretty safe place!'

'Yeah.'

'And if that doesn't tick the boxes?'

'I've got plenty of time to find this freaky creep and hopefully another girl that's missing. Might see if Elaina's place of employment needs an errand girl. At best, I'll be useful and out of everyone's hair while seeing who's also around the traps!'

'You want me to make enquiries?'

'Please. I'd prefer to avoid working with men this time around, if you don't mind me saying so.'

'Totally understandable. Tiny and Spook would be relieved too!'

'Peachie, they're friends, not my guardians!'

'I've got to roll on to the grid. Take care, Darlene, and stay in touch as often as you like.'

'Thanks.'

She smiled at his genuine kindness and waited for him to disconnect the call.

Thumbing through the local directory, she took a photo of the address of the shop she wanted to see. Time to go shopping for one more item. A long barrel and portable telescopic sight.

As evening fell, she had dismantled, cleaned and rebuilt the .22 rifle several times. Putting it away in its new case, she e-mailed the president of the range and submitted the appropriate 'permit to carry' form, along with the message that she'd be a visitor again the following day, and requested a private meeting.

Leaving a message for Radar, she explained she was available to discuss job options and detailed her immediate availability.

Afterwards, she stood in the kitchen and diced up all the ingredients for a chicken curry while sipping on an ice-cold beer. Then the arduous task of keying contact details into the blue phone. The black one was purely her 'Just in Case' phone. Halfway through the second beer was message-sending time. To Cassie, Elaina, Asta, Bev and Amy she sent a simple text:

New phone. All's well. See you with bells on. Darlene Adams XX

She knew darned well they'd all pass the information on to Deputy Sergeant Troy Oscane.

Her parents and siblings received a slightly newsier message without saying too much:

Hi Family, all's well over here in the wild west. Sunbaking, swimming and looking for work, not necessarily in that order! My new phone number for you to add to your contacts. Mobile coverage not the best everywhere. Keep well, love you all. Darlene the Dreamer XX

Lunchtime after the early morning raid and its disappointing outcome, Bev and the two constables were seated around the boardroom table with the three dogs asleep at their feet. The darkened room with its massive blank investigation board was the ideal place to watch the team lead's body cam footage. Troy was leaning up against the opposite wall, sipping a black coffee.

The fake shop facade at the rear of the building concealed a driveway and massive half-shed. It was obvious it had once housed another prime mover with its black-widow-spider decorative concrete pad. Along the wall, a not-so-obvious passenger access door opened outwards. Directly in front of that entrance was the outline of a prime mover which loomed behind thick plastic curtains. There wasn't much clearance between the exhaust stacks and the mezzanine floor, but there was obvious evidence that the rig used to be purple. Whoever had been stripping it back hadn't gotten around to behind the sleeper cab. The ugliness of the colour represented the ugliness of the truck driver's reputation. The massive shed doors behind the tail lights slid back silently. It was a very tight fit.

Troy sucked in his breath. He hadn't been privy to the debrief. Bev had insisted he see how the dogs behaved when they picked up Max's scent.

'Boss, pay attention now. Check out these dogs!'

He watched the video intently. All three dogs had suddenly dropped to their haunches and whimpered as they crawled along the furthest wall, behind a row of substantial toolboxes, which led into a dimly lit hallway. Together, they sat in front of an extremely detailed trucking and marine mural that filled the entire wall. One at a time, they'd nose the wheel of the truck then scratch at the bottom of the vessel's hull, bark twice and stare halfway up the wall. They repeated this several times then barked liked they were possessed.

Bev paused the video and said, 'We eventually managed to settle them down and get them out of there. At least we know why the purple rig hasn't been seen. But there's no sign of any women, boss.'

'Not an obvious sign, no, but clearly there's something behind that mural. The dogs were showing us that. Did anyone investigate further?'

'No. They canned it at daybreak. There was a disturbance down at the marina which took nearly all their resources. Some woman went ballistic with a Stillson pipe wrench. We were stood down for essential rest. What's on your mind?'

'Officer Bev, we need to get back into this shed. Can you organise an escort immediately, please? And you guys, get me information on that marina incident. What's this woman's name, where's she being held? I want to interview her. Leave the dogs and their treats with me.'

'Yes, sir. Onto it.'

He closed the door behind them, slipped on a pair of headphones and replayed the audio component of the recording. He was sure there was another sound drowned out by the barking dogs. Slowing down the sound waves, he listened carefully. There! A definite spike. Watching the video at the same slow speed, the peculiar sound in correlation to the dogs' incessant barking was instantaneous. Troy rewound the video and hit pause. He removed the headphones and got the dogs' attention with some liver treats. He stood in front of the screen displaying the static mural, poured several treats in his hand then dragged it halfway up the image. The dogs watched and waited obediently. A soft rap on the door didn't distract them.

'Come in.' A slight pause. 'Paul, you're going to need to see this. Please take a seat. But I think we need to get back to the site in question ASAP.'

'Go ahead, Troy, but what's that stench?'

'Liver treats for the dogs, Sarge.'

He ignored the grunt of disgust and explained the scenario, then replayed the tape at normal speed with volume. The dogs were on their feet immediately. Initially, they were confused that they could see other dogs but couldn't smell them, then their focus was on the treats. They watched the amplified video, unsure of what to do. On the fifth replay, they copied their own behaviour and growled softly when they heard the barking. Troy then cut the audio, rewound the video and replayed it. The dogs behaved exactly the same way but cocked their heads and put their paws halfway up the screen when they couldn't hear the barking.

'I'm now going to kill the visual. We're familiar with what happens. There is a loud foreign noise just before the dogs go crazy. It's minuscule, but it's there. I'll project the sound waves and pause when it peaks, replay it twice, then put it all together. It'll be interesting to see how the dogs behave.'

'Go ahead.'

Troy commenced the exercise. He was just about to replay the whole recording when Paul stopped him.

'Mate, you haven't been watching the dogs' reactions. They're ready to play the game. I suggest we don't wait any longer. Let's take these boys, your three colleagues and four of mine right now. I concur. There is something behind that picture.'

Cordoning off access to the entire block, they proceeded to enter the shed, except this time, the dogs led the way. They immediately went to the large mural, stood on their back legs and pawed halfway up. One of the local constables removed a listening device from his backpack, gently eased his way between the dogs and positioned it where they'd started scratching at the wall. It took a lot of encouragement to get them to stop.

'Sir, there are very faint but unfamiliar sounds back there. They're muffled, intermittent...?' He beckoned his boss to confirm his reasoning.

'Get in there,' Meyer commanded shortly afterwards.

All hands felt along the imaged wall. The dogs kept returning to the one section and ended up squabbling amongst themselves out of frustration. Bev took control and led them away from the wall.

'Enough,' she said, just loud enough for everyone to know she meant business. 'Sit. Stay.'

She walked one dog at a time back to the wall, gave him a treat then made him follow another one with his nose. Marking the wall with chalk when he let the treat get further away, she walked him away, gave him another treat and repeated the action with the two other dogs. All three behaved the same way. Nobody could feel anything unusual in the marked spot. No recess nor keyway. But it was obvious that was where whoever opened the door appeared, and must have for a very long time for the dogs to be so familiar with it. Troy began to wonder how often Max had actually taken Reg's dogs away from the yard. He didn't want to think of why.

'Get me that drone image,' Sergeant Meyer demanded. 'DS Oscane, would it be conceivable for that loud sound to be a heavy door?'

Troy scratched his head. 'It's possible, sir.'

'Right, I want to see another aerial shot of the area. Now.'

Bev had the electronic notepad with the imagery on the screen at the ready and handed it to him. 'Sir, from what we learnt, the street-facing walls are solid, except for the fake facade, which was how we entered the premises. The barbed-wire gate led to another dead end. This has to be an access point. If the peak in the sound waves was a door slamming, there was definitely someone here. But there aren't obvious surveillance cameras, nor sensors for a tip-off. I'm suspecting it was the woman who caused the scene at the marina. It's too coincidental to not be associated, but who is she?'

One of Oscane's constables had been shining a torchlight over the mural at different angles. He marvelled at the artist's deception loudly.

'Hey, check this out. Whoever painted this was way out there or sick in the head. Don't reckon even Salvador Dalí was this weird.'

'Voice your vision, Constable,' the sergeant encouraged.

'Yes, sir. From behind the truck's outline are spindly tendrils crawling over the cab. In the wake of the container ship, there's an octopus with the head of an arachnid, a sea urchin which is wearing a judge's curly wig, an ugly mermaid with a crooked nose wearing a pointed hat, seahorses with dog heads, a king smoking a cigar waving a conductor's wand, and if you peer closely at the porthole, you can make out a picture like a Roman orgy.'

Troy took a deep, shuddering breath. He felt so ashamed he knew who each one represented, but perplexed about the mermaid depicted as a witch.

'I need some fresh air. I'm feeling claustrophobic,' he said quietly.

Staggering outside, he leaned against the cool concrete wall, closed his eyes and tilted his head backwards. Imagining having a conversation with the ghost of Reg Oscane, he waited for the epiphany to come. Eventually, it did. Everything fell into place. Max was the local legend who secured the contract at the marina to which he was bringing in drugs and the illicit tobacco. He and Stevo swung both ways in their sexual preferences and both loved their drugs just as much. Spider, aka Graham, the abductor who drove the trucks, brought back empty trailers or was only ever seen in just the prime mover. And Reg Oscane? The conductor with his beloved dogs.

But how to get into that back room? It couldn't be that difficult. These were cunning but lazy crooks. They all had liked the same thing – what was it? Money? Driving? It wasn't drugs. Reg did not like drugs. Nor did he approve of derogatory behaviour. It came back to money or driving.

In a flash, Troy saw a ship's wheel. *Steering the wheel. That's it!* He snapped his fingers and raced back inside.

'Where's the ship's wheel? Can we see a ship's wheel?' he asked enthusiastically.

They all studied the mural. Nothing. Troy stood back several metres from the picture and scanned every inch. His eyes rested on the area where Bev had marked the dogs' interest. Those weren't the sun's rays disappearing into the horizon. The image within the image was incredible. The close-up viewer would easily see the obvious, but standing back and focusing on one thing, the viewer was looking out from a ship's steering room. Troy could make out the massive window frame with water droplets from the waves that it was carving through. He moved slightly to the right and put his hand out. It practically rested on the top quadrant of the ship's wheel. The perspective was genius.

With that image in Troy's mind, he asked for space and walked towards the wall. His right hand resting on the handle, he pressed the spindle with his left. The marked area on the image. A distinctive click was heard. Instantly, the dogs were sitting with their tails wagging around his feet. The wall slowly came ajar following the curved line of the window frame. Using their noses, the dogs forced their way in, then immediately walked backwards, growling and snarling quietly.

With guns drawn, Bev held the dogs back as the door opened wider. The minute they stepped inside, five sensor lights flooded the room. Lying on the floor with his hairy back to them was a semi-naked man with tubing around his upper arm, two boys cowering against the far wall, facing him with a shotgun lying between them. The smell of gunpowder still hung in the air.

'Don't move,' Sergeant Meyer commanded.

'He won't anymore,' said a timid voice. 'He can't.'

The two senior officers approached the body to discover the front of the man's face blown away. Troy recognised Stevo instantly by the tattoo of a ruby covering his shoulder.

'Get them away from this view,' Meyer hissed.

Bev raced over to the boys. 'Are you hurt?' She commanded the dogs to be gentle.

'Not this time, but can we play with the dogs, please?' the tall, blonde-haired boy asked quietly.

'Be gentle, they're still learning. Let's get you out of here.'

'Yes, please. We hate this place... so do they. We couldn't see anything after the lights went out. We didn't do it. We didn't. We promise.'

'It's okay, lads, it's okay, we believe you. But who is *they*?' Bev spoke kindly to them as she squatted down to their eye level.

'The ones down in the cellar. We can show you.' The little boy had the deepest blue eyes she'd ever seen.

Bev took one of their hands in each of hers and stood up with them. 'Did you want to lead the way, or just point?'

'No, we'll have to show you. It's weird, but I'll lead the way,' the taller boy said bravely.

The boys counted to twenty out loud as they walked around a wall that curved to the right, then with each step, recited the phonetic alphabet. Stopping at 'Papa', the taller boy gave the shorter one a leg up, and he felt up the wall.

'Please don't turn on a light,' the shorter one said. 'It's too blinding, and it's scary. It's like a cave...'

'And there are sixteen steps. Can the dogs come too?' the other one asked.

'Yes, they're here. Shall we adults go inside first, do you think?' Bev suggested calmly.

'No, we can. The witch left through the heavy door long after she shot the man. We thought we could hear dogs, but...'

'It's okay. One thing at a time. You boys are being so brave. You're going to be heroes.'

Another distinctive click, and suddenly, a hidden door slid to the left, revealing soft purple lights along a stairwell, which simplified the descent.

'Wait,' one boy said very quietly. 'You adults have to talk in a whisper, but only us two can talk together from the twelfth stair. That way they'll know it's just us.'

'Have you boys done this before?' Bev whispered.

'Yes, a lot of times, to give them water.'

'You ready?' the other one asked.

'Yes,' several adults whispered in reply.

They silently walked down the stairs, listening to the little boys' soft counting. On the twelfth step, the boys spoke in perfect harmony as they continued down the stairs.

'It's us.'

Then, in a timid voice, one of them said, 'Um... you talk, Robbie.'

'Okay, Tommy. We brought better things than water today. Some police and some nice dogs. Close your eyes, we need to put the lights on. Remember to open them slowly.'

Urgent, muffled sounds of sobbing erupted.

'Lights are going on now,' the boys said together in a normal voice.

'Oh, God,' the officers said in varied tones of shock as they rushed to help the seventeen gagged captives dressed in a variety of dancing costumes with their hands tied behind their backs.

The boys helped by unsealing and handing out the supply of water bottles that were stashed in the cabinet as the hands and mouths were freed. Radio back-up was called, as well as several ambulances and extra paramedics, with instructions to set up an extended roadblock.

'Where's my mum? There should be eighteen of us. Where's my mum?' A tearful lad of about eleven years old urgently called out for her. 'Mum, Mum, it's okay. Come out, Mum. Mum?'

Bev gathered him in her arms. 'Talk to us, son.'

'The witch was here last night. The sicko was here four days ago. The other sicko hung around upstairs. I could hear my mum crying last night, but she started dragging herself away. Then I couldn't hear her.' He buried his face into Bev's shoulder and sobbed his little heart out.

'We'll do everything we can to find her.' She clicked her tongue and one of the dogs crawled on his belly towards them, gently nuzzled the boy's hand and nudged him until he sat down. He pulled out a pretty handkerchief and shoved it into the dog's nose.

'Fetch,' he murmured and crawled alongside the dog. 'I seen it on TV. Hope it works.'

In an instant, the other two dogs were following suit. Robbie and Tommy weren't missing out on anything and joined in the search. Bev supervised silently while her colleagues attended to the women, who they guessed were aged between nineteen and thirty. Some Australian, a few Danish, but mainly Russian.

'Ladies, I'm Sergeant Meyer. We're going to get you out of here, but we need your names and next of kin details, please. Medical transport is on its way, including translators. Your well-being is our absolute priority. Your statements will be taken over the course of the next few days—'

The caring spiel was interrupted with pained yells of help. Troy hadn't heard Bev's voice in the calamity and desperately followed the sounds. Pushing through the dense carpeted wall one of the dogs was standing beside, he saw her desperately performing CPR. There was a lot of blood. The woman on the floor had miscarried.

'Lads, stand aside with the dogs, please—'

'Priority one. Faint pulse. Aviation medevac,' Bev instructed at each decompression. 'Towels. Blankets. Anything. Water. Now.'

The boy gripped his mother's hand tightly and begged for her to stay alive while the radio calls were dispatched. Robbie and Tommy raced back and forth with water bottles and anything that resembled a clean towel and stood patting their new friend's shoulder gently.

'Teach me.' He looked at Bev imploringly. 'Teach me how to do that. I want to try and save my mum too.'

There was a deep-set anger in the boy's eyes. He wanted revenge, but he needed his mum. Bev relented and gave an urgent lesson in cardiopulmonary resuscitation to three eager participants. They were still taking turns when the paramedics finally arrived. Bev restored the woman's dignity while the boys persisted with their new skill. Her pulse remained awfully weak.

'Ma'am, we have to take her now. Right now,' the aviation paramedic insisted.

'Copy that. Take her son too. He's been here with her the whole time.'

The first responders shared the same look of dismay then swiftly returned to their professional posts. 'Yes, ma'am.'

Troy encouraged Robbie and Tommy to stand out of the way, impressed by Bev's control of the situation.

'I need to know which hospital, and I want regular updates. It is critical you keep me informed. I'll inform dispatch of my details.'

'Yes, ma'am.'

She reached over to the lad. 'Son, we can walk with you to the helicopter. You'll be going with your mum. Did you have mobiles or wallets? Clothes?'

'Don't know where they are.' He tugged on the paramedic's arm. 'Mister, will my mum...?'

'If we go now, she'll have a better chance of staying alive.'

'DS Oscane, you look after those two,' Sergeant Meyer said authoritatively. 'I'll accompany this lad; you do what you do best down here, Officer Bev. Find everything you can that belongs to these poor souls. We'll catch up later.'

Meyer shook her hand and spoke with confidence to the boys. 'You said the witch left through the heavy door. How about you lead the way? It might get us to the chopper quicker.'

'Sure thing! Can we go with?' Robbie and Tommy asked together.

The co-pilot smiled as they secured the woman onto the gurney. 'Lads, we would love to give you your own personal flight after. Maybe the police lady can make that happen. You three brave young men are going to be mates for life. Now, we must go. Son, you can ride with your mum on the way to the helicopter once we're upstairs. You two lads, walk close to your policeman and listen to what he says. Let's go.'

'Yes, sir!' all three lads replied.

After navigating the way out, Sergeant Meyer and his senior constable, Jack, escorted the lads, behind the medevac personnel, through the heavy door. A container door. The young boys stood wide-eyed between the senior officers, staring at the helicopter, covering their ears with their hands. Everyone watched in awe as the lad and his poorly mum were strapped tightly together to the gurney, which was clipped to a winch. They shielded their eyes and saluted or waved at the pilot as the helicopter lifted off.

'DS Oscane has to talk to my boss now, so come with me, lads,' Jack said encouragingly and pivoted them towards the door. 'You need to be with the ones you also saved. We go straight downstairs, please.'

'Yes, sir.'

Troy nodded his appreciation, shook hands with the lads then followed Paul to the forensic team.

Bev had taken the dogs back through to the women and offered as much assistance as possible.

'Over here,' the local constable called out.

One side of a rather large, ambiguous piece of furniture housed a secret wardrobe which contained an abundance of sex toys, dress-up costumes, drug paraphernalia and a lot of Pepsi. The other shelves contained neat rows of purses, handbags, mobile phones, shoes and either folded or hanging normal clothes. After the victims were helped to their feet, they rushed for the wardrobe, frantically disrobed and got dressed in their own clothes. The costumes were swiftly bagged and removed. One pretty floral maternity dress, beige sandals and a matching handbag were left in the wardrobe. They were respectfully bagged. Everyone knew it belonged to the woman on board the helicopter.

The slow, sorrowful process of guiding the victims up the stairs brought about delayed anguish, terror and rage. It was with huge relief that the body was covered by a cloth-draped timber crate and the shotgun removed. Forensics discreetly stood with their backs to the procession as the victims were guided towards the sunshine through the winding maze.

'Thank you for your support, Paul,' Troy said as they stood in the background. 'Let's pray that lady survives and they all get through this ordeal. Please ensure they and your staff have counselling at their beck and call. Reach out if you need extra funding or assistance from my region.'

Additional female officers had arrived and comforted the victims while accompanying them in several ambulances. The two boys were assisted into another, along with a social worker and a local policewoman. Sufficient personnel were already stationed at the hospitals in preparation for the media vultures.

Watching the last ambulance disappear around the corner, Meyer took Troy aside.

'You recognise the deceased?'

'Max Chandler's son, Stevo. Him and his brother grew up believing someone else was their father.'

'Reg?'

'Correct.'

'He was too much of a gentleman to treat people like this.'

'Exactly.'

'The other son?'

'Graham, aka Spider. The usual driver of the once-purple rig. Gone to ground. Will crawl out eventually. You've got enough on your hands, Paul. We'll let your team run with this particular investigation. It's your jurisdiction.'

They shook hands, nodded to each other's remaining personnel respectfully and went their separate ways.

'Officer Bev?' Sergeant Meyer called out. 'Consider getting your dogs professionally trained as support dogs. I'm sure they'll be very useful in the future, but in the meantime, I'll get permission from the hospitals for you to take them in for visits. I believe a lot of the victims will take comfort in that.'

Tears welled up in her eyes. 'Thank you, sir. Yes, I will investigate those options. Good day.'

Oh, Milly, please be alive. Her heavy heart was almost breaking with dread. She might need the dogs before anyone else.

Troy walked away, sick with disgust, his phone glued to his ear.

Tiny stood rooted to the spot as he disconnected the call from Troy. Two perplexing phone calls in the same day was particularly unusual and annoying. The brief summary of discovering twenty abducted persons in Port Pirie and a formerly purple rig was the most recent. It included the whammy of being asked if he had any knowledge of a woman involved in the criminal activities. That left a particularly bad taste in Tiny's mouth.

Trixie. He shook his head. She'd sworn she'd distance herself from the activities and leave the state. It had been years since her name had been mentioned, let alone any sight of her, for which he'd been relieved. It was not comforting to discover she'd hung in the shadows like the cruel witch she was. Tiny really didn't want to reopen that can of worms. He wasn't about to take a drive to Port Pirie, either.

Shoving that issue to the side for the interim, he thought about the first phone call that upset the rhythm of the day. An out-of-the-blue conversation with his former commanding officer enthusiastically describing his amazing interlude with a beautiful woman who was a crack shot. Her unnerving account of a research scientist with a colourful history was quite the concern; as such, he had gladly employed her as his training assistant. Which then explained the change in mobile phone number and message received from Peachie. All of this only slightly pacified Tiny's racing pulse and compounded his headache. He wondered if leaving Elaina with Darlene in the west was a wise decision.

He frowned when Troy phoned again. 'And now?'

'Listen, mate, a woman was arrested for taking a pipe wrench to several boats in the marina. Max Chandler has gone to ground. I'm going to interview this woman, and I'm going to be asking several questions. I don't want to involve you, or Uncle Reg for that matter, but help me out here. You were too vague earlier. Can you give me something? Anything?'

Sighing heavily and shaking his head, Tiny knew there was no point in withholding information. *Send it through to the keeper and get on with life.* He could hear Reg giving him that advice.

'Troy, her name is probably going to be Trixie, and her fingerprints will be on file. She was a drug courier, a hooker and Max's mistress along with Ruby. Her reputation preceded her around several naval bases. Long story short, she had a fantastic figure, but her face didn't come with the same beauty. It matched her awfully sadistic, nasty streak. She was paid handsomely to leave the consort. But obviously, the white stuff and lure of flesh were too tempting. Your turn now. Has anything new turned up for any of Max's contacts?'

'Ta. Duly noted. Nothing. Burner phones are a bastard to trace when we don't even know the number!'

'Nothing unusual pinged either side of the border?'

'Nope.'

'Righto. Good luck with it all. We're taking the rest of the year off.'

'Half your luck. I'll be retired by Christmas and secretly relieved this recent discovery was out of my jurisdiction. See ya, mate, and thanks. Take care.'

A huge weight suddenly lifted off Tiny's broad shoulders. He returned the mobile phone to the windowsill of his home gym, finished off the last set of one hundred push-ups and set off to run his usual five kilometres with Nova.

CHAPTER SIXTEEN

He'd gotten in late, coasted into the normal parking spot in neutral and pushed the truck door shut as quietly as he could. His spider had been moving about erratically on the way back to the farm in anticipation of the night ahead.

'Snake Girl, come out to play,' Spider sang softly as he approached the caravan. 'We've missed you.'

Turning the key in the lock, he swung open the door and was hit with a gust of warm, stuffy air. Fumbling around for the light switch, he cried out in horror to find the caravan empty.

'No. No. No. No.'

Where is she? Did she run away? Who took her? She escaped. What are you going to do now? Your spider is lonely. You are all alone now. Reg's dead. Snake Girl gone. She gone. Where's Max? Where is Snake Girl?

His strangled cry of anguish bounced off the empty walls as he looked inside the cupboards, in the under-bed storage, raced outside, looked inside the laundry then stopped suddenly. *The yellow Ford Focus. His car. Bluey's car. Max's car!* As quickly as his long, bony legs could take him, he loped awkwardly to the furthest shed and ripped off the tarp covering the vehicle. *Phew!* Then he frowned. Why wasn't the boot lid closed properly? Why wasn't it locked?

Did you lock it? Can it lock? What is in there? Is Snake Girl in there?

Banging the side of his head to quieten the annoying questions, he flung open the boot and flashed the beam of the pocket torch. No Snake Girl. Slamming it shut loudly, he tried all the doors. They were all locked. When he tried the boot again, it wouldn't open. He couldn't remember where he'd hidden the keys.

Snake Girl. Where is she? We want Snake Girl. Snake Girl. Snake Girl.

He had never killed anybody before and imagined wrapping his large, skeletal hands around the neck of the first person he saw. Their eyes bulging, their face turning blue, then grey. Then nothing.

Stupid. Stupid Spider. Where is the answer if you don't ask it?

With deliberate steps, he slunk back to the caravan, sat heavily on the bed and dialled his boss's phone. It went to message bank. He hung up and dialled again. He methodically repeated the behaviour until it was answered.

'What the bloody hell is wrong with you? It's after midnight.'

'Where is she?'

'Somewhere else.'

'Where is she?'

'Spider, listen to me. Max reached out to me–'

'Max did?'

'Yeah, I need you for several more weeks. It's big bucks. Can I rely on you to finish working for me before you go back home?'

'Why so long?' he whined.

'Well, Max has been doing some shonky things and doesn't want you to get caught up in it. He'll have an extra-special bonus for you and then a nice long holiday.'

'A holiday? A bonus? More toys and money and Pepsi?'

'That's what he promised you, but you have to stay and work for me until then. Will you be man enough, knowing about all those things you've got to look forward to?'

'Where is Snake Girl?'

'She's quite poorly, in a secret location, getting better.'

'Oh. Will she die?'

'We hope not. You don't want that, do you, Spider?'

'No, suppose not. But...'

'Good. Get some sleep. You bring your truck to the filling point in the morning.'

'Not Albany again.'

'No, for the next two weeks, you're doing shorter trips, but on the third, you have to stay over.'

'Now I sleep.'

'That's the Spider we know. Sleep well. Tomorrow's pay day.'

'Good night, boss.'

He crawled further up the bed and curled into a ball, whispering the names of all the girls he'd kidnapped and nicknamed until he fell asleep.

Leaning into the plump pillows against the crushed apricot-coloured velvet headboard, Darlene was still too excited to sleep. The conversation about training potential Olympic shooters played repeatedly in her mind. She'd be teaching them in the hand-gun disciplines then participating as a student in the long-barrel training under the watchful eye of Radar. His regimented posture, purposeful walk and dead-eye accuracy were not to be contested. She concluded the day's adrenaline also kept her awake.

Radar had explained about reading the wind and other elements incessantly, then proved the lesson when he took them on a brief shooting adventure. Several targets had been established covering every five hundred metres over a five-kilometre area in difficult terrain. They were all allowed one shot each after he had his. Using their binoculars, they could all tell if the target had been penetrated. Much frivolity, competitive banter and encouragement filled the afternoon. But absolute awe-inspiring accuracy surpassed every aspect of the day. Bullseye after bullseye. The man was an absolute legend, and she was going to learn from the best.

She had acquired two targets but wasn't a murderer. On that matter, she was going to have to ask for advice. Jotting down several ways of ridding the scourge and the associated pros and cons of each method, she decided she needed to talk to one of three people. Radar, Peachie or Deputy Sergeant Troy Oscane.

Gliding out onto the patio, she blew a kiss towards the moon and gazed longingly into the starry heavens. Tiny was never far from her mind. She couldn't believe how quickly time had flown, yet it had dragged. Still, she had things to do. But the question weighed heavily on her mind as to who to phone and ask for help.

After several Tai Chi movements, Darlene was back in bed and clicked off the lamp. She shimmied under the covers and watched moonbeams dance on the window. The answer would come to her after a good night's sleep.

Tiny gazed westwards and searched in vain for a shooting star. His second phone buzzed quietly in his pocket.

'Tango Mike. How nice it is in the sunshine,' he answered quietly.

'Lima Bravo. As it is in the moonlight!'

'Thanks for getting in contact. Are we coded?'

'No, mate. All clear for a little while. No sign of a yellow Ford Focus. Suspect it's under cover. What's been happening down there?'

Tiny acknowledged the update and reported the recent discoveries in brief terms, then highlighted the continuing disappearance of two cockroaches and another girl. A mutual buddy in the south-west of WA had established contact, who, along with a trucking cohort, may provide an insight into their whereabouts.

Tango Mike relayed his intel. 'The grain harvest has kicked off and, on all accounts, it's going to be a record-breaker. Everyone will want their hands in that pie. Your trucking cohort surely isn't Spook?'

'Not this time. He's at home and in retirement mode.'

'Ah-ha! So, it was you doing the piggybacking on the return leg. Us lads up here weren't sure who was riding who!'

Tears of laughter were streaming down their faces as the nonsense continued for several minutes.

'Need I remind you, Lima Bravo, turn your receiver off when you're stargazing with anyone. I might get jealous.'

'Funny prick, Tango Mike! Are you familiar with the name Gavin Milne? A research scientist or some such thing?'

'Can't quite make the correlation there, but no, not yet. Will advise accordingly.'

'Potential threat or target... depending on the results of your research.'

'Sure thing. We're itching to hone our skills. Anybody or anything else?'

'Not yet.'

'Righto, we're turning. Great chat. Greater laugh. Thanks, boss.'

Tiny grinned at the sentiment.

Never in her life had Milly baked so much bacon, poached so many chicken breasts, made loaves of bread and boiled so many eggs. But her biggest achievement was the moistest, tender, tastiest roast beef. All four and a half kilograms of it. Watching her boss rub her hands with glee as she was about to devour several thin slices piled atop the still-warm crust of wholemeal bread at seven o'clock in the morning was simply the best thing Milly had seen for an extremely long time.

'Oh, man! I've got to call my husband in. Did you want to hang around?'

'I need to, boss.'

'Good.'

Milly couldn't stop smiling as she continued to peel eggs for the sandwiches. Only two dozen to go! Switching between slicing the lettuce and peeling the eggs gave her hands a bit of a break from being in the one position. The staff were allowed to sit or stand, as long as they alternated, and, at least once during their shift, walk one kilometre on the treadmill in the coolroom while they planned the next cooking foray. That was something she had yet to do, but she still had to get into the rhythm of the menu she was responsible for.

Milly greeted the man with a broad grin as he entered the kitchen from the house.

'Bo, you have got to get your laughing gear around this,' Jody said as she handed him a hearty roast beef sandwich.

'I could smell the bread from the office! That's torture in itself,' he said and smiled at Milly.

She watched as he took a massive bite. The muffled groans of delight and other smothered words of joy were music to her ears. He walked towards her, held out his hand and politely waited for her to wipe hers on her apron before shaking it heartily.

'That was marvellous. So glad you're here, and even happier you're working for my wife. I need to talk to you both. Jody, you got a minute?'

He gathered the women into the coolroom. 'Milly, if you haven't used the walker today, take this opportunity now, please. It is so important to be active, even if you're sitting or standing for long periods of time. Your feet cannot withstand that much strain constantly. They need movement for circulation and hydration. You walk, I'll talk, and Jody, my gorgeous wife, please listen.'

'What's going on?' She looked at him sideways with a raised eyebrow.

'I'm going to interfere in your business, hon, and urge you to bring on Elaina's guardian, Darlene Adams. She's just won some shooting comp over here and is hanging around until the harvest is finished to take Elaina back east. Anyway, according to Peachie, she wants to help you by picking up your orders and delivering them.'

He watched his wife thumb her chin thoughtfully. 'Why? Why hang around, and why is Elaina so important?'

'She was an abductee, currently lying low, and this other lady is making good on a promise to get the girl home.'

'So, why does she want to work here? Has this got something to do with that creepy character who pitched up out of the blue?'

Bo took a deep breath. 'Not entirely. Milly, feel free to speak whenever you like. You could be the key factor here.'

'I do have something to add,' Milly said, 'but first, you have to know I want to work for you until harvest is finished. It's the least I can do to repay your kindness, and honestly, I'm happy to work for free. You have probably saved my life.'

'Bo, what have we got ourselves involved with?' Jody demanded quietly.

'Honey, listen carefully. Elaina was last seen in Port Lincoln, then some time later was saved from disappearing permanently. The men who saved her are best mates of Peachie. This Darlene Adams inadvertently fell in with their convoy, and they all helped each other in one way or the other. Their bond is like cement now. Anyway, this woman's niece and her friend were also abducted, then rescued, but it opened up a can of worms about a whole whack of missing people. Not only that, it was recently discovered another girl from the same joint has been abducted, and nobody has seen her.'

They automatically looked at Milly.

She switched off the walker and looked at them shyly. 'I was also in Port Lincoln, then unwillingly taken further away. My own stupid fault, admittedly.'

'Do something about him, then,' Jody hissed at her husband.

'My dear wife, listen to me. There's an even bigger fish to catch, and we will. We're drawing in the net and it's long overdue.'

'Ma'am, I will not say anything to Elaina, and I have my own reasons not to let anybody know where I am. I know there's a bigger fish, and I think I know who it is.'

'Do we have time for this?' Jody asked. 'And what of your health, Milly?'

She lightly rested her hand on Jody's arm. 'We have to do it this way, boss. There are several bastards who need to die, but not by our hands, and not by a competition shooter. But by someone who is rightfully allowed to do that. Let's help them. Elaina need not be involved, and I don't need to meet this other lady until it's absolutely necessary. My health and finding my mum are my only priorities when I get home. Um... but I should go back with Elaina.'

Jody patted Milly's hand and sighed. 'Harvest is a priority. Above all else, our staff's well-being is paramount. You have a way with words. Very convincing. Okay, we'll do this.'

'Thank you, ladies. But, Milly, will you do something for me, for us, right now?' Bo asked.

'Of course! Name it.'

'Sing. Sing *Summertime*, just the way you did the other day.'

Milly blushed and stammered, 'I... I'll just have to have a little drink of water.'

With her back turned to her newly gained audience, she exercised her mouth, tongue and jaw before swishing around a mouthful of water and swallowed it slowly. When she turned around, her bosses were in a dancing stance. Forcing back tears, Milly hummed the introduction softly then broke into song. And she sang her heart out. She sang it for all the people who'd been abducted, who had and had not gotten home. She sang it for her mum. She sang it for herself.

Gavin Milne lowered the placard at the domestic terminal in Perth as the younger muscly man stretching the seams on his clothes strode towards him. They shook hands and didn't speak until they were in the black 4WD station wagon.

'Good trip?'

'Yeah, flight attendants were good eye candy. Where's my envelope?'

'In the glove box. Five grand, as promised. You a body builder or addicted to juice?'

'Bit of both. What's your flavour?' Oliver Cady thumbed through the notes and shoved the wad into his backpack, scrunching up the envelope into a little ball.

'Women and powder. Not necessarily in that order.'

'We'll get on just fine, then. What's your plan?'

'We go bush. There are some feral goats that need putting down north of here, which will give you some good practice. Then we go and take out this bitch.'

'How do you know she's still even here? It's a bloody big state.'

'Gut feeling she's down Albany way.'

'Good enough for me.'

Rubbing the sleep out of her eyes, Darlene knew she was to ask Peachie for help. She looked at the time and couldn't believe it was almost nine o'clock. She chided herself for being so lazy and swiftly got on with her day. One text and one voice message were waiting for her by the time she took her breakfast out to the patio and sat down with the plate of simple bacon and eggs.

Radar's apologetic text message for postponing their telephone catch-up due to an impromptu camp-out with his shooting team left her feeling a little disappointed, but the invitation to a private function at the shooting range in two weeks had her on the edge of her seat with anticipation. The mysterious dress code of 'terrain-ready' got her imagination working overtime. Momentarily losing her train of thought, she watched the wayward dance of the pretty yellow and white butterflies match that of the wispy horsetail clouds drifting across the sky.

She had deliberated enough, and listened to the voice message, savouring the last morsel of bacon.

'Ms Adams, Jody here. Elaina's boss, everything is fine. A mutual friendly driver indicated you were looking to help out during harvest. I'd like to discuss this further, but we're not just down the road. Give us a call when you're available. Cheers.'

Saying two silent prayers of thanks, she didn't waste another second and returned the call.

'Thanks for calling me back, Ms Adams.'

'You're welcome! Thank you for the call, Jody. Please call me Darlene.'

'Righto. What are you doing tomorrow?'

'A day off, actually – how can I be of assistance?'

'I do all my shopping in Mount Barker. Is that convenient?'

'Indeed.'

'Goodo. The outlets will pick and pack my order as per usual, and you collect them, drive for two hours, have something to eat on the house. You can do as you please on the way back to your place, but I usually get supplies every five days, the mail run every second trip. Incidentally, do you have a reference?'

'Sure! I'll send it after we've hung up. Please send me all the instructions and give me directions for where to drop your groceries off. I would prefer not to have a sight-seeing trip, and I don't want to drive at night-time.'

'That sounds fair. I anticipate an invoice for six hours plus five hundred k's in fuel. Am I close?'

'You're providing the meal, let's just make it five hours and the fuel. Did you have a budget in mind?'

'Uh, not yet!'

They shared a genuine laugh.

'Let's thrash out the costs together,' Jody said.

'Done. I'll send a message when I'm on my way to you.'

'Excellent. That's when I'll tell you where to meet me, and you can follow me into my kitchen. That is the only way you need to know.'

'I'm more than happy with that! I look forward to meeting you tomorrow, Jody. And thank you. I really appreciate you doing this.'

'Ugh, we need to thank our mutual friend, actually, but believe me, any extra reliable help during harvest is a blessing. Good day, Darlene.'

Not wanting to leave the retreat for its comfort, safety and discretion, Darlene discovered that calculating the outgoings with an ambiguous income was particularly frustrating. Two hours later, she decided a swim would help clear her mind.

Pushing herself to her absolute limits, she stretched her fingertips and just touched the wall on the thirtieth lap before rolling onto her back and sucking in some very deep breaths. How on earth was she so unfit? She could run ten kilometres without a problem. She had done exactly that the previous night at the gym.

'Ma'am,' a gentle voice called down to her from the edge of the pool, 'you booked yourself in for a pampering day. Are you still interested?'

Was she ever!

'Absolutely! Thank you for reminding me, I'll be right out.'

'Perfect. I'll walk with you. The rain shower will be your first stop–'

'That sounds perfect,' she said kindly. 'Please lead the way, thank you.'

Darlene didn't want to know any more. Hearing the plans for the day wasn't necessary. She didn't want to be organised for once in her life, just to feel carefree and be taken from room to room for pampering.

Everyone on the two-way had copped a blast of Spider's foul mood. Everyone, including the boss. Cutting him off before he reached the highway, Bo literally dragged the spindly, lanky younger man out of the truck. They wrestled until Bo landed a punch in the hollow of Spider's gut, briefly winding him.

'I'll sic Max on you, you bastard. You'll die. He hates bullies.'

'Bring it on, you little punk. I saved you from being dropped off the cliffs at the Bight when you were a whippersnapper. Now, you listen to me, and you listen hard.'

Bo roughly shoved Spider up against the tyre and informed him sternly how the near future would be playing out. Playing to Spider's schizophrenic traits, he managed to talk to three different characters. Having two sisters in the medical fraternity, both highly respected in their own fields of psychology, had helped tremendously over the years.

'So, if I work really hard,' Spider whined, 'you'll pay me big heaps of cash, then I can drive the yellow Ford Focus and have the rest of the year off? Back home?'

'Yes. See, Max is looking after you. He has funny ways of showing he cares, but he does.'

'And Snake Girl? I really miss her. Can I take her back?'

'She isn't very well.'

'Can I find a new toy?'

'Well, how about we see how you go at the end of harvest?'

The little-boy giggle freaked Bo out, as did the erection that protruded from Spider's trousers. Refraining from showing any discomfort, he gripped the younger man's wrist and yanked him to his feet.

'Best you go and earn your money now, Spider. You're behind time. One less load, one less payment. You know the rules.'

'Yeah, boss. I bend, I spend. It's not my truck, so I mustn't push my luck. Thanks for the chat. I have work to do.'

Bo stepped back and watched as Spider spit-polished the chrome bullbar before climbing back into the driver's seat and pulling the air horn. Bo's guts churned. He'd repaid Max's favour tenfold. It was time to step out of the equation. Fondling the key in his pocket, he detoured to the sheds before heading back to the house.

Gritting his teeth and thumping the spare tyre, he swore on his dearly departed mother's grave that Max was going to hell. Max knew that Bo detested drugs. He also knew that Bo detested everything he stood for.

Acknowledging the message that she was to wait at the first intersecting northern road past the turnoff to Jacup, Darlene dialled Peachie's number and slipped into gear.

'Hey, what're you up to?'

'Thanking you for putting in a good word for me! I'm on the job as we speak.'

'Too easy. Say, keep an eye out for a yellow Ford Focus... it's been stolen from another farm. The guys would rather sort it out themselves.'

'Of course. Yes, I will do.'

'You packing?'

She burst out laughing. 'Just in case I fear for my safety.'

'Good girl. Any sight or sound of that bloke from Albany?

'No, thank goodness. I will admit something, though, I do get spooked every time I see a dark-coloured 4WD station wagon!'

'That's fair enough. Keep your wits about you, anyway. Hey, word from the east is the boys miss you and love your cooking. Care to tell me more?'

'Trade secret, but have you ever tried Tiny's breakfast of eggs benedict?'

'Noooo... but I could, right this very minute. You?'

'Hell yeah!'

'What's the go with the training job?'

'Will let you know when I know more.'

'Yes, please. I'm your guardian now!'

'That you are, Peachie. Quick question for you, where do you reckon I go for some tranquilliser darts?'

'Geez, Darlene! You're a little out of your depth, aren't you?'

'Not really. A gun is a gun.' She paused then laughed. 'Don't worry, I think I've just answered my own question. Thanks for hearing me out!'

'I'll try not to worry, but I'll be keeping an eye out for you, too. Signal's breaking up. Bye for now, my little sharpshooter!'

That made her giggle. She'd had many nicknames, but never one so cool. Acquiring a tranquilliser gun and darts was the obvious solution, and she churned over several ideas as she drove towards Jacup.

Bo looked down at the ringing phone. That little punk had the nerve to phone him again?

'Yes, Spider?'

'I'm lonely. Can I talk to you for a while? Please?'

His scared little-boy voice begged for a caring ear. Softening his own tone, Bo listened to his outpouring of grief with the loss of his mother at an early age, how all his toys were always shared with Stevo and Max and how he was always sent away on errands.

'Who sent you away this time, Spider, and how'd you get here?'

'Reg. Reg Oscane, but not all the way over here. I was never allowed to call him Father or any such thing. I sometimes believed Max was my father. Stevo hit me then felt sorry for me, but made me get more toys. Reg sure didn't like it. He didn't even like me having my toys hidden. He knew, and he released some too. Then a job got canned, and I had to pay Bluey for Stevo. Something like that. Don't know. Don't care.'

Bo swallowed the bile that tickled the back of his throat. 'Perhaps I should talk to Max, but I usually call from my other phone. You would know his number off by heart, wouldn't you?

'Yes, of course I do, but I'm never allowed to say it. I'll text it to you.'

'I'm glad you've pulled over to use your telephone. You don't want the police to give you a fine.'

'Oh, no. They cannot do that. No police. Not ever. Here you go. You should have it soon. I must go to work now. Thanks for talking to me. Bye-bye.'

That poor, twisted, confused, damaged boy, Bo thought. Then rage almost exploded out of him when he remembered the cunning, manipulative, cruel beast that abducted women and his depraved influences. Answering Spider's third call automatically, Bo listened to the threatening, arrogant character.

'Reg Oscane's dead. The soft old bastard died. Max is looking for his car, which Bluey owed Stevo. Be careful who you phone, boss man. I'm only doing this job long enough to be forgotten, earn some dosh, get my Snake Girl and leave. The end.'

Chuckling at the information that had inadvertently been spilled, Bo hedged his bets. Perhaps the competition shooter who was delivering the groceries would provide a link to obliterating the entire corrupt and deviant connection.

Nine days later, Darlene bounded out of bed at 4:00 a.m., jogged down to the gym and ran three kilometres on a ten-degree incline. She then pushed through twenty laps, jogged back to her suite, showered and dressed in white jeans, a blue checked shirt and sneakers. Both she and her Jeep needed new shoes. She'd been itching to put on a new set for ages, and as Radar had cordially reminded her of the upcoming private function in two days, she needed to go shopping.

Albany, here we come, she mused. There was also a large parcel waiting for her at the post office. Rubbing her hands with glee, she slid through the gears and reached touring speed in record time.

The tyre shop had just rolled up their garage door as she drove in. As Darlene stepped out of the classic vehicle, the men buzzed around her like bees near a honeypot.

'Geez, haven't seen one of these for a while! Nice rig. It's in good nick, too! Yours?'

'Sure is. My pride and joy. Guys, five new Mickey Thomson shoes, please! How long do you need her for? I've got a whack of errands to run.'

'We'll do it right now, if you like,' the older of the men said. 'The kettle's hot in the waiting area inside. May be a tad longer than an hour.'

'Fabulous, thank you. Please balance and do wheel alignments. Oh, do you accept cash?'

'Even better,' he said and waited until she'd removed her suitcase before escorting her inside the office. 'We'll be as quick as we can, miss.'

'Much appreciated, thank you.'

An hour and twenty-five minutes later, Darlene was navigating her way through the already busy streets of Albany. The second-hand shop was her next port of call. Breezing in through the open door, she was amazed at the amount of clothing available. Terrain-ready, Radar had reminded her. Easily fitting into a pair of khaki chinos, she found another dark-brown pair in the same size. Lots of pockets, just what she wanted.

Boots. She needed sturdy boots. The selection was limited, but she reached through the rack and retrieved some work boots from the back, banging the heel out of habit. A shotgun casing fell out. *How bizarre*, she thought. Knowing not to put her fingers in dark places, she tapped it upside down and saw an edge of paper sticking out. Sliding it out and unfolding it, she broke out in goosebumps. The crayon had been sharpened with precision and the writing was small and neat. Although it was a little bit smudged, Darlene easily read: *SOS. His name is Spider. Arm tattoos are sleeves. Abducted from Port Lincoln. Jacup. Farmer is a nice man. M.*

Her hands trembled as she carefully rolled up the note and returned it into the casing before slipping it inside her jeans pocket. Those particular boots were too small, and there weren't any others. Adding a couple of long-sleeve plain brown shirts to her collection, she slowed down her breathing. After eventually regaining her composure, she took the clothes to the counter.

'I would have thought all the harvest jobs were filled,' the older woman said politely.

'They probably are. I'm going on a bush walk.'

'Watch the weather, there'll be a shearer's warning in a couple of days. Best you grab yourself a beanie and jacket of some sort, miss.'

'Oh! Thank you. Say, have you seen anything peculiar lately? Maybe a young woman with a lanky bloke?'

'Why? You a cop or something?'

Darlene chuckled. 'Nothing like that.' Then she crossed her fingers as she told a fib. 'I saw them a couple of weeks back, and they were looking dodgy. Not serious, they just stood out like sore thumbs.'

The woman held her gaze. 'Must have stuck in your mind if you're asking about them. I recall a young lass was horribly pale a while back and used the bin outside to spew. She kept pulling her shirt around her neck, and the bloke jammed a big hat on her head. They didn't steal anything. They paid cash. He was tall and gangly.'

'Oh, the poor thing. That was during that oppressive heat. Hell, I nearly passed out myself.'

'Yeah, it was bad.' The woman screwed up her eyes and scrutinised Darlene intently. Dropping her voice, she said, 'Lady, I'm not supposed to take anyone into the back room, but it is my discretion, being the manager of this outlet. You look trustworthy. Would you recognise them, you reckon?'

'Can only give it a shot.'

'Go and get yourself a jacket, then wait near that back room. I'll set up the security footage.'

'You know exactly when it was?' she asked, desperately trying to quell the rising excitement in her voice.

'Yeah, I gave her my bottle of water. I'd switched handbags and left my wallet at home, taken some money out of the till to get some lunch, and my colleague had no end of trouble balancing the end-of-day. The receipt had got caught up in some notes. Anyway, we've watched the tape over and over and both commented on the oddity.'

Twenty minutes later, Darlene had the video recorded onto her phone.

241

It was him. The mobile tattoo parlour. She suspected the girl with him was Milly. She hoped it was. She was feeling excited, nervous and sick all at the same time. Thanking the woman for her kindness and assistance, she walked swiftly back to her vehicle and put her suitcase and shopping bag on the floor of the passenger seat.

Sliding into the driver's seat, Darlene fumbled with the keys, trying to put them in the ignition. Swearing under her breath as she dropped them, she rested the side of her head on the steering wheel and reached down. In doing so, she caught a glimpse of the rear quarter panel of a passing black 4WD Landcruiser wagon in the passenger mirror. She gasped. The hair stood up on the back of her neck and goosebumps swelled on her arms. She needed a disguise. She still needed boots. She had to collect her parcel. She wished she wasn't alone.

Constantly peering cautiously in every mirror, she drove around the block and parked behind the post office. A horrible thought occurred to her as she pulled on the handbrake. There weren't too many 90s-model Jeep Wranglers in Albany with Queensland number plates. Gavin Milne had walked near her vehicle after he'd left the café. Darlene prayed the jerk wasn't observant.

With the post office blissfully empty, she showed her ID paperwork and collected her parcel. Unwrapping it in the backseat, she lifted the cardboard lid and smiled. Her brand new long-barrelled dart gun, complete with its beautiful American walnut stock, supply of CO_2 cartridges, darts, syringes, tranquilliser fluid and handsome carry case. It was time to go to the police station at the opposite end of the carpark.

Balancing the cardboard packaging along the length of her suitcase handles, she confidently wheeled her belongings across the concrete, up the ramp, and was met at the door by a young constable.

'Miss? Can I help you?'

'I hope so. I need to register a weapon, acquire a permit to carry and prepare an AVO.'

'So early in the morning, too! I was about to get coffees for the crew. You'll be here for a while, can I get you one?'

She smiled politely. 'No, thank you.'

'No worries. See you when I get back. The bloke behind the far counter will help you.'

The bloke behind the counter was very obliging, considering he'd been checking out the tall beauty ever since she'd gotten out of her vehicle. He escorted her to an interview room where the verbal questionnaire begun. After he scrutinised her driver's licence and keyed in her details, he grinned.

'Ms Adams, you have quite the reputation. Congrats!'

'Thank you. I love target practice.' She returned his grin.

'Care to explain the dart gun?'

She comfortably explained her previous role in sedating rogue bulls from a helicopter, then, at great length, the man who'd offered her a job, her refusal, his subsequent outburst, her change of mobile numbers, her further research into the local feral goat problems and her need for stable income until the week before Christmas.

'You've had a DVO on you recently squashed, and I see you returned serve with an AVO.'

'Yes, that is correct. In fact, I would like to take out another one, please.'

'You in trouble, Ms Adams?'

'No. I like to be prepared, sir.'

He raised his eyebrow, pressed his lips together, scratched behind his ear and slid his business card across the desk.

'At your service. Let's get this paperwork done. Are you staying locally?'

'Thank you, I appreciate your assistance. No, I'm not, and would like to leave town as soon as I can. I just need to buy some boots...'

'Boots, ma'am?'

'Yes, a couple of friends and I are going on a hike through a national park.' She slid up the leg of her jeans, revealing her smooth shapely calves and slender ankles, and said, 'These sneakers won't cut it.'

'Ahem. No, probably not,' he said, dragging his eyes back to the computer screen. 'Ah, the name of the person on the AVO would be?'

'Gavin Milne, and here's his contact phone number,' she said and slid her phone across the desk.

Forty minutes later, he countersigned all the necessary documents and handed them over. She thanked him, opened her suitcase and slipped a copy of the paperwork inside.

'You're aware the original needs to be lodged at the courthouse, which I can do on your behalf. However, with regards to your weapon, protocol is I have to observe it being stripped and rebuilt. I will also need you to describe its features as you're doing so to deem you confident and competent in your weapon. Can you do that for me, please?'

'You know I can! I don't understand.' Darlene raised an eyebrow. 'You've already issued me the paperwork!'

'Yes, that's correct. Please don't turn around, but behind you are some very curious eyes who would be delighted to listen to you recount your experience in and knowledge of this weapon. They've worked out who you are. Make their day, Ms Adams. I'm switching on the audio now.'

Accepting the challenge, Darlene verbalised the memorised stats of the dart gun, right down to the available simultaneous viewing of the manometer and telescopic sight, while she stripped the weapon with confident, fluid movements. As she cleaned it, she described a couple of exhilarating rides in a mustering chopper, hanging on for dear life while tranquillising some mighty feisty rogue bulls, much to the amusement of the policemen watching her intently. Swiftly rebuilding it and resting the stock against her shoulder, she aimed it at the wall with her trigger finger running the length of the barrel, and grinned.

'You're good, Ms Adams. Put your weapon in its case. We'll get rid of the packaging.'

'Thank you very much. I'll just peel off the address label and dispose of it appropriately.'

'Certainly. Is there anything else we can do for you?'

She paused, then said, 'How familiar are you guys with all the vehicles in town?'

'Out-of-town number plates stand out, like yours, by the way. Why do you ask?'

'This Gavin Milne bloke, he drives a black 4WD Landcruiser wagon. He might be in town.'

'Duly noted. Would you like an escort to your vehicle and accommodation?'

Blushing under his concerned look, Darlene replied kindly, 'Thank you all the same. I will be fine.'

'Uh, you said you needed boots?'

'Yes, but I might do that another day. I really would like to leave town now.'

He nodded and held open the door for her. His colleagues grinned as she slung the case over her shoulder and wheeled her suitcase past them.

'Thanks for all your help. Have a great day,' she called out as she walked down the ramp.

'You'll be welcome back anytime. Take care,' the young constable said loudly.

Darlene returned her suitcase to its rightful position, slid the gun case alongside the centre console and waved to her audience as she climbed in behind the wheel. Revving the engine gently, she grinned. Her hands were steady. Her mind was made up. She was in control.

Cassie desperately needed to talk to her aunt. She was getting itchy feet. The hospital staff were overbearing, the boys were happier with children their own age at day care, their mother was getting stronger, and talk was she'd be home by Christmas time. It had been suggested that an au pair wouldn't be required for much longer. Spending a couple of days with Asta had been fantastic, but being in a stable was not Cassie's cup of tea. It took a special person to spend a day in the company of horses. She and Amy had also forged a beautiful friendship. Under her guidance, Cassie had voluntarily participated in palliative care a couple of times. Now she wanted to learn more. It was always a good time to phone her favourite aunt.

Smiling broadly at Darlene's effervescent greeting, Cassie didn't even wait for the pleasantries to continue and poured out her dilemma.

'What should I do, Aunty Darlene?'

'Believe in yourself. You're certainly very happy talking about it. Find out about online courses, and maybe there are agencies that can place you with an elderly person. Do your homework, though. I don't know much about changing nappies for a baby, and I know even less about it for adults. Do you?'

'Oh. Oh, I didn't think about that. Maybe I should do more work experience with someone who is still able-bodied and has all their faculties?'

'That's a sensible approach! What else has been happening over that side of the world?'

'You mean you haven't heard?'

'Heard what?'

Cassie described the latest media feeding frenzy about the missing people being found, a disfigured corpse whose identity hadn't been revealed and a missing public figure.

She continued with her rant. 'I haven't turned the TV on for days. The way they shove the microphones into those poor family's faces, asking idiotic questions. How dare they intrude so callously!'

'Best you turn that passion into something constructive, Cassie.' Darlene chuckled.

'Yeah, yeah. What are you doing now?'

Darlene hoped her regular fitness regime would be a source of encouragement for her niece, then explained about the grocery deliveries to an amazing farm kitchen where the farmer's wife and staff cooked five-star meals for their harvest workers.

'Oh, wow! You're having a ball. Do you want to come home?'

'Surely I'm not the only one counting down till Christmas?'

'Hell no! How long is the harvest over there going to continue? It's been an average one here so far.'

'It's a huge harvest, suppose it'll finish when it does...'

'And then?'

'I'll pick you up, we'll have Christmas somewhere, see the oldies for New Year then... well... I'm going to go to find some more platypus.'

'I'm so jealous. I'm craving rolling green hills, not the rainforest so much, but open space.'

'Affirm that's where you'll be. And back yourself.'

'You always make me feel good about myself. Thanks for talking, Aunty Darlene. I cannot wait to see you!'

'Likewise, kiddo. Take care, look after yourself and pursue your dream. It is your life, after all.'

They hung up simultaneously. Cassie instantly researched available online courses and how quickly she could obtain that diploma. She'd taken six months off each of her other courses and qualified, and had every intention of breaking those personal records.

With Albany in her rearview mirror, unfortunately, the discoveries and sights remained at the forefront of Darlene's mind. She desperately needed to clear her head and changed directions on a whim. She hoped the endless sea views and rugged coastline would help. Following the winding path to Shelley Beach, her excitement grew the closer she got to the lookout. The clean white sand that disappeared into the turquoise waters beneath the towering limestone hills took her breath away.

Three hours later, a sudden chill in the wind snapped her back into reality. She had to get back to the retreat before nightfall. Aside from being totally famished, she still needed to get her thoughts together.

Time seemed to have stood still since the successful recovery of the missing women and boys, yet the concluding group therapy session organised by Bev laid the foundation of eternal friendships. Amongst the tears of happiness and sadness, the three Rottweilers also appeared to relish in the endless pats and play time. Troy proudly stood by her side as they waved their goodbyes. Everybody's physical health had been thoroughly investigated and cleared of any untoward illnesses. Their mental health, though, was a sad, sad tale.

'What are you going to do now, boss?'

'Retire. I hereby formally announce my retirement, Officer Bev. Let's organise a party. You decide which house you'd like us to live in, and I'll start my guest list! We party one month from today.'

She threw her arms around him and planted butterfly kisses all over his ruddy face. Deep down, they secretly wished they could share in a happy ending by having Milly at home.

Tiny discreetly stepped back into his office before Granny saw him and answered the slimline phone.

'Tango Mike, long time no hear.'

'Lima Bravo, nothing to report until now.'

'I'm all ears.'

'Danish Pastry safe. Our Pretty One has been busy. Database updated with two AVOs. Original troublemaker plus latest possible target.'

'You know the code names?

'Affirmative.'

'What's your take?'

'The CO has it in hand. No other news to relay. Still looking for yellow vehicle.'

'Acknowledged. Can you sweep the area from the last fireworks display for thermals?'

'Roger. Will advise accordingly. Out.'

His hands were tied, and he was so frustrated. Nova sensed her master's anxiety and leaned her body against his legs in comfort. He suddenly gasped in dismay. Granny had wanted a dog! They'd talked about it, then he got so absorbed in pining he'd let her down. Chastising himself angrily, he set about making amends. Striding into the kitchen with his spare laptop in hand, he gently wrapped his arm around his gran and steered her to the dining room table.

'Granny, I apologise for my behaviour,' he said sincerely. 'I'll finish preparing dessert while you scroll through this website of dogs that need a home.'

She wiped a small tear from her eye. 'Oh, Sonny, thank you. You were so preoccupied... I didn't want to be a bother.'

'You will never, ever be a bother. It's me who's neglected my promise. Forgive me, please.'

'Shush now, I'm looking for a dog!' she chided gently and smiled.

'Thank you, Granny.'

Tiny turned to the stove and smiled sadly. He had never let her down so awfully.

The strains of Chopin's *Nocturne in E Flat* caught Darlene unawares as she stepped out of the bathroom. With her hair wrapped up in a towel, she wriggled into the oversized bathrobe and dashed over to the bedside table. She smiled broadly as she answered.

'Evening, Radar. This is a pleasant surprise!'

'Ms Adams.' His deep voice rumbled through the phone. 'Not too late, I hope.'

'Not at all. How are you?'

'Very well, thank you. How did your shopping expedition go?'

'Pardon?'

'I just presumed you didn't have terrain-ready clothing in your suitcase...'

'You're right, I didn't. You just caught me off-guard, like you were in Albany today and saw me.'

His chuckle was warm. 'I would have insisted you join me for a meal if that were the case. Speaking of which, would you care to have breakfast with me at the range before the private function commences?'

'The day after tomorrow is what I have in my diary, is that correct?'

'Yes.'

'Certainly! What time?'

'I'd like to collect you at zero five thirty hours. You will be away from your accommodation until twenty-two hundred hours. Will that be a problem?'

Darlene paused. 'Nobody knows where I'm staying, Radar, and I'd prefer to keep it that way.'

'You can trust me, Ms Adams. Nobody will see you get in or out of my vehicle. Besides, I change it every day.'

'You do?'

'Yes. Less noticeable, believe it or not.'

'Might be taking a leaf out of your book, sir. Okay, how secure is this line?'

'You are a suspicious one. What's going on?'

Darlene explained her reaction to the sighting of the black 4WD Landcruiser wagon, the horrid thought of Gavin Milne and how she wasn't about to argue with her instinct. She then happily described her purchases for the day but omitted the discovery of the shotgun shell, note and the video.

'A dart gun? I want to see that. Bring it with you.'

'Sir, my blue suitcase does not leave my sight. It contains everything I own now.'

'It'll be more secure at your location during your absence. Just bring the ammo for your favourite handgun, the long barrel and this latest weapon. I want to play.'

Darlene laughed. 'Radar, it does come with seventy-two-gram cartridges of CO_2.'

'Range?'

'One to sixty metres.'

'Oh, we are going to have fun. See you in under forty-eight hours at precisely zero five thirty. You can text me your address. By the way, text me that Milne's phone number as well.'

'Why?'

'I have access to things you don't.'

His authoritative tone instantly made her bite her lip. Regaining her composure, she replied politely, 'Of course. I will send it soon.'

'Very good. Night, Ms Adams.'

Before she had a chance to respond, Radar disconnected the call. Peachie phoned before she'd put it anywhere near the tabletop.

'How's my little sharpshooter?' His jovial voice easily made her smile.

'Doing well, thanks. How're you going, Peachie?'

'It was a good day. Long. But successful. What's news?'

Darlene blurted out her day's events and left nothing out when she read the note.

'Jacup, you said?'

'Yes. I drive past that sign. Do you see Elaina when you go to the kitchen?'

'No. Nobody sees the staff. I've only ever met Boss Lady once, and that was when she collected Elaina. But by golly, those women are mighty fine cooks!'

Darlene then described how she got to form a friendship with the women in South Australia, who her and Elaina had had a video call with.

'Discreetly ask this Bev for a photo of her daughter, then compare it with that video. This is getting pretty heavy for us non-trained personnel. Reckon we can handle it?'

'Well, yes. I'm not a murderer, yet I will have no trouble shooting someone if I fear for my safety, or that of someone in my company. I need you to see this video, Peachie. You might also recognise this creep that Elaina reckons was in Albany the other day.'

There was a long pause before Peachie spoke again. 'Darlene, let's coordinate something the next time you're dropping off groceries. Maybe we can meet on the road. I don't want you to do anything to jeopardise yours or anyone's safety.'

'Yours included. I get it. I'm more of a solo competitor, but this is not a competition. Oh! By the way, I'm going out for the whole day with the Olympics shooting trainer the day after tomorrow. We're going exploring, and I think we're testing weapons. I'm so excited.'

'You certainly sound it. I feel better knowing you're in his company... Do you think we should bring him into the fold?'

'Not yet. He did ask for Milne's phone number, though, which I will dutifully give him after we've hung up. I'm happy to leave him with that problem child! But I realised too late that there are some questions I shouldn't ask.'

'Lesson well learnt. Hey, I've got to cut this short. Dinner's ready, and I have an early start. Keep me in the loop and we'll try and meet up. Thanks for the chat. Always good to hear from you. Night. Take care, and have fun. I want to hear all about it. Bye.'

Peachie's normal way of hanging up by saying everything at once didn't surprise her one iota. What did surprise her, though, was his statement of 'lesson well learnt'. Not wanting to overthink things, she knew it was late but sent a message to Tiny anyway.

Hey Tiny, it's the shooting star in the West. Hope all's well as it is here. D X

He replied in record time.

Hello Darlene! Great to hear from you. Yep, all's well. Granny wants a dog older than Nova. Any experience in that department?

The bigger the dog the bigger the poop! LOL

LOL Good point!

Consider adopting one. They need a loving home. Do recommend you both take Nova with you. The dogs have to get on too. Nova's been your dog since forever and although you're the Alpha male LOL her size is important to her because it's important to you.

Granny made similar suggestions. Say, how's Elaina?

She's enjoying her job! Am I the go-between here?! Hey, if you are going to adopt a dog, from what I've seen in the past, some have had a horrid previous life. They need to learn how to trust again, as do humans I suppose.

And love?

That too.

It was too late. Darlene had already sent the message. When he hadn't replied by the time she'd clicked off the lamp, she opted for the thought that he'd fallen asleep, because that was exactly what she was going to do.

Radar sat back and grinned as he hung up the phone from Gavin Milne. *Let's see how good a shot you really are, weasel.* He then burst out laughing, knowing full well how easily the jealous prat took the bait of believing Radar was the beautiful Ms Adam's latest flame. Milne was tongue-tied with rage when he learnt she was waiting in anticipation on a secluded island. Radar went to town on Milne's inane ego and finally drew out his threat of tracking Radar down and taking him out, then doing the same to Darlene after he had taught her a lesson. Teasing a former sniper in such a manner sounded like fun, so he set up the location.

Radar hoped like hell Darlene Adams wouldn't be seen or take a stray bullet at the upcoming private function. She would have to be on the opposing team, for her own safety.

Milne and Cady eyeballed each other. Their blood pumped angrily as the veins in their necks pulsated.

'Best get some more cash out, Milne,' Cady growled. 'Winner takes all.'

'Suits me,' he vented, before spinning the chamber on his pistol. 'How dare he? How dare she lead me on like that? Bitch. Bitch. Bitch.'

'That's it, buddy, get worked up. You got this. I'll have your back, just find out which secluded island she's on and give me the word.'

Milne slid his nose along the glass table and lounged arrogantly against the back of the couch. 'Yep. Done. They're going down. They have no idea who they're playing with.'

Cady smiled evilly and didn't say another word.

CHAPTER SEVENTEEN

Darlene followed the tell-tale sweep of the headlights as the vehicle traversed the hilly landscape. Radar had sent her a text with his ETA. She was ready and waiting as her watch displayed precisely 5:30 a.m.

'Morning, Ms Adams. You do look the part! Your sneakers will not be white by the time you get back here, though.' He grinned as he slipped the rifle cases off her shoulder. 'Your holster can stay under your shirt.'

'Morning, Radar. My pockets are laden, and I've got a backpack.'

'Good job. Right, let's go. I've ordered breakfast and trust you like bacon and eggs. We've got a big day ahead of us. Incidentally, you are going to be the only female. We will be taking appropriate breaks for ablutions, but it's bush style. Nothing like this fancy resort thing you're staying at! Hop in, we've got a lot to get through.'

In order of topic, Darlene responded accordingly as she clipped the seatbelt in. 'Very happy with the breakfast menu, thanks, and quite accustomed to bush-style breaks.'

'Oh? How so?'

She described the variety of rugged bush roles she had at the remote station, much to Radar's interest and appreciation of her diligence.

'Ever shoot anyone?'

'Yes. I feared for my safety.'

'Ever kill an animal?'

'Only one silly kangaroo that zigged instead of zagged. I've never had to put one out of its misery, thankfully. However, I have tranquillised animals for their safety and that of colleagues.'

'You're an honest person, aren't you?'

'Yes. I'm not a fan of deception.'

'Good. We'll all learn more of each other's characters during the day. I intend to split us up into teams, and we won't be using live bullets. Ever played paintball?'

'No. Don't they sting?'

'Only if you get shot!'

They shared a very loud laugh and were still chuckling when they walked through the private entrance of the shooting range.

'Ms Adams,' Radar drawled, 'Beyond the boundary of this range is my own private playground, hence my freedom to come and go as I please.'

She nodded respectfully. 'Very nice arrangement, sir.'

By the time she had racked her weapons, breakfast was served. In genuine chivalrous fashion, Radar helped push her chair in closer to the table then took his seat. He raised the glass of freshly squeezed orange juice.

'To a fine friendship.'

Smiling graciously, she raised hers and replied, 'To a true friendship as well.'

'Indeed! Tell me about this missing girl.'

She nearly choked on her mouthful and swallowed hard. 'I will ask you two questions. One: which girl?'

'I know one has been found and you're taking her back home with you. The other one is from Port Lincoln.'

'Second question. How do you know about her?'

'Your name came up in a conversation with a mutual friend, who... shall we say... is a friend of a friend of a friend, who indicated you were on a personal recovery mission.'

Darlene ate her breakfast politely, washed a pesky crumb down with several mouthfuls of the orange juice then dabbed at her mouth eloquently with the crisp white linen napkin. She watched Radar polish off his double serving with a poker face. Connecting the dots with the coincidences, she pinned the tail on Peachie.

'Your source is quite correct, Radar. I do intend to find this other girl and take her back with me as well. She is the daughter of a newfound friend, who rescued and still keeps an eye on my niece and another Danish girl in my absence.'

'I thought you weren't a murderer.'

'I'm not. But a snake can't be charged with murder if it tags a human. A strategically placed tranquilliser dart can also render someone useless if I fear for my safety. Both are pretty apt penalties for certain scourges of the earth, in my opinion.'

'Do you know how to ask for help?'

'No.'

'You best learn today.'

With that, Radar pushed back his chair and tapped his watch.

'Meet me outside in fifteen minutes, and bring your weapons. You are going to have a lesson with the .22 LR first, then we play with the dart gun, but they both stay here under lock and key until we return.'

Staring at the bathroom mirror, Darlene was at a total loss about how to feel. Her own face didn't even give her a clue. With Radar's words of advice clanging in her ears, she collected her weapons and stood beside him exactly fifteen minutes later. A faint golden glow lit up the eastern sky.

He handed her a pair of binoculars. 'Ms Adams, to the right of centre approximately seven hundred and fifty metres away, locate the darkest green tree. Now, study that tree and tell me what you see.'

After several minutes, she described the foliage, the trunk, the shrubbery at its base, the bird's nest at the crown and the unnatural square box sitting on the third branch from the top.

'Very good. That's a camera. It shouldn't be there, but you cannot remove it. How would you make it inoperable?'

'Put a bullet through the centre of the box.'

'Can you?'

'This particular .22 LR has a good reputation for distance, according to the salesman. But here? It'll be a challenge in this light and at ground height, but I'd give it a go. Ideally, though, I'd like to be at eye level or higher. It's always easier shooting downwards than upwards. Agree?'

'I'm asking the questions. You have three shots. Do your best with what you've got to work with.'

With that, he slid the binoculars from her hand and stepped backwards. Taking a steadying breath and exhaling quietly to quell her rising ire, Darlene prepared her rifle, took up her stance, focused the telescopic sight, observed the breeze, took a deeper breath, closed her eyes and shut out all the noises of the world. She opened her eyes, released her breath slowly, curled her finger around the trigger, aimed and squeezed.

Radar's deep voice quietly informed her of the known result. 'High by an inch. Two shots remaining.'

Repeating her preliminary breathing exercise, she imagined she was taking out the trash. Two bullets. Three pieces of trash. Discount Oliver Cady. He wasn't in the west. Two pieces of trash. So, which one first? Milne or Spider? They may both be coming to hurt her. She feared for her safety. She imagined Milne's cold stare. She heard his tirade of abuse. With her rifle at the ready, she focused through the telescopic sight, observed the breeze, took a deep breath, closed her eyes and shut out all the noises of the world. She opened her eyes, saw Milne lunging at her with his fists clenched, released her breath slowly, curled her finger around the trigger, aimed and squeezed.

She vaguely heard Radar's voice. 'Bullseye.'

Completely absorbed in her self-protection mode, she reloaded and envisioned Spider stalking and trapping her in his web. She had to shoot first. She had to get the girls home. After another quiet, deep breath, she released it slowly, curled her finger around the trigger, aimed and squeezed.

'You missed.'

'No, sir,' she said as she lowered her gun. 'That bullet went through the previous hole. I staked my life on that shot.'

'I do believe you did. Well done, my girl. Now, let's put away this lovely piece then go into the thicket. I want a go at this dart gun.'

'One request, Radar. Please leave me some darts.'

'Well, bring the CO_2 cartridges, then!'

His deep, bellowing laugh echoed across the lawn and rippled through the trees as sunrays painted golden stripes in the sky. After an hour, they both felt a bit dissatisfied with the dart gun, secured it alongside her .22 and hightailed it deeper into the shrubbery behind the range.

'The lads are going to meet us at Point Charlie. Let's go, Ms Adams.'

Twisting his lips into a wry grin, Tiny answered Troy Oscane's phone call.

'I believe congratulations are in order, Deputy Sergeant! You helped save a lot of people a lot of heartache.'

'Thanks, mate, yeah. Touch and go with one lady, but she pulled through, thankfully. It's just her and her little boy in this world. I'm telling you, I would have adopted him at the drop of a hat.'

'Far out. What happens now?'

'You were right about Trixie. She turned in order to save her bacon, which was futile. She actually did the world a favour and blew Stevo's head off, but Max is still unaccounted for.'

'Anything I can do to lighten the load?'

'Yeah. I'm going to send you a few loose ends that are beyond my pay grade to investigate. Don't mean to put pressure on you, but I'll be formally announcing my retirement tomorrow and having a party in four weeks. You and Spook are invited, and bring your dear Gran. How is she, by the way?'

'Bloody hell! You're a piece of work. Gran is fighting fit and dangerous, thanks for asking. She'll be living her days out with me. Repaying the kindness in her twilight years she showed me in my wayward youth.'

'I always envied you, Tiny.'

'Yeah, mate. Blessed, is what I am.'

'Yep. So, see you all in four weeks, then?'

'Congratulations, Troy Oscane, on a fine career and finishing it on a high note. Very sensible. Send us all those details and we'll be in touch. Thanks for calling.'

Tiny looked to the sky and nodded his head. *Reg Oscane, you old dog, your gift to your nephew will make his retirement very comfortable.* Walking back inside with a boyish smirk, he wrapped his arms around his dear grandmother and hugged her tightly. He told her how blessed he was, then made her sit down while he poured the tea.

'Say we were to go to South Australia, Gran, how would you like to travel and what scenery would you like to pass?'

'Gosh, Sonny! Let me see, it's an awfully long way, so how about we fly then drive? Um, scenery... somewhere near the Flinders Ranges. I've never seen them, and remember, we'll have two dogs to think about soon.'

His smile was enough to express his agreement. Staring unseeingly into his cup of tea, he sighed loudly.

'Make a phone call, you nincompoop!' Gran said wisely. Her eyes twinkled with mischief. 'Heavens, you've been pining ever since you got home. Go on, skedaddle. I'm going to settle into my reading nook.'

He just nodded and took Nova for a walk.

Radar's familiar ear-piercing whistle, like that of an eagle, sounded the much-needed lunch alarm. In silence, both teams tried to sneak up on each other, which proved more hilarious than tactical. Each of the twelve competitors had been shot once with a paintball, with the majority in the backside, given it was the meatiest – although not necessarily the largest – target. Hence, not many sat down to snack on muesli bars and replenish their water backpacks. Amid the frivolity was the bold competitive streak of each opponent. So far, they were all on the same level. No authority. No leaders. All team players.

Up to that point, the 'red' team Darlene was in were leading the challenge. Radar read out the scores of the latest accuracy challenges. The 'blue' team, Radar's team, had nailed all the static targets at least once, while the red team had missed four. This now brought the two teams together on even scores.

The afternoon's competition, however, was fraught with trying demands. Two competitors in each team would be mimicking an injury of their choosing, but one person had to be blindfolded. The hardest aspect was choosing who was going to be that person. Nobody on either team volunteered to be injured, either. Egos were riding high. Darlene wasn't good at relying on anybody. Never had been. But she felt it was about high time she learnt.

After the hour-long break, Radar retrieved the topographical map and pointed out the relevant checkpoints, the essential targets, the critical recoveries and the bonus point captures contained within the two-square-mile area. The 1800-hours rendezvous was a clearing in a gully where target practice would round off the day's competition. Its coordinates would be revealed at each of the two checkpoints, creating a puzzle for the players to solve.

Except this time round, there was to be a team leader. Radar led his squad in the opposite direction and blended in with the tree line. Foxtrot, the self-appointed, wannabe drill sergeant, led the red team towards the ravine. They slid down on their behinds, crawled up the rise and waited for instructions. In his obnoxious manner, with a tendency to be manipulative but clever in strategy, he pointed to Darlene and tossed over the bandana.

'My arm? My leg?' she challenged mischievously.

'Your eyes.' He looked at her smugly. 'Ever shot a gun blindfolded?'

'Not yet! Who's the injured one, then?'

'I'll do the honours and walk with a limp!' he retorted.

'Let's do this. Time's a-ticking,' she quipped and promptly tied the bandana around her eyes.

Slowing down her breathing, she concentrated on the confusion of noises around her then on the feeling of something being tied around her waist and tugged three times. All day, three of anything had meant 'go' and one had meant 'stop'. They'd communicated by hand signals or warning calls only. The afternoon was going to be exhausting. Stumbling and cussing under her breath, she wrapped one hand around the rope, making it easier to feel which direction to follow. She silently cursed herself for hastily volunteering.

By the time they'd reached the first checkpoint, she'd taken three shots – both ankles and one in the shoulder – and she was furious. She hadn't had the opportunity to shoot at anything. She'd been too busy trying to keep upright. Ripping off the bandana, she saw all three shots had been friendly fire. Eyeballing each team member, she walked in front of them, one at a time, and inhaled. Smelly deodorant. She'd detected it three times as it drifted past her. Bad BO. Yeah, she'd been following it for too long. The other two team members were scentless.

'Problem?' Foxtrot challenged, as she caught the stale smell of cigarettes.

'Yeah. Next time I get capped by friendly fire, you're all going to get one in return. Are we here to win this competition or humiliate me?'

The two scentless men instantly lowered their heads. Smelly looked away and smirked, Foxtrot clenched his fist, but Stinky glared at her. She returned the contemptuous look and stared him down. He took one step towards her, and she pointed her weapon at him, stopping him in his tracks.

'Don't. Or I will shoot you.'

He took a large step closer, and she shot him in the upper thigh, about two inches away from his groin. He scowled at her. His face was rife with anger. Foxtrot stepped in between them.

'She warned you. Serves you right.' He roughhoused Stinky. 'You're with me. Right, you lot, let's make tracks.'

Darlene saw that Smelly had hold of the rope. She reloaded her gun, eyeballed her teammates then retied the bandana. The whole dynamic of the team had shifted. Suddenly, it was a bunch of egotistical independents, and she was a burden.

A long while later, it was too quiet, so she stopped walking. The rope didn't pull her along. She listened. There weren't any footfalls on the dirt, or twigs snapping. The birds had stopped singing nearby and the crickets had fallen silent. She felt around for a tree, shimmied against its trunk and pulled the rope towards her. She pulled and pulled until she'd measured fifteen metres of rope. Too proud to call out for help and too pissed off to cry, she visualised Radar's map. She couldn't stay there blindfolded. That was daft. She had to break the rules. She had to take on her own team as well as the competition. Tying the rope into knots at one-metre lengths, she looped it through her shoulders, listened, then removed the bandana.

Using their careless footprints, she tracked her team, lost them through the pine needles but recovered swiftly. Travelling parallel to them and silently, she fired a few shots behind them. Knowing them better than themselves, she predicted they'd return fire in the direction they'd just come from. Jogging ahead of them, she came upon the edge of a clearing. She needed height. Scaling the nearest tree and scraping her hands in the process, she was almost three metres off the ground when she saw a peculiarly shaped pile of leaves to the left of her position, further away from her team. Shimmying down the tree and pulling out splinters while getting her bearings, she froze. A hideous brown snake slid across the path and disappeared into the brush.

Sprinting to where she figured the pile of leaves was, she caught some gunfire. Blue paint coloured the nearby trees. She returned fire madly, with several targets yelling out in pain. Another volley could be heard further away. Using the trunks as protection, she dodged her way to the pile. It was water. She took two of the six bottles, picked up the discarded plastic wrapping, which once contained another half dozen, shoved everything into her pockets and paint-blasted the trees behind her as a decoy. Now she was ready to hunt down her team.

Three hours later, she'd tracked them to the first checkpoint. They looked totally dejected. From her lookout, she saw the blue team approach from the other side. They were also one person down. No blindfolded one. No injured one. No Radar. Big mistake. Huge mistake. The two teams shot at each other several times, gathered the clues and scarpered off in opposite directions. All ten of them with no signs of injury.

Darlene had to find Radar. There was no way he'd have left himself vulnerable and blindfolded. No man in their right mind would do that. Nobody leaves their mates behind.

Her level of respect for the competitors had plummeted. She backtracked, saw fresh evidence of urination and hoped they weren't doing anything else when she did find whoever it was. Rapid fire of red and blue painted the trees above her head. She returned fire and ducked down behind the nearest trunk. Time for elevation. Spotting a fairly decent tree with dense foliage, she prayed there weren't any more snakes, waited for three minutes and climbed it easily. The branches weren't the strongest, but staying close to the trunk, she studied the ground level. Movement. No movement. She fired high deliberately. The return fire was low.

Then she saw him. Radar, no blindfold but actually limping. She was about to shimmy down the tree when she saw his adversary sneaking down the slope of the gully. Cunning buggers. It was a trap.

She stifled her gasp. No it wasn't! There were ten competitors at the checkpoint. Who the hell was this, then? Retrieving her rifle scope from her calf pocket, she couldn't hide her gasp this time. Gavin Milne. *What the hell? No. This cannot be happening.*

Surveying the ground cover for Radar, she found him. There was a dark stain on his calf. He moved like a giant unstable gazelle. Stealthily. Smoothly. But with a limp.

She needed to do something. As quietly as she could, she climbed down the tree, jogged towards them, climbed another tree, looked through the scope and focused on Radar's last known position. *There.* She swallowed hard. Milne had a long barrel and was about one hundred and fifty metres behind him. She was packing her Smith and Wesson. Darlene swiftly removed it, checked the magazine and removed the safety. *Game on, you bastard. Time to take out the trash.*

Listening carefully to the sounds of nature as she landed softly on the dirt, she concentrated on anything unusual while silently running towards Radar. Loud panting made her freeze against a broad tree trunk.

'Where the hell is he?' a voice squawked through a two-way.

'Bastard just disappeared. What's the range?' Milne's familiar, nasally tones replied.

'Too bloody far. Too many trees. You're going to have to do it. I lost you in the ravine, so stay high.'

Darlene's blood drained to her feet. She recognised the first voice. Oliver

Cady? What the hell was he doing over here? And with Gavin Milne? Had Radar set her up? She was momentarily paralysed when she heard Cady speak again.

'He was playing you about the bitch, Milne.'

'Yep, I realised that when I straightened out, but I don't believe she's at this party. Bloody sure she's not on some island neither. His lover, my arse! I'll have my way with her first, then we take her out. Not too many old Jeeps in this part of the world. Let's nail this bastard. She'll be an easy target then.'

'Righto. Stay high.'

'Best place to be.'

The sound of Milne heaving off the ground and jogging away noisily gave her the chance to breathe normally. She waited thirty seconds, fired a couple of shots in the air behind her with the paintball gun and listened to the rapid fire of something heavier further away. Darlene jogged towards it for a count of three hundred paces and climbed another tree. Cautiously using the scope, she scoured for movement. She focused the lens and saw it was Milne with a rifle slung over his shoulder. She knew he was too far away for an accurate shot. Scurrying back down the tree, she stuck to the soft earth and jogged for another one hundred paces in his direction, paused and fired a few shots behind her with the paintball gun, crouched down. An echoing volley answered, but the crack of a powerful weapon reached her ears rapidly. He was close.

Stepping quietly around several trees towards the sound, she found the one that was begging to be climbed. The magnificent red tingle tree. Another crack of the high-powered weapon made her dive for cover. She fired the paintball gun behind her to be met with silence. Without hesitation, she nimbly scaled the tree and sat astride a decent branch, her back resting against the beautiful trunk. Using the scope, she surveyed the ground for movement. The sun glinted off something metal about sixty metres away. *No!* Zooming in, she gasped. The bastard had a Sig Sauer.

In a split second, the scope was in her mouth and her Smith and Wesson was in her hand. Looking through its sight, she could make out Milne drawing the rifle up to his shoulder. In her mind's eye, she aimed for his hand. That ugly hand that was going to wrap itself around her neck. Breathed out slowly and squeezed the trigger several times. Calmly adjusting the scope, she saw him writhing on the ground, clutching at his wrist. Then she heard one shot, and suddenly, he wasn't moving anymore.

Darlene took stock of the surrounding area without looking at Milne, caught a glimpse of Radar, identified three landmarks, put away the scope, changed out clips, tucked her Smith and Wesson into the waistband of her pants and climbed down the tree. Treading silently, skirting Milne's location, she made her way to where she'd last seen Radar. Picking up on the blood trails, she followed them then lost them in a lot of leaf litter on one side of the path. Standing still, she listened for anything unnatural. Hearing a squelch echo through the still air, she made a beeline towards it, then stood stock-still.

'Where the hell are you, Milne? I've lost sight of you.'

Silence befell the radio. She listened carefully. In the distance, she vaguely heard heavy, uneven footfalls, but she couldn't find any more traces of blood. She'd lost the trail. Over her shoulder, in the distance, she caught sight of someone through the trees, then lost him. Shooting a couple of times into the air with the paintball gun was replied to with similar sounds behind her. He'd backtracked. Darlene pivoted on the spot and used the tree trunks as barriers on every fifth duck or weave. The sound of the two-way was louder.

'Dammit, Milne. Respond.'

She raised her paintball gun and stepped around the tree at the exact same time Radar did. Their faces reflecting mutual relief.

She rushed over to him. 'Bastard got you, Radar. I'm going to need your help, because I cannot carry you.'

'See, you do know how to ask for help!'

They both emitted a strangled laugh.

'It's good to see you, Ms Adams. I've lost a very important phone, and I have to find it. It's critical.'

'We've got to stop the blood first.' She whipped off her bandana and assisted Radar onto the ground. 'Any idea where you lost it?'

'Nope, I was about to make a call when he found me the first time. That's when I dropped it.'

'Can you use the method for tracing your own phone that you used for Milne's?'

'If I do, you are sworn to secrecy for the rest of your life.'

'Of course! Here, drink some water. I see you found a more practical use for your bandana! Stay still, I'm going to add mine to the mix.'

Darlene couldn't help herself and erupted into relieved giggles while tying her bandana on top of his blood-soaked one. After removing her backup phone from her calf pocket, she unlocked it and handed it to him with a grin.

'Here you go, Radar!'

'Walk away, please. You cannot hear this conversation. I hereby inform you that I will retain the use of this phone.'

'That's okay,' she said as she waved her usual phone at him. 'That's a just-in-case one. Go for it. I'm going to hug a tree!'

She walked fifteen paces to her right and dry retched. A smelly whiff reached her nose. Immediately, her 9mm was in her hand while she hid and listened to the approaching footfalls. It was Stinky. She counted to five, stepped out from the tree and shot the dirt in front of his feet.

'Stay where you are,' she said loudly.

'Listen, woman, things are going downhill quickly. And that ain't a paintball gun! Some bastard is taking pot shots at us in the clearing.'

'Anybody hurt?'

'No. Where's Radar?'

'Not available at the moment. He'll make contact when he is.'

They stared at each other until Stinky broke eye contact, groaned and sat heavily on the ground at the base of a tree. He looked at this watch, glared at her, frowned, closed his eyes then rested his head against the tree.

'Why did you leave the others?'

'Foxtrot knows I'm the better tracker, so he sent me.'

'You reckon?'

He just grunted.

Darlene barely breathed. Her voice dropped to a hissed whisper. 'Uh, whatever your name is, you might want to very slowly move away from that tree trunk. There's some sort of snake uncoiling itself above your head.'

'If it can climb trees, it's not dangerous,' he said flatly without opening his eyes.

'You're kidding yourself. Good luck.'

Suddenly, a large shadow loomed up behind her. She dropped to her knees and spun around with her pistol drawn. Radar's raised eyebrow and finger against his mouth made her blush. She nodded, stood up silently and did not move.

In three large, silent steps, he helped the snake from the tree, put it on the ground and gently put his heavy boot on its head while he held its writhing tail at shoulder height.

'MOVE!' he bellowed.

Well, Stinky nearly crapped himself as he tried to scramble to his feet, misplacing them both and falling flat on his backside with a look of mixed horror, relief and fright contorting his face.

'Sir. That's a huge snake. Sir,' he managed to say as he scrambled to his feet.

'Yep. And it's getting very angry. You best get back to where you came from. NOW.'

As he said that, Radar lifted his foot.

Darlene passed out.

'Hey, hey, Ms Adams, welcome back!' Radar's gentle voice brought her back to the land of the living while he flicked water over her face.

'Where's Stinky?' she asked while wiping the droplets off her nose.

'Who?'

'Stinky. The amazing tracker,' she said and swallowed hard.

'Oh, he went to lead the pussies back to the range. Now, we need each other's help. Firstly, let's go and find my phone. Secondly, can you remember Cady's number?'

'He's here, Radar. Stinky said someone was taking pot shots at the boys in the clearing, and I heard him talking to Milne on the two-way.'

'He's not going to hang around in the trees in the dark, that I can guarantee you.'

'Did you know? Did you know they were both here?'

His withering gaze prevented her from asking any further questions. 'As I said, Ms Adams, we're going to need each other's help. Do you have his number?'

'Yes.'

'Good. Take my hand, and I'll help you to your feet. Find the number while you catch your breath then read out the digits very clearly. Then say nothing else. Afterwards, you are going to have to listen very carefully. We'll be tracing my phone.'

She obeyed, then heard all sorts of peculiar noises as he took the phone away and put it in his shirt pocket. Together, they followed the pinging, which gradually got louder. The shadows were lengthening. Very soon, they'd be without any natural light. Eventually, the harmonious pinging filled the air, almost causing them both to celebrate loudly. The dirt around the screen illuminated with a green shadow. Darlene picked up the glowing phone and handed it to Radar, screen down.

'Thank you.' Then he spoke into his pocket. 'Thank you, Overwatch.'

'Yes, sir. Out.'

She stared at the phone then back at him, her mouth agape. She gazed skywards and felt compelled to blow a kiss.

'Let's get out of here, Radar. I've got an image of one of those thick chunks of rib eye replacing a thousand questions.'

'That's all the incentive I need. Do you know the way?'

'We can work it out together by looking at that map. Looks like we've both learnt a few things today, sir.'

'Indeed. Wasn't hard, was it?'

She chuckled and didn't reply. Their headlamps clicked on simultaneously as they cross-referenced the GPS coordinates with the topographical map.

Amongst more cuts, scrapes, and bruises, and with both limping, Darlene and Radar met their teams halfway across the floodlit shooting range.

'On behalf of all of us, we owe you both a massive apology,' Foxtrot gushed.

'Make sure you've prepared a report for me by noon tomorrow,' Radar commanded. 'Every single one of you, and heaven help you if they're exactly the same. DISMISSED.'

The ten men scurried away with their tails between their legs.

'Yellow-bellied pussies.' Radar scowled.

Darlene knew better than to say anything and helped the injured man to the waiting paramedics. They dressed his wound, and commented on the loss of blood, but after much encouragement, they agreed he would not require a hospital. Her ice-wrapped sprained ankle wouldn't take long to heal if she rested it appropriately.

'What about that steak?' Radar asked as he hobbled into the kitchen.

'You cook it, I'll make the sauce and salad. But only after I go and clean up.'

'Copy that.'

Radar made sure he was alone when he spoke quietly into his phone.

'Confirmed hit, Tango Mike?'

'Affirmative, sir.'

'Excellent. Need a clean-up crew.'

'Acknowledged.'

'Any luck on the leak?'

'Not yet. Will advise, sir.'

'It was a close call.'

'Relieved you're still walking.'

'Thanks for the assist.'

'Our visual was obscured. We're lucky our Pretty One had your back.'

'Indeed.'

'Our lips are sealed. On the turn. Out.'

He smiled with relief. Nobody would have forgiven themselves if the beautiful crack shot had been taken out. Radar would finish removing the trash when he discovered who let the cat out of the bag.

They both sat down to a particularly hearty feast, clinked their beers together and thanked each other for the day.

'Am I safe, Radar?'

'Yes, Ms Adams. You certainly are.'

'Thank you. Now I can eat without getting indigestion!'

'Likewise. Incidentally, our mutual friend will happily give you a lift back to your accommodation after dinner.'

'I'm not going to ask.' Darlene winked cheekily.

'You're full of nonsense. Now, go on and eat your dinner, young lady. Nice sauce.'

'Perfectly cooked steak. Thank you, sir.'

As suspected, Peachie arrived forty minutes later. Radar recounted the day with much humour, leaving Darlene to think he had an absolutely fat time. He insisted he'd be resting up for several days and would be in touch. The farewell felt almost final.

She let Peachie initiate the conversation as they pulled into the retreat. Up until then, they'd been lost in their own thoughts.

'Hope you're not disappointed in me?'

'No, not at all. Thanks for pitching in, Peachie. I was way out of my depth.'

'When you're ready, we'll have a look at the footage and go from there. But right now, you've had one hell of a day. I'll wait until you're inside the lobby before I roll. Good night, Darlene.'

'Thanks again. Good night. Please travel well.'

'Always.'

She slid out of the front seat with her weapons and quietly closed the door. When she blew a kiss, he pretended to catch it and put it in his pocket. She nearly burst into tears and managed to smile broadly before turning away as the waterworks escaped.

She desperately needed a hug, desperately needed to talk to someone. She was desperately alone. Void of any coherent thought, she showered, then on autopilot cleaned her weapons and collapsed onto her bed.

Shouldering the rear door of the Jeep closed two days later, Darlene carried the last of the grocery boxes into the pantry. Putting away and sorting out the items in shelf-life order, she then straightened up the other shelves, vacuumed, mopped and sterilised the storage benches. Seated at the staff table to the side of the pantry, she folded the freshly laundered tea towels, aprons and bandanas while waiting for Jody and Bo. Their regular meeting was conducted when neither of the staff members were on shift. The mouth-watering aromas of pizza and garlic bread made her stomach growl. She'd deliberately had a light breakfast and was famished.

'Hi, Darlene, thanks for doing another trip so soon – the drivers are either hungry or just plain greedy,' Jody said with a chuckle. 'Today, we're sampling coffee beans from the South Pacific. Are you hungry?'

'It's no problem at all, thanks, and yes, your pizza is killing me. It smells amazing!'

'Good. New recipe for the base. Hope you like thick and loaded.'

They were sharing a good laugh as easy as old friends did when Bo walked in, removed his cap and promptly scoffed a crust off the steaming hot garlic bread. In all the deliveries to date, at no stage had Jody discussed her staff, and she quite often steered the conversation away from the harvest. Her prized stud rams were always the butt of many jokes, as were Bo's combine harvesters. They were all trying not to drool while the pizza cooled down enough to slice when Elaina burst through the door.

'Boss Lady, come quick–' She looked at Darlene wide-eyed, smiled, started to cry, then spluttered, 'Um, we need your help.'

'Wait here,' Jody commanded.

Bo and Darlene looked at each other and took their seats.

Within thirty seconds, Jody's bellow reached their ears. 'Get in here now, you pair. Need extra hands.'

Pushing open the accommodation door ahead of Bo, Darlene gasped in horror. A dark-haired young lass in a simple cotton shift with a scarf around her neck was lying on the floor in a pool of blood. Her skin as pale as the buttermilk-coloured walls.

'Good God, what on earth?'

'Girly troubles, and she has them bad... Bo, those towels. Darlene, do whatever you can to prepare a moat in the shower. Elaina, dab her brow.'

Calling out from the shower that it was ready, Bo helped as best he could without getting in the road. 'Ladies, I'll tend to the kitchen. This is your department.'

The girl tried to grip Jody's arm and struggled to whisper, 'Leave my... scarf... on... p-please.'

'Yes, okay. Now, this is Darlene Adams, Elaina's guardian. She's here to help out. Stop fussing, child, and let us help you get sorted.'

The poor girl couldn't stand. She either clutched her stomach or her head and cried out in agony. Darlene helped support her and insisted Elaina either get hot water bottles or warm up the towels. Heat on the stomach would hopefully ease her discomfort. It still worked for her. Anything hot on her stomach, even in the middle of the stinking hot summers.

Eventually, the girl had a bit more colour in her face and could speak coherently without screaming out in pain. With several hot water bottles strategically positioned, Darlene and Jody made themselves useful and cleaned up the evidence in the donga. Elaina volunteered to do the laundry.

'How long as she been like this?' Darlene asked quietly.

Jody attempted to explain. 'For the last six months now. Apparently. She missed her doctor's appointment due to circumstances beyond her control...'

'What on earth is she waiting for?'

'That's another story.'

'I can tell her, Boss Lady,' the girl said weakly and leaned against the door frame for support. 'I think I'd better be home soon after the next monthly visit.'

'Should you wait that long?' Jody asked.

'Yes. The hot water bottles have worked better than anything else. How the hell can I strap these around me?'

'It's not a fashion show. We can make a plan,' Darlene said kindly. 'While you rest, perhaps I can be useful?'

'Boss? Will that be okay if I do rest for an hour?' she almost pleaded.

'I expect you to. How's your head?'

'Yeah, having the cool wrap around it has helped, thanks. I dread this time of the month, but I am eternally grateful to you, Jody. Thank you too, ma'am.'

Jody nodded her head but shook it sadly as soon as the girl had lain down and shut her eyes, leaving her bedroom door open. Indicating that they would talk outside, Darlene gently placed another damp towel over the girl's forehead. Lightly squeezing her shoulder, she whispered, 'I'll leave my number for you. Phone anytime, you poor little poppet.'

'Boss, I'll stay for an hour with her, then finish off my shift, if that's okay,' Elaina suggested.

'Yes, that's fine. Thank you.'

The women conferred outside in hushed tones about possible remedies, both old-fashioned and new, to ease the onslaught of cramps. The headaches were Darlene's greatest concern, though. A blocked pituitary gland could cause an awful amount of havoc on one's metabolism and reproductive organs. She should know.

Lunch was a quiet affair, with Bo making himself scarce, given the circumstances.

'Jody, I never travel without my suitcase, so I can stay tonight and do the young girl's shift... um... it's not my business, but nobody calls anybody by their name?'

'You're right, it isn't your business. Just know that my staff don't socialise. They've met, they share the donga, but they're here to work. You will be introduced to the young lass when she's ready. It is unusual, but it's necessary.'

Drama aside, they couldn't stop eating the delicious meaty gourmet pizza. It was the best one Darlene had ever had the pleasure of devouring. Topping it off with the perfectly grilled homemade garlic bread, it was no wonder Jody's Kitchen was on the top of Peachie's list of places to eat.

Jody poured the deliciously aromatic coffee and said, 'I'd better take some pizza to Bo and have a chat with him. In the meantime, I will take up your offer of helping out until Elaina's back on shift. She was probably getting things ready for the pepper steak pies and making croutons. Make sure the rosemary is added before baking, please. Can I leave this with you?'

'Absolutely. I don't have any commitments tomorrow, nor I am expecting to be paid extra. Go on, you've got a business to run.'

'You're an earth angel, Darlene. You just don't know it yet.'

After Jody left, her words rang in Darlene's head. The memory of Jimmy saying the same thing to his matron poured out her eyes like the grief tap had just been turned on full blast. Eventually composing herself, she donned an apron, bandana, hairnet and gloves and got back into the kitchen. It was like she hadn't left, but this was a kitchen like no other.

Tiny chided himself for leaving such a goofy message. 'Hi, Darlene. Hope you and Elaina are well. We've got a new old dog! Um, you girls seen any shooting stars? Oh, it's Tiny calling. Bye.'

He, Nova and the latest addition to the family, Pluto, a Jack Russell, ran around stupidly for the rest of the afternoon. Almost breathless, he answered Spook's call.

'Hey, mate!'

'You going to Sarge's retirement party?'

'Yeah, thinking about it. Granny said she'd like to fly down then drive. What say you?'

'You taking Nova?'

'Of course. And Pluto. Her new dog.'

'Instant family. You need a woman now!' They shared in another laugh.

'How's your family, Spook?'

'Thanks for asking. Grandma is like a cat on a hot tin roof every time the phone rings. We've been told to expect the twins to grace our world any day, and even though we've heard it so often I don't think she'll consider leaving the area! I'm excited, too, but can't do much except wait.'

They discussed the available options and would make suggestions with their companions once the actual invitation had been received. Peachie came up in conversation, as did Elaina and Darlene. Spook thought Tiny's message was hilarious and teased him the whole time he walked back to his office.

271

Sitting heavily in his chair, he called Spook a few choice names then fell silent as he clicked on the attachment to Troy's e-mail.

'Bloody hell,' he whispered.

'What's up?'

'I've got some work to do. Hey, Spook, you heard about that sting at Port Pirie?'

'Yeah. It's still all over the news. Sick of it, actually, and willing to bet those Russian families can't wait to get the hell out of the place.'

'True.'

'You sound preoccupied. Anything I can do to help?'

'Yeah, follow up with Peachie about the Ford Focus. Thanks. Reckon we're missing something.'

'Righto. Talk soon. Ciao.'

Tiny studied the report, drew up an investigation board with all the known information and came up with absolutely no leads whatsoever. Even Spider had crawled down a hole. He circled the name and added a large question mark. Dialling Troy's number, he wasn't surprised by the cautious answer.

'Already?'

'No. Can you give me the missing one's last known number and tell me, that event out at Penong, what was its outcome?'

'That was a mystery to all of us at my level. The perp is still a blubbering mess, pleading mental illness. Under surveillance in a hospital ward down south, I believe. I'm not privy to how long they can keep him. I'm suspicious but have nothing to back up my claim. I'll flick that through as well. Hey, this is all covert.'

'Do you think there's a connection between all this and your colleague's missing daughter?'

'My guts say there is.'

'Good enough for me. Send through everything you've got. No promises – and hurry up and send through your invitation, I need to make arrangements.'

'You'd be there?'

'Wouldn't miss it, Troy. We need to have that drink, remember.'

'Yeah, yeah, for sure. Thank you. Now that I know you'll be there, I'm sure Spook will be too, so I'll make it an easy place, but sorry, it'll have to be in this neck of the woods. Any suggestions?'

'Orroroo. Peterborough. Somewhere with the Flinders in the background.'

'Thanks, Tiny. Really look forward to seeing you guys again. Oops, got to go. Sending now. Bye, mate.'

Tiny drummed the desk impatiently. There had to be a connection. It reeked of rogue drivers that many decent ones had been getting rid of over the years.

'Darlene?' Jody called out as she entered the kitchen. 'Bo and I have discussed it. You can stay and work. Manage your own fatigue, but you have to have eight hours sleep before you leave tomorrow. My crew should be firing on all cylinders by then. Take the middle room in the donga, and no talking all night. In saying that, you'll be driving out of here after midday.'

'I'll do my best tonight, Jody. Where's the to-do list?'

Satisfied that she was quite competent in working autonomously, Jody handed her the menu. Pointing to the highlighted items, she grinned. 'Just do what you can, Darlene. I'll check in with you before 10:30 p.m.'

'Thanks, boss. I'll shift in now before it gets dark and have a break.'

Removing her kitchen attire and stepping into the donga, she swiftly made up her bed. In desperate need of a strong coffee, she listened to the telephone messages while she stirred the cup quietly. Almost bursting out laughing at Tiny's dorky one, she did wonder why he just didn't contact Elaina himself, but still couldn't get the smile off her face and went and stood by her V8. He had phoned her, not the other way around. Things were looking up! She felt warm all over until she listened to her father's message. Leaning against the front bumper, she replayed it before returning the call.

'Hey, Dad, thanks for calling. Guess where I am?'

'In trouble, by the two men that are looking for you. What have you done?'

'Being a crack shot isn't always what it's cracked up to be. How long ago did they phone?'

'Oh, almost a fortnight ago. Yeah, I'm a bit slack in getting the message to you, but your mother and I squabbled every time the subject came up. Anyway, they weren't threatening, they just couldn't get a hold of you and expressed their concern. Mum wanted to give them your new number, but I discouraged her. That's what you would have wanted, no doubt.'

'Absolutely. Thanks. You're right, it is an old message. We caught up, everything is sorted. Anyway, how are you all?'

He enthusiastically explained her mother was out at a Pinot and Paint class while he was waiting for his lift to go to the local men's shed. They both felt they'd finally grasped the retirement thing.

'We're over halfway through November already. Cassie has said she can't get home for Christmas – do you think you can?'

'New Year, definitely. Why?'

'We're all going to hire houseboats at Echuca and have Christmas lunch on a paddle steamer.'

'Gosh, that does sound exciting!'

'New Year celebrations might be quiet, given the week-long sojourn on board, although we will all be together at Cassie's home. Is that enough information for you to work a plan?'

His rumbling chuckle brought tears to her eyes. 'Oh, Dad. I really could do with one of your hugs.'

'There'll be plenty waiting for you, pet. Take care, love you lots.'

'Love you too. Please block those pesky numbers...'

'Already have. Bye for now.'

Sighing loudly, she gazed skywards and smiled. Someone up there was watching over her. She knew it. Blowing a kiss towards the heavens, she also said a little prayer to Jimmy and wiped at a stray tear.

Draining her coffee cup, her thoughts turned to the frail dark-haired young woman nearby. She dialled Bev's number.

'This is a surprise!'

'Hi, Bev, only a quick call, but I was thinking of you. How're you doing?'

'Keeping the chin up and dosing on the positive thoughts. I can only make it a quick call too. I've got to fly – have a party to organise, Darlene. Great hearing from you. The girls are well and behaving! Bye for now.'

A party! Darlene loved a good party, and it had been such a very long time since she'd attended one, let alone organised one. Refraining from feeling sorry for herself, instead she replayed Tiny's funny message. With a broad grin on her face, she strode purposefully into the kitchen and met the cooking challenges with gusto.

CHAPTER EIGHTEEN

Seated in the darkened corner of the remote pub, Spider was eyeing off the display of potential toys. He'd gotten tired of being alone. With his truck and trailers stashed at an abandoned rail siding out of town, he'd stuck to the scrubby tracks leading to the pub on nightfall. With his plan to take some time off, he paid cash for a room for a few nights.

After the shocking conversation with Max, Spider had decided to fulfil his obligations to his boss, retrieve the yellow Ford Focus and then pay a visit to Bluey. All without Snake Girl. He realised he hadn't missed her at all. There was no point in going back to Port Pirie now all his toys had escaped and Stevo was also dead.

Smiling now as a leggy brunette with every crevice of her ears laden with sparkly piercings walked towards him, he very slowly got up, showed off his bulging pants and strolled out the side door towards the accommodation units. Waiting in the shadows, he crept silently behind her and wrapped his arms around her as she turned around.

'Feel like playing, Blingbling?'

Her giggle turned him on even more. 'Lead the way, Daddy Long Legs.'

'Goodie, we can have a midnight picnic. I've got Pepsi.'

'What are we waiting for, then?'

'No questions. Do not ask questions,' he said and tightened his grip on her arms while steering her towards the furthest motel room. 'I hate questions. You will play nicely.'

'It's five hundred for the night. You pay upfront.'

'I pay nothing at all. You're mine now.'

She tried to struggle, and the minute she opened her mouth to say something else, he shoved a balled-up, drug-laced handkerchief into her mouth. Almost immediately, she stumbled. He gathered her into his embrace and disappeared into the darkened room, swiftly locking the door behind him. If anybody had been watching, it would appear he was the perfect gentleman supporting a rather inebriated friend. Securing her hands and feet, he removed the gag, wrapped her in a blanket and took off her shoes. No shoes on the bed.

Yay! We play. Don't work tomorrow. Let's play.

With a sly curl of his lips, he forced Blingbling to sip on the straw sticking out of the Pepsi bottle and patted her head gently. Leaving her wrapped up, he sent a message to his boss. *Am tired. Need a break. No loads tomorrow.*

Humming his happy little tune, Spider prepared himself for a mini holiday.

Thousands of kilometres away, one out of four minuscule pings faded into the network of monochrome lines filling the computer screen. Its activity had been minimal, with only one other communique to somewhere along the southern end of the Dingo Fence in South Australia. However, that number had been particularly active between Yalata and Penong. Overwatch entered the data into his report.

Three days later, Radar grinned broadly as Darlene entered the shooting range foyer.

'So glad you could make it, Ms Adams. You're going to make a young lady very happy.'

'Nice to see you again, Radar. You and Peachie have a strong connection, I gather!'

'Indeed. Care to have a couple of practice shots with your long barrel while we're waiting?'

'Actually, I would, thank you!'

She selected her preferred targets and commenced her routine preparation.

Radar smiled and nodded appreciatively as he watched the projectile of her .22 LR successfully obliterate the bullseye at one thousand metres.

'You're getting good at this. You sure you don't want to go on tour with me?'

Chuckling as she prepared to take the maximum two-thousand-metre shot, she said, 'No, thanks. I've got some loose ends to tie up, then I'm heading home for New Year.'

'Peachie will be arriving soon; I'll make myself scarce, if you like?'

Darlene lowered the weapon, turned to look at him and smiled. 'Only if you feel that's necessary.'

'I'll hang around in the shadows, if you don't mind. Would you care to join me for lunch afterwards?'

'Thank you, that would be nice.'

'Excellent. The wind's picking up, Ms Adams... let's see how you go now!'

'Challenge accepted, Radar.'

Tucking the stock of the rifle snugly into her shoulder with a firm stance, she looked through the telescopic sight and focused on the distant leaves swaying intermittently in the breeze either side of the target. With the wind blowing from the left, she'd have to adjust her aim appropriately.

One shot. She only had one shot. Imagining she was shooting to save her life from being abducted, she shut out all noises, slowed down her breathing and focused. Her trigger finger resting lightly on the undercarriage of the barrel, she counted down from five. On two, she curled her finger around the single-stage trigger. On the count of one, she squeezed.

'You nailed him,' a quiet voice said with admiration. 'Well done, Ms Adams.'

Jubilation built up in her like she'd never experienced before. Her trip home with the girls was going to be a lot safer now.

Peachie watched from behind the perspex screens as she capably stripped down the rifle, cleaned and rebuilt it before wrapping it up in its soft cloth and inserting it snugly into its case. She truly was a wonderful markswoman. He'd arrived early enough to watch her nail all the bullseyes with the pistols and rifle. Studying her counterpart's mutual respect, Peachie discreetly snapped a photo and sent it off to Spook and Tiny with the message: *Danish Pastry in good hands. This one has a sharp eye.*

It was at that moment Darlene turned around, stared at him with a broad grin and shook her finger. 'No photos, Peachie!'

She walked around the barrier and hugged him tightly. 'It is so good to see you again.'

He wasn't about to divulge that Spook had been in touch with him and returned her hug. 'You're a sight for sore eyes! I'd be in deep strife if I didn't take a picture, Darlene.'

The genuine greeting between him and Radar was quite heartwarming. She and Peachie went to a quiet section of the clubhouse and spent the next hour sharing their company with his gorgeous twenty-eight-year-old wheelchair-bound granddaughter, DeeDee. She'd been sixteen when she got pinned in the bunk of a truck after the driver had fallen asleep at the wheel. She should never have been there. She never finished her shift at the café and was abducted from right under the noses of the owners. Her being alive had changed Peachie's attitude towards life for the better, and he'd made it his mission in life to ensure hers was as peachy as he could make it. His circle of friendship with Tiny and Spook had got thicker afterwards. That driver did not survive. The owners sold up and left the state.

Darlene was determined to do everything she could for the young woman and promised to visit her before the end of the year.

'Please can I have a signed photo of us together when you do come visit, Ms Adams?' DeeDee asked.

'Absolutely. Would you like to have a shoot too?'

The next thirty minutes were spent discussing all sorts of options, with suggestions of hand and arm exercises to strengthen the muscles needed to squeeze a trigger. They reluctantly ended the conversation with promises of extending DeeDee's social network with Darlene's new circle of South Australian friends.

'Thank you so much,' Peachie gushed. 'You've made a young woman very happy, and I'm delighted to have been in your company again.'

'It's the least I can do. I uphold my promises, as you're well aware. Maybe we can return east via convoy, or are you hanging around after harvest?'

'Only for the party at Jody's Kitchen, then I'm heading out. I might even think about retiring soon.'

He had just finished breaking the news when Radar joined their table and heartily slapped him on the shoulder.

'What a jolly good idea!' Darlene exclaimed.

'What about you, young lady? What will you do when you go home, wherever that is?'

She playfully punched Peachie on the other shoulder. 'Go where the platypus play. And that's all you need to know right now! I have a sneaking suspicion you'd let one too many secrets out of the bag... again!'

He chuckled and shook hands with Radar. 'You pair can shoulder-tap me anytime! I'll leave you to enjoy your lunch. Stay in touch, Radar.'

The farewell between Darlene and Peachie was warm, with them promising to reconnect before the harvest party. Neither had mentioned the video or the note. Darlene was going to fight this battle alone.

Tiny stared at the screen while a lump formed in his throat. It had been a long while since he'd seen his former commanding officer. Nobody would ever realise his hips were prosthetic under his smart black trousers. Tiny's bravery in rescuing the Alpha Unit bordered on a death wish, but he owed it to the memory of his own unit to save this one.

The buzzing of his slimline phone jolted him into reality. From experience, he knew that coincidences like this weren't always a good thing but answered calmly.

'Tango Mike. How nice it is in the sunshine!'

'Lima Bravo. As it is in the moonlight!'

'Thanks for getting in contact.'

'Looks like the band's getting back together.'

'Do tell.'

'CO is looking well and met the large round one socially.'

'Is that it?'

'Yes, boss. Thought you'd like to know. No sighting of the yellow vehicle. Will update on the old hot spot.'

'Copy that. Anything else?'

'No, boss. On the turn. Out.'

Frowning at the ambiguity, Tiny suspected there was more to the social gathering, but he'd have to wait for Peachie or Spook to spill. He shook his head forlornly. They were good. They never did. Nova sensed her master's anxiety and paced the studio alongside him. He missed the adrenaline of a good hunt but was enjoying calling the shots from the safety of his secret location when given the opportunity. Replying to Peachie's message, he thanked him profusely.

Tiny then informed Spook of the latest update on the yellow vehicle; Spook would naturally bring Peachie up to speed. He sent a text message to Troy confirming acceptance of the retirement party invitation. The glamping options outside of Peterborough sounded like the perfect weekend's celebration.

'Come, girl,' Tiny said to Nova. 'Let's go and see if Granny and Pluto are up for a stroll through the rose garden.'

He smiled and watched his treasured pooch bound up the stairs and wait at the landing behind the ancient display cabinet. Keying in the digits, he stepped out from behind it and inhaled deeply. The aroma from Gran's freshly baked apple and rhubarb pie filled the room nicely.

Pacing angrily along the walkway in between silos, Bo couldn't believe Spider would be so stupid and go walkabout. Dialling Max's number exacerbated the situation when his mobile also went straight to message bank. Trying to find solace in the last of the sunrays painting the wheat gold, Bo grinned mirthlessly. He had longed for the day he'd be rid of the South Australian connection. Spider had just fast-tracked it.

The tell-tale sign of the dusty cloud behind his wife's 4WD would bring a tender smile to his face until the day he died. There would always be some culinary delight to share after their warm embrace, even with the troubles they battled together.

'Bo, honey, how would you feel about harbouring another stray until the harvest party?'

'If you're talking about Darlene, I've got no problems with that. It'd make things simpler for them to depart all together anyway. Is Milly's health deteriorating?'

'No. Darlene needs to keep a low profile for a while. With her here, I can go and get the groceries. There's banking business which is overdue as well, and Christmas is around the corner.'

'Sure. Go for it. Listen, Spider's gone underground. If you see my truck in your travels, let me know! Little bastard. That was the last straw. Max has got to go as well.'

'About bloody time. And get rid of that flipping car. There's something not right with it. It's poison.'

Bo wiped crumbs from his lips after finishing the still-warm apricot pie and gathered Jody into his arms. He hummed their favourite tune and rocked her gently. This was their special time together.

Spider listened to Max's rant while slouching against the glass of the public phone box on the outskirts of town. Rolling his eyes, he focused on his passenger, fast asleep against the truck window. Four days of play were what he had needed. He still needed to fulfil his obligation then meet up with Max sooner rather than later.

'Shut up and listen to me, you old fool,' he hissed. 'Max, I have the yellow Ford Focus. I took it. I told you that. I will be driving it back, and you and Bluey will be meeting me at the Mundrabilla Pass. I will need another truck or vehicle of some sort. I have a new toy.'

'You will not bring any toys. The police are combing the hills for you and me.'

'Are not.'

'Yes, they are. Come home earlier, Spider. I miss you. We have lots to talk about.'

'Liar. You're a liar, Max, and your pants will be on fire. Your nose will grow as long as a telephone wire. So there.'

'Listen to me, boy. Come home soon. Don't worry about finishing that job. We can go on holiday.'

'You like boys. I don't. No. Not going on holiday with you. Not. Not. Not.'

'Get back here, or I'll come and fetch you.'

'Don't you dare threaten me, and don't ever tell me what to do again.'

Spider slammed down the phone. How much longer did he have to do this job? Climbing back inside the truck, he gently pulled Blingbling onto his lap and made his way back to the farm. It was going to be very late when he got back to the caravan and would be able to stash his new toy without any trouble.

While waiting in line at the silo and auger bins for the first load of the day, Spider smiled evilly, knowing he had a toy stashed away in the caravan. Then he tuned into the hot topic on the two-way. News of the missing prostitute travelled quickly in the remote region. The locals were familiar with the pierced harvest hussy who preyed on the newcomers. She'd returned like a bad rash for the last nine harvests.

A rash? Have you got a rash?

Spider thumped the side of his head and eyeballed the boss as he strutted along the walkway. Anticipating the ringing phone, he answered it first.

'I'm here, as you can see, boss. Where am I off to today?'

'Albany.'

'I'm getting tired of this job. When do I finish?'

'Couple of weeks.'

'And then?'

'You can take your car and your cash and go home. Never to return.'

'Suits me fine. I'll work hard every day until then. Thanks, boss.'

Spider waved happily at the bloke beside the auger as he rolled past and obediently followed the hand signals until the three trailers were full. Trundling along and blocking the view to the caravan, he climbed over to the passenger side, crawled out and crept into his caravan, retrieved his sleeping toy and managed to fold her into the floor-well of the passenger seat then quietly shut the door.

With his bag slung over his shoulder, he locked the caravan, waved up to the boss and strolled around the trailers while winding down the tarps. Spit-polishing the chrome bumper bar, he slid behind the wheel and rolled the tattoo sleeves down the length of his arms while slowly navigating the dusty farm road. A lovely lazy day where all his spiders could play. He liked Blingbling's bling.

Smiling and looking forward to the brunch the girls were organising, Bev snuggled into her recently retired partner. Drawing love hearts in his lightly hairy chest and listening to his steady breathing, she was in two minds as to joining him in retirement or continuing with the job she was so passionate about.

It was Sunday and one week away from the private retirement party. Troy's almost instant family had spent a terrific weekend at Cowell Beach, with the girls barely containing their excitement about glamping in the rugged foothills and celebrating their much older friend's retirement. Cassie had made Bev promise that she'd arrange for Darlene to make a surprise appearance by video link. When asked why, after the long-winded description of how much the woman loved a party, it came down to the fact that she wouldn't have been to one in a long while.

Bev's wishes and affirmations for her daughter's well-being were repeated endlessly. Whether she was making up for the years she hadn't prayed or setting a precedent for future years, she hadn't decided. Either way, she whispered her morning prayer.

Yawning silently as she slipped the invoice into Jody's folder, Darlene closed her room door and leaned against it. She had the next twenty-four hours to herself and was really looking forward to having lunch with Radar again at the shooting range later that day. Through the lacy curtains, she saw her beloved Jeep sitting under the cover in the carport. Waiting. Waiting for a long run. Peeking out from under its protective layer was one sexy looking front grill and fat tyres. Desperately missing the luxury and peace of the retreat, she finally accepted the decision she'd made.

Totally exhausted and grateful to have two extra pair of hands in the kitchen, even though they were like ships in the night, Darlene wasn't sure if it was her age or experience that had encouraged the senior role. It just seemed a natural transition. The weekly meetings were professional and productive. Jody appeared to be far less stressed, and together they had decided on introducing a new dessert, given Christmas was just around the corner. And the weather was hot. The trifle cups had become the most popular sweets item on the menu, the feedback box overflowing with requests for them to be available at the harvest break-up party. The other overflowing requests were wanting the date of the party! Darlene needed to know as well so she could make plans.

A soft knock on her door broke her reverie. The youngest lass with the long, thick dark hair nervously played with her fingers. The two women looked at each other shyly, but the minute Darlene stepped back, the girl swiftly moved inside and closed the door. Standing with her back against the furthest wall from the windows, she stammered before regaining a bit of confidence.

'Ms Adams... um... Jody and Bo told me who you are. Please can I bum a lift back to South Australia with you? I'll contribute to the fuel.'

'You have a distinct advantage over me – I don't even know your name! In saying that, yes, I'll happily give you a lift. In the very brief conversations I've had with Elaina, she speaks very highly of you and treasures your friendship. So, whereabouts in South Australia?'

'I love her accent. We haven't had much time to talk, but we clicked when we first met. It sort of feels like one of those lifetime friendships, even though we didn't know each other before. Totally weird. But totally special too. Um... do you know where Port Lincoln is?'

Darlene's instinct did somersaults. She could almost feel the fireworks exploding in her eyes, it was that strong. She clasped the girl's pale hands.

'I won't tell a soul, but I am praying you have a snake tattoo hiding under that beautiful scarf.'

Milly crumpled into Darlene's arms and sobbed as she poured her heart out. She told her the whole story, from running away from home, getting the snake tattoo, living with her best friend, Amy, not knowing if her mother was alive and not knowing where to start looking for her, being abducted, drugged and used as a sex slave then rescued. With her health the way it was, she knew there was something wrong but didn't want to die before talking to her mother. That was the only thing that kept her going. Darlene rocked her gently until her tears had lessened and let her step out of the embrace.

'Ms Adams, please don't tell anybody this, but I want to kill that freaky schizo bastard, except I'm not a murderer. I've heard you're a crack shot, though I don't reckon you're a murderer either. He has got to die. The car he stole is under a tarp in the shed. Bo nearly sprung me, and I definitely don't want him or Jody to be involved. I owe them my life. A debt of gratitude. How can I repay them?'

'Seeing as I still don't know your name, I'm going to call you my younger sister.'

Milly's smile brought her face alive. She truly was a beautiful young woman. Darlene explained that things worked out when they were meant to and that she and Milly would need to bide their time like they had so far. The undeniable theory had already proved itself.

'Yeah, but he's got to die.'

'You mentioned a shed?'

'Yep. One of Bo's.'

Darlene excitedly grabbed Milly's hands. 'Then Bo will know when he's finishing up. If our bosses are aware of your circumstances, I'm willing to bet this mongrel won't be around for the harvest party.'

'Damned straight. I'll ask them on my next shift. Ms Adams, do you know of anybody who has the right to shoot someone?'

'Dear girl, shooting someone in fear of your safety can be mentally damaging in its own right, but killing someone? I'm not going there. However, if a type of animal should bite a human...'

Milly gasped. 'Like a spider? Better still, a snake.'

They looked at each other and grinned.

'Your secret is safe with me, little sister. Now, before you skedaddle, I want to show you something. Two things, actually.'

Digging around in her suitcase, she handed Milly the shotgun cartridge. 'You had several guardian angels looking after you that day!'

She gasped and promptly shoved it into her pocket. 'Oh, wow! You found it. You? Wow!'

Grinning and nodding, Darlene slid her phone off the cabinet and located the photo she was looking for. Before showing Milly, she explained the wonderful network of strong women she'd gotten involved with. Their motto was empowerment and positivity.

'That's my mum,' Milly whispered as she stared at the screen. 'You know her? Oh, God, that's Amy! Who are the other two?'

'My niece, Cassie, and another Danish girl, Asta, who came over to find Elaina. We all had a virtual chat when she was ready to divulge her secret of being alive. She's been trying to nail the bastard that took her, but through a series of coincidences, I've met two, three, now four wonderful men, five when you count Bo, who have looked out for us girls without us even knowing it.'

'My mum... she's still so beautiful. I always admired her natural looks and wished I'd inherited them.'

'You have, you just haven't looked inwards yet. Now, little sister, I need some sleep.'

Darlene winked and gently ushered Milly towards the door.

'Thank you so much, Ms Adams. I feel so much better knowing I'm that much closer to seeing my mum.'

'That you are. Enjoy your shift.'

'Did you leave treats?'

'When have I not?'

They giggled quietly and hugged each other before Darlene gently closed her door. Collapsing onto her bed, she said a prayer of thanks and slipped into a happy, dreamless state.

CHAPTER NINETEEN

The drive back to the dusty motel hadn't been a complete waste of time, but Foxtrot was seriously getting tired of the pub scene and the limited range of hookers. Although the behaviour of a spindly bloke covered in tattoos did have him intrigued. He annotated in his diary the nefarious pattern. Every third day, the bloke would carry his passenger inside his motel room, lock and leave, then return on foot. It was obvious the passenger was female and drugged. A cunning fellow. Light entertainment to pass the time, but Radar was now the target. Not some freaky, lanky bloke who had left early that morning with his blanket-wrapped pleasure toy.

Totally flummoxed by the disappearance of his two cohorts, Foxtrot took advantage of sifting through the files on Milne's laptop. Clearly the man liked fantastic-looking women in sexy lingerie. A particularly interesting e-mail about nailing Darlene Adams furrowed the brow above Foxtrot's steel-grey eyes. If only he'd known earlier, he'd have taken them all out and collected the lottery on offer. For a sweet two grand, all he had to was to tag Radar, which was as easy as slipping a custom GPS tracker inside the man's backpack. Either Milne or Cady was going to have the honours of taking him out. Only if they failed was he to step up and continue with the plan, given his close proximity at the next training session.

They had failed. Miserably. Foxtrot rubbed his hands with glee. He too liked beautiful women, but he preferred really easy money. Utilising the illegally sourced software on the laptop, he resorted to tracking the new number activated in the outskirts of the shooting range and guessed it was the primary target. Radar. He suspected the old sniper swapped out his mobile phones like he changed his vehicles, but finally he had made a mistake.

Foxtrot fondled the fat brown envelope. Soon, he'd be a very, very rich man, but his work wasn't done yet. He had ethics. He would collect when the time was right.

'We'll see how good your radar is,' he mumbled. 'You're mine, you old bastard.'

Following the pinging triangle on the screen, it navigated several roads in and around Mount Barker then headed westwards. One hour. That was all that was separating him and his target. Then the image of the beautiful bitch brutally nailing his brother with the paintball gun fuelled his ire. She was definitely next.

Swiftly zipping up the leather jacket after tightening the buckles on his boots, he loaded up the backpack with magnetic explosives and clipped the silencer onto his long-barrelled .357 magnum. His gloves and dark-tinted full-faced helmet disguised him perfectly.

The moment he was out of the town limits, he twisted the throttle of his sports bike and screwed it on until the needle hovered around 160 kph. Someone was going to die today.

Increased police blockades conducting thorough vehicle inspections with the assistance of K9 units had commenced in the southern region from late morning. The missing prostitute had created a lot of interest, particularly as word filtered through of the sordid discovery in the neighbouring state. Practically exhausting local resources, the Federal Police had provided several dozen officers to assist. Hearing this on the two-way, Spider had a decision to make. Dump his drugged Blingbling or return her to the pub. Both meant drawing attention.

A black dot in his side mirror grew incredibly large, zoomed past then disappeared into the distance. *Wow! You need a motorbike! Ditch the car! Buy a bike! Nobody would know it's you! You'd be invisible!*

Oh. But you don't know how to ride one. Stupid idea.

Damn Max. Get the car. Go home.

Boring. Get more toys.

Spider looked at the drugged toy and scowled. She hadn't been much fun. It was a bit callous to leave her on the roadside, but he couldn't afford to get caught with her.

The motorbike rider! You could be a hero! Yeah! Yeah! Find a shady tree.

Do it. Let's go home. Boring.

With his mind throwing suggestions in all tones, he eventually agreed that it made sense to find a tree, lay her down on the blanket with all her clothes and a hat and all the water she needed then get on the two-way saying he witnessed a motorbike take off quickly. He would broadcast that there was something that looked like a body lying under a tree.

Yeah! Yeah! Do that. You'd be a hero. Nobody would know it was you.
Yeah. Yeah. Hurry up.

He slowed the truck to barely a crawl and listened for another ten minutes to the two-way while he searched for a large enough tree. Given the heat of the afternoon sun, it'd have to be decent.

There! On the opposite side of the road was a nice clearing and three trees. He angled the truck and trailers to block the view of both directions of traffic and dragged her limp body across to the driver's side, unrolling her gently, which consequently unravelled the blanket. Smacking away his spider the whole time was futile. He just had to do what he had to do.

Trying to dress her was awkward, but he managed. Eventually. He propped her up against a bent Mallee trunk, wrapped her hand around the bottle and gently patted her on the head before positioning the hat like a snoozing Mexicano having a siesta. He giggled. *Sí, senorita. Say sí, sí. Say nothing is better.* He splashed a bottle of water on her face and watched the droplets slide down her neck, then forced her to drink from another bottle. He listened carefully for oncoming traffic, but all he could hear was his own truck. *You have to go now. Don't waste another second. You'll get caught. The cops will find you. Max will find you too. Go. Now.*

Climbing back in behind the wheel, he checked for traffic before crossing the lane and headed towards the farm. The lack of oncoming trucks indicated he was nearing the roadblock, and he promptly reached for the two-way. He also knew the police scanned the channels.

'Did anyone see a motorbike come this way?' he asked quietly in a mature voice.

'Yeah. Some cops are chasing him, why?'

Spider hung the two-way out the window, intermittently depressing the transmit button during his reply.

'He... out... some trees... saw... something... past...'

He got bored and returned the receiver to the cradle.

'Where are you?'

Don't answer any more questions. One was enough. Stop it.

Spider turned off the two-way and dialled his boss. 'Hey, boss man, roadblocks will delay my return.'

'Just get back here and park up, Spider.'

'Yes, boss.'

Tiny jumped at the vibration of his slimline phone and swiftly stepped out of earshot.

'Tango Mike. How nice it is in the sunshine,' he said quietly.

'Lima Bravo. As it is in the moonlight!'

'Sitrep?'

'Not much. But live entertainment is always the best.'

'Copy that! Keep me apprised on the cockroaches.'

'Will do. See you on the flip side. Out.'

On high alert with another ambiguous message, Tiny left the dogs to babysit Granny and returned to his office. His mind was on the Dingo Fence line in the bottom half of South Australia. Something was gnawing at his guts.

In good spirits after a particularly entertaining lunch with the delightful Darlene Adams, Radar had deliberately waited two hours after they'd said their farewells before he headed towards the national park west of the shooting range. Summer had squashed the cold snap into oblivion, making it too hot for tourists to venture into the remote area. Which was the ideal location for him to implement his plan.

While waiting for his lunch date to arrive, Radar had studied the varying reports from the debacle of the training day for the third time. One author's account stood out like iridescent gonads. Foxtrot. Radar set the trap and used his permanently borrowed phone to communicate with a dead number and consequently draw the rat out of the hole. A black dot finally appeared in his rear-view mirror, bringing a smile to his face.

This time, Radar followed the proper channels and reached for the burner phone. Dispatching the code then deactivating the scrambling device, he waited the three seconds for his earpiece to activate.

'Yes, sir?' Tiny responded, astonished.

'Got a bogie on my tail. A bloody fast motorbike, actually. Been dogging me for fifteen minutes. Any word from up top?'

'Acknowledged. Stand by, will make connection.'

'Copy that. While waiting, I had the pleasure of being in the company of our Pretty One for lunch.'

'Oh?'

'She's an exquisite woman, and my God, can she shoot! Wouldn't mind her by my side right now.'

'Why's that?'

'Focus, lad!'

'Trying to, sir. Stand by.' A pause, then, 'Switching you to Overwatch, three, two, one. Go ahead.'

'Reading you loud and clear, sir,' Overwatch said.

'Suspect a target is due east of my location.'

'Stand by... stand by... acquiring your location, sir. Stand by... affirmative. Single rider on a motorbike approaching quickly.'

'I'm going to play a game with him. Not much he can do with a bike, but tell me if he goes to attach anything to my vehicle. I'll swing hard on the wheel, and you help take him out. You read me?'

'Loud and clear.'

Tiny was gobsmacked. 'What's going on?'

'Not your mission, Tiny. Overwatch and I have this under control. Two ears, one mouth, remember.'

'Sir, yes, sir.'

Slowing the Hummer down, Radar straddled the centre line, forcing the motorbike to follow suit or play chicken. Watching as the rider hurtled alongside the passenger side and put his right arm inside his jacket, Radar jerked the wheel towards him, straightened up then put foot. For several kilometres, the game of chicken continued.

'Gun!' suddenly blared in his ear.

'Copy that. Stand down,' he commanded. 'You have your orders.'

'Sir, yes, sir. Bike pulling back. Again. Stand by... he's doing something with the backpack at a really slow speed.'

'Acknowledged. I'll drop my speed so he can catch up. Minimising collateral damage.'

'Keep alert, sir, he's accelerating in your direction. Increase your speed to one twenty. Keep the wheel straight. Steady. Nice... nice. Sir, without applying the brakes, drop your speed in five, four, three, two, one. NOW. Alert. Driver rear quarter panel, stretching arm out. Left hand down in three, two, one. NOW.'

Radar watched in his side mirror as the bike and rider went flying through the air at the same time a projectile penetrated the fuel tank.

'You didn't see anything, sir. What is your destination, please?'

'Manjimup. ETA forty-two minutes.'

'Final destination for this soiree?'

'Bunbury.'

'Copy that. Have a good day, sir. We've got some paperwork to attend to. Over.'

'Thanks, boys, love your work. Out.' Radar puffed out his chest and grinned. 'Now, lad, talk to me about this other creature causing grief. I'm kinda enjoying this.'

'You've mentioned our Pretty One a few times and no Danish Pastry.'

'Just answer my question, Tiny.'

Tiny replied very quietly, 'Acknowledged. Sir.'

Reluctant and somewhat preoccupied, Tiny summarised the sordid South Australian connection. He then channelled the conversation towards Radar having another rendezvous with their mutually reliable informant, Peachie.

'Sir, given the relationship with our Danish Pastry, who is now, I believe, in the same location as our Pretty One...'

'Are your feelings compromised?'

'Conflicted, sir.'

'Carry on with your initial train of thought.'

'Yes, sir. Suspicions are strong the target known as Spider is crawling around the region. Recommend getting to know the farmer soon. Harvest will be drawing to a close in the south-west. Farmers' talk amongst farmers. Drivers' talk amongst drivers. From what I can determine, the ladies cook up a storm in a place called Jody's Kitchen. And you like a hearty feed, sir.'

'Copy that. I'll consider the suggestion while I'm kicking around some sand.'

'Yes, sir. Have a good break.'

'Our Pretty One is a very capable woman; therefore, the Danish Pastry is also in safe hands. Over and out.'

Radar heard the distinct final beep of the connection, waited thirty seconds to ensure complete disconnection then spoke quietly. 'Overwatch?'

'Line's secure. Read you loud and clear, sir.'

'Did you get all that?'

'Affirmative. Sir, I can get boots on the ground with appropriate notice.'

'Good. Get on with it. I think it'll be fitting if our Pretty One takes out the last piece of trash.'

'If you say so, sir.'

'Speak freely, son.'

'The acquisition of the IG may prove useful. Will discuss and make contact.'

'Copy that. Arrange for the location of the recently departed rat to be cleaned, then report back to me.'

'Acknowledged. Lips are sealed, sir. Out.'

Radar's grin dissolved into a very loud yawn, and he frowned at the same time. As much as he liked tying up loose ends, he was tiring far too early in the game and far too quickly after the rush. He knew Tiny would forgive him when the lads all got together.

Tiny ran his fingers through his short grey-white hair and swore silently. He trusted his former CO and crew above the clouds implicitly, yet he could not deny what his instincts were bellowing. He also knew Peachie and Spook would not divulge anything, which exasperated him no end. Staring blankly into the late-afternoon sun, Tiny sighed heavily and secretly wished he was thousands of kilometres away.

Darlene awoke to the faint strains of Chopin and sat bolt upright. Totally disoriented, she couldn't even think of what the day was as she answered the phone.

'Hello?'

'Darlene! It's Bev. Hope it's a good time to call?'

'Yes, yes. How are you all?'

'Super excited. Troy, my... um... my... oh, what the hell, the man I'm madly in love with has formally retired and we're hosting a party. The girls want you to be a surprise guest.'

'Me?'

'Yeah! Cassie said you loved a good party and hadn't had one for a while.'

'Funny girl. So what's the party all about?'

'Troy's retirement. He wants to adopt Amy, we both do. We want to get married, but we won't until Milly is back home. It's an agreement and pledge we've made to each other. If she doesn't come home, we'll continue the status quo.'

'Oh, Bev. I pray frequently too.'

'I suspected you would. Anyway, how's everything with you?'

'Going well, thanks. Keeping out of mischief and loving the harvest! No time to go sightseeing, but I am looking forward to calling in and seeing you on my way through. We'll make a plan when I have dates. In the meantime, send me through the details of how I can make this surprise a surprise!'

'Will do. Okay, I won't hold you up. But the day after tomorrow will probably be the best time. Some VIPs arrive progressively today and tomorrow. The party has already started. The girls are doing a wonderful job in setting the scene with decorations, and they've been doing all the cooking too.'

'Fabulous. I look forward to joining the party!'

'Wonderful. Okay, must go. Bye. Take care.' Bev hung up.

Now Darlene was in a dilemma and slumped back into the pillows. Was it up to her to tell Milly's story? Completely obliterating those thoughts was the incoming call from Radar.

'Hello, Radar! This is a lovely surprise.'

'Yes, I thought you'd say that, Ms Adams. I take great pleasure in informing you I believe most of the trash has been taken out.'

'Oh. Gosh. I'm flattered! You borrowed my line. Thank you very much. I know better than to ask questions about how, so I'll just say thank you again! How can I repay you?'

'Well, there is one thing you can do for me first.'

'First? Okay, I'll do my best, sir.'

'I'd really like to see Peachie again and have an early Christmas drink or meal with you both. Is there any way you can coordinate that?'

'Leave it with me. Did you have a date in mind?'

'Oh, within the next nine days would be best for me. My schedule is quite congested leading into the new year.'

'I'll come back to you within two days with a plan. Does that work for you, Radar?'

'Absolutely! Looking forward to seeing you already. Thanks, Ms Adams.' He disconnected the call.

Totally wide awake, she knew Jody was on her way to collect the groceries. A perfect time for a chat.

'You're awake early, Darlene! All good?'

'Hi, yes, thanks. I do have a question for you, though. A mutual friend of Peachie's and mine would like to have a really early Christmas meal before he departs, which is soon. I'd like to buy the foods for it and plan a menu. Given the busy time we're all dealing with, would it be inappropriate if I hosted it in the courtyard? Just this one time? Please?'

'That's three questions! Mind you, this is very intriguing and sounds possible. By the way, your younger sister posed a question to Bo and I about an early departure for one of the drivers, thereby minimising any interaction on the highway heading eastwards. Bo's particularly keen, and I'm pushing hard to have that eventuate sooner rather than later. I have a question for you now.'

'Anything.'

'Would you mind if Bo, the girls and I joined you and your guests for dessert?'

'I would love that very much.'

'Good. Have a look at the roster when you're back on and see what time and day suits best. I suggest a three-hour lunch overlapping the one-hour breaks for the two girls. Let me know as soon as you can. I'll put it to Bo, and he can organise it with Peachie.'

'Great idea. Thank you so much, Jody. I'll catch up with you soon.'

Feeling positively excited, she dialled Peachie's number. Hearing his puffing and panting, she was quite concerned when he took a while to speak.

'Darlene!'

'Peachie, are you okay?'

'Yes, a tad unfit and battling the heat, but I'm back in the aircon and talking to you. So now I'm fantastic!'

She chuckled and enthusiastically explained the arrangements in place for their upcoming lunch and cryptically mentioned that most of the bothersome people in her life would no longer cause any issues.

'I am so relieved about that. Lunch sounds great, too. I'll work in with Bo. Incidentally, when are you heading home?'

'I think it's only right that Jody has help with the end-of-harvest party, but it is her call. We haven't discussed it yet. Us girls will not be attending, so maybe we depart the morning of. I haven't really given it much thought. Why's that, Peachie?'

'I figured convoy style would be a good idea.'

'We'll play it by ear, but where's your destination?'

'Home is in Blue Mountains. Yours?'

'Let's sort out lunch first.' She laughed as they hung up simultaneously.

With the party for Troy's retirement now into its third day, Bev was delighted with the turn-out. The guests were still mingling beautifully, and the girls absolutely doted on Tiny's grandmother. He wasn't small by any stretch of the imagination, but the bond between him, Spook and Troy obviously went deep. The three were almost inseparable. All the meals and finger foods were terrific, and the atmosphere was better than expected. She'd noticed Neil, the interstate senior police officer, observing the interaction from afar. Being a late arrival and warmly welcomed, particularly by Troy, Bev saw he was without conversation and approached him.

Holding her glass of wine in one hand and offering him a beer, she grinned. 'So glad to have you here, Neil.'

'He's a special man, that one, my dear. Troy's late father was the most chivalrous gentleman I ever had the pleasure of working with, and he was highly respected. I owe his son a drink now. He beat me to the retirement decision! When's a good time to get him alone? It's high time he heard some stories of his old man.'

'He'd like that very much. As you can tell, I'm particularly fond of him too! In about twenty minutes, a dear friend is going to make a surprise video call. I'm not sure why I suggested it, or why the girls insisted on it, but Darlene Adams is going to join us for a drink. Troy hasn't said much about their acquaintance, but I suspect it was on one of the routine truck checks when he caught up with Spook and Tiny. In answer to your question, sir, after that I will make sure you two men have the opportunity.'

'Thank you. The old dear is making eyes at me, if you need to mingle.'

Both laughing at how they obediently danced to the tune of the elderly, they took their drinks and continued mingling. Bev let the girls discreetly corral the guests and positioned herself so she could see the clock.

Cassie cornered Tiny as soon as he was on his own and introduced herself. Declaring her recent studies in caring for the elderly and her outright admiration for his grandmother, she boldly explained that if the situation arose where he was seeking a carer, she would jump at the opportunity.

'How come you don't look like your aunt?' Tiny blurted out without thinking.

Cassie looked at him, totally surprised. 'My aunt? Aunty Darlene? How do you know what she looks like?'

'I've met her. I've... never mind how, Cassie. I'm just curious, that's all.'

'Yeah, I bet you are! But now I am, so how did you–'

Bev's loud clapping interrupted everyone's conversation and immediately captured their attention. As silence fell in the room, her phone rang. She answered it and pressed the video accept button the same time Amy and Asta swivelled the TV screen around. Cassie dragged Tiny to the front, putting Troy in between him and Spook. Darlene's beautiful face filled the screen as she poured an icy cold beer into a tall, chilled glass.

Grinning broadly, she sang out, 'Troy Oscane! Congratulations on your retirement. A job well done, and now there's no excuse but to smell them roses! Here's to Troy!'

She raised her glass, as did everyone else, and they called out his name before downing their drinks. Cassie blew her kisses, as did Amy and Asta. Darlene automatically blew kisses back. Bev pressed play on the karaoke machine, and James Taylor's *You've Got a Friend* belted out through the speakers. Those precious few minutes with everyone singing together would remain with them all for the rest of their lives. Stuttering and stammering, Troy thanked everyone, and especially Bev for organising the amazing party. Then he looked at the large screen.

'Good to see you, Darlene, and nice to hear from you too,' Troy said with a mischievous grin when the din quietened down. 'I reckon you could talk the whole time!'

She burst out laughing. 'You keep reckoning that. Wishing you all the best in your retirement, and I hope our paths cross when I come back through.'

Tiny and Spook put their faces closer to Troy's, and on the count of three, they all blew a kiss. She returned their kisses jubilantly and joined the party for several more minutes before reluctantly waving goodbye.

'Yep,' Cassie said to Tiny, 'you pair had better get together.'

'It's not as easy as that. But you had better go and tend to my grandmother, young lady. Her glass is empty!'

Cassie squealed with delight and skipped away.

The men converged, leaving the women to fuss over themselves and prepare the food for the next course. Bev sent a message to Darlene thanking her very descriptively.

Much later that night, Troy was still seated beside the fire pit with his senior colleague listening to the heroic and mischievous stories about his father. The two men shared experiences, trials and tribulations and a bottle of tawny port. Not once did Troy's late uncle come into the conversation, even when they raised their glasses to absent family and friends. Neither man spoke for a while, respecting each other's privacy and revelling in the silence. It hadn't been often in their lives that peace and quiet could be enjoyed. The unspoken bond between them cemented their perpetual friendship.

On the way to their respective accommodations, Tiny cornered Troy and encouraged him back to the fire pit.

'Man, I can't have any more to drink! I'm done.'

'Not even coffee?'

'Oh, I will not say no to that. You got any chocolate?'

They laughed.

'Tiny, I see you've met Cassie. You know she's Darlene's niece?'

'Yeah. How's that work? She looks more like Elaina than her niece!'

'Yep. Caught me by surprise too. But I have to admit my guilt... it's been eating me alive.'

'What guilt?' he asked and stood up.

Troy shuffled his feet, huffed and puffed and buried his head in his hands.

Tiny stirred up the embers with a solid stick, sat back down and asked quietly, 'So, what's eating you alive, then?'

'I listened to Cassie talking to her aunt about their experience.'

'So? You're a cop. Isn't that your job? Okay, you're a retired one now.'

'Not usually without their consent. Mate, she described the truck and the driver that they got caught up with.'

'Go on.'

'It's the same bastard that got DeeDee.'

Tiny sucked in air through his teeth. 'It can't be,' he said adamantly.

'Then he must've had a double, because the description was so damned similar. I ran the deceased's name through the system, and there aren't any known relatives. My colleague, Neil–'

'The OIC from the Alice?'

'Yep. He's got the same information. But all that aside, whoever this other maggot is, he's still out there. Just thought you needed to know.'

'What else you got for me?'

Troy sent Tiny a voice file containing the snippet he'd recorded before officially retiring.

'Best you listen to it in private, mate.'

'Copy that. Let's change the subject.'

Bev's humming got louder as she carefully walked towards them with a tray of coffee and biscuits. 'Here you are, gentlemen. We've decided brunch would be a better option. See you then. Always remember something, you two – you've got a friend.'

Troy was instantly on his feet, tenderly kissing her on the cheek and taking the tray graciously. She blew them a kiss, smothered a yawn with a peculiar grin and toddled off into the shadows towards the furthest glamping tent possible. She'd insisted on their privacy!

The two men reminisced, and eventually, the subject got around to the late Reg Oscane. Hours later, Tiny handed Troy the envelope he'd been harbouring for just the right length of time.

'Mate, the old rogue said I'd know when you should have this, and he was right. You should have it right now.'

'What's this?'

'Not my business. But I will impart some of his advice. Read it in private, and consider the options. You'll know what to do.'

'Bloody hell. Thanks for fulfilling his wishes. I don't want to talk shop, but what of the cockroaches?'

'A complete mystery, but a belated retirement gift would be nice!'

'Yeah, or an early Christmas present!'

'Don't want much, do we?'

Troy stabbed at the fire as he got up, bade Tiny goodnight and left him stargazing.

At long last, it was the day of the luncheon. Bo had been looking forward to having a conversation with these men for what seemed like an eternity. The days had felt a lot longer than usual, but as always, harvest came first. He checked the tonnage and released three drivers. Two were recommended to other farmers with more grain available for cartage. One was waiting for him by the auger bin, rather impatiently.

They walked towards each other. 'Boss, what's going on? Where's my truck?'

'In for its service, Spider. Just about drove the wheels off her this year.'

'What am I supposed to do, then?' he whined.

'Have the rest of the day off, get your laundry up to date, clean the caravan and get ready to go home. There might be a few more loads to Albany. I'll know by the end of the day, then you'll know. Anyway, here's your pay for this week.'

Spider took the packet and shoved it into his trouser pocket. 'Is my job finishing soon?'

'Yep. We're wrapping up for the year, and you've got to go home. All cashed up!'

'What about Snake Girl?'

'She's not going anywhere for a while, Spider.'

'Oh. She was the best toy. Ho hum. Okay. See you at nine o'clock in the morning, then. Bye.'

Bo's guts churned as he watched the gangly, awkwardly tall man saunter towards the caravan, then practically crawl inside and disappear. The most appropriate nickname he'd ever come across in all his sixty-two years. Jody's text message reminding him to meet them in the kitchen for lunch then join the guests for dessert was like a breath of desperately needed fresh air.

Seated between Radar and Peachie, Darlene sat back and listened to the two men converse generally about war games, weaponry and the latest in aircraft technology. A common interest, it seemed, and she was happy to play the hostess and learn more about helicopter improvements. The girls had done an amazing job with the entrée of prawn cocktails, and the selection of roast meats, potatoes and perfectly made roast vegetable salad. The rosemary dinner rolls were also the best she'd ever eaten. They had insisted they do the first two courses if she made the dessert. Her bûche de Noël had been the best-kept food secret; even the meringue mushrooms were top notch. She had cheated with the ice cream, but not with the brandy snaps. Being conscious of the time, Darlene collected the plates, excused herself politely and stepped into the kitchen.

'You girls are amazing!' she exclaimed as she watched Bo and Jody polish off the bread rolls. 'I loved the way you decorated the table, and by golly, those were the finest two courses I have ever had. Well done.'

The sparkling smiles from Elaina and Milly challenged the tinsel hanging around the kitchen. The staff rinsed and loaded the dishwasher, leaving their bosses chatting quietly amongst themselves.

'We haven't seen any trace of dessert, Darlene!' Jody called out.

'I'd like to bring it out when you're all seated, if that's okay?'

'What are we waiting for?' Bo stood up, grinning broadly, and escorted his wife to the door.

'Um, do we say our names?' Milly asked.

'Are you ready to?' Jody replied.

'Yes. Yes, I believe I am.'

'I most certainly am!' Elaina said happily.

'Let's do it, then!' Darlene said as she pushed open the door for them.

Bo and Jody led the way, followed by the two girls shaking little bells. Darlene carried the basket of Christmas crackers behind them. Milly's beautiful voice filled the courtyard with *Hark! The Herald Angels Sing*. As she handed everyone a cracker each, she squeezed their hands. They all joined in the last chorus, linked hands and pulled the crackers.

The girls squealed with delight when they looked closely at the new addition to the table. A miniature Christmas tree. The crystal angel glistened in the sunlight, but it was the two crystal reindeer with gold chains that caught their eye. Peachie and Radar were standing behind their chairs wearing reindeer ears and broad grins, holding out a set for everyone. With much frivolity, they managed to wear the Christmas hats and the reindeer ears, then Bo introduced himself and took his seat. Loud, effusive compliments of the first two courses revolved around the table.

But it was Milly who took centre stage. She bravely removed her scarf as she announced herself and told her story. Elaina held her hand then told her own story, including her initial reluctance to go home a coward with slight memory loss. The nightmares had returned with the memories, yet Milly's survival and determination inspired her to help remove the scourge known as Spider. They wanted him to die by snake or spider bite if it was possible, but didn't know enough about the local poisonous creatures. Milly explained that her return home was going to be a surprise, if her health challenges didn't let her down.

Discreetly stepping back inside to prepare dessert, Darlene felt it was so important for the souls in the courtyard to get to know each other. Her primary objectives were to deliver the girls safely, somehow take out the remaining piece of trash and definitely repay the kindness of her newfound friends. The how, she hadn't worked out. But she would. She always did. By now, her former bosses would have received their tickets to Hawaii as her way of repaying their kindness. A destination they'd always wanted to visit and hadn't been shy in telling everyone about.

Peeping out the door, she saw the conversation seem to lull. It was time for dessert. Wheeling out the laden trolley sparked up the festivities. Everlasting memories were captured as they almost finished the bûche de Noël and double-upped on the brandy baskets with ice cream. Peachie and Radar handed a reindeer necklace to each of the girls. Jody was given the angel. It was fitting.

With the ladies disappearing into the kitchen, Radar gathered the men.

'Gents, this has been fantastic. Friends for life made right here. Bo, I cannot thank you enough for the hospitality, and Peachie... well, mate, you've come through for us again. Thank you. However, we have a situation. Recently, the missing prostitute was found, but her disappearance raised a few eyebrows over east. I'm under the impression there's a rogue that had the same MO in this region.'

'There is. He leaves tomorrow,' Bo stated flatly.

'Stall him. Find out where he's meeting his cohorts, then advise Peachie accordingly.'

'Pardon?'

Bo and Radar looked at each other sternly, then both softened their stance.

'Apologies, Bo. It's hard to step out of the military protocol.'

'I wasn't sure if I should salute, clip my heels or what. The last man who spoke to me like that was my grandfather. He lived with us in my growing years, and that was the only way he knew how to talk. By giving orders. I rebelled, then swiftly grew up.'

'No hard feelings, then?'

Bo gripped Radar's hand firmly. 'No, sir. Thank you for your service. Forgive me, please. I respect your change of circumstances; you just caught me off guard. But why stall this little bastard?'

'You heard the girls! I quite like the idea, actually.'

'Yeah, me too,' Bo said quietly. 'But you need to know that the yellow Ford Focus is here.'

The slow smile that spread across Radar's face was probably the second most satisfying sight Bo had seen all day. It was the first Peachie had seen that wasn't associated with food.

They shook hands and nodded their heads in silent agreement as the ladies descended from the kitchen, carrying trays of coffee, tea, cheese, biscuits and chocolates. A fine way to end a delicious feast. Reluctantly, the little Christmas party came to an end. Elaina and Milly recited a poem of gratitude to their treasured guardians. Elaina sat down and looked expectantly at Milly. She smiled, hugged all and sundry, then she did what she did best. She sang. Her velvety rich, jazzy voice filling the courtyard with the 1910 classic *A Perfect Day*. After several more hugs, the women left the men to their conversation.

The three men stood beside Radar's black Chevrolet Silverado contemplating the plans for the days ahead.

'Peachie, I'm going to ask you to cart grain between the farms locally. I'll send Spider down to Albany...'

'Sure thing, boss.'

'...but, Radar, can you give me a time frame, please?'

'Mate,' Radar said firmly, 'as soon as I have word from my unit, Peachie will inform you. Please know that after what you and your lovely wife have endured and who you have protected, your back will always be covered. We must keep the girls' secrets secret.'

Radar pressed his right ear and walked away.

Peachie encouraged Bo to walk in the opposite direction and said, 'Boss, that prostitute who went missing then was found... will you check the caravan for any incriminating evidence?'

'It had crossed my mind. I was going to destroy it after last harvest but never got around to it. I'll be sure to do it straight after this one.'

'Radar's contacts might be able to provide assistance, if you can drag it clear of all other infrastructure,' Peachie suggested with a chuckle.

'Who the hell are these guys?'

'Friends, boss. They're friends. And Radar's correct in what he said. You and your wife will be under their protection. Look at it as an extension of the kindness and protection you provided the girls.'

'Mate, I'll be glad when all this is over and done with and I can stop looking over my shoulder.' Bo shook Peachie's extended hand.

They replicated Radar's broad smile and purposeful stride, and reconvened at the bonnet of the ute on steroids. He stuck out his hand, heartily shook Bo's then gave him the thumbs up.

'Extend the driver in question for six days. Please make it happen, Bo. Huge thanks again for a terrific lunch. We'll be in touch. All the best to you and your wife – there's freedom and clear days ahead!'

'The pleasure was ours, sir. You're welcome anytime. Cheers, Peachie, see you when I'm looking at you!'

'Cheers, boss. That'll be tomorrow morning, I'm guessing!'

Bo waited until they were out of sight before dialling Spider's number and giving him the news about delaying his departure.

'Why?' he whined.

'Because you've got good records doing the Albany runs. I need you for another six days, double pay on the last two. Come on, Spider, think of all that money.'

'Aww, boss, I really want to go home. Promise it's double pay?'

'I promise, but only on the last two days. I'll have another truck for you at the auger super early in the morning, then you can do two runs and stay in Albany overnight.'

'Super early. Like five o'clock, then be back as quickly as possible to do it all over again the next day? Right?'

'Five o'clock is right. Every second night, you stay in Albany. You got it, Spider. See you in the morning.'

'Yes, boss. Bye bye.'

Sitting in the hire car waiting for Spook, Tiny listened intently to the recorded conversations from Overwatch. Even in six days, he still wouldn't get to the west in time, and Spook was about to become a grandfather, which counted him out of the mission. Shaking his head in frustration, Tiny knew he'd have to rely on his eyes in the sky. Nova's happy bark caught his attention as she romped with Pluto and the three Rottweilers. The dogs had connected instantly at the retirement party, and Granny had loved the views of the Flinders Ranges. So much so, she'd insisted they extended their stay and go exploring.

Cassie and the other girls had volunteered to supervise the dogs, giving Bev and Troy a much-needed break together, and care for Granny at the glamping venue. Everyone knew the dear old lady didn't need a carer. She was extremely capable, steady on her feet and ready to go at the drop of the hat, but it gave Cassie some work experience and enough time to worm her way around Tiny's little finger after easily doing it with Granny's. He still couldn't understand why Cassie looked nothing like Darlene, who appeared remarkably similar to Elaina.

Tiny put his mixed feelings aside as Spook climbed into the car. Spook's hasty return home was full of excitement and apprehension. This time, he was about to become a granddad! Leaving Granny in Cassie's care while he and Tiny drove to the airport was the opportune time to talk men's talk.

Spook had finally stopped to take a breath after talking incessantly on the phone to his wife and son-in-law, assuring them he was returning home immediately, when he revisited the original conversation about the development in the west.

'You saying there's another girl that's been rescued?'

'Yeah, but lips are sealed. Her health isn't the best. I'm tempted to have an aerial medevac on standby halfway across the Nullarbor but have the distinct feeling it's not my place to interfere. Plus, it's a girls' thing... her health challenge, that is.'

'Awkward.'

'Yep. Radar threw his hat in the ring to join the convoy with Peachie, but again, I can't intrude. This isn't my mission, apparently. It's Darlene's.'

'You've convinced yourself on that one. So, where are you going to meet the women, then?'

'Hey? No, no. According to Cassie, her and her aunt are having Christmas together after Elaina gets back. I'm looking forward to seeing that one. You?'

Spook looked at his mate like he was from another planet. 'Yeah, of course. So... what are you going to do?'

'Let's just wait and see how all this plays out.'

'Oh, sh... I've just remembered something. Cassie described the truck and driver. I thought that bastard had died?'

'He did,' Tiny replied gruffly.

'Man, she described him to a tee, even the beat-up old truck. Is someone playing games with us?'

'Doubt it.'

'You needed to know. Thanks for the lift, Tiny. I'm going to run as fast as I can and board this plane. Keep in touch. Have a great time, and remember that Christmas is at my place. Bring some friends.'

They shook hands strongly and quickly before Spook practically fell out of the car, landed on his feet and ran as best as his ageing legs could carry him. Once he'd disappeared through the Departure doors, Tiny blipped the horn twice, leaned over, pulled his door shut and made tracks back to the base of the Flinders Ranges.

His head was in a spin. What if Granny wanted Cassie as a carer in her future twilight years? What if she didn't? What then? What if that caused problems with the budding friendship between Elaina and Darlene? Too many what ifs! *Make a decision or it'll be made for you, man.* Spook had told him that so many times over the years; it was high time he heeded the advice.

He pulled over and put on his hazard lights. His head was bursting with all the information swirling around in it. There was something that couldn't wait any longer. With the other information Spook had revealed, along with the similar conversation with Troy about the bastard that maimed DeeDee, he listened to the recording four times then forwarded it to Overwatch.

He sighed heavily and drove back to the glamping grounds. All he could do was wait for a reply.

Tracing Santa's sleigh on the wall calendar with the longest wooden spoon in the kitchen, Jody turned to Bo and Darlene with probable dates for the harvest break-up party.

'The fifteenth is in the middle of the week, which gives the drivers the following day off, then we estimate another four days straight and we're done. Have I read the figures correctly, Bo?'

'You have. This rogue would have long disappeared by then...'

'Us three girls can clean up in here while it's quiet, and you pair can take the day off too,' Darlene suggested, pen poised atop her notepad. 'If you don't need us for shifts on the seventeenth, we'll have that day off and leave on the following one.'

'That'd only give you a week!'

'Plenty of time to get the girls home, and I get to keep a promise to have Christmas with my wayward niece, Cassie. Speaking of Christmas, what do you guys do?'

'Sleep!' they replied in unison then laughed.

Bo said, 'No, not all day! The kids have finished early, so they're hosting Christmas this year. We just pitch up with the presents, dessert and booze.'

'Then we drive to Busselton for the new year and think about going away for three weeks after that,' Jody added. 'Last year, we went to Perth. It was okay, but busy and damned hot. Probably a bit late to book a trip to the Antarctic, so we'll see.'

'Wow! Antarctica! So quiet, and the weather would be beautiful this time of the year!' Darlene quipped.

'And white and no dust!' Jody said and burst out laughing.

'What's wrong with Tasmania?'

'Absolutely nothing!' Jody grinned and threw her arms around her husband.

Together, they circled the fifteenth as the date of the harvest party, and agreed the rest of the planning was up to him. It was his staff who deserved the party. They'd busted their buns, made some big dollars and made their boss a very happy man. He wrote his catering request on the whiteboard and drew a Y-shaped tree stump with the digits '25' beside it.

'I'll leave that one for you, Darlene, because I don't know how to spell it, let alone pronounce it, but it'd be great if you could make us one for Christmas Day.'

'That I can. I recommend a hazelnut semifreddo version of the Yule Log,' she said with a wink. 'It's a lighter version of the one we enjoyed, and it can be frozen. You'll have everything available to decorate it and will have a lot of fun doing it! As will I making it.'

Leaving the bosses to their own business, Darlene disappeared into the pantry. Potato bakes, beef chow mein, pasta salads and several dozen trifle cups were her tasks to fulfil. She kept thinking of Tiny and imagining his strong arms around her, holding her tight and keeping her safe. Seeing him with Spook and Troy tugged at her heartstrings. She gathered there was a bond, and probably secret men's business, which suited her fine.

The elderly lady who Cassie was fussing over was presumably Tiny's grandmother, and if that friendship developed, there would be no turning back. Unless Elaina was already in the equation. Nobody had seen the tears streaming down Darlene's face when they'd disconnected the video call. She felt such yearning for somewhere to call home. Even with the knowledge that finally, the lucrative settlement payout had been transferred, in her mind's eye she saw her tree house and sighed heavily. The forest would have already begun to reclaim what was hers.

Darlene needed to read more of Jimmy's manuscript. His words were very comforting.

CHAPTER TWENTY

Seated under the overturned wheelbarrow in the darkened corner of the shed, Bo eavesdropped on Spider's speakerphone conversation. Only one character seemed to participate out of his three. The aggressive one.

'Listen, Max, this is how it is. I've done extra days and am picking up extra cash by doing so. Anyway, I'll be back here to get my gear two nights from now then drive to one of the sidings south of Norseman and sleep. I will have a good twelve-hour drive initially, which I will not do all in one go. No cops. Understand?'

'Bloody hell, Spider. This is messing up all the plans.'

'Too bad. I'm calling the shots now. You want this car? You work to my plan, and I will get home in a different vehicle. You hear me? My rules, my tune. Your turn to dance.'

'There is no home. I keep telling you that.'

'You don't know everything. You always thought you did. This is what's going to happen. You listening, old man?'

'Yep.'

'You will wait for me exactly eleven kilometres east of the Mundrabilla roadhouse, on the northern side. There are campsites off the road. Find the closest one to the east. Be prepared to wait another day, depending on this piece of crap I'm driving, fuel and road conditions. Got it?'

'Yep.'

'You once told me you had an old F-truck...'

'Still do.'

'Well, that's the one I want.'

'And I suppose you roll in, we swap vehicles and go on our merry way?'

'Pretty much. You go one way and I go the other.'

'That it?'

'Yes. See you soon, Max – or do I get to call you Father?'

'What?'

'You've messed with my mind all my life,' Spider growled. 'Did Stevo know?'

'Of course he did, you idiot.'

'You callous freak. And you're a cruel bastard for not telling Reg.'

'See you soon, Spider. Or shall I start calling you Graham?'

The angry flow of expletives was muffled by the whirring of the engine as it tried to turn over. Bo immediately turned his phone off.

'Come on, boss man, answer the phone!' Spider yelled into the darkened space.

After the loud thump on the steering wheel, a ferociously slammed door echoed through the shed. The redial tone was met with more frustration. Bo waited one hour before leaving his cramped position and stood behind the shed until he heard the water pump start up. He then high-tailed it through the last half of the uncut paddock. Never before had he felt so spooked walking through the wheat fields, but he knew the eyes in the sky would have pinpointed both locations.

Nearing midnight, Spider dialled his boss again. He didn't care it was late, because he couldn't sleep.

'Bloody hell, do you know what time it is, Spider?'

'Yeah, sorry, boss. I'm going to need a jump start...'

'Hey? Where are you?'

'I'm back in my caravan, all tucked up and lonely, but it's my car and I finally found the keys and the number plates! I thought I'd lost them. Anyway, can you help me get it running, please? I'm going to get a head start in two nights time for my road trip.'

'That's a long day.'

'It's okay. I've got a plan, but don't really want to muck around being a mechanic, getting all dirty, and, well... can you help me, please?'

'How about you leave me your keys, and I'll do a service on the vehicle myself? I'll even park it by the caravan if you want.'

'Wow! You will? Geez, thanks, boss. Take one hundred dollars out of my pay. It's only fair, because it might need oil and whatever. Oh, yeah, and please can you put the plates back on?'

'Get some sleep, Spider. We'll catch up in the morning by the auger.'

'Yes, we will, and that's when I'll give you the keys and the plates. Night-night, boss.'

Yay! Be nice and nice things happen! Lots of money and a big ol' F-truck! Yay! Two more days then we play! Yay! Yay! Yay!

Spider curled his gangly legs into the smallest bundle possible and wrapped his arms around his skinny body. His larger-than-normal head tucked into his neck as he whispered the nicknames of all his lost toys.

Tiny took all the dogs for a run one hour before dawn. They'd just scaled the lowest plateau in time to watch the horizon perform its colourful dance as the birdlife serenaded the magnificent sight. He'd woken up with Darlene on his mind. He had to talk to her. It was too early in the morning to expect a coherent conversation, so he sent her a message along with a photograph of the early morning view.

Great seeing you again, Darlene. It's incredible how you and Elaina have the same features and look nothing like your niece! Check this out... easier to take photos of the sunrise than capture a shooting star. Talk soon. T. X

Darlene had just turned off the light when her phone chimed. She giggled at the message but stared in wonderment at the magnificent view. Then typed out her reply.

Good morning, Tiny. Wow! What a glorious sunrise. It was so nice to see you and Spook the other night. Are you still glamping?

Yeah, we go home tomorrow. My Gran and your niece have struck up quite the relationship. You know she's studying to care for the elderly?

I believe so. My fingers are sore; would you like to talk instead?

She smiled and answered on the first note. 'That's better,' she said softly. 'Did I wake you?'

'No, I've just finished my shift. Elaina's on next, then another girl, then back to me! We cook culinary delights, you know.'

'I bet! How is Elaina?'

'She has more better days than not and is a great cook!'

'I know. Hey, did you know Cassie is pushing hard to be Gran's carer?'

'And?'

'Gran's making noises that it'd be a good idea.'

Giggling, she asked, 'Do you think they're matchmaking?'

'What? Doubt it. Cassie's not my type! Anyway, I don't even know what to suggest for Christmas. Spook's still hounding me to join him.'

Darlene burst out laughing. 'I'd like to know who and what is your type, actually! You once said you had so much to tell me. Would you like to start now?'

His deep chuckle was undefinable. 'Nope.'

She paused momentarily. 'Okay... what would you like for Christmas?'

'For everyone to be together. For once, in a very long time, to feel like a family.'

'Mm, that does sound so nice. I'm going to go to sleep with that thought. Good night, my shooting star lover... whoops... lover of shooting stars.'

Tiny listened to her soft laugh and compared it with Elaina's locked away deeply in his memory bank. He missed her, he knew it. But the women were so similar it was uncanny. He also longed to be in Overwatch's company. He looked at the phone to see Darlene had already disconnected the call. Whispering his confusion into the cool, quiet air, he planned to confirm with Granny if she still wanted to travel to Scone for Christmas. Then that decision would be made. He shoved the knowledge of who the third girl was out of his mind. That was not his call, and Christmas wasn't far away, yet the several thousand kilometres separating them were.

The buzzing of his slimline phone was spookily well timed, and he rubbed his eyes as he answered.

'Tango Mike. How nice it is in the sunshine!'

'Lima Bravo. As it is in the moonlight!'

'Plans afoot, I suspect?' Tiny muttered.

'Roger that. Feet on the ground en route to location Alpha.'

'Put your feet in the shoes of those recently rescued. How many would forgive?'

'Been following that process, actually. Some Russkis have connections in deeper places than us. Should we leave it to them?'

'Negative. Our ground. Our call.'

'Copy that. General consensus up here is to take out the remaining perps. You aware of the planned vehicle swap out?'

'Affirmative. Aren't F-trucks notorious for combustible explosions?'

'They can be. Primarily the old F150 models between 2009 and 2012 – they had transmission shifting problems, which was an extremely dangerous defect.'

'Yeah, but how old is old these days?'

'Don't go there, boss!'

'Run it past the CO for separate incidents. No other party is to be involved.'

'Affirmative. We concur. Say, boss, that's a nice place to propose. Out.'

Tiny looked skywards and flipped the bird, laughter exploding out of him. *You wish*, he thought.

Spider had already left for his first load to Albany. Expected ETA back at the farm would be 3:00 p.m. then, typically, a quick turnaround back to the Port for scheduled unload the following morning. Bo had been informed by a third party that there would be extensive roadwork delays the following day. A particularly frustrating time for anyone itching to finish up.

Rolling past the auger for the third time at 2:40 p.m., Peachie reached downwards and slipped his boss a note with the instructions for the night's plan. They didn't have much time, and Bo had a lot to prepare beforehand. The rendezvous time was 2100 hours. The farm was to be clear of drivers, all lights extinguished and complete tech silence. Only text messages between the husband-and-wife team were permitted.

Bo radioed his advice to the drivers that last load was 5:15 p.m. After that, the gates were closed until morning. Typically, some drivers grizzled, where others were overjoyed. The local pub was celebrating the harvest hussy's discovery and recovery with half-price beers. Although said prostitute wasn't available for business, she was behind the bar pulling drinks!

On the clearest of nights, the half-moon and two stars looked like a heavenly smiley face. With the back of Jody's 4WD already smelling like a mobile café, she and Milly finished loading the selection of wrapped lamb and rosemary pies, roast beef rolls, potato bake slices and pulled pork sliders into the stainless-steel warming trays. The esky was loaded with a mixture of water and soft drink bottles.

'Boss, it looks like we're feeding an army!'

'We've probably over-catered, dear child. How about you write a thank-you note on those trifle cups?'

'And *Merry Christmas*?'

'Go for it. Be quick, though. Bo will be here very soon. It's already 8:50 p.m.'

No sooner had she said that than headlights swung into the carport. Calling for Milly to hurry up, Bo and Radar stepped out of the Landcruiser and jogged towards Jody's 4WD.

'One more tray, boss. Evening, boss, sir,' Milly said politely as she rushed out of the kitchen and handed Jody the cooler containing the desserts. 'Sir, I'd like to thank your men for their assistance, but all I know how to do is sing. Do you think you'd be able to get them a recording?'

'Young lady, I will most certainly make a plan. Right now, we're on the clock. Excuse us. By golly, Bo, you'd best drive quickly – these delicious aromas are making an old man very hungry. Night, ladies. Off you go inside now. Jody, keep your phone on, please.'

'Yes, sir. Night,' they both replied obediently and swiftly closed the kitchen door behind them.

'That was easy, Radar,' Bo said quietly. 'Mind you, you do look pretty intimidating with all that Special Ops kit.'

'A man's got to do what a man's got to do. But I wasn't kidding about an old man being hungry. Put foot, son. We've received confirmation that Target One is stationary in Albany.'

Milly couldn't resist the temptation to hug her boss. 'Thank you for everything, Jody. I truly owe you and Bo my life.'

Returning the solid embrace, Jody said, 'You probably shouldn't have been aware of what was going on, but Radar gave Bo permission. That's why I juggled the shifts. We shall discuss it no more! Now, Milly, be honest with me, please... are you going to be right to travel with your cycle and all its discomfort?'

'I should be. I'll just be sleeping and have already suggested to Ms Adams that we hire a motorhome and tow her car. She's seriously considering it, given she's driven one already. Only problem is getting one around here!'

'Leave that with me and Darlene, or Ms Adams, as you prefer to call her! Right, we've both got work to do. Make sure you eat. You're a little too thin for my liking.'

'Yeah, the weight's falling off me, and I don't like it neither. I'm putting it down to stress. Anyway, I've got bread to make and more meat to roast! Thanks again, Jody. Have a good night.'

Milly disappeared into the pantry before the tears slipped down her cheeks. She had noticed how much of her hair had been falling out. Not quite clumps, but too many strands each time she brushed it. The other things that concerned her greatly were the peculiar dark brown blemishes on the bottom right of each iris which seemed to grow each month, then recede.

Sobbing quietly, Milly recited her private prayer. *Oh, Mum, I need you. Dear God, please forgive me for not telling her I'm alive. Amen.*

Bo watched with admiration and a healthy respect the swift mechanical inspection and repairs conducted on the yellow Ford Focus. He had taken three hundred dollars out of Spider's final pay to cover the costs. They'd all looked at the bricks in the spare wheel well with contempt and left the compartment untouched. DNA samples taken off the shoes, toys and old clothing lying around the boot were bagged accordingly. Peachie assisted under Radar's murmured instructions. His unit were dressed in dark clothing and night-vision goggles, with blackened faces. They all had a job to do, and conversation was kept to a minimum.

It wasn't long before Radar gathered his men for their opinions on snakes and arachnids. He proposed utilising a fake roadblock in an unpopulated area along the Great Australian Bight. While the driver was preoccupied, nature's passengers would enter the vehicle. Rumbling tones of agreement filtered around the group until his right-hand man spoke up.

'That is possible, sir. Booby traps and innocents aren't acceptable combinations.'

'Indeed. Where are we at with the vehicle?'

'Completed, sir. Do we wash it?'

All headlamps swivelled around and settled on Bo.

'No, but I did say I'd leave it by the caravan.'

'Copy that. Let's do it, lads. We're going to need this space for the scrumptious meals provided to us.'

'There's a washroom opposite the caravan, men,' Bo offered.

'Bo, Peachie, you're with me,' Radar commanded.

'Yes, sir,' they said respectfully.

Stepping out of the shed and away from the men, Radar removed his headset and stared at the heavens, stifling another yawn. He was looking forward to finishing this mission and disappearing into the wilderness. Too many people for too long.

'Bo, that young lass with the voice of a jazz angel; do you think she'd be willing to sing in front of the men while they ate dinner instead of the BS with a recording?'

'I think we should ask.' Bo pulled out his phone and posed the question to Jody via text.

Her response was instantaneous.

The roasts are in and the bread machines are doing their stuff. Yeah! Milly has a break now anyway and she will love that. When shall I bring her?

This is team lead. If the other dames would like to sit in the glow of the moonlight and listen, bring them as well. Now, I've been salivating for too long, how quickly can you get to the shed?

Very quickly! Within ten minutes.

Good.

Radar waited until Bo had pocketed his phone before shaking his hand. 'Come on, lad, we've got a stage to prepare. What else is under those tarps?'

'My grandpa's old Indian motorbikes, his Leyland flatbed truck and the chairs for the harvest break-up party.'

'Let's get cracking, men. We've got a show to prepare for, but the only light shining will be pointed upwards behind the singer. The rest of us must remain unseen.'

Peachie clapped his hands and did a very small jig. 'Radar, thank you for this gift. Bo, you and Jody are two very special people.'

'With some extraordinarily special friends,' Bo replied in awe. 'It is us that need to thank you guys.'

Milly was overjoyed and rapped loudly between Darlene and Elaina's bedroom doors. 'Ladies, wake up, get dressed and come quickly. You're going to sit in the moonlight while I sing. We're leaving in five minutes. Hurry up!'

Well within the time frame, the four women were excitedly nattering while Jody drove carefully, dodging kangaroos and foxes on the way to the vehicle sheds.

'Us three have to stay out of sight,' Jody instructed. 'Milly, it's your show, but you won't see your audience, okay?'

'That's cool. Ooh, I'm so excited. I wish my mum could hear me. Ms Adams, I've been thinking, it'd be awful if something happened to me and I never got home and you had to keep my secret forever. That'd be so unfair. On all of you, actually. I think she should know I'm alive, but I doubt I'll be able to sing if I told her, because I'd be bawling the whole time.'

'Leave it with me.'

'Girls, Radar has to have the final say,' Jody instructed as they pulled up alongside him and Peachie.

Milly rushed over and, while gripping his arm, told him her request and asked if he was comfortable with the situation.

He patted her hand as they walked together a little further away and pressed his finger to his right ear. 'Scramble our location on my mark and record.'

'Wow, that's power,' she whispered.

'No, dear child, that's authority. There's a huge difference. Peachie and I will escort you inside the shed; your friends will be quite fine, comfortable and safe out here. Sing your heart out. It's your thanks you want to extend.'

Milly hugged Radar with all her might, then stepped back. 'Thank you so much. You're awesome, sir.'

'Come with me and listen to the instructions I give Ms Adams.' Radar clasped her hand and led her to the other women. 'We have a very small window to play in, and fingers crossed this works. Using your phone, start texting Mama Bear constantly with blank messages until she wakes up. When she responds, these two phones here will sync. That's when you hold this one towards the stage. She'll be none the wiser, and nobody must know. Ever. We want to hear three taps confirming the arrangement.'

'Yes, sir.'

Radar pressed Darlene's 'just-in-case' phone firmly into her hand. 'I need that back afterwards, Ms Adams.'

'Of course, Radar. Thank you.'

He and Milly dissolved into the darkness of the shed. The air was warm, and the aroma was mouth-watering, yet it was pitch black aside from the diffused orange spotlight sitting underneath an old milk crate pointed upwards. Its pattern created a soft diamond pattern on the rusty old corrugated roof.

No one else moved. No one else spoke.

'Young lady, Bo and Peachie will help you onto your stage. Are you ready?' Radar asked.

'Yes, sir,' she replied confidently.

Her greatest wish was about to come true. She could hear quiet breathing. Finally, she heard the creaking of chairs as the three men sat down and Radar's quiet command of 'Now.'

Waiting for half a minute, Milly prayed her mum was on the phone.

Outside, Darlene had finally roused Bev with the incessant string of blank text messages. Eventually she'd responded with a single question mark.

You have to listen to me carefully, my dear friend. This is not for public knowledge. Do not call. I repeat. Do not call, just put me on speaker and wake up Troy, then listen carefully. Do this NOW. Lots of love.

Thousands of kilometres away horizontally and hundreds vertically, several other sets of ears were on standby.

Milly heard the three soft taps coming from the door of the shed and smiled. With her mouth and tongue exercises complete, she turned around and threw out her arms. In a smooth melodic voice, she opened her show with a little speech.

'Ladies and gentlemen, for all I cannot see, for all I cannot hold, all I can do is sing my love and gratitude. Merry Christmas, and thank you for being in my life. I love you, Mum. I'm coming home.'

Her opening song of Glenn Miller's *Moonlight Serenade* set the mood for the evening. For fifty minutes, she sang unaccompanied, covering a beautiful selection of classy jazzy numbers from the 1930s through to the 1950s. Her last number was *I'll Be Home for Christmas*. Several minutes of silence filled the shed, with the exception of a few quiet sniffles drifting in from outside, before the eruption of 'Encore, encore!' and rounds of applause bounced off the shed walls. Curtsying gracefully, she sang James Taylor's *You've Got a Friend*, encouraging everyone to join in the chorus. They did. Even those that were separated by the atmosphere and bitumen joined in the heartwarming song.

Darlene was crying and sent another message to Bev. *It's a long story, but it's hers to tell. Trust me. Do not tell anybody else. Sleep well. D XX*

Peachie and Bo helped Milly down from the stage while she sang out her thanks and well wishes for the wonderful people around her. The applause followed her out the door. She threw her arms around Radar, Peachie then

Bo, swiping at the happy tears that streamed down her face and trying to talk at the same time.

'You're an amazing young woman, Milly, our canary,' Radar said gently. 'You have just created an everlasting memory for a lot of people. Best you leave us men to our now-softened hearts.'

'Will I see you again, sir?' she asked and leaned against Jody for support.

Clutching Darlene's hand, Elaina asked, 'Will we?'

'I hope so, but that's a conversation for another time. Off you go, ladies.'

'Night, sir, and thank you,' Milly and Elaina said simultaneously and giggled.

Darlene hung back and handed Radar his phone with a watery smile. 'You're an absolute godsend and a legend, man. Thank you. Bev knows to keep tonight a secret. Good night, Radar.'

'Night, Ms Adams. We'll be in touch.'

She returned to the huddle of women and hugged Milly. They chattered happily as they climbed into the vehicle and didn't stop talking even when they got back to the kitchen.

'I'm too wide awake now to sleep,' Elaina said. 'What can I do to help you, Milly?'

'See how you feel when you put your head on your pillow,' she replied kindly. 'If you're still awake in thirty minutes, find me and ask me then.'

Darlene couldn't stop yawning. She thanked Jody and congratulated Milly one more time before quietly slipping away to her room. Elaina's foot in the door halted her, as did the picture on the phone being held up to her face.

'Uncle Spook's a granddad! Look, look, he's got one of each to spoil!' She wiggled her wrist, which revealed a delicate dolphin bracelet.

Large hot tears trickled down Darlene's face. 'Oh, that's so gorgeous. Give him my regards when you reply, Elaina.'

'I already did. He's invited us for Christmas too! Even Amy, Asta, Cassie, Bev and her boyfriend and some dogs! Apparently, they were all at a retirement party together. Even my gorgeous... oops, I mean the not-so-little one! What do you reckon?'

'As long as you do not ever repeat what you witnessed tonight to anybody. It isn't our place to do that. You do understand, don't you, Elaina?'

'Oh, totally. It will be our forever secret, and the big army man is to be listened to. It'll be so good to see Uncle Spook and the not-so-little one again. He gives the best hugs.'

Darlene tried not to stare at the bracelet and pondered on that comment before replying. 'I'm getting worried about Milly's health and am seriously considering putting you girls on a private plane.'

'What about you?'

'I'll still drive.'

'No. I mean, it sounds great and all, but you'll be alone...'

'Not really.'

'Yeah, but still, no. We talk to Milly. I too am worried about her health. There was huge hair ball blocking the drain, and she's the only one with long dark hair. I didn't tell anyone, just cleaned it up, but have you noticed how much weight she's lost? Her things are going to coincide with our trip, too.'

'Exactly. That's why I think the sooner she's back home, the better. She needs her mum, Elaina, and you need to make arrangements with your own family too.'

Darlene caught the girl as she broke down. 'I will. I'll see if they can come over for Christmas. But it's all come so quickly... I'm scared to be alone with Milly. What if she...'

'Oh, Elaina, we mustn't feed those thoughts. I'll request a medic on board if possible.'

'That would make me feel much better but still be worried about you.'

'You're sweet. I'll have Peachie to overtake!'

That made the younger woman smile weakly. 'I don't think I'll go back into the kitchen, but I do think we sit with Milly and Jody to discuss. It's important decision needing all of us.'

'I totally agree. That's a lovely bracelet, is it new?'

'No, my not-so-little one gave it to me. I just felt like wearing it.'

'It suits you! Well, we both need some sleep. Your shift is before mine, so I'm happy for you to arrange the meeting. You've all got my number. Sleep well – we've got a very busy time ahead.'

'Has it ever not been?'

She smiled wanly and closed her door. It would be in Milly's best interest if she got home sooner rather than later. The long trip eastwards could actually do her more harm than good. It'd be in Darlene's best interest if she knew exactly how Tiny felt... or if she'd convinced herself there was something! She groaned at the sound of an incoming message. Cassie's text prevented her from shutting her eyes. *Please can we talk, Aunty Darlene?*

She smothered another yawn and dialled her niece. 'You're up early, Cassie!'

'Oh, Aunty Darlene, I don't know what to do! My parents are dumping the guilt trip on me again, big time. Even Granny and Granddad are dropping hints that I should be home for Christmas. I promised to have it with you. That nice man, Uncle Spook, has just become a granddad, and he's invited everyone that was at Uncle Troy's retirement party to his place for Christmas. Even the dogs! I almost phoned you last night, but hoped sleeping on it would provide the answer. But it didn't! What do I do?'

'Okay, take a deep breath. Our families are going on a houseboat, right?'

'Yes. They're away from the twentieth to the twenty-eighth, in the Woop Woop up the Murray River near Echuca! Then they fly back to Tamworth for the New Year celebrations, and Granny and Granddad get a lift back to Coffs.'

'Talking about grandmothers...'

'Oh, she is a darling. I love her to bits. So sprightly and quick-witted, and man, you should taste her chocolate cake! We're back at Tiny's place in the hills behind Bathurst. OMG, Aunty Darlene, you should see this joint! It's amazing. Rolling green hills, but no rainforest. Anyway, Granny has got her own self-contained chalet; my unit is close by, yet far enough away from the main house without being shoved down the boondocks.'

'I take it you're caring for the elderly now? What happened to the au pair work?'

'They all went home! Asta's moved in with Amy and working down that way until Elaina gets back.'

'You've suddenly acquired several more aunts and uncles, I hear?'

'Yep, how cool is that! But when are you getting here?'

'I don't know yet, and I don't know where "here" is, either! Let's get back to Christmas, shall we?'

'Yes, we'd better. Uncle Spook lives outside Scone somewhere, which isn't that far from here, as in Tiny's place. I wonder if I should start calling him Uncle Tiny... hmm... it's got a nice note to it... By the way, I've looked at the map, and it's damn well closer to the Gold Coast than it is to Echuca. But my God, it's a long haul from Port Augusta! Can you imagine that? With three big dogs?'

'And miles and miles of bugger-all in between.'

'That's funny! Aunty Bev reckons a change of scenery would do them all the world of good and talked about the zoo at Dubbo. But I don't know. I would hate to encroach on the families, even though Granny seems keen, and honestly, Scone sounds so much more peaceful than a flotilla of houseboats! It's a logistical nightmare and awfully expensive to try and do both. I'm leaning towards Christmas at Scone and New Year at Tamworth.'

'You've raised some good points. What about your responsibilities there?'

'Granny's going to talk to Uncle Tiny about it in the next few days. He's been very aloof, which is normal, apparently, for this time of the year. What are you going to do, Aunty Darlene?'

'You're cheeky and a tad presumptuous. I've got loose ends to tie up in Queensland, Cassie, and I'll need a hand if I could borrow you for a few days. I'll get you back to your posting.'

'It'd be so much easier if you and Uncle Tiny would just hook up and stop being so bloody scared. From what I can see, you both need someone, and it's pretty damn obvious you've got the hots for each other. Geez, the screen almost melted at the party!'

'That is quite enough from you, young lady. I think you're making all this up! Now, your aunt needs to get things done. Work out the pros and cons of what we've discussed, have a conversation with Aunty Bev and co and we'll catch up in a few days. Put your ego back in its box when the oldies pressure you.'

'Yeah, right. How do I do that?'

'Try asking how they got around the exact same challenges when they were growing up. For instance, how did they overcome trying to be in two places at once? You'll get the hang of it! Cheers, kiddo. Behave yourself now.'

'Nova's a great dog, too, and you should see Pluto. She's so playful – you wouldn't believe she's older than Nova. You'd really love it here, Aunty Darlene. I reckon more than where the platypus play! Bye, and thanks for talking with me.'

With the words 'logistical nightmare' ringing in her head, as well as Tiny's ambiguity about almost everything, Darlene tossed and turned until she eventually fell into a restless sleep.

Shoving his mobile back into his top pocket, Bo watched as Peachie rolled his first trailer under the auger. It was the fourth phone call from Max he'd ignored in twenty minutes. He'd felt compelled to answer the first 'unknown caller', only to be bombarded with a thousand questions. Then the abuse started, so he'd hung up and had tried to concentrate on the job at hand ever since.

They were emptying the last silo and dropping the lower-grade barley off to the local brewery. Controlling the flow to minimise the itchy grain dust, his thoughts turned to Spider. Was it really the kid's fault he was so twisted? Should his life be taken? His MO was to abduct and play; he'd never actually killed anyone, but he had hurt them for life. Max, on the other hand, did deserve to cease breathing. Bo couldn't afford to have any trace of either one of the rogues back to the farm and had almost pushed the risk for far too long.

He lapsed into the historical abyss when, decades ago, his inadvertent acquaintanceship with the newly elected Port Pirie Councillor occurred with the sale of his late grandfather's catamaran. The men had gone for a sail prior to concluding the transaction, but unbeknown to Bo, Max had already been on board and stashed a very young Filipino woman and a spindly, large-headed toddler named Graham in the cabin. They had just trialled the electric winch for the main halyard when Max went below and brought up his guests.

That was the first disagreement. The child had sobbed and tugged at Bo's hand. Max had taken photos. Then he took photos of himself in compromising positions with the Filipino and forced Bo at gunpoint to pour the white powder onto the table. Max's thirty-two-year threat of releasing the photos to Bo's wife unless he did Max's bidding was forever over his head. Even though Bo had not participated in anything sinister, before, during or after the meeting with Max – he had always detested drugs and resented poor behaviour to women and children in the same capacity – Max had haunted him ever since. Even when the bastard demanded Bo meet him at the Bight. If he didn't, Max threatened to toss his own kid off the cliffs. When Max called in the favour of hiding Spider, he had sworn on the child's late mother that all evidence had been destroyed and the slate was clean.

'Whoa! Boss. The auger's screaming!' Peachie called out.

Bo cursed loudly and punched the emergency stop button. It was the first time he had ever lost focus around machinery. Climbing down the stairs, he met Peachie at the third rung.

'Mate, are you alright? You look like you've seen a ghost.'

'Just want these next few days over with, man. Can you get a hold of the top dog for me? We've got to find the hole where someone's hiding. There's some history that needs to be destroyed. And I need to go and see Milly.'

'Sure. One thing at a time, hey. I'll make a phone call.'

'Hop back in your cab, Peachie – I'll roll your tarps. Another truck's on the way in. Most of the others are going to get caught up in the roadworks. If you're keen, there are about three more loads to the brewery.'

'I'll take them, boss. By the way, the top dog will want to know if you're seeing the rogue off or leaving his pay in an envelope on the dash.'

Bo looked at Peachie as if he'd grown another head. 'Yeah, no, I'll just have it in an envelope. I've got to phone Jody.'

'Roger that, I'll get out of your hair.'

'Thanks. You're a lifesaver.'

'We both are, Bo.'

Tucking the phone in the crook of his neck as he rolled and secured the trailer tie-downs, Bo asked Jody to prepare the final wages for the driver departing that night and bring Milly with her when they met at the shed.

'Why Milly?'

'She said something a while back. I just want confirmation I'm doing the right thing.'

'You are! We are. We'll be rid of the scourge forever, Bo.'

'Please just do what I ask, Jody. I'm hanging up now – I'm expecting another call. See you as soon as possible.'

Tiny was nervous. Very nervous. Pressing the contact button, he waited.

'Lima Bravo. How nice it is in the moonlight!'

'Tango Mike, as it is in the sunshine! Sitrep?'

'Top dog otherwise engaged. Roadworks occurring as we speak. Target One detained as planned.'

'Copy that.'

'Overheard health condition of our Canary is on the decline. Pretty One considering private air charter for our Canary and Danish Pastry.'

'Copy that.'

'We're getting hungry. There's been talk of chocolate cake and scone, singular.'

'Stop teasing.'

'Yes, boss.'

'Make tentative arrangements on medevac, bounce it off the top dog with solution. Advise accordingly.'

'Copy that. Out.'

Tiny's heart fluttered. Even if it was Christmas at Spook's place, it would still be the best if Bev's daughter could survive the trip and everyone was back safely. He'd also received feedback from Peachie that the fondly nicknamed Canary's health was of great concern.

He depressed the contact button again.

'Yes, boss?'

'Keep up the great work, but contact me when I can be useful.'

'Acknowledged. Are you okay?'

'Torn, mate. Really bloody torn.'

'Don't wait until you're an old man to have another love, boss.'

'When are you back on land?'

'When there's a reason to celebrate. On the turn. Good chat. Out.'

Tiny smiled and sighed heavily. He'd done the right thing.

'Bo?' Jody called out the window as they pulled alongside the first storage shed. 'Milly and I'll wait here with the aircon running.'

He walked around the corner, waved in acknowledgement and pointed to the phone glued to his ear.

'How bad are you, Milly?' Jody asked.

'Getting worse. All indications are my things will be early, which usually means they'll be worse, and I am not looking forward to that. We've got mouths to feed and a party to cook for, and I don't think you should be a pair of hands short!'

'Your health is our priority. Would you consider flying back with Elaina?'

'What? No way. Ms Adams is meant to be taking me home. What about her driving all that way by herself?'

'That's how she came over, dear girl!'

'Jody, I think we need... oomph... argghhh... to talk to...' Milly had just gotten out of the vehicle in time and vomited while clutching her stomach.

'Let it all out, Milly. You ate far too much of the lemon and white chocolate cheesecake in one sitting, greedy guts!'

She groaned and greedily drank the plain mineral water Jody handed her, before draping the damp towel back over her head.

'I must look quite the sight. Hot water bottles strapped to my guts and a wet towel on my head!'

'Don't forget about the green gills!'

'Yuck, sorry about that. What a waste, but it was so addictive!'

Bo approached cautiously. 'Am I right to come around, or is this secret women's business?'

'It's safer on boss's side of the car,' Milly groaned. 'I just overindulged in cheesecake.'

Bo leaned against the hood of Jody's vehicle and looked at Milly. She really was going downhill quickly and ought to be home. Catching Jody's look of impatience, he got to the point.

'Milly, a while back, you said you'd heard some names when you were in the truck with Spider. Can you still recall them?'

'Hell yeah. Reg, Max, Stevo and Bluey. Oh, and Ruby Oscane. Bluey was at Yalata, where we got the car from, I remember that much. But I have to tell you something about this Max bloke. I reckon it's the same one that I read about when I first worked at Port Pirie, then sort of stalked. He was campaigning for the election thing on the council, and just looking at him gave me the creeps. Still does when I think of his pockmarked face.'

Milly shivered in revulsion.

'See, I'd scored a tuck shop job, and some of the women in the kitchen didn't speak very highly of him. They all said they'd never leave their kids alone in his company. Anyway, here I am, late teens, new place, a runaway, brave as anything and stupid too. Picked up on his election tour and followed him around. I don't know why I kept at it, but it took three weeks to know his routine. Every third day, he'd go to the pool and watch the kids' swimming training. Another dorky sloth of a human pitched up on alternate visits, and they'd sit together. While in Spider's truck pretending to be out of it and listening to his schizo conversations, I reckoned this Max bloke is the same councillor in Port Pirie and probably the same one who owns that yellow car. There was something dodgy about the whole deal, but it's too fuzzy in my head to try and explain. I can draw you a picture of the sickos.'

'Now?'

'Oh, she can draw anytime!' Jody said with a wry smile. 'This girl doesn't need pencils or paper, either. By the way, Milly, I'm keeping that notepad of yours.'

Bo pulled out a tattered delivery docket from his back pocket and handed Milly a pen, then his phone rang.

'Excuse me, ladies.'

'We're staying in the aircon anyway, Bo,' Jody said and closed the window.

She watched in amazement as Milly sketched out the scene she'd described; the way she captured the two voyeurs was exemplary.

'You must have been pretty close to them to have seen those marks on their faces.'

'I was. Just suntanning on the grass, facing them, with a book propped up, blocking the view of my drawing pad. They weren't looking at me, anyway.'

'Oh?'

'No. It was a boys' school.'

'Oh, that is sick. How do you feel about them dying?'

'I'm fine with it. I just hope they haven't bred. Imagine all the parents, grandparents and siblings that have endured a lifetime of anguish and heartbreak. Prison won't hold people like this. They're too corrupt. No. They need to die.'

'Not only the families have suffered, but the victims too,' Jody whispered.

'Yes. Some may never have been rescued.'

'And of these other names you've mentioned?'

'A bit fuzzy, but I think this Reg is dead,' she mumbled. 'Ruby Oscane definitely is, but Bluey's a blur. That's about all I can remember. There. Done.'

Milly handed Jody the very concise drawing of two creepy looking sexual predators. She flipped it over quickly in disgust.

'I don't care to look at them any more than that. I think we should have a heart-to-heart with Darlene and Elaina. You need to see your mum, Milly. She needs you too.'

'I know,' Milly whispered. 'I don't want to go alone, and Elaina panics when I'm sick. You're strong...'

'I can't come with you, dear child!'

'Aww, you and my mum would get on like a house on fire!'

'Yes, we probably would. I hope to meet her one day and enjoy a fine roast beef sandwich on that rosemary bread with you waiting on us!'

'Her birthday is in January! She's sixty!' Milly's childlike excitement brought tears to Jody's eyes. She gathered the girl into her arms and shared a sobbing session. 'I just hope I live that long, Jody. I'm not well at all.'

'Try not to feed those thoughts. You need to go home soon; we'll make it happen. Okay?'

Nodding her head and wiping her eyes, Milly said, 'Yeah, let's talk to the girls. I should probably be in hospital while I suffer out my monthly visitor. I pray it's a simple fix.'

'We all do. You've been so brave, so strong, so tenacious for so long, and now you're being sensible. Bless you, dear child. We'll get you home.'

Bo had watched the interaction from behind the vehicle and waited to catch Jody's eye in the side mirror before approaching the driver's side.

'That was Radar. Everything's on track. I'll take that envelope, thanks, Jody. Now, Milly, I have another question for you. Are you okay for these men to die?'

'Absolutely. I am grateful to you all for making it happen and pray that the only thing on the conscience of those involved is knowing they did a good thing for mankind.'

Jody handed him the envelope, which he tucked into his trouser pocket, then he took the scrap of paper from her, flipping it over. The colour drained from his face as he staggered backwards. Both women fled the vehicle and caught him before he collapsed onto the ground. Dragging him into the shade of the shed, Milly raced around trying to find some water. Eventually finding a clean bucket, she filled it and barely managed to empty it over Bo's head. Jody sat beside him, dumbstruck. Coughing and spluttering, he looked at her, wide-eyed. His fist clenching the scrunched-up piece of paper.

'I'll dial triple zero in two seconds if you do not speak, Bo,' Milly commanded, placing the towel off her own head onto Jody's.

'Thanks for the dunking,' he murmured.

'Unclench your hand. Tell your wife your name, where you are, today's date and when you were born.'

Bo dutifully obeyed in the exact order of instructions and consoled his sobbing wife. 'Sorry, love, didn't mean to scare you.'

Milly slid down the side of the shed and wept in relief.

'You can't die before me, Bo. You're not allowed to.'

In between sniffles, Jody answered Bo's phone and handed it to him. 'It's Radar.'

'Sir?'

The two women watched as a string of emotions danced across his face. Milly retrieved three bottles of water and a soft drink from the 4WD and handed them around. Bo drained the soft drink in one go, hung up and drained a bottle of water.

'Right, ladies. We've got the green light. Thanks for the refreshments. Now, we've got our own things to attend to.'

He got himself upright, hugged them both and grinned. 'Be assured, the love of my life and our little Canary, everything is going to be fine.'

Waiting for them in the kitchen, Elaina and Darlene had brewed a fresh pot of herbal tea and prepared a platter of savoury muffins.

'Yum!' Milly exclaimed as she walked in. She then pivoted on one foot, rushed back out of the kitchen and promptly threw up.

Elaina fought back tears. 'Oh no.'

'She ate too much cheesecake, Elaina!' Jody hissed. 'Think about that instead.'

Behaving like nothing was out of the ordinary, she kicked off the meeting with the date of the harvest party and the executive decision Bo had made that it was going to be a BBQ. Several of the farmers around had their own onsite butchers and would provide the meat. The only requests from the kitchen were potato bakes, coleslaw, bread and bread rolls, and a large supply of trifle cups.

'Does that mean we can go home and have an early Christmas?' Milly asked hopefully.

'Yes, it does.'

'We'll be sad to leave, Jody,' Darlene said. 'Really sad. Maybe Jody's Kitchen would consider having us back for next harvest? What do you say, girls?'

'Oh, that'd be awesome!' Milly squealed.

'I'll book our tickets from Denmark as soon as we get home!' Elaina said enthusiastically and kissed her dolphin bracelet.

Jody looked pleadingly at her oldest staff member, who took the cue in her stride and said, 'Girls, I've been thinking long and hard about how we get home. Organising a motorhome is possible but time-consuming. However, it's a long drive without being able to stretch the legs. Facilities, while available, are cramped, if you get my drift!'

They both nodded solemnly. Darlene went on to explain the knowledge she had recently gleaned from Cassie, and Bev's confirmation about their driving holiday – one man, three women and three male dogs – and that she had made preliminary enquiries at the Dubbo Private Hospital, renowned for its exemplary women's health services. The hopeful looks from the women in front of her confirmed her decision.

'I'm yet to get word, but, my little sisters, I suggest you fly in the first instance. I've done the groundwork with my contacts, as well as at the hospital. They're expecting you both within the week. I can get you to Dubbo–'

Darlene's mobile interrupted the conversation. She excused herself and took the call from Radar.

'Ms Adams, I need to speak with you privately and immediately, please.'

'Excuse me, I have to take this call. Girls, I hope your laundry is up to date!'

She didn't wait for approval and stepped into the pantry. The minute the door was shut, she confirmed her availability and listened intently.

'Pardon the eavesdropping, and forgive me, too. I sense the urgency – we all do. I can accompany the girls as far as Dubbo. How do you propose they get there?'

'Geez, Radar! I don't know where the hell you've got those listening devices, but in this instance, I am not going to argue. I've paid for a private charter to be on call. They're on the ground in Esperance. Getting the girls from here to there is the challenge. Any suggestions?'

'Send me the details of the charter company and leave the rest with me. How quickly will they be ready to go, or should I talk to Jody?'

'Best you have a conversation with her, please. Shall I put her on?'

'Affirmative. I'll stand by.'

Darlene forwarded the relevant contact details to him, whipped open the door to the pantry and rushed over to where Jody was peeling potatoes.

'It's for you. Team Lead calling!' Darlene winked.

'I'll take it in the secret room.' Jody smirked.

Darlene sighed loudly and whispered her thanks to whoever was watching over them and listening, too. She wondered what other conversations had been overheard, by whom and how. It wasn't for sinister reasons; she was confident of that.

Knowing full well the potatoes for were gnocchi, she continued with the meal prep. Eventually, Jody returned, wiped her tears and handed back Darlene's phone.

'Radar's organising a helicopter. He said he'd tell you the rest when it was confirmed.'

'Oh, Jody! Did he give some sort of time frame?'

'ASAP! The cheeky sod made me repeat it. ASAP. He gave me permission to use it on Bo when I needed him to do something quickly!'

The women laughed until the tears started. Comforting each other, their fears for Milly's health remained silent. Working together, they knocked up the batch of gnocchi and packed the sliced potatoes for the freezer.

'When will you leave?'

'The eighteenth, if I'm not an imposition or in the way.'

'You would never be in the way, but you don't have to wait.'

'Thank you. I know, but I want to.'

'Your call.'

Darlene set up the production line of trifle cups, and between them, they had that task completed in record time. Radar's phone call made them both jump out of their skins. Neither had said a word the whole time.

'I'll put you on speaker, if that's acceptable?' Darlene asked.

'Go ahead.' He paused, then said, 'The day after tomorrow, zero seven hundred hours, a chopper will land in the front yard. I will disembark and personally escort the girls on board. They need to travel light. Your jet charter will meet us at a predefined airstrip halfway across the Nullarbor and take three passengers directly to another one outside Dubbo. Road transport will transfer the patients and myself. I will verify I am their designated guardian until advised otherwise. Do you read me?'

'Loud and clear,' Darlene replied.

'Who do you think should contact Mama Bear?'

'The primary patient.'

'Affirmative. You're getting good at this! Might have a job, if you're interested...'

'Spare her for next harvest, if you don't mind,' Jody called out. 'I'll definitely have a job for her!'

'I'll make a reservation right now! Okay, ladies, you know what you have to do. See you on the lawn. I'll instruct Bo accordingly.'

'Roger that,' Darlene said swiftly. 'Zero seven hundred hours. Good luck, and thank you.'

'Over and out.'

Jody volunteered to talk to Milly and make the necessary phone call while Darlene coordinated Elaina in preparation for the flight.

'Answer your phone, Tiny,' Radar commanded to the ringing tone in his ear.

'Sir?'

'Yes. Listen up. I have coordinated a medevac for our Canary and your Danish Pastry ex location. Dubbo is the destination. Canary's kin being advised. Suggest you arrange suitable accommodation for a large contingent.'

'I owe you a debt of gratitude, sir.'

'Negative. This stuff keeps me young, but I am in dire need of wilderness. See you on the flip side, and get ready for Christmas.'

'Christmas, sir?'

'Correct. The dames are coming home.'

'Sir, yes, sir.'

'That's my boy. Out.'

Tiny sat back in his chair with his fingertips pressed together. The similarities between Elaina and Darlene had him so perplexed he knew he had to challenge Cassie. He found her playing fetch and tossed another tennis ball at her.

'Tiny! I had a good teacher at cricket, if you want a game.'

'Another time, maybe. Maybe! Hey, how come you don't look like your aunt?'

'This again? So soon? That's not my story to tell! Why are you so curious, anyway? Do you like her?'

'I think I told you it wasn't as easy at that.'

The young woman screwed up her eyes at him. 'You'd make an awesome poker player!'

Granny's call from the patio made them turn instantly. 'Telephone, Cassie.'

'Thanks, Gran! Race you, Tiny. Run, Nova! Run, Pluto!'

Cassie lay on the lounge room floor and spread the road map out before her. She hadn't thought her aunt's landline telephone call peculiar at all, given her explanation that mobile service was unavailable. Trying to contain her excitement, she circled the planned rest stops in blue ink then scrawled a big yellow star around the town of Dubbo and a red question mark off the coast of Central Queensland. From Dubbo, they could share the driving if the pending weather event up north didn't eventuate. But it was the long days of driving beforehand which her aunt had to endure that caused concern.

'Going somewhere?' Tiny asked her as he walked past.

'I could be, but Amy and Asta told me they were going to Dubbo, and I was just seeing how far away it was.' Cassie crossed her fingers and tucked her head into her shoulders like a child who wasn't telling all the truth.

'And the blue marks?'

'Oh, just some places Aunty Darlene wanted to see.'

'And the question mark?' He grunted and looked at her sternly. 'Cassie, let's get this straight once and for all. If you need something, you have to ask. I don't do hints very well. So, spit it out.'

She sat up, drew her legs up to her chest and sighed. 'Geez, you ask a lot of questions without waiting for an answer.'

'And? I'm listening.'

'Tiny, I have to ask for time off.'

'And Christmas?'

'Um... well... Aunty Darlene already promised to have it with me.'

He mock-frowned. 'I'll go and talk to Granny. What's she up to, anyway?'

'Making you something for Christmas, so make a noise!' Cassie giggled.

Tiny mimicked her. '*So make a noise.*' Then, more loudly, 'I don't do that, either!'

Cassie was left with the sound of his laughter echoing through the house.

Knocking quietly on Darlene's door, Milly leaned up against the jamb to steady herself. The dizzy spells hadn't been as bad as the previous night, but she still felt weak.

'Milly! I was about to make a cup of tea; would you like one?'

'Yes, please. I'll sit at the table.'

'Of course. Talk to me.'

'My mum's expecting me to be on my deathbed! She's already blowing everything out of proportion, and it's doing my head in. I always reckoned she overreacts.'

'No matter how old you are, you'll always be her kid. Try and remember that, little sister. Hell, I'm nearly twenty years older than you and my folks still talk to me like I'm young, naïve and inexperienced in the matters of the world. In some ways, I am. But one day, they won't be here. One day, you'll wish to hear them nag, or tell their silly jokes, or blurt out the blunt truth!'

'Unfiltered, more like it!'

They both laughed, then Milly said, 'I'm eternally grateful to you for... well... everything. I suspect I'll be staying in Dubbo for a while. Either way, I can't believe I'm seeing my mum again so soon! It would have been a horrid surprise if she had seen me in hospital. At least this way, she'll have support, and Amy's been there for her the whole way. You know I've reached out to her, hey? I used Elaina's phone. Her and Asta also had a chat.'

'I suspected that.'

'Cool. By the way, nobody has mentioned me singing. Anyway, Amy reckons Mum and this Troy Oscane are going to get married and then adopt her! They've already done that with the three dogs, which are going to be handful, but I do remember her being good with animals.'

She listened to the young woman talk out her fears, hopes and dreams for the future without her reproductive organs. Milly and Jody had done some research, and in reality, it was probably the best solution. When the young woman did eventually find the man of her dreams, they'd adopt a boy, a girl, a dog and a goldfish.

'Will I ever see you again, Ms Adams?'

'Yes! Here, next harvest!'

They both shared a hearty laugh.

Then Darlene said, 'I plan on meeting my niece Cassie somewhere, and I would like you girls to meet.'

'I'd like that too. Amy wanted to yell it from the rooftops when I talked to her!' Milly laughed. 'She told me they were all hitting the road and would meet Elaina and me at the hospital. Where will you be for Christmas?'

'I'm not sure yet. I've got loose ends to tie up in Queensland, and my parents are expecting me to join them for New Year's. In Tamworth!'

'That's some miles you'll be covering. How're you getting over there, anyway?'

'I'll drive.'

'And Peachie?'

'I don't know. He's been very aloof, but he's got lot on his plate at the moment. I'll talk to him in a couple of days. By the way, how is your packing coming along?'

'I'm done! Jody's given me an apron and a bandana. So cool!'

Darlene gently hugged the frail young woman and kissed her tenderly on the forehead. 'Believe in yourself, little sister. You've got this. Feed the right wolf.'

'I will, I promise. Are you going to see us off in the morning?'

'Of course! Radar is going to have two very dear friends to look after; I'll just give him some advice.'

Milly giggled. 'Treats and kindness. That's you all over, Ms Adams. Thanks for the cuppa. I'm going to get some sleep, and you've got to get ready for work.'

They squeezed each other's hands. Their eyes conveyed the message of hope, and both looked away as the tears fell.

CHAPTER TWENTY-ONE

Troy looked at the calendar. It was still fifteen days to Christmas, and he was getting impatient. The contents of the envelope from his late uncle were never far from his mind, plus he had some exploring to do around Lake Windamere in New South Wales. Not fully comprehending the inheritance, the map nor the abundance of land, he'd hoped to have the opportunity for a longer chat with Tiny. The bundles of cash would be particularly useful for the festive season, too.

Being home didn't help, because all he wanted to do was eat. Bev had already made two batches of shortbread and fruit mince pies, which he had eaten practically on his own, and she'd kept moving the Christmas cake and puddings. The only presents under the tree were the gifts he was giving the women in his life. He felt it was imperative they be in Dubbo before Milly arrived.

As he walked past the girls' bedroom, Asta reminded him that her parents were joining Elaina's in the flight over and would make their own way up to Dubbo. Troy automatically put another five handkerchiefs in the open suitcase lying on the bed. His own surrogate family had a twelve-hundred-kilometre journey to cover. The dogs would adapt to the confined travelling arrangements. Then he laughed; they all would. They could all drive, and they had talked about sharing the trip. It really wasn't far with that many drivers. What were they waiting for? It was Bev's last day at work, and it was midafternoon. He dialled her number and bombarded her as soon as he heard her voice.

'Hi, honey, why don't we leave really early in the morning?'

'Gawd, you're scary when you read my mind!'

'Well, I'll take the first shift. The motorhome's ready to go. The girls are just bumming around, tripping over themselves or hiding all the treats from me. It's not fair! I'm not doing anything but going stir-crazy. I want to marry you, woman!'

They laughed loudly. She had blossomed when she'd heard Milly sing, had cried a lot, but ever since the conversation with her daughter, Bev's energy had been admirable. She was going to announce her retirement in the new year. On her sixtieth birthday. Troy was determined to marry her during the month of January. They had some exploring to do and decisions to make. Either live inland with plenty of acres and a lake view or on the top floor of an apartment building with sea views.

'Troy! You haven't heard a word I've said… you've drifted off again. What aren't you telling me?'

'No, I thought I'd found the cookies, but I was wrong,' he fibbed and crossed his fingers. 'What were you saying?'

'Yes, let's do it. Get the girls to knock up sandwiches for the road and freeze everything that's perishable. Have a catnap; we might even leave tonight. Got to go, see you when I get home. Love you.'

Troy danced around like a madman, fist-punching the air. He prayed and prayed Milly would pull through. The information Tiny had drip-fed him prepared him for the worst, thereby enabling him to support Bev should things take a bad turn. He was just about to rustle up the girls when Tiny phoned.

'ESP, man. I was just thinking of you.'

'Uh-oh. What were you doing?'

'Preparing to head eastwards within the next twelve hours with a full motorhome.'

'Like the Griswolds, except with the addition of three dogs?'

'Yeah, but right now, I wouldn't want it any other way! What can I do for you, anyway?'

'You know it's about a thirteen-hour drive? Christmas is still a while away.'

'Yep, but Dubbo's the primary destination. That's where Milly will be… is that still on?'

'All systems are a goer,' Tiny said quietly. 'How long are you going to be staying in Dubbo?'

'That depends on several things. Bev and Milly, the pending arrival of the international Danes and if I can go exploring before heading to Spook's for Christmas. Why?'

'Well, I've just booked a massive farmhouse until the end of January. All seven rooms have their own ensuite, and the joint sits on a large grassed block a couple of clicks from the zoo. The girls can sleep in your RV if it doesn't accommodate everyone appropriately. It'll be like a zoo at times, anyway. There are even chooks and a bloody rooster! I'll be bringing Granny, Cassie and our two dogs. How about we leave the hen house, and you and I go exploring?'

'You're a legend. Crunch the numbers, and let me know. What a damned fine idea. Get there as early as you like! We can't all loiter around the hospital all the time. Besides, you and I need to hang out for a while so you can tell me a bit more about these properties.'

'Those are for you to discover, Troy, but by all means, I'll have my ears on. I'll flick you the details of the farmhouse. Just leave a nice room for Granny and Cassie, please.'

'Of course!'

'Listen, if we do get the opportunity to conduct secret men's business, I'm going to see if Spook can get a leave pass. You right with that?'

'Hell yeah. Good on you, mate. Looking forward to being in your company again. Travel well.'

'Sure thing. You too, Troy. Thanks.'

Standing in the long shadows between the silos along the elevated walkway, Bo had watched Spider wash the truck and trailers, tip them enough for the water to drain then detail the prime mover. That was the good boy Spider; then, the angry one came out to play. The bucket was dropped into the laundry tub, noisily cleaned and dumped unceremoniously upside down on the concrete floor. The caravan door slammed back on its hinges, and his heavy stomping echoed into the night air until it suddenly stopped. Silently and creepily, the real Spider emerged from the caravan, stepped into the washroom and, a long while later, loped around the yellow Ford Focus then made his way back inside his abode. His shadow from the spotlights created one spooky image.

Stepping out shortly afterwards with a bag over his shoulder, he carefully put it on the front seat through the driver's door, slipped the envelope into his shirt pocket and yelled out his thanks. Nobody replied. Under the light of the interior, he removed the SIM card, crushed it and the mobile phone then dusted his hands into the rubbish bin. Several other pieces of paper torn out of a notebook went in the metal drum before he dropped a match. He swayed to the little flame, recoiling when it hissed and several embers floated into the air. Bo knew darn well the typed nameless note indicating the final pay would hold no relevance to Spider. He read it slowly, nodded his head, screwed it up and tossed it into the smouldering rubbish. Quietly shutting the caravan door, he left the keys to it and the truck on the table outside.

Folding his lanky frame into the small car, Spider turned over the ignition, yelled out his thanks again and drove slowly down the dusty farm road for the last time. Bo squelched the two-way radio three times, received one squelch in acknowledgement then looked skywards. Somewhere up there, they were tracking the transponder built into the aerial of the sound system.

'Bye, Graham,' Bo whispered. 'Bye, Spider. Goodbye, son of Max.'

Hours later, he climbed down and, under torchlight, walked home. The burden of being guilty by association lifting slightly off his shoulders as he sat on the porch until daylight.

The sound of the air being chopped by a swift-moving helicopter gave the women goosebumps as they huddled together inside the carport. Milly's ashen face was alive with anticipation as she clutched the hands of Darlene and Elaina tightly. Their eyes were as wide as a startled deer's in the headlights. Darlene couldn't resist and craned her neck around the corner. Aviation was a secret passion of hers. The sleek blue and white Mercedes-Benz of the sky, or industry termed Eurocopter EC145, was almost impossible to see. Then, all of a sudden, there she was, slowly lowering until she hovered above the ground like a beautiful overgrown dragonfly. The pilot gently settled the skids onto the freshly mown grass.

'Girls, you make sure you follow Radar's command,' Darlene called out. 'Keep your heads low, and don't jump up and down when you're on board! I am so, so envious of you right now! These are magnificent aircraft, and it is a spectacular day to be in the air.'

'We wish you were coming with us!' Elaina yelled.

Their farewells had already been said in the kitchen, the dongas, the courtyard and the carport. Blowing kisses, Radar looked quite the foreboding travelling companion, but his grin said it all.

'I'll carry our Canary,' he said loudly. 'Elaina, wrap your arm inside mine, and hold on tight. A colleague dressed similarly to me will stow your bags and assist you on board. We will all be wearing helmets. Ready?'

'Yes!' both young women said as loudly as they could.

Jody and Darlene clutched each other's hands and watched as the precious cargo were swiftly deposited and secured on board the helicopter. The seven-minute turnaround was impeccable. Darlene stepped out and saluted. Watching the pilot lift the helicopter through shielded eyes, she did the wing-wave symbol. He was almost one hundred feet in the air when he dipped ever so slightly and waved. She grinned, waved back furiously and blew kisses until they were out of sight. *One day*, she mused. *One day.*

'A secret interest of yours, young lady?'

She jumped. Bo stood beside her, his arm casually draped around Jody's shoulders.

'Uh, yeah. Anything loud, fast and sleek! But man, that is a sexy helicopter. One of the most comfortable. It's fast, with great fuel capacity, and geez, the pilot had a light touch!'

Bo slipped her an envelope marked *'private and confidential'* while Jody was straightening up a few pot plants. He walked over and assisted with the larger ones before encouraging her towards the courtyard.

'If we're not on a time limit today, I'll cook you pair breakfast.'

'Let's make it brunch, thanks, Darlene,' Jody said. 'We've got some other business to attend to. Say we sit down at 11:30 a.m.?'

'Done. And thank you again for absolutely everything.'

They both smiled and turned away.

Watching idly as the digital clock ticked over to 8:00 p.m., Darlene put the empty beer bottle on the table and lay back on the couch. Brunch had been a success, and she'd had an extremely productive day in the kitchen afterwards, albeit a very long shift, but she had some space to herself again. Sliding the two open-dated airline tickets out of the envelope gave her a great reason to celebrate. She wasn't sure if her plan would come off, but the charter company had kept their promise of two return trips from Perth to Hobart. Radar hadn't let her pay for the medevac flights, but he had let her pay buy the tickets for Jody and Bo and one for him to the same value. The little note on the back of a coaster from the Emu Café in Albany brought tears to her eyes.

Darlene Adams, you're the rarest friend anyone could have the privilege of knowing. Our paths will cross again, of that I am sure. I am going to enjoy my holiday – thank you. On the rear passenger wheel of your vehicle is a burner phone. Only use it if you cannot handle the situation. There's someone watching over you and smiling down upon you. Until we meet again, yours in trust. Radar.

The Emu Café? Peachie! She dialled his number again in the hope he'd answer. He'd been off the air for a couple of days, and her emotions were in upheaval. He was still unreachable.

A good news bedtime story was Milly had been successfully reunited with her mother and immediately rushed into emergency surgery. Mother and daughter had both prayed and cried together beforehand, although a complete hysterectomy was the safest option. But the bad news was Milly had slipped into a coma during recovery. Bev had described it as if her body had gone to sleep, even though her vitals were strong and the brain activity was above average. A quick chat with Elaina had assured Darlene that all the girls and Troy were rallying around Bev, doing their best to be supportive without being in the way. Everyone on both sides of the country was on tenterhooks for very different reasons.

Three days later, Peachie returned Darlene's call, feeling very glum, and failed to sound as happy as she did when she answered.

'I'm not peachy at all. Did the girls get back home okay?'

'Yes, Milly had an operation and is in some sort of recovery coma or something, but nearly everyone's together in or near Dubbo. What's happened to you, Peachie?'

'I've had a suspected heart attack and am in Perth waiting for a flight home. The heart surgeon in Sydney has been in touch and recommends a triple bypass. I, too, will be home for Christmas! I asked Bo and Jody to keep it under wraps until I knew exactly what was going on. My truck's going to stay at their farm until I can organise something, but I have a huge, and I mean a huge favour, one that's bigger than me, to ask of you.'

'Oh no, I am sorry, Peachie. What can I do?'

'Drive the motorhome to Perth or take it back east. Either way, I'll pay the rental fee.'

'Where is it?'

'At the farm.'

'You can't drive back with me?'

340

'No, pet, they won't hear of it. Stay on Channel 38.'

'Done. I'll take it east as far as Port Augusta. Please keep me in the loop with your plans, and I hope everything will work out. It has to!'

'Will you get to Dubbo?' he asked quietly.

'I will make that a destination, and before Christmas, but I also need to go to where the platypus play.'

'Unfinished business, by the sounds of that, young lady. I'll leave you with your thoughts. Let's stay in touch. And, Darlene, thanks for doing this for me.'

'Too easy, Peachie. Take care. Bye for now,' she said softly and hung up.

Contemplating the preoccupied farewell, Peachie sent a message to Tiny: *If you don't make a decision, it's going to be made for you, mate.*

He didn't expect a prompt reply and read it wide-eyed. *Too late for that.*

The head nurse put her head around the doorway. 'Peachie, that's such a cool nickname! Glad you're off the phone. You've either got contacts in very high places or you're a very important man – either way, you're being flown out from the rooftop at 1:00 a.m. Get some sleep, please.'

'Thank you, ma'am. The less said, the better. Merry Christmas. Good night.' Peachie grinned and silently thanked his contacts in very high places.

Milly's private hospital room was abuzz with activity. Physiotherapists attended to their patient's joint and muscle stimulation, while nurses supervised and monitored her chest cavity when reducing her reliance on the ventilator. It brought great relief when the results of all the tests indicated benign abnormalities and there was no sign of a stroke or aneurysm. The medics couldn't explain why Milly wasn't waking up, but after several days of the body repairing itself, they were going to reduce her pain medication and change the settings on the ventilator to see if she'd try and take a breath by herself.

The doctor gently squeezed Bev's shoulder. 'We're going to have to experiment to bring her out. You understand that, don't you?'

'Yes, doc. When?'

'Firstly, you need to stretch your legs and get some fresh air. Your daughter's not going anywhere; her vitals are strong. She's sleeping. Are you familiar with what her workload has been like recently?'

'Long hours, but her voice was so strong when she sang...'

'What? I mean, what did you say?'

Bev almost revealed the secret and simply smiled. 'What I meant was a neighbour described her voice as smooth like fine whisky and thick like melted chocolate. Milly has the most exquisite jazz voice. Sarah Vaughan-style jazz, true classic jazz.'

'Right. Well, we have to try something, and it might as well be music. I don't care how, but get a hold of some recordings of the early jazz musicians. I've only read about the power of music as therapy. Bev? Are you in agreement?'

'Absolutely! Her and Amy also performed the most beautiful duets in choir when they were younger.'

'Well, get Amy in here as soon as possible, too. I've got a phone call to make.' He excused himself and bustled out of the room with his phone pressed to his ear.

Amy stood nervously in the lift beside Troy, her hands covering her mouth while she did her exercises. She'd already explained she hadn't sung for several years and was concentrating really hard on trying to remember the lyrics to the last song she and Milly had ever sung together. It had been at an end-of-year concert at the old people's home several years earlier. Their duet of *Wind Beneath My Wings* was supposed to be the last performance. They had sung it facing each other and burst into tears when they received an encore, deciding on the uplifting song *That's What Friends Are For.* Their rendition brought the house down.

Pacing impatiently outside Milly's room, Bev rushed over to Amy and Troy as soon as she saw them step out of the lift and almost dragged them with her while she talked urgently.

'Amy, my darling, we have to try and get Milly to wake up. There's nothing sinister in her results. She's healing well, and although she's going to be very weak and disoriented, it's critical we encourage her to wake up.'

'Why do you need me?'

'Because you're her best friend, and you sang with her! They're going to try and force her to breathe on her own, and we're all going to pray that music as therapy is as strong as what the doctor has shared.'

'Go ahead, hon, sing your heart out,' Troy encouraged.

'What about the other patients?'

'It's live music, and you also have a beautiful voice. Sing, Amy. Sing for Milly. Sing for all the heart-sore people.'

They fell silent as they stepped inside Milly's room. The soft beep of the heart monitor seemed awfully loud. Swiping away hot tears, Amy kissed her best friend's forehead, whispered how much she missed her then took a deep breath and stood up straight.

Their signature song was what she opened with, before moving into her preferred genre of 'soul'. Voices of accompaniment drifted through the corridors, as well as ripples of requests or encores every time she paused for a break.

Amy decided to stand in the doorway. Staring at the cross on the wall behind the nurse's station, she sang to her parents in heaven before walking and performing what she could of the multitude of requests. After generally entertaining the entire ward for several hours, she blew kisses to her audience. Milly was still sleeping, though breathing ever so lightly on her own; every now and then, she'd forget how to and the ventilator would kick in. Amy buried her head into Milly's shoulder and burst into tears while begging her to come back to the living world.

With the change in travel plans, Bo and Jody had relentlessly pestered Darlene to drive the long haul earlier rather than later. She'd finally given in.

'Not sure if you're stubborn or just plain independent!' Bo said as they lowered the hoist. 'Always suspected you didn't mind getting your hands dirty.'

'Yeah, I'm not sure which, either! Thanks for doing all the crappy stuff. I hate doing the bearings, but I know how to if I need to.'

'Would love to have you back here next year. We both would.'

'I'd like to bring some friends with me!' she said with a grin.

Jody arrived with a small selection of ready-to-heat meals and made herself at home stacking the fridge while Bo and Darlene manoeuvred the borrowed car trailer into position. They'd successfully welded a barrier across its nose to deflect the wind and protect the front end of her Jeep. With the shed light swaying gently in the breeze, the south-westerly gusts indicated a change in weather, and not one for the better. Another sheep grazier warning had been issued, with cold, wet and windy weather to be expected during the next two days. Bizarre for so late in the year, but not unusual. The previous day's temperature had ranged from four degrees at dawn to a high of thirty-eight by midafternoon. Weird weather patterns on opposite coastlines raised eyebrows. An early tropical low developing off North Queensland was an indication of the forthcoming wet season, just as Jimmy had predicted. Darlene prayed she'd get to Mackay before Christmas.

No sooner was the trailer secured to the motorhome than the three of them headed to the enclosures to ensure the sheep and lambs could not be exposed.

'My God, he is gorgeous, and doesn't he know it!' Darlene said, in awe at the size of the prize stud Merino ram.

'Yes, it's a bit late to show you my other boys,' Jody said, 'but I've put a couple of calendars in the motorhome for stocking fillers. Now, come on, we've got a dinner to enjoy.'

Seated in the kitchen, Darlene discreetly wiped at her wet eyes.

'Thank you both so much for everything. I'm going to miss you.'

The delicious chicken and zucchini lasagne was accompanied with a delightful salad, the signature garlic bread and several beers, amid a swag of storytelling and good humour. She handed her wonderful hosts their thank-you present and happily listened to the wish list the pair created on the spot amid constant expressions of gratitude.

'Where will you be pulling up, Darlene?' Bo asked, genuinely concerned.

'Norseman for fuel, and I'll cram as much as I can in all the tanks and jerry cans, then the same places I did coming over. I'll be listening to the two-way for information. It's not really a big deal. All my friends will be close by.' She winked.

'Who else knows of your journey?'

'My niece, who I promised we'd have Christmas together, has probably let the cat out of the bag... I'm anticipating a welcoming party at Dubbo, but secretly, I want it to be a surprise.'

'And then?'

'I have some unfinished business to attend to further north, but the weather up there isn't looking pretty. Then New Year with the family back south.'

'Nobody waiting for you? No home?'

'No. Nothing official, anyway!' She semi-scoffed and briefly fondled the dolphin bracelet.

'Right, we're cleaning up,' Jody insisted. 'You go and get a good night's rest. See you at 4:30 a.m.!'

Bidding them a very good night infused with endless words of gratuity, Darlene closed the door to the kitchen for the last time that year. She really was going to miss the pair of kind-hearted souls and grinned at the thought of them discovering the yule log in the freezer.

'Lima Bravo. How nice it is in the sunshine!'

'Tango Mike, as it is in the moonlight!' Tiny responded automatically and zipped up his duffel bag.

'Signals from both sides of the border have been stationary since last contact. Please advise, boss?'

'Monitor all primaries regularly.'

'Copy that. How's our Canary?'

'Recovering slowly and positively.'

'Good news. And the dames?'

There was a long pause before Tiny replied, 'You'd have a better idea than me, Overwatch. I expect you'll be monitoring those numbers as well.'

'Affirmative. You okay?'

Tiny crossed his fingers. 'Still in two minds.'

'Best make a decision before one's made for you. We're on the turn. Out.'

Tiny scoffed at the repeated advice in such a short time. *Best pay heed to it,* he surmised and dialled Darlene's number. Frowning at having to leave a message, he realised he hadn't thought of what he was going to say and hung up. It was time to drive to Dubbo.

Cassie really was great for Granny and was diligent in maintaining her studies, surprising both her guardians. The consistent high distinctions were equally impressive. Granny had encouraged her to push her limits and learn a foreign language at the same time. She'd accepted the challenge and decided on German. But Tiny finally got to know what having a pesky little sister was like. Always wanting to hang together, buzzing around, talking, asking questions, wanting to learn or watch when he was working on the machinery. His only escape was disappearing into the strictly out-of-bounds areas of the house and his shed.

He exceeded everyone's expectations when they checked out the farmhouse not far from the zoo, found their rooms, and explored the property before temporarily leaving the dogs at the pet resort. Nova and Pluto had bounded excitedly to where the three Rottweilers were housed independently, then carried on to their own kennels opposite the males. Everyone agreed they could bark to their hearts' content for as long as they liked.

En route to the hospital to meet up with Troy and co, Cassie's navigational skills were highly amusing as she mimicked the inbuilt German navigator.

Humming happily, Tiny discreetly sent Troy a message announcing their arrival and walked around to open Granny's door. Cassie bounded out, manhandled the wheelchair and insisted she assisted her elderly companion.

'Tiny, I have to be seen to be doing my job in public.' She winked cheekily. 'Now, please hand me the crocheted blanket.'

'You still haven't told me why you and your aunt look so different but have the same mischievous wink!'

'That's because it's not my story to tell. Now come along, you pair, we've got dear friends to see and a special young lady to meet.'

Cassie animatedly explained Milly's beautiful singing voice, according to Amy, and how wonderful it would be to hear them sing together. Fumbling in the pocket of Granny's wheelchair, Cassie sighed loudly.

'What's up?' Tiny asked.

'Nothing! I just had to check I had Milly's Christmas present, and I do, so... oh! That's Uncle Troy!' She waved madly and left Tiny to push the wheelchair as she raced over and gave the man a hug. She only stopped talking when they entered the hospital.

'Ladies, I need you to wait here for a couple of minutes, please. Tiny, a word?'

The men stepped away and walked towards the canteen. Troy grabbed Tiny's hand and shook it heartily. 'Mate, I'm going to propose to Bev very soon, and, well, would you do me the honour of being my best man?'

Totally caught off guard, Tiny just stared at him before realising what was being asked. 'Uh, yeah. Geez, Troy. I'm the one that should be honoured! Yes. Congratulations, mate. I take it things are looking up?'

'Thank you, thank you so much. Bev's upstairs, obviously. Milly's understandably weak but has been sitting up, clear-eyed, a little brain-fogged, and is asking all sorts of questions in between a lot of sleeping. The poor kid's almost pleading for answers, because she doesn't remember getting here.'

'That's fantastic news that she's awake! Have you told Spook and Darlene?'

'No! That's your job. Anyway, these questions Milly's asking, I'm going to be looking at you for answers.'

'Not in mixed company, Troy. I'll steer the conversation away gently. Trust me on this.'

'Righto. So, you'll be my best man?'

'Yes! Let's go and tell Granny and Cassie about your wedding!'

On the way to them, Tiny concealed a pang of jealousy by asking Troy if he was too old for a buck's night. His reply was a stark contrast to his positive expression of the news.

'I knew it, Uncle Troy!' Cassie gushed and excitedly danced around. 'I knew you two would eventually acknowledge the chemistry. Took you long enough! This means Aunty Bev's daughter is recovering. Oh, it's going to be a wonderful Christmas. Where's Asta and Amy?'

'Uh, waiting with Elaina in the carpark for the arrival of the Danes. They bussed it to Dubbo and hired vehicles from town. They'll be here soon. But I think we go upstairs now before Milly's totally overwhelmed. Cassie, be extremely gentle with her, and refrain from asking too many questions.'

'Of course. The poor dear has been through an awful ordeal.'

Granny laughed quietly and patted Troy's hand. 'Congratulations, Troy. I'm already looking forward to another party of yours!'

Troy knocked softly on the door and held Bev tightly as she wept into his arms. 'She's sleeping again, Troy. We had a little conversation, then her eyes got heavy. Oh, I'm so sorry to have gotten everyone's hopes up.'

'Hey, hey, come outside, honey. We've got visitors.'

Granny was standing with the aid of Cassie and held out her arms to comfort the pained mother. Bev's loud sobs tore at everyone's heart.

Cassie peered in the door and blew Milly a kiss. 'Gosh, you're beautiful, Milly. I can't wait to hear you sing. Here's an early Christmas present for you. I'll just leave it on this table thing. Ha ha, I'm a poet.'

Tiny gently pushed his way into the room and closed the door. He smiled at the crocheted yellow canary, read the medical chart, observed the monitor output and saw the girl's chest rising and falling steadily on its own. He sat down on the chair, introduced himself and told her how he had met Darlene. He declared his admiration for her courage and that very few people knew of his military connections, of Radar's tremendous leadership and influence, and of Peachie and Troy's eternal mateship. When he talked about how grateful he was to have participated in saving another young woman, he paused mid-sentence when Milly raised three fingers.

In a hushed voice, she asked, 'It was you who saved the beautiful Elaina with this Uncle Spook?'

'Yes, Milly.'

'She never stopped talking about you! Did Spider and Max die?'

'Not yet.'

'And Bluey?'

Tiny's sharp intake of breath was louder than he'd anticipated.

'He has to go too. Please... make that happen. He had bags of clothes, kids' shoes, drugs, money and guns... the yellow car... if he's connected to them, he has to go.'

'Yes, ma'am,' Tiny said respectfully.

Milly sort of laughed. 'Who's the girl that blew me a kiss and thought she was a poet? And what is that?'

'I knew you weren't sleeping, you scallywag. Her name is Cassie. She's Darlene's niece, and that's the crocheted canary she made for you.'

'How thoughtful! Ms Adams is a beautiful, funny, kind-hearted woman and a great cook! I'm getting tired, Tiny... although you're not. One day, I hope to know your real name.'

'It's been an honour talking with you. Merry Christmas, and a speedy recovery, please. You're going to be inundated with visitors very shortly.'

'Tiny,' Milly murmured, 'did they really hear me sing?'

He wiped his eyes. He tried to speak, but he was choked with emotion. Eventually, he managed to say, 'Oh, Milly, our Canary, that's your code name. How Cassie knew that is beyond me. Yes, there wasn't a dry eye in the house or in other places. We all heard you, and we all want more, too.'

He reached over and very lightly brushed away the tears that trickled down her face. 'Keep getting stronger. You're an amazing young woman. I'd better let the others come in to meet you, and while they're doing that, I'm going to make a phone call. Thanks for listening and talking to me.'

'Thank you for who you are.'

Tiny squeezed her hand gently, said a silent prayer and walked out with a bowed head.

Bev gripped his hands. 'Did she talk, Tiny? Did she say anything?'

'A few murmurs. Poor kid didn't get a word in with all my drivel! There's a nice colour returning to her face.' He looked at all the expectant faces and spoke kindly and firmly. 'Folks, in my experience, it's best not to overwhelm the patient by bombarding her with questions and the like. Instead, talk to each other, so she can listen to your conversations, but include her. She is in the room! Plus, it's nearly Christmas. Happy talk. Okay?'

Tiny's huge stature naturally pulled everyone into line as they filed into Milly's room. Troy's look of appreciation didn't need words, and Granny's smile confirmed he'd said the right things. He stepped out of the room for space and almost bumped into Asta and Amy, who greeted him shyly and raced inside. As soon as he was alone, Elaina ran towards him and threw herself into his waiting arms. He hugged her tightly and swung her around in the air while she planted kisses all over his face.

'Thank you so much, you gorgeous man. I knew you had something to do with this, somehow, but the nice army man swore us to secret.'

'Secrecy, that's how you say that phrase. Your English has come along really well, and you look great.'

'Yeah, mate, you too!' She giggled and steadied herself on the floor.

'Very funny, Elaina.' He grinned and indicated with his head towards Milly's room. 'You need to be in there.'

'I know. Will we see each other again?'

'We have to, but we'll always have company, and Christmas is around the corner.'

'Yes, I behave, and I wish you merry Christmas in a special way, then.' She blew him a kiss as she closed the door.

Sliding into his car, he sent the signal and tapped the steering wheel impatiently. It seemed ages before the connection was successful.

'Lima Bravo. How nice it is in the moonlight!'

'Tango Mike, as it is in the sunshine! Canary advised of a missed target.'

'Repeat that.'

'We have a missed target. The original location of the yellow Ford Focus.'

'Negative. Midnight Arachnid and surrounding area taken out. Solo perp in solitude.'

'Solo perp guilty by association to last known targets.'

'Stand by... thank our Canary, will advise before Santa's sleigh departs the North Pole. Out.'

Resting his head into the luxurious headrest, Tiny breathed a sigh of relief. He now owed Milly a debt of gratitude. The circle of implications grew thicker, yet the friendships gained were everlasting.

CHAPTER TWENTY-TWO

Filling up the fuel tank to the brim at Norseman, Darlene had no intention of stopping at any of the roadhouses en route to South Australia. Afterwards, she tucked herself in behind the roadhouse, had a light breakfast then slept heavily for three hours. Wearing her usual travelling garb, including her Colt 45, she inspected her vehicles before repositioning them at the wash-down bay and using the equipment available.

'You look nice,' a childlike voice called out.

Darlene paused momentarily, ignored the comment and continued with her task.

'I said, you look nice.' This time, the voice was cold.

She worked her way swiftly to the opposite side of the vehicle and saw the creature sitting on the bonnet of a yellow car. Desperately trying to keep her breakfast down, she realised the creep was clearly eyeing her off. Reeling in her panicked thoughts, Darlene ignored him completely.

'You don't fill out your clothes, pretty lady. I am not a fool.' A threatening tone had replaced both voices.

Rapidly winding up the hose and snatching the receipt from the slot, she took her mobile out of her pocket and hurried back to the motorhome, waving at a trucker as he rolled in behind her. He climbed down from his rig and eyeballed her. The bullbar of his Volvo was splattered with blood and guts and positively stunk.

'You nearly finished here?' he barked angrily.

She nodded furiously and pointed at the yellow car with a trembling hand, all the while dragging her foot in the damp soil.

'Well, get a move on, then!'

She watched as the creature slid across the bonnet, climbed into his car and took off in a hurry. He sped past several stationary trucks and turned right. He was heading south. She was heading east. Darlene whistled like she was calling a dog and pointed at the ground when the trucker glared at her. In the dirt she'd drawn 'SOS'.

She hurriedly got into the motorhome, dialled up the two-way to Channel 40 and listened for the wide-load convoy she'd overtaken two hours earlier. If she could get in between them, she'd be relatively safe.

The only chatter on the radio was another wide-load escort travelling eastwards, causing westbound truckers to complain. They were thirty kilometres ahead of her. The blast of the air horn behind her was all the encouragement she needed.

She easily caught up to the wide-load escort vehicle, was encouraged to overtake the convoy tail and spent the rest of the day watching the behind of a massive haul truck on a flatbed covering almost two lanes. The vehicles that did overtake were very fast sedans or motorbikes. When they pulled into a rest area midafternoon, she did the same and tucked herself out of sight from the highway. It was only then that she contemplated the morning's scenario and consequently broke out in ginormous goosebumps.

Spider. It was Spider. But he should have been long gone by now. She eyeballed the burner phone and swiftly dismissed the thought. She wasn't in trouble. Retrieving her short barrels, she slipped a magazine into the Smith and Wesson and put it in the console between the seats. She prepped the Colt 45 and hung the holster over the headrest of her seat. She rehearsed reaching for it while her left hand comfortably gripped the steering wheel.

She slipped into the same position as the wide-load escort pulled out. They had permission to drive another four hours then, by law, had to pull over for the night. That was not in her plan. Nor had she travelled enough kilometres. She was far too wide awake by nightfall and pushed onwards. There hadn't been any sighting of any yellow car. Taking her mind off the what-ifs, she dialled down to Channel 38 and phoned her parents.

Much later, she was still sighing with relief. Their conversation hadn't been as daunting as she'd anticipated. Her parents would be attending their traditional Christmas street party and were particularly excited about getting away the following day. Darlene explained she'd had travel complications and would definitely see them at Tamworth, with Cassie, for New Year's Day. Her mother had expressly told her of their granddaughter's exciting new job and how she had fully encouraged the girl to pursue the opportunity. There had been a joint telephone conversation between nearly all the aunts and uncles and parents about refraining from being selfish and letting the twenty-somethings meet their partners or job obligations, only on the proviso that on New Year's Day, and for as long as possible afterwards, they could all be together.

Bright spotlights were swiftly filling her side mirror about an hour east of Cocklebiddy and started weaving erratically all over the road, before straightening up and overtaking her. Mumbling a rather impolite name at the driver, she didn't give the vehicle another thought as the taillights disappeared. Not long afterwards, she hugged the left of the lane as two long-haul truckers overtook her. The second one did the indicator dance, and his deep voice penetrated the air of the motorhome.

'Got your message. Will keep an eye out. Keep them straight. Out.'

Darlene had no qualms about not responding. Instead, she yelled out her thanks.

Tiny was just about to walk back inside when his slimline phone vibrated in his pocket.

'Sitrep?' he answered swiftly.

'Mobility cancelled. Mission aborted due to delay on Target One. Dual presence with Target Two. Seek advice.'

'Stand by.'

Swearing under his breath, Tiny used his normal phone, deactivated caller ID and dialled a number he knew he would never be dialling again.

Her raspy, fake-seductive voice crackled through the phone. 'Ahh, the little lost lamb. Was wondering when you'd reach out. Looking for some comfort after all these years?'

'Not comfort, Trixie. Only your whereabouts.'

'Ooh, coming to find me, big boy? I'm excited, but what did you do with Bluey? He's a blubbering mess. I hope you're going to have an old-fashioned duel with Maximus Powderpuff... oh, hang on... he'd like to deal with you. Shall I put him on?'

'Let's just keep this conversation between ourselves. Why'd you hang around?'

'Easy money and the thrill of the catch, I suppose. Stevo got greedy.'

'Was that all he got?'

'Guilty as accused and got away with it. You going to look me up?'

'No. Where is Bluey?'

'Where he always is.'

'Goodbye, Trixie.'

'Forever this time?'

'Yes. Forever.'

Tiny disconnected the call, reactivated caller ID, switched phones and said, 'How do you read?'

'Loud and clear. Location confirmed for Target Two. Continue?'

'Affirmative. Target Two. I repeat: Target Two. Make it look like an accident before they reach the border. Targets must not meet. I repeat. Targets must not meet.'

'Read you loud and clear, boss. Instructions on missed target?'

'Make it look like another accident.'

'Copy that. Out.'

Three and a half hours later, Darlene had slept, showered, eaten a bowl of pasta salad and made a coffee for the road. She felt alive. Not seeing any vehicles nearby while peering out of every window, she silently stepped out to check hers, gazed into the night sky and smiled. The stars twinkled against the cloudless black curtain as a satellite traversed its path. Suddenly shivering, she rushed back inside, locked the doors and turned the key. Another long drive ahead following the dotted lines.

Nearing 2:20 a.m., the swerving tyre marks on the highway looked peculiarly fresh, and it was obvious the vehicle had veered off the blacktop, bounced its way back on then continued on its way. She immediately thought of the idiotic driver that flew past her.

Checking her mirrors and ahead, there were no headlights in the distance, so she pulled off into the rest area, slowed to a stop, lowered the window and turned off the engine. Listening to the sounds of nature, she focused on anything unnatural. Nothing. Taking the opportunity to top up with fuel, she felt like a pistol-packing mama.

She wasn't far from the Mundrabilla Roadhouse and grinned. They weren't going to get her hard-earned cash on this trip, either. About ten clicks past it was the rest area where she had intended on snatching some more sleep.

Sweeping headlights in the distance gave her the hurry-up. At night-time, it was impossible to judge the distance on a winding road, particularly with powerful spotlights that seemed to go on forever. Securing the empty jerry can, she shone her spotlight over her dust-covered Jeep and pouted, twanged the tie-down straps and felt the hubs on every road-hugging tyre. Double-checking her surroundings, she blew a kiss into the sky and carefully manoeuvred the vehicles over the jagged shoulder, onto the blacktop. Last thing she needed was a flat tyre!

Just as she'd changed into top gear, an approaching vehicle flashed its headlights, blared on the hooter in a friendly manner then sped past. Her hands remained firmly on the wheel and did not return the interaction. She was an unidentifiable anonymous driver in her baggy clothes with a Colt 45 and Smith and Wesson at the ready. Besides, nobody knew where she was. She hadn't activated the burner phone. Then she began to doubt her belief that it was a different vehicle to the erratic behaviour of the... oh, God... it was also a yellow car. A little yellow car. The image of a human spider popped into her head. Darlene swallowed the bile that rose to her throat and turned up the volume on the two-way.

Just before the first rest area of twelve pull-in zones spaced evenly on opposite sides of the highway, Darlene yawned loudly. Her heart fluttered when she saw a long-haul truck tucked away in the westbound campsite, and she swiftly dismissed the notion it was someone she knew. The two-way was ominously quiet, but her eyelids were getting heavy. There was a truck in the third rest area heading east, two more on the other side of the road heading west. She smiled when she saw the fourth camp area was empty. Far enough away but close enough.

She tucked as far back from the road as possible, using the shrubbery as a barrier, but towards the front of the cleared area, enabling a quick getaway if needed. Disabling the interior light and turning off the ignition, she stumbled around in the dark, locked all the doors and covered all the windows. Knowing full well her vehicle was locked, she didn't venture outside and sighed loudly in relief that she had enough fuel in the tank to get her to Border Village. Using her mobile phone as the only form of light, she got out a change of clothes and prepared the shower cubicle. Just as she turned on the tap, the two-way came to life. One hand flew to her mouth to smother a shriek as the other turned off the water. A childish, leering voice sang through the speaker.

'Hey, pretty lady, come out to play. It was you I saw at Norseman today, then you drove your two vehicles away, but hey, pretty lady, come out to play.'

Without a sound or any light, Darlene got dressed, took the safety off the Colt 45 and sat on the edge of the bed. Contemplating her next move, her heart almost seized as the crunch of a very slow-moving vehicle cruised through her camp area and continued eastwards.

The same singsong voice punched through the speaker. 'It's okay, pretty lady. I'll park up here and wait. I go to sleep now, but I know you're all alone. My spider's all alone. Hey, pretty lady, come out to play. Tomorrow, we go on a date.'

'Oi. Stop being an idiot and get off the radio,' a particularly angry voice bellowed. Darlene dashed off the bed, turned down the two-way and promptly sat in the driver's seat as stiff as a board.

'Don't you ever talk to me like that,' a snarl replied. 'Mind your own business. Tomorrow, lady, enjoy the sunrise.'

Not wanting to hear any more, she clicked it off and gnawed the inside of her cheek. She wasn't tired now. Her hand automatically reached into the glove compartment for the burner phone, then stopped. Radar had indicated she was to use it if she couldn't handle the situation. She could handle this situation. She had four weapons!

Then the consequences of using each one played out in her mind. The obvious one to use was the injection gun. Silent and untraceable. She knew she could walk silently; she'd proved that to herself at the shooting range. She didn't know if anyone had her back then. Did anyone have her back now? She still didn't know.

For the first time since being in Peachie's hired motorhome, Darlene thanked him for having the most spacious model. Climbing into the berth above the cab, she cupped her hands around her face against the small window and waited for her eyes to adjust to the darkness. An oncoming semi-trailer was cautiously straddling the verge and camping area on the opposite side of the road. At the same time, dull headlights swept into her campsite from behind the trailer. She pulled away from the window and watched as a little yellow car cased her camp, drove forwards slowly then followed the verge ahead of her vehicles before disappearing behind some shrubbery. Darlene knew full well there were two more campsites on the northern side of the highway. Spook and Tiny always camped in the one she was in on their way home, because it accommodated both their trucks. She nearly burst into tears at the sudden feeling of loneliness.

Pressing her face against the window, she watched and waited. The men had talked about the pea soup which could sometimes come in before sunrise, making it nigh on impossible to see five metres in front of one's hand this close to the Great Australian Bight. She prayed this would be the case and that it would be in her favour. Shoving all thoughts of Tiny out of her mind, she imagined a hideously creepy spider skittering towards her. It was going to make her break her promise to Cassie. No. No, it wasn't. Nothing was going to force her to go back on her word. She was going to take out the trash. Her gift to everyone. Her secret, until she could talk to Radar.

Overwatch didn't like the thickening cloud interfering with his visual. He knew Target One was in close proximity to the Pretty One. His lips were sealed. No collateral damage. He had to return his attention to Target Two and the missed target, then report.

After two hours and no further interaction, Darlene's mind was made up. She switched her mobile to silent, readied both pistols, loaded four darts with enough ketamine to take down two rogue bulls and prepared the injection gun. As quietly as possible, she key-locked the motorhome and threaded her way through the scrubby, bush-filled camp areas.

Darlene prayed she knew what she was doing as she worked her way to the northern aspect of the next campsite. As suspected, the yellow car had reversed very close to the tree line. A snapping twig beside her boot forced her to crouch down and hold her breath for a count of ninety.

The rear passenger door opened as the interior light filled the misty space, making the spindly silhouette appear alien. The hair on Darlene's body stood on end. Her guts twisted into a knot. It was a human spider. Gangly legs and arms, big head, puny body. He contorted and curled into the back seat. His long arms and bony fingers stretched upwards and fumbled around for the interior light. As it plunged into darkness, she heard the threatening tone.

'Pretty lady, I remember you now. You got away, but not this time. In fact, my spider wants to play.'

The interior light flickered. He sat up, then he somehow crawled out of the back seat and disappeared out of sight. Darlene didn't breathe. She raised the injection gun and couldn't see her own hand. She very slowly ducked down.

'Aw, no fair. I'm tired. Spider sleepy. Sing me a lullaby, pretty lady. Tomorrow, we get wired.'

The chilling giggle hung eerily in the dense mist. The hazy light of the car's interior was further diffused when, she realised, he crawled back in. She slowed down her breathing and stood up very slowly, slipped the injection gun off her shoulder and nearly shrieked aloud when one of the trucks fired up its engine. Its air whistle pierced the thickened silence. She took one step forward just as the interior light came back on. Taking advantage of the echoing sound and cloaking mist, she approached the light very slowly, bent down and felt around for a pebble.

'I know you're out there,' a calm tone called. 'I knew you'd come.' Then, instantly, it changed into a growl. 'Never, ever ignore me again. You won't see daylight. You won't feel the rain.'

Darlene froze as the threat sat up, pushed the car door open even wider and stretched its legs. The worming, scrawny feet swirling the dense air. She was ten metres away.

'I can see you, pretty lady. Let's have another drink together...' The voice changed to that of a whining boy. 'I'm tired. It's been a long day, and you aren't playing nicely. Why? Why? Why?'

Slowly pulling herself to full height, she watched the creature shrink back down onto the seat just as a gentle breeze blew from behind her. She tossed the pebble onto the roof of the car.

'Don't. Just don't, or else,' the ugly, threatening voice growled.

He sat up and twitched towards the door. He was coming to get her. She aimed the gun at chest height and fired. He groaned and fell backwards. She listened. The idling truck was a nice sound. She reloaded. He sat up again. She shot him in the stomach. He fell backwards. She put a dart into both bony feet hanging out the door.

Two other trucks fired up their engines in unison. Darlene crept closer and shone the torch at the body of the mobile tattoo parlour. The spider tattoo sleeves were rolled down its arms and legs. She did not look at the face. *Never ever look at the face, just in case the eyes are open. Just in case. Never look.* She flicked off the torch, walked backwards for fifteen paces, spun and raced back to the motorhome. With her heart in her mouth and arms out in front, she stumbled and fell, hitting the dirt hard. She lay there, forcing herself to breathe slowly, then rolled onto her back. Her mobile started buzzing. Ignoring the incoming call, she activated the torchlight and shone around the ground. It was alive with crawling bugs.

In a flash, she was on her feet. She made sure she had everything and had just gotten to the door of the motorhome when the first truck rolled out of his campsite. Waiting until he'd driven past, she unlocked the door, leapt inside, locked it behind her and instantly laid the weapon on the bed before swiftly stripping off.

'Merry Christmas, everyone,' she said quietly and frowned at the incessant ringing mobile phone. Again? An unknown caller, at this time of the morning? She ignored it, put a load of washing on and took a very long shower.

Berating himself for repeatedly dialling her number, Overwatch patched a call through to Radar.

'Sorry to bother you, sir.'

'Go ahead.'

'Target One and our Pretty One in close proximity. Location Oscar. Zero visibility. Failed comms. Requesting intercept.'

'Ah, the old pea soup. Sitrep on remaining targets?'

'In progress. Clean-up crew waiting in the wings.'

'Request approved. Border Village.'

'If a no-show?'

'Pray and continue to last known location.'

'Copy that. Thank you, sir.'

'You did the right thing, son.'

'Lips are sealed, sir.'

'Out.'

Overwatch sighed loudly and pressed redial. He listened to her voice message again, then disconnected the call. Saying a silent prayer, he set up the intercept accordingly and coordinated his immediate transfer to terra firma. He had some Christmas shopping to do.

Wearing washing-up gloves, Darlene secured the wiped-down, dismantled injection gun and looked hesitantly at the ownership papers inside the outer pocket of its case. They had to stay in place until she crossed the border. Even though she had no further use for the weapon, she really needed to speak with Radar, yet wasn't prepared to use the burner phone.

Visibility was horrendous as the dawn approached. Only then did she confirm that it definitely was the pea soup of the Great Australian Bight. In another hour, she'd be nearing the South Australian border. It'd be safe to sleep there during daylight hours. With that decision made, she turned up the volume of the two-way, listened to the truckers' road report and followed behind the slow-moving procession of taillights. She didn't look sideways but asked herself the obvious question.

Now what are you going to do? You left the darts!

Tiny let out the breath he'd been holding and looked at his watch. Three and a half minutes. A personal best out of water. He sat down heavily on the bed and again checked his watch, for the millionth time. Sleep had failed him. Nova had jumped on his bed and rearranged the blankets around her, and now watched him intently. He was about to attempt another personal best when he heard the tell-tale click.

'Lima Bravo. Team Alpha leaving clean sites.'

'Acknowledged. Anything else?'

'Negative.'

'Copy that. Out.'

He felt better knowing that he could give Milly some good news.

The blasting early rays of the sun were the best thing Darlene had hoped for as she rolled off the verge and into the temporary parking zone of the border. This time, she did answer the incoming call.

'You are persistent,' was all she said in a calm voice.

'Ma'am, thank you for answering. The pea soup caused quite the consternation. Simply returning the favour, I've had your back since Jacup. Can you stall your travels for a few hours?'

Darlene gasped and bit back tears. 'Are you a friend of Radar?'

'Yes, ma'am. Please answer the question.'

'Uh, yes. Yes, I can.'

'Excellent. A rendezvous is being arranged. Lips must remain sealed. How do you read?'

'Loud and clear.'

'Good. You are in transit in a dual vehicular setup, correct?'

'Yes.'

'Where is your destination, ma'am?'

'New South Wales.'

'Clarify.'

'Dubbo.'

'Excellent. At approximately thirteen hundred hours, two APVs will meet you on the South Australian side of the border and lighten your cargo.'

Darlene listened intently and responded accordingly. 'Copy that. There is a situation which requires attention approximately seventy clicks west of my current location.'

She was met with silence.

'Hello?'

'Thank you, ma'am. That is not your concern.'

'The evidence may be.'

'Negative. Confirming the rendezvous and cargo swap at previously stated ETA.'

'How much cargo?'

'Whatever is necessary for you to continue on your journey. Cross the border soon, please, ma'am. Good work, and good day to you.'

'I will graciously accept your assistance. Thank you, bless you and merry Christmas.'

'Merry Christmas, ma'am. Make it a special one. Out.'

She swiped at the tears that filled her eyes and followed the convoy until the border patrol officers indicated for her to stop. They were extremely thorough with any accumulation of weeds and seeds, scrutinised the receipts from the wash-down bays and grilled her incessantly about the abundance of weapons. Her valid 'permit to carry' documents and folder of shooting certificates had them intrigued, but the small trophy satisfied their curiosity, enabling her to cross into South Australia without further delay. Parking well out of the way of all traffic and pedestrians, Darlene secured and darkened the interior of the motorhome. Sleep. She desperately needed sleep.

Sitting bolt upright at 12:33 p.m., Darlene's waking thought was of a bacon and egg roll, and she promptly got on with it. Seated on the motorhome's side step, gazing into the sparse flatland while devouring the simple breakfast, she sighed heavily and loudly. She was still hungry. After cleaning up, she conducted a swift check of all her vehicles, leaving the engine bay of the motorhome until last. She'd just closed its bonnet when ahead and across the four-lane highway, several uniformed men alighted from their vehicles. The time was 1:26 pm. The moment the team lead pressed his hand to his ear, she knew he was her contact. Radar had done it a couple of times. The simultaneous chime of her mobile confirmed her suspicion.

Standing by the passenger side and dutifully shaking hands with an average height, extremely solid, bearded man, she followed him out of the visual of the passers-by until they stood at the entrance to the motorhome.

'Ma'am, I believe you have something for us?'

'Yes, sir. The package is in its own carry case, with all the appropriate paperwork; however, the missing cartridges are affixed to–'

'That situation is under control. You have no further need of the IG?'

'No, thank you. It's served its purpose adequately.'

He removed his sunglasses, and his brandy-gold eyes fixed her with a concerned look. 'Are you okay, ma'am?'

Darlene put her shoulders back, raised her chin and smiled. She returned his gaze and said quietly, 'Yes, thank you for asking. I believe I will be.'

'Very good, ma'am.' He nodded and slipped on his sunglasses. 'Where is the destination of the motorhome?'

'Port Augusta.'

'And the trailer?'

'I'm to leave it in the yard of the hire vehicle premises for collection by a third party.'

'Excellent. We won't hold you up any longer, ma'am. If you could produce said cargo, we'll be on our way.'

Without further communication, Darlene handed the injection gun to the man's second-in-charge. They nodded formally, then Darlene and the team lead shook hands once more.

'Merry Christmas,' they said in unison and grinned at each other before turning away.

She straightened up the back of the motorhome, hung the washing and headed east.

Nine hours later, Darlene drove into Ceduna with a smile that challenged that of the rising moon, buoyed by hearing Bev's news that Milly was recovering steadily and had been given a forty-eight-hour pass from midday on the nineteenth, subject to change. The only glitch was they wanted it to be a surprise for everyone at the farmhouse, but all the men were going away from the eighteenth to the twenty-third on secret men's business. For the first time in a long while, Darlene hadn't taken it upon herself to provide the solution. Dubbo was still two thousand two hundred kilometres eastwards, and December the nineteenth was less than three days away.

With plenty of time to contemplate the near future, a very full tank of fuel and an extremely large and strong black coffee, she drove through the night. Although fatigue was creeping in as the sun announced its presence, the sight of the Big Galah at Kimba, smack bang in the middle of Australia, did make her smile with relief. Taking advantage of the well-equipped rest area, she freshened up then slept heavily. Twelve hundred and ninety kilometres to go.

Frustration was eating Tiny alive. The multitude of voices and dogs, as well as the incessant buzz of conversation, had him on edge, plus the lack of sleep and lack of communication from his buddies in the sky were exacerbating his level of anxiety. He had received no update on Target One. Even though Milly had gratefully received the news of Bluey's demise, then revealed the story behind her snake tattoo, he was still pent up. Tossing and turning, he was glad he wasn't going to be flying the chopper that morning. He longed for the sunrise.

He tried to lighten up his mood when he met Troy in the kitchen before anybody else emerged. They both added a tot of brandy to their coffee and grinned like two schoolboys. The next few days were going to be a blow-out. Exactly what he needed. They jogged to the furthest paddock from the farmhouse as the sound of an inbound chopper disrupted the peaceful early morning.

With their kits casually slung over their shoulders, they embarked on the waiting civilian Eurocopter Super Puma. Shaking hands with the pilot and co-pilot and giving them the coordinates to follow, they belted themselves in and enjoyed the scenery. Tiny pointed to a broad span of water as they searched in vain for a Tudor-style home beside the lake. Troy grabbed his attention by clutching at his arm. From the elevated position, they got a bird's eye view of a quaint chalet's rather glorious pitched roof, with several smaller ones attached to it, all surrounded by a 360-degree timber deck.

Troy pointed across Tiny's vision. 'That's mine, you reckon?'

'Could be. Looks like you're up for a road trip sometime!'

'Scary that I'm in the middle of you and Spook in proximity... just bring beers.'

The party really started when the new granddad climbed on board, buckled up and handed out perfectly chilled beers. 'Thought this might be a mini buck's gig, Troy! Here's breakfast in a can, and cheers to many years of happiness for all!'

The deep voice of the pilot rumbled through the headset. 'Watch out, Newcastle! The boys from the bush are back in town.'

Tiny paused mid-sip and switched to direct comms. 'Sir?'

'That's right, lad. I wouldn't miss this for the world. I need to see my Canary sing again.'

'Who else knows?'

'Some of our men in the moonlight. Just need to know if our host will take on another stray. From what I can gather, there are a few of us.'

'That won't be a problem, I can vouch for that! You tagging with us, sir?'

'I'm leading, lad. Tango Mike is my co-lead.'

'You sly dogs! No wonder you've been quiet, Overwatch.' He leaned forward and squeezed the co-pilot's shoulder.

'I've covered a lot of miles in very little time, dude!'

Tiny couldn't get the smile off his face.

The five men crept into Peachie's hospital room while he stared blankly out the window, scratching at the scruffy beard covering his chin.

'Time for the enema,' Radar said in a quiet voice.

'Not today, thanks. I'm expecting my granddaughter.' Peachie replied without turning around.

'We won't take no for an answer.'

'Well, I–' He turned, then gasped. 'You bastards!'

Tiny pushed the door shut, locked it and twisted the blinds in its windowpane in the hope of abating the laughter somewhat. Troy snuck Peachie a tot of port as they all took turns to bring him up to date with the latest news. Christmas was still on at Spook's, and they'd do everything they could to accommodate Peachie and his granddaughter. He didn't commit to anything.

'Men,' Overwatch said quietly when the nonsense subsided, 'some time back, a certain ring-wearing paedophile renowned for the black circles under his eyes went to hell. I formally advise that another of the same description, along with an old truck, will never be seen again. No passengers were harmed in that incident. Just thought you'd like to know.'

The celebration was silent as they all took stock of news in their own way. Twenty minutes later, the senior nurse rattled on the door. Spook unlocked it, and they all stood as calmly as one would expect in a ward of heart patients.

'Goodness gracious, I saw you lot come in and instantly, I knew there would be trouble! How much did he have to drink?' The stout matron stared up at Radar.

'Just a wee drappie, me lady... from Santa, of course.'

She puffed out her chest and pretended to scoff. 'Yes, of course. Well, one hopes Santa knows who else has been good around here! The doc will be by in fifteen minutes. Stick around for some news.'

Cheekily chucking Radar under the chin, she waltzed around and closed the door. The snickers and guffaws had barely subsided when several knocks on the door stopped them in their tracks. Spook, playing the doorman, opened it to find a remarkably pretty young woman in a wheelchair with a broad grin resembling Peachie's.

Radar held the floor. 'He's been misbehaving something chronic, miss. We're his personal security.'

'Oh, I can imagine the nonsense you lot would get into!' DeeDee quipped and rolled over to Peachie's waiting arms then hugged all and sundry to the best of her ability.

They were all chatting merrily when the doctor breezed in, took one look at his audience and stammered, 'B-bloody hell, Peachie, if I knew you had bodyguards, I'd have been here earlier!'

'The best people in the world are right here in this room, doc. A couple are MIA, but hey, we're blessed with who we have. So, tell me, how'd I go?'

'Great news! You can go home tomorrow. From the looks of you blokes, you'll be wanting a medical clearance certificate so he can fly at some stage?'

'Yes, please,' Troy replied.

'Well, just accept it'll be well into the future, but vehicular travel is acceptable for the interim as a passenger only.'

The doctor shook hands with them all, wished them a merry Christmas and thanked them for their service, then advised that Peachie would be ready by ten o'clock the following morning. He respectfully nodded to them all and closed the door behind him. Festive excitement was beginning to build, yet nobody had the fortitude to mention the elephant in the room. DeeDee informed the men that she'd be collecting her grandfather the following morning and he'd be convalescing with her in the Blue Mountains. Nobody argued, but all agreed to provide assistance, which was graciously accepted.

The freedom of being behind the wheel of her V8 put paid to the inconveniences Darlene had endured at Port Augusta. After picking at some fruit then snatching a catnap at the foothills of the Flinders Ranges, her energy levels were surprisingly recharged. But it was the eventual sight of the roadhouse at Broken Hill that brought tears to her eyes. The sudden onset of sobbing forcing her to veer off the highway and stop in a clearing. Climbing across to the passenger seat, she leaned into it and wailed. Delayed shock hit her like a tidal surge, buffeting her against the seat. Clasping at her knees, then clutching at her stomach, she bawled continuously. She grieved for Jimmy. The platypus. Her tree house.

Eventually, she caught her breath, wiped at her awfully swollen eyes and stepped outside. The oppressive temperature brought beads of perspiration to her body immediately. With her fuel gauge sitting just above 'E', she let the air escape from the fuel tank before squeezing the last drop out of the last jerry can. She'd fill up at Broken Hill and not have to worry when she got to Dubbo. Then she cried again. She finally admitted to herself loneliness was not the best feeling in the world.

Washing her face and having a long drink of water, Darlene realised she was also hungry. She knew the roadhouse's burgers were good and began to salivate as she parked her Jeep right in front of the grimy cafeteria window after refuelling. Not recognising any of the trucks, she pulled down her big hat, adjusted the shoulder holster, untucked her baggy shirt and pushed open the dusty glass doors.

After paying cash for her purchases, she claimed the corner seat and sent a message to Bev asking what their plans were. Her prompt reply brought a watery smile to Darlene's face.

While the boys are away, us girls get to play! Milly's getting stronger every hour. The Danish fathers have taken themselves off on a tour and also get back in the evening of the 23rd. Milly and I are thinking about taking the bus to the zoo... the farmhouse with expanding walls isn't far from it. She only needs to come back for a check-up after Christmas then is officially released. How are you?

Darlene put her phone away and graciously accepted the mighty fine hamburger placed in front of her, along with the large, strong, sweet black coffee. It was midafternoon. Dubbo was still eight hundred kilometres away. She was in no-man's-land and ahead of schedule. Savouring the delicious burger with the juiciest beef patty, perfectly cooked bacon and crispy fried egg, she watched the world go by and considered her options. Desperately needing a decent shower and more comfortable bed, she investigated what options and facilities the most expensive hotel in Dubbo had. It had everything she needed, including a bathtub and in-room laundry. Successfully booking and copping the late fees on the chin, feeling more enthusiastic, she replied to Bev as she drank her coffee.

I'm going okay, thanks. Will let you know when I'm closer. Take care. XX
Thank you. Travel well. So looking forward to meeting you! XX

Spook, Radar and Overwatch took charge of the food and booze shopping expedition, while Troy and Tiny disappeared into the jewellery shop. Forty minutes later, they met up at the designated rendezvous and continued their secret men's business.

As night fell, so did the revolting heat, affording Darlene the pleasure of winding down her window and listening to the beautiful V8 burble. She smiled, hung her head outside and blew a kiss wildly into the heavens. Then the most sensible idea popped into her head. Spend a day and two nights with the women, fly to Mackay, tie up the loose ends and arrive at Spook's with Milly on Christmas morning. She loved giving surprises as much as she loved receiving them. Devising more items in the mischievous plan, she felt more invigorated the closer she got to Dubbo.

The minute she had full phone coverage, she dialled her favourite private airline charter company, thanked them for their assistance with the mercy dash, apologised for the lateness of the call and thrashed out an itinerary. She'd covered another three hundred kilometres when she received the confirmation of her flights. Switching playlists, she sang along to the Crooners of Christmas as the lights of Dubbo filled her windscreen. She had to regather her Christmas spirit.

The morning of the nineteenth, Cassie was like a cat on a hot tin roof. Not helping the situation was Nova and Pluto being excessively clingy. She'd been unsuccessful in reaching her favourite aunt and expressed her concern to Granny while they were collecting the eggs for breakfast.

'No news is good news, dear. That's been an age-old saying, and one that Sonny has grown up with.'

'Yeah, I know, but still... I don't have a horrid feeling, so that's also a good thing.'

'Indeed it is. You have to feed the right wolf, Cassie. It's vitally important. Now, how's your German version of *Silent Night* coming along?'

Cassie giggled and replied favourably then explained how she, Asta, Elaina and Amy had been practising under the arbour the previous evening but then got attacked by mozzies. They all spoke French very fluently as they raced back to the house.

Granny chuckled. 'You do have a wicked sense of humour. I am looking forward to meeting your aunt.'

'She's a special lady. Ever since a young age, we've had a connection, but she doesn't have my short fuse. She's more refined, but I daresay she'd be a shield maiden if she had to.'

'A shield maiden? Goodness, where on earth did that come from?'

'You'll see. She's beautiful and strong.'

'Now I have a completely different image to that of the demure, delicate princess I conjured up.'

'Oh, she's that too!'

'Are you trying to befuddle me, child?'

'Absolutely not, Granny!'

'Well, let's just wait and see what Santa brings. Come along, I'm getting hungry and you need to feed these jolly dogs!'

They both laughed as the pooches scampered ahead of them and tumbled over themselves.

Pushing her suitcase, forcing a pathway through the already busy hospital canteen, Darlene ordered a hearty breakfast, fruit juice and a cappuccino before placing several orders with the florist. Finding a seat inside the canteen was nigh on impossible, but eventually a vacant table came up right at the back corner. After the thirty-six-hour rest, she was feeling fresh and her skin was glowing. She sported a very stylish and flattering shoulder-length haircut, and her spring green and white sundress complimented her disposition.

It was a mighty fine breakfast, and the coffee was sublime. Passing on her compliments as she departed, she collected two of the impressive bouquets and proceeded to the 'Ward of Positivity', as promoted on every available noticeboard. As she stepped out of the elevator, she heard Milly singing to her audience before she actually saw the young woman. With her back to Darlene, she sang several medleys, curtsied and returned to her room. Then stopped. Backtracked, turned around and looked directly at her older friend. With a loud sob, she rushed forwards and almost tripped over her portable drip, falling into Darlene's arms.

'You're here! Oh, wow! How can I ever thank you?'

'By accepting these flowers, introducing me to your mum and getting off my toes!'

They giggled, hugged and wiped their tears as Milly led her towards the blubbering, smiling Bev. An hour later, with the best news that Milly had been officially discharged under strict orders to take thing easy, they loaded the boot with bouquets, chocolates and hampers. After some more retail therapy, the three women non-stop nattered until they arrived at the farmhouse.

Only Cassie recognised her aunt's Jeep. Sobbing loudly, she threw herself at her aunt, dragging her out of the vehicle in a bear hug. Then ear-piercing squeals of delight from Elaina and the other women filled the air as they realised who else was with her. Nova wiggle-waggled as she made her way over and received abundant pats from Darlene. Pluto just followed suit. Non-stop laughing, crying, food and drinks continued until the late hours of the night.

Eventually, Darlene and Granny got to have a heart-to-heart conversation.

'I take it the men don't know of your whereabouts, young lady?'

'That's correct.'

'I am not an interfering old biddy, but your niece has wound herself tightly around both our fingers. I daresay it wouldn't be difficult for you to do the same.'

'Duly noted. I have a private and urgent matter I need to attend to in Queensland, and I'd like to borrow Cassie for a couple of days. We'll fly. It's just too far to drive.'

'What about Christmas?'

'I promised to have it with Cassie.'

'And I need her at Scone.'

The two women looked at each other levelly. Their eyes revealed what they both were not prepared to say.

Darlene eventually grinned. 'Strictly between us two, do you like surprises, Gran?'

'I will grant leniency on this occasion and will insist that the women keep a secret close to their chests.'

They hugged each other and enjoyed a nightcap before bidding each other goodnight.

On the way to the airport two days later, Cassie was in a sour mood. Trying to lighten up the atmosphere, Darlene said, 'I am so proud of you, my dear niece. You have a lovely network of empowering women.'

'Well, you started it,' she said bluntly.

Waiting several minutes, Darlene said, 'Spill it. What's got you fired up?'

'You should have told Tiny, or at least Uncle Troy.'

'Why? They'll be right. The men are enjoying their own company, and it is vitally important for them to have their own space, as it is for us women. Always remember that, Cassie.'

'Do you like him?'

Darlene couldn't hide the blush.

'Sprung!'

'Instead of trying to play Cupid, young lady, how about you get together a shopping list and think about the dress you're going to wear?'

'We've already got ours, thanks. But you need a dress, something Christmassy and classy, just like the ones we used to have, and pyjamas. I didn't like the ones I saw. Plus, I've got everyone's last-minute lists in my phone and a wad of cash. It seems we all like to play with cash.'

Darlene smothered her grin as she parked in the secure lockup, the flight attendants greeted them at the private gate before escorting them across the apron towards their waiting aircraft. The sleek Citation Mustang. Cassie was agog.

'Who are you, Aunty Darlene?' she whispered as they took their seats.

'Just a woman who likes loud engines and sleek aircraft. Now, buckle up and enjoy the ride!'

An unfortunate delay upon arrival at Mackay saw them finally picking up the hire car too late in the afternoon to go and visit the rainforest. Instead, they checked into their accommodation and had an early night.

As sunlight kissed the world good morning, they both burst into tears when they walked up the winding path. Darlene because of the memories, Cassie because she got to personally see the final piece of the picture she'd grown up with. It was meant to be a short visit to say some prayers and to say the final goodbye, yet time stood still for Darlene. Gazing skywards, she grinned at the round puffy clouds and touched her left cheek as a soft breath of wind caressed it. They went for a stroll through to Jimmy's resting place and were received beautifully by the orchestral lyrebird and a burst of butterflies. Cassie stared in awe at nature's magnificence and Jimmy's legacy.

Back at the tree house, it took some doing, but they managed to wrestle the spiral staircase into position. Darlene, like a gazelle, bounded up the rungs and left her niece standing on the ground, shaking her head in bewilderment. It didn't take long before she too was beside her aunt with tears streaming down her face as they admired the spectacular view.

'I get it now, Aunty Darlene,' she whispered. 'Thank you for everything.'

Together, they forced the door open and stepped into the tree house, then swiftly stepped back again, dragging the door with them. Nature's critters had already moved in. Without any further delay, they were back on the ground, hiding the staircase. Cassie gave her aunt a moment to herself. Taking one last look at the magnificent view, she wished for the forest to hurry up and reclaim its own.

With a very heavy heart, Darlene drove away, drawing on the strength of Jimmy's friendship. Cassie was respectfully silent, even after they'd ticked off all the items on the shopping list and returned to their ocean-view villa.

Reminiscing and sharing stories while enjoying room service and several icy cold beers, they were in between conversations and jumped then giggled when Chopin's *Nocturne* filled the patio. Darlene excused herself from the table and took the call in her bedroom, enjoying the blast of cold air. The humidity was revolting.

'Hello?'

'The beautiful Darlene Adams! How goes it with you?'

She smiled. 'Peachie! Going okay, thanks, just having a rest. How are you?'

'Yeah, all good. They put in a stint but insist I have to lose weight before a triple bypass.'

'That's good news!'

'No, it's not. It's Christmas. My favourite food fest of the year!'

Sharing a laugh, she listened to Peachie's exciting news that he and DeeDee were going to surprise Spook and co on Christmas Day.

'Oh, that'll be wonderful for everyone.'

'Your plans?'

'I need to attend to some private business, but we'll keep in touch. You take care, now. Talk to you Christmas Day, and please give my love to DeeDee. I haven't forgotten my promise to her.'

'Will do. Travel well. Oh! Before I forget, Bo and Jody send their regards to you and the girls.'

'That's lovely. I'll be sure to pass it on when I'm chatting to them. Cheers, Peachie.'

'Okay, take care. Bye for now.'

She hadn't fibbed at all. But did she want to be by herself early on Christmas morning? Again? Like she had for so many years? No. No, she didn't. Stepping back onto the patio with another couple of beers, she sat down and smirked at her curious niece. In between mouthfuls of the salad, she sipped at the beer to conceal her blooming smile.

'Cassie, tomorrow I need to go the post office, collect and redirect my mail. I hope he doesn't mind, but can you give me Tiny's postal address?'

'Yes,' she blurted out, then leaned forwards. 'What are you up to, Aunty Darlene? You have that look in your eye I haven't seen for a hell of a long time.'

'How much shopping have we got left to do?'

'Only your dress, now, and hair appointments. Gawd, how the hell did you survive this weather? It's like the air's been sucked out of the atmosphere! Anyway, I believe the men were sorting out the booze, and Tiny and Uncle Troy have already settled up with Uncle Spook for the catering over Christmas. I think we should contribute with some more hampers, though. There's a lot of extra mouths to feed, and I think the Danes are on a fairly tight budget. And I owe you money and beer.'

Darlene suddenly stared blankly at her niece. 'I feel as if I've lost a day... what's the date?'

'Today's the twenty-second of December.'

'Oh, hell. Okay, I have to make a phone call.'

'Can I listen in?'

'Alright, but don't say anything, please.'

'You got it.'

Dialling the after-hours number of the airline charter, Darlene toyed with her dolphin bracelet, frowned and stopped. After the Christmas greetings, she explained she was feeling lousy about taking the crew away from their families over the Christmas period. The conversation from the operator flowed easily about how the customers paid the wages then continued with the rest of the marketing spiel.

'Yes, that is true. But can you please contact the pilot and ask if they'd mind flying us back tomorrow? Early afternoon, hopefully, but we'll work in with them. That way, everyone gets to wake up on Christmas morning with the ones they love. It'll mean so much to me if you can make this happen.'

Cassie jumped out of her chair and did a silent happy dance.

'Thank you. I'll stand by the phone and expect his call anytime. I don't care if it's midnight tonight! Bye for now.' She hung up.

'Oh, Aunty Darlene. You're going to be the best gift Santa ever brought anybody!'

'Let's hope so. But we're going to have to order the hampers now and just hope they'll be ready for when we get back. Then I need to get you back to the farmhouse before the men return. I almost stuffed up.'

'You choose the hampers, I'll phone Granny. Isn't it normal for women, wanting to know if their men will be home for dinner?' she stated candidly.

'You are so right! It won't be too late to call her, will it?'

'Hell no,' Cassie replied with sass. 'I'm her carer. I check in whenever I like!'

'Their men? I heard you, you cheeky little sh–'

'Don't swear, Aunty Darlene. It's not very becoming of you!'

Their giggles erupted simultaneously.

Darlene answered her phone in the kitchen and couldn't contain her excitement. The pilot was grateful and overjoyed. They'd meet at the airport at midday.

Cassie bounded into the living room and called out, 'Granny said Tiny had checked in and they'd be home for an early dinner.'

She wasn't about to let her niece know exactly what she had planned and happily poured them each a nightcap.

'Excellent. You'll be home before them, and then I'm going to disappear...'

The sudden loud sob from Cassie took the wind out of her sails, and she rushed over to gather her niece into her arms.

'You can't just go. That's so cruel,' Cassie wailed. 'You promised we'd have Christmas Day together. You've never broken a promise. Why?'

Rocking her from side to side, Darlene couldn't help but chuckle. 'Not forever, you ninny, just for two nights. I'll be there Christmas morning.'

Cassie's blush was a beautiful shade of crimson.

After the younger woman had composed herself, her excitement grew. 'Are you going to let me in on your secret?'

'No. But you know already half of it – you just have to keep it to yourself! Now, we'd best pack our bags and get to bed. Tomorrow morning is going to be hectic!'

In unison, they said the word 'hectic' like a pair of hippies and fell about the place laughing.

The men were seated around the campfire, lost in their own thoughts. Tiny was typically stargazing when Tango Mike casually said, 'You don't have to look for me skywards, bloke. I'm right in front of you!'

Guffaws filled the night air, along with some colourful descriptions.

'You're not the shooting star I was going to make a wish on this time! But damn, it's great to have you here with us, man. Thanks for everything you've done, and more so recently.'

'A pleasure. It's been entertaining.'

Radar joined the conversation. 'Men, when we're in mixed company, Tango Mike here is going to be called Overwatch. Aside from you fellas, only Peachie and the beautiful DeeDee know his real name, and I'd rather keep it that way. Anyway, here's some news you blokes will want to listen to.'

He broke all the rules and turned on his mobile phone. After he finally convinced his men that he would be reading from a couple of screenshots, they settled down and listened carefully.

'An investigation into a corrupt official in a South Australian council who was long suspected of being involved with shifting drugs and housing sex slaves came to a sudden end. It appears a love tryst had gone very wrong in the remote dunes along the Great Australian Bight. Both participants died of gunshots from the firearms found lying beside their bodies several metres away from their burnt-out vehicles. Evidence of illicit drugs was also found. The police are not treating the incident as suspicious. A media ban has been issued after this press release.'

Resounding, heartfelt cheers filled the night air. Radar put his hand up to settle down the jubilant celebrations and continued to read.

'In what can only be described as a fatal accident, it appears a single shot from a homemade gun ricocheted off a metal target and struck the shooter between the eyes, killing him instantly. The deceased male was known to police. No other information was available at the time of the press release.'

Again, the celebrations were loud and eventually petered out.

Troy addressed the elephant in the room. 'Any update on the last cockroach?'

'You're retired, bloke!' Radar stated bluntly. 'When we know, you'll know! Enough shop talk. It's our last night out here, let's rock on!'

'Copy that!' came the unanimous reply.

CHAPTER TWENTY-THREE

Heads turning as the dark-haired stunner and older blonde bombshell stepped out of the beauty parlour put a zing in their stride. They completed their errands in record time, including the purchase of the prettiest red and white ruffle wrap dress for Darlene, and enjoyed a leisurely morning tea before returning to the villa to check out. With the hire car loaded, their Queensland visit had come to a rushed end.

'Will you miss it, Aunty Darlene?'

'Some aspects, yes. But this weather is going to get ugly. It'll be an unpleasant festive season for the people up here. To be honest, Cassie, I am looking forward to a whole new chapter in my life.'

'Good! So am I. Do you think we'd be able to live with each other?'

'Hey? He's a gorgeous man, but let's not get ahead of ourselves!'

'You pair are made for each other,' she grumbled.

Tailwinds and daylight savings time saw them touch down an hour and a half after departure. They wished the pilots and crew a merry Christmas, showered them with gift cards then swiftly loaded up Darlene's Jeep.

'Cassie, I am going to need your help. We've got to find a huge box, wrap it up and stick it under the tree.'

'What's going to be in it?'

'Not much. It's a prank I've always wanted to play.'

Their giggles were identical.

'Count me in! We need a huge bow, too. We'd better hurry, though, particularly if you need to be somewhere else before nightfall. Good luck in explaining that to Granny!'

The nearest whitegoods retailer was most apologetic that the washing machine box didn't have a bottom but very obligingly managed to get the folded cardboard in behind the front seats. Almost emptying the cheap shop of wrapping paper, sticky-tape and ribbon, the two zoomed back to the farmhouse.

It was clear the women there had been busy. The place oozed with Christmas baking, handmade decorations and even more presents under the tree. After everyone's shopping had been distributed, they all thought Darlene's prank was hilarious and unanimously agreed it should be for Tiny, given he was the biggest man. She locked her trusted blue suitcase, stashed it on the floor behind Cassie's bed and slung a simple cloth bag over her shoulder. All she needed was her phone, sunglasses, purse and keys. The rest of the necessities were already in the vehicle. The only intention she had for the day of Christmas Eve was to do absolutely nothing except lounge around in her nightie and read Jimmy's manuscript. And try not to worry about not having her suitcase, or any weapons on or near her.

'I have one request,' she said loudly. 'Even though we're pretending the box is going to be for Tiny, make it easy for me to slip a stuffed Christmas stocking in the bottom of it. I'm coming back, but it's going to be awfully late.'

Darlene's sudden announcement caught everyone off guard, and the girls stopped wrapping the box. While she had their attention, she continued to talk.

'I've never been here, and Cassie's never left. Please, it's very important you all play along.'

'You will be here in time to open the presents?' Cassie insisted. 'It's always early, you know that.'

'Yes, I remember. I promise you, I will be, but you all have to promise me that none of you will say anything.'

Elaina and Asta approached Darlene with her little fingers pointing skywards. 'We winkie promise!'

After the hilarity had subsided, the two young Danish women had another phrase to add to their vocabulary. Darlene repeated her request with a broad grin.

They all promised. Even the five dogs sat on command by the lounge door.

'You had better leave if you've never been here,' Granny said firmly. 'The men are usually early instead of being on time.'

After the hurried farewells, the plentiful hugs and lots of giggles, Darlene bolted to her vehicle and fired up its engine.

Cassie rushed over to her, grinning broadly, and said loudly, 'Stop revving it, Aunty Darlene, you're like a big kid! Your dress and shoes are in my wardrobe. Granny said she'd phone you later. Love you. Thank you for keeping your promise. See you on Christmas Day.'

She planted a noisy kiss on Darlene's right cheek and raced back to the house. 'Hurry up and go,' she yelled and pointed to the sky.

Racing down the concrete driveway and breaking the speed limit for twenty minutes, Darlene eventually blended in with the normal highway traffic into town. She was confident only the women at the farmhouse knew what type of vehicle she owned.

She checked back into her room at the hotel and ordered dinner for several hours later. Relaxation was her priority. She had half-made a huge decision, and she had to be convinced she was going to go through with the rest of it. After hanging out her washing and filling the tub with lavender-scented bubble bath, she poured herself a cup of cold herbal tea. For the next forty minutes, Darlene reflected on the last four months of her life, watching the bubbles slowly dissolve around her.

Did she have any regrets? No. Was she comfortable in all the decisions she'd made? Yes. Did she have any issues from her previous relationship? Not anymore. Did she want to be on her own? Definitely not. Had she fallen hopelessly in love with Tiny? Absolutely. Could she live with two other generations? She paused, contemplated the alternative and slid underneath the bubbles. Exhaling loudly underwater, she made her decision. Yes. And came up for air. Did she know if Tiny loved her? No. No, she didn't; she just hoped he had the same feelings as she did. Did she have a contingency plan? No. For the first time in her life, she did not have a just-in-case, and she felt peculiarly light-headed.

Almost looking like an Egyptian mummy with her head wrapped in a white fluffy towel and body wrapped in a white fluffy dressing gown, she spoke through the door, requesting room service leave the trolley for her to collect. Peering through the fish-eye, she waited thirty seconds, opened the door and whisked it inside then swiftly locked her door.

The delightful aroma of the filet mignon, pepper sauce and loaded potato tantalised her taste buds. Pouring an ice-cold beer, she treated herself to her own company until the next evening, tucked away in her hotel room, relaxing and reading.

As the sun lit up the shimmery western plains on Christmas Eve, Darlene read the last of Jimmy's poetic ramblings and sobbed her heart out. The already healthy monthly remuneration from the proceeds of his book sales brought a watery smile to her face. Shutting her eyes and drawing in a deep, slow breath then exhaling calmly, she said a silent prayer of thanks then another one for guidance.

The traffic finally abated. It was a noisy hotel, with Christmas festivities happening, and she was alone by choice. She imagined the farmhouse and the raucous evening they'd be having. It was going to be her last night alone. She hoped. She had just wrapped herself in the large bath towel when Granny phoned, who spoke quickly and quietly.

'We have all kept our promise to you. The laden Christmas tree was the focal point, and everyone's in good spirits. The men have had several huge days and nights, by the looks of them, and were very heavy eyed after an early dinner again tonight. Christmas morning is traditionally an early start, and tomorrow will not be any different. Anticipate everyone emerging in their Christmas pyjamas by 5:30 a.m., followed by a light breakfast. Nova has not left Tiny's side. Pluto is with Cassie. We don't know what you're planning, but we did as you asked and modified the opening to the box before the men arrived home.'

'Thank you, Granny.'

'Just who is this surprise for?'

'Everyone, I suppose, but it's something I have always wanted to do. Let's hope it doesn't backfire on me! Please see if someone can take candid photos, regardless of the outcome.'

'Okay, well, the laundry door will be unlocked. What time will you be arriving?'

'After midnight.'

'Make sure you eat the cookies. Have a little bit of milk, leave some carrot, but drink most of the beer, then hang on.'

They both giggled.

Then Granny said, 'I'll help you. Let's meet in the laundry at 4:30 a.m. It's the darkest hour and generally when people sleep the heaviest.'

'You don't, Granny?'

'Not this Christmas morning, I won't be.'

'Thank you for doing this. I'll see you in the laundry at 4:30 a.m. Night.'

'Night, and thanks for making this a truly special Christmas.'

Darlene practised her Tai Chi, meditated, then set her alarm for 3:00 a.m. Taking up the entire king-sized bed for hopefully the last time in her life, she slept honestly and soundly. Stirring at the sound of a text message, she fumbled for her phone and smiled. She'd only been asleep for thirty minutes, and it was from Tiny.

Hello Darlene. Wishing you an early merry Christmas and hope you're travelling okay. It was wonderful seeing Elaina again, so glad Milly got home in one piece too. Thanks for whatever you had to do with it all. The Danes arrived too. That was one tearful occasion to witness. We're all heading to Spook's place after Christmas breakfast from Dubbo. Have you got his address? All's well here. T. X

She didn't respond and fell back asleep. Waking up five minutes before the alarm with a childlike sense of excitement, she swiftly showered, and after styling her hair, she got dressed in her Christmas pyjamas. The cheeky elf pattern was ideal. After a minute's hesitation, she eventually clipped the delicate dolphin bracelet onto her left wrist. Leaving a fifty-dollar note with a Christmas card and a thank-you letter for the purchase of the dressing gown, she wrapped herself in it. Taking all her things, she quietly closed the door, crept down the stairs and climbed into her lovely clean Jeep, smiling broadly as she turned the key. So far in her life, there was nothing better than the sound of a V8 early in the morning. Laughing loudly as she rumbled down the highway, she blew several kisses into the heavens.

Getting to the driveway entrance with twenty minutes to spare, she killed the lights and ignition. It was so quiet. Not even the chooks were clucking, and the rooster was unusually silent. The stars above shimmered magically. Leaving the gear in neutral, she pushed her vehicle up the driveway and was puffing like anything by the time she got it behind the shed. Securing it and catching her breath while thanking the weather gods for keeping the heat out of the day, Darlene crept stealthily to the laundry door. It was 4:27 a.m. She pushed it open to find Granny wearing her matron-style 'Mary Christmas' nightie. They wished each other merry Christmas, stifled their giggles, shared the cookies and some of the milk, broke bits off the carrot but couldn't do the beer. Most of that went down the laundry drain.

Granny gave her a tube of mints, took her bag and dressing gown and went back to bed. Under the twinkling Christmas lights and the faux fireplace, Darlene contorted her way in behind the beautifully decorated Christmas tree and smiled broadly when she felt how they'd modified the box. Chuckling softly, she watched the pastel brushstrokes of mauve and blue turn into gold, announcing another dawn, said a prayer of gratitude and, at the first sound of running water, sat down cross-legged with the full Christmas stocking on her lap and shuffled into the box. The finger hole and tinsel to pull it closed behind her was a brilliant initiative! Saying a silent 'thank you' to whoever turned on the air conditioner, she waited and listened to the gradual increase of excitement. Christmas carols filled the room, and she wiped silent tears from her face.

'Heck! That is still a huge box.' She was sure it was Troy who spoke excitedly. 'Bet it's for me!'

Similar sentiments were enthusiastically shared, with the levels of eagerness swelling when the Danish fathers took on the joint role of Father Christmas. Everyone was a big kid at heart and loved every minute of the early morning fun. Even the pooches got spoilt and played noisily with their toys. Eventually, the big box was the only present left.

'We can't move it. It's too heavy,' the one father said.

'Whose is it?' she heard Troy ask.

'Um... looking for the tag,' the other one said. 'Oh, here it is... let's see.'

He slapped the top of the box. Darlene nearly squealed in fright and quickly covered her mouth with her hand.

'Of course! Big box for big man. Tiny, merry Christmas.'

The fake groans and pretend moans were replaced with boisterous mirth.

'Who's it from?' Tiny's deep voice, filled with excitement, brought more tears to her eyes.

'It's yours. You come and find out,' one father said loudly and burst out laughing.

Tiny rocked the box. Darlene tried to rock with it and suppressed her giggle.

'Pull the bow,' Troy called out.

'Come on, Tiny,' Granny nagged cheekily. 'The eggnog is getting warm!'

Tiny chuckled, undid the bow and tore off layer after layer of the three-sided wrapping paper, until the last, which was actually glued onto the box. She did her best to hold it shut. Eventually, he just lifted up the box, and there she was, staring up at him with a wide grin.

'Merry Christmas!' she called out, sobbed happily and lifted her arms to be picked up. Their voices were drowned out by the loud gasps, hoots of laughter and applause.

The big man scooped her up and held her midair.

'There's something you need to know,' he said while gently lowering her enough that she could stand.

'I can't wait to hear it,' she replied and kissed him as he turned his head.

'I have to tell you something!'

'Well?' She almost had to yell out to be heard as the lounge room filled with raucous laughter, squeals of delight, plenty of sniffles and happy tears as everyone wished each other a very merry Christmas all over again. Darlene, Cassie, Milly and Elaina were inseparable as she handed out her gifts. The prized ram calendars were a huge hit!

Troy couldn't contain his excitement as he handed her a very welcome glass of eggnog. 'Who else knows you're here?'

'Only the people in this room,' she replied with a grin from ear to ear.

'Oh, you amazing woman. Spook is going to love this!' he said and slapped his thighs rhythmically.

During a very light breakfast, they all agreed to continue the surprise and that Darlene should be the last one to arrive at Spook's. They had a three-hour journey ahead of them and were to arrive no later than 1:30 p.m. The residents had clearly worked out a routine, and in under two hours, nearly everyone was standing on the broad verandah dressed in their classy Christmas outfits. The five dogs wore their bling collars happily. Their bells jingled each time they shook their head or romped around. Only Tiny, Granny and Cassie were tardy in their arrival onto the verandah.

The Danish fathers sported red suits with white trim matching their white shirts, complimenting their wives, who wore layered green and gold dresses in the design of tinsel draped over a Christmas tree. Elaina and Asta's cold-shoulder dresses adorned with reindeer on a soft orange background flattered their youthful figures. Milly and Amy rocked the matching 1950s-style green and white snowflake-covered A-line dresses, and when they twirled, the Christmas-tree-scene borders flared out beautifully. Troy's dark green shirt and black trousers, set off by the holly-and-Christmas-cane tie, extolled Bev's lacy green and black cap-sleeved A-line dress. Darlene simply loved her red and white ruffle dress and was twirling with the girls, admiring their pretty dresses, until Tiny stepped outside.

When he caught her eye, he took her breath away at the same time Elaina gasped. The white trousers, dark green shirt and white tie were bordering on knee-weakening. When he turned to assist Cassie, the snowman and carrot on the back of his white waistcoat started up fits of giggles. Cassie joined him, wearing a beautiful white sweetheart-neckline, full-skirted dress elegantly adorned with a Christmas bauble pattern. Her Nordic gonk hat looked fantastic. The buzz of excitement grew as Granny made her appearance. Her ankle-length, three-quarter chiffon-sleeved dress with a Christmas tree and snowmen around the border topped off the fashion parade brilliantly!

From behind her back, she gracefully popped on her snow-encased reindeer-antler hat, tilted it to the side and sang out, 'Merry Christmas! The Danes made us do it!'

With everyone in great spirits, they travelled in convoy style. Darlene quite liked the look of Tiny's Mercedes and suggested he lead the way. She'd tag behind and bring up the rear.

Two hours into the journey, she got bored of the view and floored it past the four other vehicles. Blipping her hooter as she overtook Tiny, she did the indicator dance and tucked in front. She answered his phone call with a laugh.

'What's under your bonnet?' she asked cheekily.

'A lot more than yours,' he replied in a voice thick with emotion.

She giggled. 'I'll drop off my speed when you tell me to, Tiny, then wait down the road from Spook's driveway for ten minutes. Sound like a plan?'

'Sure does.'

They rung off. Darlene burst out laughing and answered Peachie's call excitedly.

'Merry Christmas, you two!'

'Merry Christmas. Where are you?' Peachie asked, concerned.

'Oh, leading a convoy. Where are you?'

'Behind a bunch of slowcoaches,' DeeDee answered. 'We watched an old square thing overtake them all, but now we're on a windy stretch, so it's impossible to overtake.'

Darlene laughed loudly. 'That old square thing is powered by a V8, and I'm driving it!'

'You're kidding!' DeeDee and Peachie said in unison.

'No, I surprised a houseful at Dubbo this morning. Spook and co don't know anything about this. I'll be waiting down the road for about ten minutes... care to join me?'

'You bet. They don't know we're coming either, so we'll follow your lead.'

'Done. I'll be dropping my speed on Tiny's call, then pulling over. You may want to hang back a bit to avoid being recognised.'

'Will do,' DeeDee said pleasantly. 'This is going to be a truly wonderful Christmas, Darlene. So exciting. Listen, we're both in wheelchairs, so bear with us.'

'Of course! See you soon, you wonderful people.'

'Let us overtake.' Tiny's voice boomed through the two-way speaker as they hit the overtaking lane.

She depressed the button twice and decelerated. Tailing them at a reasonable distance, she saw where they turned down a side road. Following them, she slowed right down and answered her phone.

'Darlene, in three kilometres, there's another driveway off to your right. Travel at walking speed for almost a kilometre. You'll spot where to park. See you there.'

'You bet! Thanks, Tiny.'

Pulling up under a large tree, she got out and watched as a blue Toyota Camry rolled in behind her. She hugged DeeDee and Peachie through the windows as they wished each other merry Christmas. The matching elf shirts also matched their broad grins.

'Hey, Peachie, can you please do me a huge favour and get a message to Radar wishing him a merry Christmas for me?'

'Will do. I recall the second driveway is pretty wide – should we go in side by side? It'll be better if we're on your left.'

'Yeah, let's do it. We'll have a slow race!'

And they did. It took them another fifteen minutes to arrive.

Darlene gasped when she saw Spook's full white beard, which matched his shock of white hair. He really did look like Santa, and his blue and white suit matched his wife's amazing snow-scene dress. A stunningly beautiful younger woman stood beside her, positively glowing in her blue and white dress with Santa's sleigh travelling around the full skirt. A man in an elf suit was beaming proudly beside her. Each parent was holding a tiny baby wearing a combination of their outfits.

The partygoers were walking towards the approaching vehicles, except Tiny, who baulked. Darlene briefly flicked her left indicator on and watched their delighted surprise unfold. It was the proper thing to do. She was so preoccupied that she jumped out of her skin when her door opened and there stood the real Santa.

'Radar!' She burst into tears and flew into his arms. 'Oh, Radar, thank you with all my heart. Merry Christmas.'

'Hush, Ms Adams, we'll discuss it another time. Yes, merry Christmas. There is someone who urgently needs to speak to you.'

He stepped aside, and a man sporting a left prosthetic hand and a patch over his right eye, in similar attire to Tiny minus the waistcoat, stepped towards her and gripped her hands tightly.

'Ms Adams, may I congratulate you on several tasks very well done. I'm Overwatch. But most importantly, thank you for saving our CO's life.'

Darlene gasped as tears welled up in her eyes. 'The training exercise that went wrong! Well, actually, it went right. Honestly, sir, I am the one that ought to thank you. It's an honour being in your company. I don't know how you sorted out the last bit, but I am so glad you did. Thank you.'

'Boss is heading this way. Let's chat another time. Merry Christmas, ma'am. You're a remarkable woman.' He bent down and kissed her lightly on the cheek.

She was speechless and got bustled into Spook's embrace before she could say another word.

'Oh, Darlene! This is a wonderful surprise. You've made this a truly special Christmas. Come and meet the rest of my family.'

'Spook, I had several good reasons, but honestly, everyone here is making this a truly special Christmas.'

'Indeed,' Radar said, then quickly added, 'Shush, now. My Canary and choir are about to sing.'

They followed his gaze as the faint ringing of bells drifted down from the first-floor balcony. Suddenly, two unaccompanied, beautifully harmonised voices filled the air with a medley of Christmas carols. The gasps were quickly replaced with soft sniffles. Milly and Amy stood on a raised platform and performed the repertoire brilliantly. Cassie, Asta and Elaina stood behind them in true choral fashion and supported the lead singers perfectly for several more

Christmas songs. They curtsied gracefully at the outrageously loud applause and calls of 'Encore!'

Darlene saw Cassie smile broadly and wave to Granny, who clutched at Tiny's hand. In an unrecognisable mellow tone, she sang *Silent Night* in German as her personal backup artists accompanied her superbly. The girls continued to sing through the accolades, with melodies including *Stairway to the Stars, Somewhere Over the Rainbow* and *A Wonderful World*. The five singers finished their set with *Summertime*, before Milly and Elaina raced down the stairs ahead of the other girls. They threw themselves at Peachie and Radar, whose smiles were the broadest anybody had ever seen.

After the plenitude of hugs, kisses, handshakes and festive greetings, using the bucket of the front-end loader surrounded by support, Peachie got lifted up to the landing. DeeDee was so small-framed in comparison, Overwatch and Tiny easily carried her mode of comfort up the stairs. Spook, Tiny and Elaina were inseparable.

'Folks!' Radar's voice boomed across the verandah. 'Overwatch, Peachie and I have a message for our female WA contingent. Please give us five minutes before we rejoin and continue with the festivities.'

Tiny hung back until Radar discreetly dismissed him. He frowned and reluctantly turned away, encouraging everybody else to move to the other end of the verandah as Darlene, Milly and Elaina gathered around the three men.

'Girls,' Radar said quietly and firmly as he retrieved his phone from under his Santa suit. 'Listen to this news report from the other day. There was a single vehicle discovered off the highway towards the Great Australian Bight, where the sole occupant had presumably camped, taken far too many drugs, attempted to burn his tattooed arm and body stockings and consequently died from snake bites, possibly dugite. In quite a perplexing scene, the evidence of amphetamines and cocaine may have brought about delirium, given the dense spider pattern on the articles of clothing. A timely reminder about the dangers of taking drugs and the importance of not walking around barefoot in the remote outback, particularly as tourists flock to coastal areas for Christmas.'

It was impossible to stifle their jubilation for several minutes. Their smiles were wider than the Grand Canyon as they joined the party.

Tiny instantly drew Overwatch aside. 'What was all that about?'

He squeezed the taller man's shoulder and grinned. 'Take that up with the CO... here he comes now.'

Tiny spun around as Radar adjusted his Santa hat.

'Son, the girls had to be told first. It was their suggestion, the way the last cockroach died.'

'And?'

'Snake bite, of course!' Radar chortled loudly.

His and Overwatch's laughter was so contagious, Tiny had tears rolling down his face as the three men held each other until the developed belly laughs subsided.

'Merry Christmas!' Radar said loudly and buzzed a streamer at Peachie, who returned fire, kicking the party off once again.

In exemplary fashion, their hosts, Spook and Maureen, who insisted everyone call her Grandma, lead the procession past the amazingly decorated lounge room, through the breezeway, then paused for dramatic effect. Together, they pushed open the white timber doors, revealing an exquisitely wide, bright dining room with white country cupboards adorned tastefully with decorations. A dramatically long table, with its elegant gold, red and white tablecloth, provided enough room for the families, waifs and strays to fill the room comfortably. Ice buckets containing bubbly, sparkling wines, beers and pre-mixed spirits were strategically positioned, along with an incredible selection of glass drinkware and appropriate quantities of finger foods.

Spook lightly tapped his tall glass of beer and, in a voice thick with emotion, spoke a toast. 'My beautiful family, our beautiful friends, old, new and forever, thank you for joining us and making this Christmas a very, very special one. To absent friends and family, we give thanks. Merry Christmas, everyone!'

The unanimous, joyous cries of 'Merry Christmas!' and 'Thank you!' filled the room. Eyes swivelled to Milly and Amy, who naturally took the cue and started singing the duet *Baby, It's Cold Outside*. The round-robin duet was tear-jerking. It evoked raw emotions, as if everyone released all their cares at the same time. The room shone with love, devotion and friendship.

Troy couldn't wait any longer and tapped his glass before placing it on the table. He held everyone's attention as he gently took Bev's glass from her hand and placed it beside his, then escorted her into full view. Nimbly getting down on one knee, he took a deep breath and retrieved a delicate teal-coloured velvet box from his pocket.

Opening it up facing her, he said, 'Bev, please do me the honour of becoming my wife.'

She wiped a stray tear and smiled broadly. 'Yes, Troy. I would be honoured.'

The room went berserk, with several rounds of celebratory drinks and speeches before they were all ushered outside to the northern aspect of the spacious verandah. The view was extraordinary, but the incredibly decorated table and delicious aromas that filled the air took pride of place. Everybody milled around, talking pleasantries, sharing stories and laughing loudly. The men went in one direction and the women went in another. As is the usual thing at a party.

Santa, aka Radar, then made an appearance, naturally commanding attention. His loud, jingling bells echoing through the surrounding valley.

'Ladies and gentlemen, we have another announcement that needs to be shared during this momentous occasion and celebration.'

He stepped aside as Tiny and Overwatch waltzed around the corner in each other's arms. Darlene gasped and held back a sob. *Oh, God, he's gay. He said there was something I should know. He also said he had so much to tell me,* she reminded herself and stared in utter disbelief.

Nobody said a word. Nobody caught anybody's eye. The birds fell silent. Even the wind dropped off, and the dogs stopped playing. Suddenly, the theme from *Love Story* filtered through the open windows. Darlene stopped breathing as the men awkwardly danced. Their faces concentrating on their dance steps. They stopped their twirl and faced each other. Her knees nearly gave way, and she felt for the railing as she drew in a very deep, quiet breath. Cassie semi-supported her by leaning into her trembling body. Overwatch took a step backwards and reached into his pocket. Somebody gasped. Tiny then took a step towards him and reached into his pocket. Somebody else gasped. She swallowed hard. They both retrieved a jewellery box.

Darlene fainted.

She came to in a darkened bedroom with Granny and Grandma gently fussing over her. The sounds of raucous laughter drifted through the slightly opened door. The gentle scent of primrose made her sneeze noisily. It always had.

'Oh, good, you're awake! Heavens, you gave us all a scare, young lady,' Granny said and handed her the box of tissues.

Struggling to sit up, she blinked rapidly. 'I gave *you* a scare? Hell, how do you think I feel?'

'Why, what on earth happened?' Grandma opened the curtains a bit more.

'They're gay!' she blurted out.

Their peals of laughter, mixed with peculiar giggles, were actually quite contagious.

'Oh, my.' Grandma snickered. 'I think we need to adjourn. Here's your handbag, dear. We'll wait for you in the passageway beside the lounge.'

'Thank you.' Darlene applied some lip gloss, shook her head slightly and fondled the fat envelope.

'Can I go in?' she asked softly as she approached.

'Of course, dear.'

Darlene slipped off her sandals so she didn't wake the sleeping babies, and padded softly to another amazing Christmas tree. Propping the envelope '*for Spook from Santa's little helper*' in between two branches, she grinned and tried hard not to think about Tiny.

'It's Christmas. Let's get merry!' Darlene murmured and smoothed down her dress as she slipped back into her sandals.

She was met with a round of applause as the elderly women ushered her to the chair between Cassie and Elaina. The men politely took their seats afterwards, and the delicious festive Christmas feast commenced as if nothing had happened.

Hours later, after several games of French cricket and badminton, they were all barefoot and seated underneath the marquee on the lawn, enjoying the delicious array of desserts as the shadows lengthened. It had been a rather extraordinary Christmas Day. As the last of the sunrays painted the hilltops, casting a pretty, burnt-orange glow across the sky, the familiar strains of *Love Story* drifted down from the verandah. This time, mixed giggles and sniggers rippled through the partygoers, which gently subsided as, once again, with arms entwined, Overwatch and Tiny waltzed around the corner of the house towards the group. A lot more alcohol had been consumed, and scarily, they were a lot better.

Darlene watched in horrified fascination. The bastard. *You silly cow*, she admonished herself and played with the dolphin bracelet. *I sat in a box for you*, she thought as she perved on his amazing physique. Her eyes travelled downwards, then she squeezed them shut. *No. No. No.* She reached for another iced beer and refilled her glass.

By the time the two men had faced each other and retrieved the jewellery boxes, she'd consumed two more drinks and started to giggle. Several of the younger women joined her and promptly bit their lips when the two matriarchs gave them 'the look'. Darlene caught DeeDee's eye across the circle, and at the same time, they shrugged and shook their heads in total bewilderment. Tiny twirled Overwatch around twice. Overwatch twirled Tiny around twice. Darlene poured herself another drink and snacked on some more camembert, grapes and biscuits. Still holding out their jewellery boxes, they saluted each other and marched through the seated, semi-inebriated patrons. Tiny disappeared, so Darlene turned her head and looked at DeeDee.

Love Story was on its third round when Overwatch dropped to his knee. Darlene gasped. He was in front of DeeDee. She jumped when she felt light pressure on her knee and turned her head to find Tiny in front of her. With military precision, he flicked open the white satin box. Darlene lost herself in Tiny's eyes and mirrored his twitching lips.

'You ready, boss?' Overwatch asked loudly.

'Absolutely,' Tiny responded.

The men spoke in unison until the names.

'Will you do me the honour of being my wife, please, Darlene?' Tiny asked and presented her with the most exquisite rose-gold ring studded with diamonds.

'I, um... I, um... are you sure?' Darlene blurted out.

The silence was deafening.

'Why do you ask such a question?'

'Because a while ago, you said there was something I should know, and you never let on anything this whole time.'

Tiny stared at her and grinned. 'I love you, Darlene. It just took me a while to admit it to myself.'

Darlene and DeeDee caught each other's eye again and burst out laughing.

Clutching at Overwatch's hand and in between fits of giggles, DeeDee called out, 'You... you also... thought... they were gay!'

'Uh, yeah!' Darlene replied loudly and reached for Tiny's hand.

They joined in with the raucous laughter until it subsided. Then, as a wild swan on a distant pond called to the rising moon, DeeDee's voice faded into the background. Darlene heard nothing except her own voice as she gazed lovingly into Tiny's eyes.

'Yes, Tiny. Yes, I will marry you.'

He gathered her into his arms and kissed her tenderly as they swayed to the same melody. He held her at arm's length and grinned.

'I thought you liked pranks!' he said with a lazy wink.

She giggled. 'I do. I *did*! You cheeky sods, you really had me going!'

Tiny roared with laughter. 'Is that why you passed out?'

'Yes!'

They laughed, they cried, they laughed some more. They agreed the theme from *Love Story* was not going to be played at the wedding. The festivities and everlasting unions were celebrated long into the night. It was a wonderfully memorable, merry Christmas for everyone.

EPILOGUE

The gifts of a truly special Christmas kept on giving when, during the traditional Boxing Day champagne breakfast, the three couples announced they'd like a triple high tea wedding. Much to the delight of all and sundry, Spook and Maureen very kindly offered the use of their amazing home and garden for the venue. With plans afoot for January nuptials, prior to the Danes returning to their snow-covered homes, Bev asked if it would be appropriate if the date could coincide with her sixtieth birthday, being the twelfth. Everyone assured her it would be most fitting and enjoyed a round of celebratory drinks. She then announced that she'd be formally retiring on the same date, and another round of celebratory drinks flowed amid a lot of laughter.

It was the simplest planning and coordination meeting Darlene had ever attended. The military men assigned themselves the transport, accommodation and facilities logistics. Peachie's brother-in-law was to be the marriage celebrant. The younger women would be the bridesmaids and jumped at the opportunity to help with the wedding favours and floral arrangements. They would also sing as the brides walked down the aisle and at the signing ceremony. Spook's daughter and family were immediately embraced as the assisted ring-bearers, flower girl and pageboy, with all seven dogs at their respective masters' feet. The Danish parents insisted they source the hire furniture and accessories. The two grandmothers volunteered to do the celebration cakes. The only items left for the brides and grooms were to coordinate the bouquets and caterers, cover the costs associated with the wedding and invite the guests.

Until the wedding day, Darlene and DeeDee were forbidden to be left alone with their future husbands, and nobody argued with the matriarchs. Much to the dismay of the two younger brides-to-be and their betrothed, but to the amusement of everybody else.

Tiny had already been nominated as Troy's best man; Spook was going to be Tiny's, with Radar to be Overwatch's. All the men would vacate the premises by the ninth of January and be at the garden church in time to receive their blushing brides. Troy announced that a former colleague, Neil Chalkham, who had worked with his late father, would give Bev away. Peachie announced he would give DeeDee away. Amid a lot of gaiety, Darlene announced that she and Tiny had yet to speak with her parents. They'd been unsuccessful in reaching them on Christmas Day. Cassie had the same situation with her parents.

With promises of returning to Scone for celebrations on New Year's Eve, the convoy returned to the farmhouse in Dubbo with full stomachs and laughter lines. Radar convinced Darlene that her suitcase would be very safe in the backseat beside him, and she had the pleasure of his and Overwatch's company, where they got to talk more about their passion for fun, loud cars, aviation and shooting.

Radar leaned in between the two seats and said, 'Ms Adams, with reference to the ownership paperwork of the IG, please know that it has been filed accordingly with the transfer documentation. You have no need to worry yourself about that any further.'

Her sigh of relief was loud.

'Thought you'd be happy to know that!'

'You bet. Thanks, Radar. Guys, are Jody and Bo aware of the result?'

'They are, and they're also having the best Christmas with that knowledge.'

'Thank you both so much for everything.'

'Of all the gifts everyone has received this Christmas,' Overwatch said loudly, 'eternal friendships have been the greatest.'

'Hear, hear!' Darlene and Radar said simultaneously

'Hey, Overwatch,' she said, casting him a sideways glance, 'I have to know... who taught who to dance?'

Peals of laughter ricocheted off the interior as she put foot and floored it past the slowcoaches in the convoy.

Four days after Christmas, Darlene and Cassie finally got to wish their respective parents a belated but blessed Christmas during a rowdy telephone conversation. They didn't have much option but to listen to the exciting account of the houseboats, a great grandchild due sometime in March and all the fun the families had together. Neither of the pair had the opportunity to talk about their Christmas or share the exciting news.

Darlene accepted it a lot more easily than her niece, who flew into a fit of rage with indignation and fled from the farmhouse. It didn't take long before she was discovered halfway up a tree with her pants leg caught on a twig. Her embarrassment was quickly replaced with fits of giggles and the admission that she had finally learnt to put her ego back in its box. She heeded Granny's advice and accepted that the right time for talking would present itself.

It did. On New Year's Day. They arrived for lunch at the red-bricked home of Cassie's parents, commenting on the ever-present jacaranda trees as they drove up the driveway. The rumbling note of the V8 echoed through the air until they stopped. Once again, the peaceful country air was silent. Nobody came out to greet them. Cassie sniffled quietly then put her shoulders back and fulfilled her carer's role with Granny. Taking the opportunity of the precious few seconds, Tiny pulled Darlene into his arms, and they kissed passionately.

'Unhand that woman,' her father yelled out from the patio. 'You don't know where she's been!'

'Actually, I do, sir, and I know where she's going to be for the rest of her life.' Tiny had pulled himself up to his full height and walked towards his future father-in-law with his arm around Darlene.

She couldn't get the smile off her face as she did the honours of introducing the two men to each other. Cassie got the warmest embrace from her grandfather, who then gently shook Granny's hand. After the pleasantries, he encouraged Cassie to take their two new family members into the house and do the necessary introductions.

He hugged his adopted daughter tightly and shed several tears as he kissed her head. 'Congratulations, my Darlene the Dreamer, you are beautiful. I've missed you awfully and hope you'll come and see us after you're married. I should have told you this a long time ago, and more recently, but I am so proud of you, your achievements, your integrity and honesty. I love you, my girl.'

She let her tears wet her father's shirt as she hugged him back.

'Always know, Dad, that I loved you first, and now I have another family who will also share my love. Yes, we'll come and visit you. But come, we need to go and save my future husband. He's probably in shock with all the ebony-haired people around!'

They both laughed as they wiped at their eyes and walked around to the verandah to see her mother and Granny in deep conversation on the swing seat, Cassie holding the stage with her mother and the other women and abundant children in the outdoor kitchen. Tiny was at the bar with the men and looked very comfortable with a beer and set of darts in his hand. Silence fell until her mother sobbed loudly and put her arms out. Winking at her future husband, Darlene greeted her warmly and hugged her, wiped at her tears and kissed her gently on the forehead. The older woman couldn't speak and just dabbed at her tears.

Eventually, after Darlene was hugged and talked over by her extended family, her oldest brother gave her a bear hug and handed her a perfectly chilled beer and a set of darts.

'I'll always be your brother; we will always be here for you, but man, we are so relieved this big fella has got your heart. Congratulations, sis. We'll be there on your wedding day.'

Darlene smiled broadly, thanked her brothers for who they were, winked at Tiny and had a mouthful of beer while she compiled her thoughts. She didn't get the opportunity to say anything further. With not a lot of encouragement, Tiny challenged her to a game of 501, competition rules. Ladies first. Closest to bullseye always starts. She nailed it dead centre. Their audience fell silent. Tiny took his turn, speared the back of her dart and split its feathers. The nearby forlorn caw of a crow was the only sound that could be heard. She returned Tiny's challenging look and took her second throw. Left centre of the double bull. He damaged the feathers on that dart too. The bullseye was pretty congested. She could only go to the right of centre or below. The right lessened the chances of her competitor. She closed her eyes, envisioned the gap to be a mile wide, aimed and threw, nailing right of centre, awfully close to the wire. A buzz of excitement filled the air.

She looked at Tiny and fluttered her eyebrows. 'Do your best, kind sir.'

He simply smiled and said, 'Oh, I always do, lovely lady.'

Standing side on, she watched Tiny as he closed his eyes, slowed down his breathing, gradually raised his arm, opened his eyes and threw the dart. Centre bottom, but his first dart fell out. Darlene won! Their audience went wild. It was the loudest and happiest New Year's Day celebration she'd ever had the pleasure of experiencing.

After a drawn-out farewell, at long last, they were seated in her Jeep, all talking through the windows above the rumbling note. Cassie promised everyone would receive a digital wedding invitation as Darlene slipped into reverse. Her family walked and talked either side of the vehicle all the way down the driveway. Eventually, the four were pointed in the direction of Scone. With arms waving madly until they couldn't be seen anymore, the four occupants sighed loudly and burst out laughing.

'Welcome to the family,' Cassie said with a giggle. 'I'm so glad you insisted that their presence was the only present you wanted, because can you imagine how many dart boards you'd receive?'

Granny chuckled and said, 'You'll need a bigger home, Tiny! But I long for some peace and tranquillity. Perhaps we ought to sneak back home for a few days reprieve!'

'That's awkward, because there are a few things I need to do before I carry Darlene over the threshold...'

'You can do it beforehand, you know,' she said candidly.

'He will not,' Granny said and joined in the laughter.

The rowdiness and happiness continued long into New Year's night at Spook's. The bright, clear day that followed made it easier to clean up after the extended celebrations and tremendous breakfast. It was decided that none of the grooms should be alone with their future wives at night leading up to the wedding, so to make it easier, all the men in the bridal party except for Spook would join or follow Tiny on the trip back to his place. Everybody else, including DeeDee, would stay at the Dubbo farmhouse and do wedding things. The Danish fathers would be rescued for a few days of secret men's business. Granny and Cassie would return to the farmhouse on the ninth then travel up to Scone the following day. The lengthy Tamworth farewells paled into insignificance.

Just as the misty morning sun adorned the top of the rolling hills on the day of the combined celebrations, Bev, DeeDee and Darlene looked down upon the magnificent wedding setting and inhaled the delicate fragrance of the bouquets filling the house, mingling with the jasmine from the flowering shrubbery along the fence line. They drank in the peaceful surrounds in between sips of perfectly brewed coffee.

The men had created a fantastic environment and sensibly positioned the already decorated tables along the outside of the marquee walls, under its awnings. During the photographs, the walls would be slid back and the furniture rearranged to provide an informal but personal seating plan. Tall tables would be strategically positioned for easy mingling, with adequate seating placed around for simplified eating and chatting. Before the men had departed to conduct their secret business, they had showered all the women with bunches of roses and bouquets of daisies and chrysanthemums, as well as chocolates and champagne, with humorous instructions not to be late.

The massive white marquee resembled the garden church with teal, mauve, apricot and ivory bows tied behind the chairs either side of a very wide red-carpeted aisle. Tall ivory-coloured vases of fresh and artificial mixed bouquets stood proudly in front of the tied-back lacy drapes. Ivory was the themed colour for the wedding, and each of their beautiful dresses featured it.

Darlene's mother, who had arrived the previous evening, along with the two grandmothers, wheeled out the cakes for uninterrupted accolades and photographs. The three-tiered ivory heart-shaped cakes exquisitely decorated with trails of teal, apricot and lavender-piped roses sat on ivory and gold cake boards. Each bride was given a choice of flavours. Bev requested traditional fruit, DeeDee vanilla and Darlene chocolate. On small gold pillars placed around the wedding cakes were the traditional round first-anniversary fruit cakes adorned with individually coloured roses. Teal for Bev, apricot for Darlene and lavender for DeeDee. Bev's birthday cake was a swirled salted caramel cheesecake and looked absolutely amazing. The elderly women couldn't get enough of the praises until every descriptive and congratulatory word that existed had been exhausted.

The acoustics and harmonies were perfect as Milly and her girlfriends rehearsed their repertoire in Spook's huge new shed. They took a short break and peered through the shed window.

'Our brides-to-be are awake,' Amy said softly.

'Those apple and cinnamon muffins smell delicious, Milly,' Cassie said. 'Can we take them now?'

'Yeah, I'm getting hungry too!' she replied. 'Let's sing *Happy Birthday* on our way.'

'Let's do it round-cuckoo style,' Asta said with a giggle.

The girls fell about the place in fits of laughter.

'It's *robin*, round-robin!' Elaina managed to say, gasping for breath and wiping her eyes.

397

After composing themselves, they gathered up the bunches of flowers and, with Milly carrying the platter, sang their way to the beautiful, beaming older women in their lives.

At two o'clock, the nerves and giggles started as their fondly called handmaidens got the gorgeous dresses ready. DeeDee shared her story of being rescued from a trucking accident and being in the same hospital as Overwatch. It was Tiny who had introduced the pair, given he knew Peachie, but Overwatch was one of Tiny's men who had been terribly injured in a different incident. The pair of almost-invalids had become very fond of each other, but distance was always a challenge. Yet over the years, while there was an unmistakable attraction, neither had declared their undying love for each other, except in the way the best of friends do. Although DeeDee had no idea about the proposal, she knew they were going to have Christmas together. Overwatch had made that promise to her earlier in the year. And that was her inspiration to keep going. Their side-splitting laughter about the men dancing together called for a fresh application of makeup.

DeeDee suddenly asked the women not to help her as she moved very carefully to the end of her chair, split the footrests and used all her strength to stand up. Gasps of surprise and smothered sobs filled the lounge room as she wobbled, teetered, sat down heavily and stood up again more confidently. She let the blanket fall to her feet and revealed two prosthetic legs.

'I had a series of operations during the year and went through a hell of a lot of rehab,' she said proudly. 'Absolutely nobody knows. These last few wonderful weeks of immobility have weakened my confidence, but I am even more determined to walk down the aisle on my wedding day, dance with my husband and be loved by him too.'

Tears flowed freely as she eventually got rhythm and walked light-footed.

'Now, please freshen up my makeup... again... then help me get dressed.' She giggled and returned the plentiful hugs, duly obeying the 'open, close, turn now, breathe in, stop wriggling' commands.

Her audience gasped as she twirled gracefully and her beautiful lavender and ivory empire-waist chiffon dress flared out and fell smoothly down her trim hips to the floor. Instead of usual-looking feet, the curved blades of the prosthetics afforded DeeDee the grace of a ballerina.

'You are a beautiful and remarkable woman, DeeDee.' Bev spoke for everyone.

'Being the youngest, we think you should walk slightly ahead of us.' She put her hand up. 'Yes. We will not hear another word about it!'

Bev was next to be assisted into her gorgeous teal chiffon dress with ivory accents around the bodice and down the back, which spilled into the small train. Her teal and diamante crown attached to a delicate lacy ivory veil complimented her outfit perfectly. She looked absolutely stunning.

Granny buzzed around closing all the curtains to the lounge room windows just as the sound of helicopter blades chopped the air. Her hand firmly clasped Darlene's when she rushed past to have a look.

'They'll still be there afterwards, my girl. Now, come along – you will not be going anywhere wearing that!'

Cackles filled the hen house, as they had for several days. Darlene's mother couldn't stop weeping and made herself useful by replenishing the glasses with fruit punch and generally tidying things up. She did perform the honours of zipping her daughter's one-shouldered beaded apricot and ivory chiffon mermaid dress, tutting the entire time in between her usual term of endearment of 'Darlene the Dreamer'.

For the first time all day, Cassie fell silent. She stood alongside her glamorous girlfriends in their matching spaghetti-strapped peacock-coloured dresses. An ivory chiffon scarf was elegantly draped over each of their shoulders and clasped at the neck by a mother-of-pearl cameo brooch.

'Wow, Aunty Darlene,' she eventually murmured. 'You sure are a beautiful woman.'

Darlene smiled, admired the girls and embraced each one tightly.

'Thank you, Cassie. You look gorgeous, and I am so proud of you. Girls, you have all achieved so much and should be so proud of yourselves, too. Always remember something – we are all beautiful women, inside and out.'

'Best of friends, forever,' Milly said loudly.

'And about to be late for your own wedding,' Granny said with a plum in her mouth, initiating more hilarity. 'Come now, the first set of important men await. Right, let's go, old ducks, we need to find our seats.'

Recently retired police senior sergeant Neil Chalkham stepped towards Bev as she was escorted onto the verandah by Amy and Milly.

'You look beautiful, my dear,' he said calmly, 'and it is my honour to give you away. However, there is a young man who would like to accompany us.'

Milly tried not to squeal as her older brother walked up the stairs in his Navy whites, carrying a bouquet of teal silk hydrangea and cream roses. 'Happy birthday, Mum!'

Bev almost fainted and collapsed into his arms, with Milly ensuring she didn't fall down. 'My son, my darling Clive, you remembered! But how? How did you know? How...'

He held his mother and rocked her gently. 'Sometimes, some questions cannot be answered, but always know this, Mum. I never forgot your birthday, nor your favourite flowers.' He gently dabbed at her tears. 'Come along, now. We can't keep the good man waiting.'

Then he looked at Milly, chucked her under the chin and grinned. 'Gee, baby sister, you've grown up to quite the pretty young woman!'

He nodded his appreciation to her stunning girlfriends and stood aside as DeeDee wheeled out of the lounge. Peachie gasped and, steadying himself with his cane, wobbled over, showered her with compliments and gently pressed her bouquet of mauve silk roses and cream hydrangeas into her hand.

'Granddad, they are beautiful. I love them, thank you!'

'Ma'am, Clive and I will carry you down the stairs,' Neil suggested kindly.

Her smile was so endearing. 'Thank you, gentlemen. Who's going to drive the loader for Grandad?'

Peachie couldn't stop wiping his tears. 'Not today, young lady! Today, I walk down those stairs.'

Then Darlene stepped out of the lounge, and her father gasped loudly.

'Good Lord, you have stepped out of a dream,' he said. 'It's no wonder your mother was tongue-tied!' With a deep bow, he presented her with a bouquet of apricot silk hydrangeas and cream roses.

'Just perfect, thanks, Dad! You look pretty dashing yourself.' She planted a noisy kiss on his wet cheek. Her hug was the tightest one she'd ever given him, and she gently kissed his forehead. 'Love you.'

'Love you too, my Darlene the Dreamer.'

She was too excited to cry. At the bottom of the stairs, they all hugged each other and tried to contain their elation.

The bridesmaids insisted they would follow the beautiful brides down the aisle, singing the song of their own choosing. Peachie pushed DeeDee's wheelchair to the corner of the house, which was out of sight from the groomsmen and guests.

'One moment, Granddad,' DeeDee said quietly as she handed Cassie the blanket. 'Please come and stand beside my chair.'

They all watched as she got her balance and grinned broadly before throwing her arms around Peachie.

'Thank the man upstairs for my improved heart!' he exclaimed as quietly as he could. 'You incredible woman, DeeDee.'

He couldn't contain his excitement and did a little jig on the spot, his broad grin mirroring that of his beautiful granddaughter.

'Check out my feet! Look what I can do now!' She giggled, hitched up her dress a bit, bounced and twirled.

'Come, ladies, let's not keep these fine men waiting,' Neil said with a hearty chuckle. 'We've got thirty seconds to get to the aisle before they send out a search party!'

The handsome husbands-to-be, dressed in dark pinstripe suits, ivory shirts and ties complimentary to their blushing brides' dresses, stood with nervous anticipation alongside their best men. At their feet sat the seven dogs, wearing appropriate bows and bow ties. Two tiny babies slept in front of them, their antique cradles adorned with silk flowers, horseshoes and ring boxes upon a bed of rose petals.

The five young women walked towards the red carpet singing *La Vie En Rose*, encouraging the overflowing marquee of guests to stand. The choir then split up and stood either side of the carpeted aisle. With DeeDee giving them the thumbs-up, Milly and Amy's hauntingly beautiful rendition of Etta James's *At Last* filled everyone's souls, while gasps, tears of joy and unadulterated love filled the air.

New Found Books Australia Pty Ltd

www.newfoundbooks.au

SHAWLINE
PUBLISHING
GROUP